THE DYING SQUAD

ADAM SIMCOX

This edition first published in 2022 by Gollancz
First published in Great Britain in 2021 by Gollancz
an imprint of The Orion Publishing Group Ltd
Carmelite House, 50 Victoria Embankment
London EC4Y 0DZ

An Hachette UK Company

1 3 5 7 9 10 8 6 4 2

A CIP catalogue record for this book is
available from the British Library.

ISBN (Mass Market Paperback) 978 1 473 23076 7
ISBN (eBook) 978 1 473 23077 4

Typeset by Input Data Services Ltd, Somerset

Printed in Great Britain by Clays Ltd, Elcograph S.p.A

MIX
Paper from
responsible sources
FSC® C104740

www.gollancz.co.uk

'Unta... ...ly or...in... l, so s...ylish and pack... ...
nou...   Rob Parker, author of *A Wanted Man*

'*The Dying Squad* is one of those books that fizzes with life. Every page has a new idea, or a funny line, and Daisy May is just a brilliant character to spend time with. Also, the ending arrives in a steel-tipped boot. Well played Adam'
Stuart Turton, *Sunday Times* bestelling author
and winner of the Costa First Novel Award for
The Seven Deaths of Evelyn Hardcastle

'Excellent. Funny, creepy and "oh no he did not just throw that twist in there" compelling'
Anna Stephens, author of The Godblind trilogy

'Whip-smart, fresh with a dash of dark humour, *The Dying Squad* is a wildly entertaining read. Highly recommended'
Adam Hamdy

'Grim, wry and inventive, a twisting tale with both guts and heart. Never has Lincolnshire seemed more desolate, or more menacing'
David Wragg

'A thrilling ride with dark humour, action and a touching side that's hard to forget'
The Sun

Part One

Midway upon the journey of our life, I found myself within a forest dark, for the straightforward pathway had been lost.

Dante Alighieri, *The Divine Comedy*

No one here gets out alive.

Jim Morrison

Chapter One

Winter hated Lincolnshire.

It sprinkled frost on its fields, squatted on the remains of its abandoned crops and draped everything in a sea of compacted fog, almost as if it were embarrassed by the place. The flatness of its Arctic landscape had always made Joe think of a disillusioned god, one who'd swiped the ground clean with the back of his hand, then shrugged his shoulders when tasked with its reconstruction. There was beauty in such bleakness, he supposed, if that was your kick.

It wasn't his, but that didn't stop him appreciating the spirit-level-flat horizon, because when you were on a stake-out, a clear line of sight was the partner that never let you down. It didn't make the beaten-senseless farmhouse opposite any prettier, or the ditch, fifty yards away and cut like a chasm along the side of the road, any more pleasant to hide in. But he wasn't being paid for pleasant.

Joe shifted on legs that were all needles and pins, ice water pooling around boots that weren't as waterproof as advertised, cursing the dew and mush that had smeared itself on a raincoat four times above his pay grade, and reviewed the facts.

He was big on facts, Detective Inspector Joe Lazarus. He blamed it on an old cop show he used to watch with his dad;

they were hungry for *just the facts, ma'am* in the *Dragnet* universe, and although much of what Joe saw of televisual police procedures annoyed him (and don't get him started on the dime-a-dozen crime books that were spewed out daily), on that score he reckoned they got it right. All there was, was facts. Determine those, and the truth followed close behind, cowed and willing.

So, fact one.

There was a county-wide epidemic of teenagers being used to sell drugs in rural towns and cities. These kids were often imported from cities like London – or, in the case of Lincolnshire (the fine county he was currently ditch-hiding in), Nottingham – but just as often they were locals from broke-arse homes, presented with the opportunity to make more money in one week than they would do in a month working the fields, or, if they were really lucky, the arcades.

County lines, that was what the media called the practice. Joe supposed it was more lyrical than *child abuse*.

Fact two: the recent rampant influx of drugs had pickled the county in addiction and despair, ripping apart Lincolnshire's locked-in-time-and-all-the-safer-for-it seams and resulting in areas like this, its inhabitants – and buildings – crumbling from pharmaceutically induced neglect and rot. Joe might not have had any great affection for his home – in fact he'd grown up outright despising it – but the point was, it *was* his home. If he simply stood by and let a ragtag collective from Shottingham – not his favourite term for the city – claim it, what did that say about him?

Nothing good, and he *was* good. Good at his job precisely because, for him, it wasn't a job, but a calling. Some of his colleagues mocked him for this (most of his colleagues, if he was honest), but that was fine; he was content to leave them to their cynicism and their office politics and their massaged arrest figures. All he cared about was justice.

4

His dad's disapproving face flashed up. He shooed the image away, just in time for fact three.

Fact three was that Joe had fought hard to head up the task force, swerving a considerably more prestigious murder investigation; the county line had to be not only disrupted but cut off for good, and he was the man to do it. The fight-back began with him, right here, right now, in a rain-bloated Lincolnshire ditch.

The gang itself (who went by the name of Pilgrims) were good, and they were disciplined. Their operation turned over hundreds of thousands of pounds each month, with safe houses scattered all across the county, money moving between them quickly and quietly.

Joe had hunted down *good* before, though – great as well – and when it came down to it, they all fell the same way. Greed, stupidity and addiction had been levelling the playing field since man had first crawled from the swamp, and it was those three anti-virtues that had led him here. A grabby solicitor in Skegness, one of the seaside towns welded on like a barnacle to the east coast, had taken a liking to one of the young Pilgrims he'd been paid to represent. The girl's drug boss had taken exception to this favouritism, and the solicitor's fear of reprisals had led him straight to Joe.

In return for his protection – and after putting the fear of God in him – Joe had been granted a look at the inner workings of the gang. Luck, that was what this game was based on. You needed it, and if you were patient enough, you got it.

Was it patience that was stopping him calling this in and raiding this safe house? As he'd lingered in the ditch, time stretching seemingly beyond meaning, there'd been enough comings and goings for him to know it was the nerve centre of the gang, or one of them. A click of the button on his radio and twenty minutes from now it would be over. A pat on the back, another foot on the career ladder, and no more ditch water.

He rubbed his arms, spasms of cold rippling through him.

No, it wasn't patience. It was something else, some wriggling-in-the-gut instinct that demanded he hold his nerve, because if he did, he would catch not only some fish, but a whale too.

So he'd wait a little longer. It wasn't like he could get any colder or wetter.

Somewhere a dog barked at something he couldn't see. Joe ignored it, because there was always a dog barking in places like this, at times like this. The young woman walking down the middle of the road towards the safe house, on the other hand, wasn't for ignoring.

Even from five hundred yards away, she made an impression. Mid teens or early twenties, it was hard to tell with her build. Tall, like she was reaching to high-five the sky, her angular limbs jutted out defiantly, a shock of bright pink hair crowning her head, which seemed slightly too large on her thin frame. Joe had seen her type before: beaten by life.

Where are you off to, kid? he wondered. As if I didn't know. Maybe I'm wrong. Maybe you're not sweating heroin addiction. Maybe you're collecting for your church group, and you don't know this is a house of pharmaceutical ill-repute.

He frowned, chastising himself. It was easy to get cynical in this job, but easy rarely meant right. If she was as drug-ravaged as her frame suggested, the people who had sold her those drugs were the problem. *His* problem. She was a casualty of a war that had started long ago, one that had no end in sight.

Joe often wondered what victory would look like – and whether his superiors would appreciate it.

Now that he could see her better, she had something about her. It was the confidence of her walk, the way she held her head aloft like she was daring the world to take her on.

Not just daring; hoping for it.

6

As though sensing this judgement, the girl turned on her heel, whistling as she headed straight for him. Joe's knees kissed dank water as he ducked down further, hand going to his radio as she reached the lip of his den. She posed little threat to him personally but considerable danger to his operation; if she alerted the gang inside the farmhouse to the copper lurking in a ditch outside, it was unlikely they'd carry on being nefarious.

'Base, this is Oscar Bravo nine,' he whispered, his voice an urgent gasp. 'I've got a problem. Over.'

His reply was an earful of static.

Then, before he had time to swear at his malfunctioning equipment, she was in the ditch with him, showing a sureness of foot her awkward lope hadn't hinted at.

'All right?' she said. 'What we watching?'

'Who are you?' Joe hissed, checking her behaviour hadn't alerted the posse of drug puppies in the farmhouse. Not so much as a curtain twitch. Satisfied that that wasn't about to change, he turned to the girl in punk's clothing. 'Well?'

'Not the most important question to ask, to be honest, mate. Being a copper, thought you'd realise that.'

Joe took his hand from his radio. 'How do you know I'm a copper?'

'Another beauty. Reports of your genius are clearly exaggerated.'

Joe stole another glance at the farmhouse. 'And how would you be receiving reports on my genius, exactly?'

'We've got the same gaffer. In a manner of speaking.'

'You're police?' said Joe doubtfully, looking her up and down.

'You could say that.'

'You don't look like police.'

'Says the bloke trailing a Paul Smith coat in a ditch.'

'What are you, sixteen?'

'Never ask a girl her age, pal, particularly when she looks as joyfully young as me. Old enough to solve crimes in need of solving, that's all you need to know.'

'So you're undercover?' said Joe. 'Bit young for that, aren't you?'

'I'm here to help,' said the girl. 'What else matters?'

'What matters is I'm the lead on this operation,' said Joe, 'and no one told me a kid with a smart mouth and pink hair would be blowing my cover.'

'Who's blowing your cover?' she said. 'You see the gang storming out?'

The farmhouse was still.

She held out her right hand. 'Daisy-May Braithwaite, at your fucking service.'

Joe looked from her bony china-doll wrist to her faintly acned face. Older made to look younger, perhaps? It was possible – he'd seen a thirty-year-old lad he'd been at basic training with pass for fifteen on an undercover operation – but still, her *eyes*. They were impossible to read, cloudy, like they were guarding a secret. This Daisy-May could be his daughter, and Joe was only scraping forty-five himself.

He let her hand linger in mid-air. 'No one else is supposed to know about this op. *I* barely know about it.'

'Well they do, I'm not bent and I'm here to help,' said the girl, hand still offered. 'Now, we taking this safe house, or what?'

Chapter Two

The mist bit the road off in both directions, like it was intent on isolating them from the outside world forever.

The girl knocked on the door.

'What are you doing?' asked Joe.

'Where I come from, we knock before we break into someone's house,' Daisy-May said. 'This is the country, after all.'

'This is a bust is what it is,' hissed Joe, looking at the door, expecting to hear a shotgun blast or the sound of fleeing feet.

The girl stepped aside, beckoning towards the door. 'Be my guest. Hate to get in the way of a man and his bust.'

They waited, the door remaining unanswered.

'We should radio it in first,' Joe said finally.

'It won't work,' said Daisy-May.

A squall of static told Joe the truth of her words.

She smirked at him. 'See? No wonder there's such a drug problem round here if you're in charge of stopping it.'

He took a step back. He knew the gang were inside, because he'd *seen* them go inside.

'Something's not right here.'

'No shit,' said Daisy-May, winking at him, then opening the door. 'You should be a detective.'

*

The majority of two boys lay in the hallway, chunks of them smeared on the walls and floor, their torsos carved apart by gunshot and violence. If they'd put up a fight, it was one they'd lost quickly and badly.

'Well,' said Daisy-May, '*they* ain't getting up.'

Joe glared at her, holding a finger to his lips. The murdered kids looked barely older than her, yet she hadn't flinched.

It was like she knew they were there, he thought. That or she's seen so much death in her life that it doesn't leave a mark any more. She has to be undercover, or at the very least an informant. Either's a help until it turns into a hindrance.

He kneeled down to check for a pulse he knew wouldn't be there, then tried to work out what bothered him most about the scene, other than two dead teenagers. He knew he should retreat, high-tail it outside and call it in to the station. This was a crime scene he could do nothing but disturb, and for all he knew, the person who'd shot these kids could be in the kitchen, making themselves a brew before their next killing spree.

The problem was, he couldn't, because his radio wasn't working.

He reached into his coat, searching for the familiar phone-shaped bulge, finding lint and negative space instead. That didn't make any sense. He didn't take a shit without his phone, let alone stake out a drugs safe house.

It had been there when he'd been hiding in the ditch.

Hadn't it?

A thud sounded somewhere above them.

This is all wrong, thought Joe. Daisy-May being here. My phone not being here. The dead boys. The dead radio. Everything.

'Sounds like we're not alone,' whispered Daisy-May, her breath cold in his ear. 'Who could it *be*?'

Joe peered up at the ceiling. 'You know what happened here.'

Daisy-May said nothing, much to his surprise. Her face was blank, like she'd slipped on a mask of neutrality. Where was the irreverence? The smart mouth?

That thud again, quieter this time, like someone had muffled it.

'I don't care whether you're undercover, a narc, or a punter looking for a score,' said Joe, his eyes drawn down to the boys with exit wounds for faces. 'Wait outside. This is no place for you, trust me.'

'Always thought trust was a thing you shouldn't have to ask for,' said Daisy-May, 'but a girl can take a hint.' She bowed elaborately, then backed away, smiling slyly at him. 'Consider me fucked off.'

Joe shook his head, waiting until he heard the door slam shut. Things had been simpler when he'd been slowly freezing to death in a ditch.

He eased into the hallway, edging past a faded white door decorated with a bullet hole in its centre, giving silent praise to floorboards that didn't so much as squeak beneath his feet.

The snail trail of blood down the centre of the hall was harder to appreciate. He followed it to the stairs, a single bulb dangling like a noose lighting the way for him, chunks of floral wallpaper hanging loose from the walls like they were trying to escape the poverty of it all.

He stopped to listen at the foot of the stairs.

Nothing. Not even the whisper of an apologetic thud.

His hand reached for the banister as his foot found the first step, wincing in anticipation at the sigh the house would make in response. It didn't come; in truth he'd never felt lighter, more alive. It was as if his senses had been stretched to their limits, his vision pinging in and out of focus, like his system was warring with fight or flight.

Up, one stair at a time, his nose twitching at the lingering smell of soured gunpowder. From the massacre downstairs, or from something up here?

He reached the upstairs landing, stopping at the first door on the left, looking at breadcrumbs of blood that were drying up but still staining the ragged tan carpet. He had that feeling, the one that told him truth was lurking on the periphery, waiting to be discovered.

He gulped down a deep breath, then took a step towards the open door.

Joe staggered slightly, grasping the door frame like a lifebelt. This was a trick; it had to be.

His eyes disagreed. The pin-sharp vision he was now 'enjoying' laid out that truth in blood-red Technicolor. He scrunched them shut, the image he'd just seen lingering, regardless.

'This is straight-up fucked,' said Daisy-May from behind him, 'don't think I don't get that.'

Joe stood there, eyes closed, the blackness in front of them marred with dance trails of red.

'Open your eyes,' said Daisy-May.

'No,' said Joe.

'*Now,*' she insisted, with a firmness and gravity that belied her years.

He did. The scene lay in front of him, unchanged.

A man in his forties. On the floor, on his back, legs stretched out, bent slightly at the knees, his arms wide, like he was trying to fly.

A shirt, once as crisp and white as his own, now red, flapping at the bottom.

A hole in his stomach, gouged out with a cocktail of gunpowder and fire.

His face turned towards them, the mouth slightly open, like *no* was trying to escape.

Joe grasped Daisy-May's arm. 'What is this?'

She patted his hand consolingly. 'Could say *not what it looks like*, but it really fucking is.'

Joe stared at the man on the floor, the one who wore the same clothes as him, the same skin as him, the same face as him.

'So yeah,' said Daisy-May, 'you're *dead*, mate.'

Chapter Three

This had gone far enough.

Joe reached for his radio, ready to call it in, something he should have found a way to do ten minutes ago, static be damned. He didn't know why they'd mocked up some poor bastard to look like him, but what he *did* know was how close he'd got to finishing this gang for good. To think they wouldn't fight back from that position had been naïve, arrogant, even. That was on him.

What wasn't, apparently, was his radio; Joe's hand found the space where it used to be.

'You look peaky,' said Daisy-May, scratching her pale, emaciated stomach. 'I'd sit down before you fall down.'

Joe ignored the girl, her voice white noise, and, crouching, shuffled towards the corpse on the floor. There was no getting around it: the similarity was uncanny. His slightly crooked nose, four-day stubble, identikit grey eyes. Only the skin was different. Waxy, the lustre bleeding away with the poor bastard's life force.

'She said you might be a denier,' said Daisy-May, shifting from foot to foot impatiently. 'Often the way, she said, with the older ones. Me, I accepted it quick, but you're too clever to see the truth. Least, you think you are, which makes you dumber than a fucking horse.'

Take a breath, thought Joe. Take a breath and ignore her babble. This is a war story to tell at an after-dinner speech in five years' time. An anecdote they'll lead with when they write super-cop books about you. The opening scene in the biopic of your life.

'There's a rational explanation for this,' he said, slowly getting to his feet.

'You're right there, pal,' said Daisy-May, popping a stick of gum into her mouth. 'You're dead. Things don't get more rational than that.'

Joe gave her a thin smile. 'So, what? You're telling me I'm a ghost? Is that it?'

'Not telling you anything,' said Daisy-May, inspecting a fingernail. 'Just leading you to the water. Up to you whether you drink it.'

Joe looked at his hand, squeezed it into a fist, breathed in, then out, then jumped up and down on the spot. 'Sprightly for a ghost, wouldn't you say?'

Daisy-May rolled her eyes. 'Prefer clanking chains and a bed sheet, would you? That can be arranged.'

Joe took a step forward, and with an outstretched finger poked her arm. The girl flinched slightly. 'If I were a ghost, wouldn't that just pass straight through you?'

'You've been watching too many shitty horrors,' said Daisy-May, 'or not enough. And FYI, we don't really use the term *ghost*, yeah? It's kind of offensive.'

Joe snorted, then went over to the grime-encrusted window, the faint sound of sirens drawing him in. He smiled.

'Now we're getting somewhere. Or are you going to tell me that's a phantom siren?'

Daisy-May joined him, peering past him at the blue lights on the horizon.

'Nah, that's the pigs all right.'

He nodded, satisfied, and perched himself on the windowsill. 'Well then, you'll be able to prove your point, won't you? If we're ghosts, or whatever the hell term doesn't offend you, they won't be able to see me, *right*?'

Daisy-May winked at him, tapping her finger against her forehead. 'There's that big brain I've heard so much about it. We're going to be like the Holmes and Watson of the astral plane, you and me.'

The sound of the sirens got louder, then died away altogether, replaced by the squeal of tyres on tarmac. As Joe heard the thud of fist on door, a sliver of doubt crept down his spine. That body on the floor hadn't begun to look any less like him; at the very least, it would give the boys downstairs a shock. Still, they'd be laughing about it back at the station within the hour. There'd be a rational explanation for it, once the facts had been ascertained. There always was.

Silence, then the sound of something metal meeting something wooden, splinters splintering, warnings yelled.

Joe swallowed, his heart galloping along with a steadily rising tide of panic. But didn't that show the girl was talking nonsense? It was hard to imagine a ghost having a panic attack. Hard to imagine the concept of a ghost at all.

Two (three?) sets of footsteps in the downstairs hall.

An armed response unit, if those shots had been heard.

Daisy-May held her finger up to her mouth, miming *shh*.

Joe ignored her. 'Detective Inspector Joe Lazarus, identifying myself. One DB, a gunshot wound to the stomach, two DBs at the front entrance, one witness.'

'Technically I didn't see you get popped,' whispered Daisy-May into his ear. 'But shout away if it makes you feel better.'

The footsteps below them stopped, and Joe felt a surge of relief.

They'd heard him.

He smiled triumphantly at her, then marched towards the door. 'If you don't want to get shot, I suggest you follow my lead.'

He placed his hands behind his neck and slowed his pace to allow her to catch up, the girl sarcastically mimicking his stance.

'I am unarmed and walking into the upstairs hallway,' he called down to them.

'I could learn so much from you,' she said.

Joe ignored her, swallowing hard and moving to the doorway as the footsteps made their way closer to them.

Then he saw them.

Two members of the ARU, one armed with a chunky SBR carbine, the other with the relatively svelte Glock 17 pistol, out in front but not too far, fingers on triggers, ready to do what was necessary, if it was necessary.

There was a moment when Joe thought it would be all right.

A second in which the ARU unit froze like they'd seen the man and the teenage girl on the landing, like they would issue the command for them to drop to their knees if they didn't want their bodies torn apart by bullets.

That second passed.

The men edged forward, looking right through them.

This isn't happening, thought Joe. This isn't happening, and in a second I'll wake up and say that out loud.

He felt Daisy-May's bony hand on his back.

'This is rough, first time it happens,' she acknowledged.

The ARU were inches from them now.

'DI Joe Lazarus,' Joe said, his voice wavering. 'One DB. Looks like he bled out a while ago.'

Like someone pouring water on your soul was how he'd think of it later, that first time someone stepped through the air he was occupying. As the cop's flak vest and gun lurched through him, Joe's senses desperately tried to process what was happening, his body refusing to obey his command to wake up. But this was real life, or whatever came after that.

The men stepped through him and into the room, pausing when they saw the body on the floor. The cop with the Glock reached to the radio pinned to his left shoulder. 'Man down,' he said quietly. 'Repeat, man down. Dispatch RA unit immediately.'

His colleague crouched down to the unmoving body, taking a pulse.

'Bit late for that.' Glock cop shook his head. 'This is a bad business. Going to be repercussions.'

'Aren't there just,' said Daisy-May, taking Joe by the wrist and turning the world white.

Chapter Four

If dying was floating down a tunnel towards a serene sea of white light, it was immediately clear to Joe that he wasn't dying. There was no way death could possibly be as painful as this.

It was like he'd been jammed into a flesh straw, then spat out: his arms pinned to his sides by the membrane tunnel all around him, fractured images of places and people that were familiar yet starkly alien playing all around as he was hurled downwards. Finally, with a sea of bile clawing its way up his throat, he crashed to the ground. He clawed at eyelids that were scrunched shut, gummed together with a sort of pay-the-boatman sleep slime.

It's going to be OK, he thought. This is all a fucked-up fever dream, and it's going to be OK. I'm not dead, despite what the girl said, because ghosts aren't real. Flesh-and-blood coppers called Joe Lazarus are. I'll wake up, and I'm going to be in bed next to my wife, my Claire, and sunlight's going to be streaming in through the window, and all is going to be right with the world. This white haze is just part of the fugue-nightmare comedown.

All I have to do is snap open these eyelids, and I'll be in business.

Here we go.

He forced his eyes open, the gunk in them thick, unwilling but ultimately pliable.

What he saw made him wish it wasn't.

Despair throttled a cry from him, sinking his knees into the coarse, sandy ground of an earth he didn't know, an earth no living person had ever known.

The landscape in front of him was pancake flat, as if some ancient demon had taken a cosmic sand-blaster to it, scouring away every last molecule of life. A thick sea of fog hovered just below his knees, stretching ominously in every direction, a river of pea soup to wade through. The sky above him churned violently, its clouds pregnant with ever-changing hues of red, black and grey.

In the distance – an unknowable, cosmically vast distance – the outline of a wall was visible. Joe turned through three hundred and sixty degrees to see that the structure encircled everything around him; it was as if someone had received funding from God to re-create the Great Wall of China. Whichever way he looked, the wall stretched. There were no joins, no bricks, even. There was simply wall and sky, and the effect of the two things hitting each other made him think of being at the bottom of an unfathomably wide well. The effect was nauseating.

Flashes of a life lost attacked him as he crouched in the dirt, people he couldn't remember and places he swore he'd never forget crushing him in a vice of guilt and regret, the insanity of the last few moments – if moments even existed any more – leaving him short of breath and shorter on hope.

None of this is real, he thought. Despite what my eyes are telling me, none of this is real.

He felt a hand on his shoulder.

Firm.

Insistent.

Real.

'Hold it together,' said Daisy-May. 'And don't fuckin' puke on me, all right?'

Joe ignored the girl, plunging a hand through the fog and into the earth beneath it, the nearest thing to his old reality that he knew. He lifted his fist then opened it, staring at the grains of grit as they tumbled downwards. 'You're telling me I'm dead.'

'Wrong tense. I *said* you were dead, and get on this: you still are.'

Joe raised his head, taking in the horizon again. 'You're with the gang. You've drugged me.'

Daisy-May barked a laugh. 'Really think you're that important? Notts gangsters don't have the production budget for this shit, mate. They'd just shoot you.'

She crouched down next to him, grabbing his chin and lifting it until his eyes were level with hers. 'Oh, that's right: they already did.'

Joe swallowed. 'How do you know that?'

Daisy-May released his face, getting to her feet and dusting herself down. 'Truth is, I don't. Not impossible to imagine, though, is it? Copper ends up dead in a drugs safe house, you can probably rule the local priest out.'

Joe rose shakily, his feet not on board with the decision. Daisy-May reached out a hand, grabbing his elbow, steadying him.

'Bad news for you is, that little trip we just took? That's as good as that journey ever gets,' she said. 'First time you pass over from the world of the living to the world of the dead, they go easy on you, send you first class. Next time? *Pure* cattle class, and that shit's rougher than your arse.'

Joe grabbed her arm tightly as he bent over.

'You all right there, old man?' said Daisy-May.

'Is that a serious question?' he said. He reluctantly opened his eyes, straightening up, and freeing himself from her grip.

He took a breath, instantly regretting it. 'Why does this place smell of chlorine?'

'Why does chlorine smell of chlorine?' Daisy-May turned on her heel and began striding away. 'Come on. She'll be waiting.'

Joe stood, hands on hips, his feet a little firmer. 'Who's *she*?'

If they were walking to a specific place – and Daisy-May's purposeful speed hinted that they were – it wasn't apparent to Joe. Not visibly apparent, anyway, because the landscape remained unerringly featureless, the shimmering wall far in the distance the only landmark of note.

'You're quiet,' said Daisy-May.

'Weird, that.'

'Things will make more sense when you've met her.'

'And who *is* "her"?'

'You'll find out.'

Joe hurried after the girl, finally matching her stride, the gritty earth beneath his feet kicking up under the blanket of fog. 'I thought the afterlife was supposed to answer all of life's questions.'

She snorted. 'Any "answer" you get here opens up five more questions. Get used to it.'

'You've got quite the bedside manner.'

'So I'm told.'

Joe stopped, tilting his head in response to a sound snared on the wind. 'Is that . . . moaning?'

Daisy-May didn't reply, and the ground began to incline upwards slightly. '*Yes* or *no* won't really do that question justice. It's the kind of thing you just need to see.'

As they reached the peak of the hill, what could have been five minutes or an hour later, Joe saw what she meant.

★

This could be Marrakech. This could be Baghdad.

Joe stood with Daisy-May at the top of a scrubby, crumbling hill, looking down upon a scene bursting with life. Or not, as the case may be. An unknowable number of men, women and children, all of them chattering, yelling and muttering in rolling, indecipherable tongues, moved below them. Some were so far away, they looked like ants. Some were closer, penned in by hills and peaks in the gnarled landscape, and they were all hemmed by those endless walls of sky-punching concrete. It was as if every being ever born on the soil had made their way here, somehow.

Joe doubted they'd come willingly. This place looked like it had been built grudgingly, like its creator resented it having to exist at all.

'Noticed the people here?' said Daisy-May. 'How they look right, but not *right*-right?'

Joe peered at the surge of bodies below them and saw what she meant. Whether in the distance or a few feet away they moved like regular human beings, but ones in a flicker book that only came to life when you flipped the pages at speed. There was a hollowness to them.

'What's wrong with them?' he said, watching a small boy and his dog running below them, just a few feet away.

'Same thing that's wrong with you and me, if being dead counts as *wrong*.'

Joe held out his right hand, staring at it intently. 'But we don't look like that.'

'We do to them.'

Daisy-May smiled as a grubby, half-translucent girl scrambled up the hill towards them, a ratty, bedraggled toy rabbit grasped firmly in her hand. She crouched down to her, kissing the young girl on the forehead, reeling off words that were no more than clicks and whistles.

The girl beamed, replying in the same manner.

'What language is that?' asked Joe.

'It doesn't have a name,' said Daisy-May, smiling at the girl, ''cos the rest of the Dying Squad don't recognise it as a language. Think the Dispossessed couldn't be capable. I think different.'

'The Dispossessed?'

'We call 'em that, because that's what they are.' She fished in her pocket and pulled out a bedraggled daisy, placing it behind the girl's ear and winking at her. 'You be good, Chestnut, all right?'

Chestnut smiled, nodded, then ran away into the throng, stopping only to give a final wave.

'How come you can understand this language, and the others can't?' said Joe. 'You can barely speak English.'

Daisy-May punched him on the arm. 'Cheeky fucker. I dunno, I can just sort of tell what it means. I hear the clicks, and I see the words in my head.'

Joe grunted, then looked from the filthy, desperate people to the waves of concrete encircling them. 'What is this place?'

'We call it the Pen.'

'I can see why. I'd have gone with refugee camp.'

'Not so far from the truth there,' said Daisy-May.

'What *is* the truth? Who are they?'

Daisy-May watched the mass of bodies below her sway this way and that, seemingly oblivious to them both. 'Ask twenty people in the Squad what the Dispossessed are, and they'll give you twenty different answers. You ask me, they're a cautionary fuckin' tale. Souls that were on the tipping point of heaven and hell, and for whatever reason ended arse-first here.'

Joe let out a hollowed-out laugh. 'Next you'll be telling me we're in purgatory.'

Daisy-May didn't reply, instead watching a teenage girl a hundred feet away. Dressed in the same rags as the other

Dispossessed, she somehow stood apart, and not just because of her shock of white hair. A group of forty or so of the dead had gathered around her, listening intently. There was an air of authority to her that was hard to define, one he'd seen before on the force, men and women who didn't need a title to lead, because it was in their very essence.

This girl, this shimmering ghost, had it.

'She makes an impression, right?' said Daisy-May.

Joe nodded. 'Who is she?'

'I call her June, 'cos she's young like me, but old at the same time. Not just the white hair, neither. *Looks* like a June, do you know what I mean? First noticed her a few weeks ago, mainly 'cos she moved different to the others. Hard to say how, other than it's like she has more frames to her. Like someone did a better job of putting her together.'

Joe saw what Daisy-May meant. The white-haired girl didn't share the shimmering impermanence of the other Dispossessed; there was a solidity to her that demanded attention. 'Is she in charge?'

Daisy-May clicked her tongue disapprovingly. 'Official word says the Dispossessed ain't switched on enough to have a leadership structure.'

'What do you say?'

She shifted on her feet, rubbing her arms against an ill wind Joe couldn't feel. 'I don't need to say anything: that girl's talking, and they're listening. What worries me is what they're hearing.'

'Which is what?'

'I don't know,' said Daisy-May, ''cos the white-haired lass won't talk to me, and neither will the Dispossessed she chats to. They're shutting me out, and usually you can't shut them *up*, they're so grateful to be spoken to. That's not all that's troublesome, neither. They're moving differently. Grouping together, when all they'd do before was straggle. The leadership here doesn't believe me – or doesn't want to – but I'm telling you, something's up. That girl connects with them in a way that even I can't, and that ain't good.'

'Every question I ask seems to lead to another question,' said Joe.

Daisy-May laughed. 'Welcome to the Pen. You'll find out more, don't worry. Then you'll be nostalgic for when you didn't know, believe me.'

They watched in silence as the white-haired girl smiled at two translucent teenagers, leaning down and whispering to them. They turned, looking straight at Joe and Daisy-May.

'That normal?' asked Joe.

'Nothing's normal in this place,' said Daisy-May gravely. 'Come on. Time to see if you're worth the crime-solving hype.'

Chapter Five

Joe felt it before he saw it. What began as a tickle under his feet quickly became a throbbing, one that vibrated every cell within his apparently undead body, the smell of chlorine, always present, gaining strength by the lungful.

'Should the ground be doing that?'

'Why don't you ask it? It's right there, under your feet.'

'It'd no doubt speak more sense than you.'

Daisy-May sneered. 'That vibrating means we're getting closer.'

'Closer to what?'

'To where we need to be.'

She stopped, digging the toe of her battered Converse trainer into the dirt and grunting with satisfaction. She crouched, wiping away dirt with the back of her arm. There was a man-sized hatch beneath her. 'Don't be afraid to help, Joey. I'm all for equality.'

'It's Joe.' Nonetheless, he began to kick away at the dirt until a thick circular ring appeared.

'Next bit's trippy,' said Daisy-May. 'But you're used to that now, right?'

As Joe descended, and his eyes adjusted to the weave of tungsten lights, he saw he was entering a room so vast it was impossible to take it seriously. It was like one of the 1970s science fiction novels he'd loved as a boy (Paul Lehr's name popping in uninvited, an irrationally random memory snippet). They were, at least, inside; after the vastness of the outside world they'd just come from, this felt like a foothold in reality. He'd never imagined four walls and a ceiling could be so reassuring, even if those walls were sky-scrapingly tall in scale.

He jumped off the ladder, his feet hitting the tiled floor slap bang in the middle of the room. He inspected the wall facing him. It ran unchecked into the distance, a long metal bench racing alongside it, trying to keep up. Looking up did nothing to quell the sense of scale: the ceiling was barely visible, hiding amongst the heavens. It felt almost deliberate, crafted to make any visitor feel insignificant and irrelevant.

That height, it should have taken us hours to climb down, he thought, yet it took only minutes. How can that be?

'Whoever designed this place never met a member of the human race,' he said wonderingly.

'Whoever designed this place *invented* the human race,' said Daisy-May, slumping onto the bench with a clang.

'I suppose you're going to tell me this is God's waiting room.'

'You see much of God in this place?'

'I don't know what I see.'

'Yeah, well, that's where the Duchess comes in.'

Now they were getting somewhere. 'Is she the boss around here?' Joe asked.

'Going to have to let go of these earthly titles, pal.'

'So she's *not* the boss.'

'Oh, she is,' said Daisy-May.

Joe sniffed and winced. 'Chlorine again.'

'You get used to it.'

'Hard to believe. What's that all about?'

'The Duchess has never said. Chlorine's antiseptic, though,

right? On the soil, you use it to clean water, purify it, control bacteria, get it into line. I think the same applies here, 'cos I don't think the Pen's always been the Pen. I think it used to be something worse. Something that needed disinfecting.'

Worse than this? thought Joe. Hard to see how that could be possible.

A crunching, grinding moan came from the wall behind Daisy-May, and the outline of a gigantic door appeared beside her. He didn't recall it being there a moment ago.

'It's like this place was designed for giants.'

'Who's to say it wasn't?' said Daisy-May, jumping to her feet. She looked at Joe critically. 'Could have smartened yourself up a bit.'

He smoothed down the coat that had just a short time ago trailed inelegantly in Lincolnshire mud. 'Yeah, you really set the standard,' he replied, nodding at her punk-grime clothing.

The girl gave him a single-finger salute then knocked once on the door. It opened inwards, seemingly by itself.

A voice, clipped and economical, commanded, 'Enter.'

Joe craned his neck as they passed through. The doorway had to be a hundred feet high – possibly a hundred and fifty – which made the room on the other side even more impossible.

It was tiny, bizarre, like someone had shaken out a head full of memories. A Christmas tree wilted in the corner, half its bulbs flickering nervously, and dozens of picture frames hung on the walls, the photographs within them aged beyond black-and-white, almost like cave paintings. The furniture seemed to span the centuries: a Victorian dresser in the corner, a 1950s wooden chunk of television to his right, its picture snowy and indistinct, a gleaming, seemingly brand-new coffee machine bubbling away to his left. The whole place seemed temporary, somehow, like an amateur dramatic set that would collapse if you pushed it too hard.

He knew how it felt.

Undoubtedly, the most striking feature of the room was the elderly woman at the centre of it all, sitting behind a mighty oak desk. Her silvery shoulder-length hair had been scraped back off her face, a style that accentuated her cut-glass bone structure. There was a waxy look to her, Joe thought, like she'd been embalmed, but the sense of authority she radiated, the blackness of her sharp eyes, suggested few would tell her so.

He felt a prickling, creeping sensation as she appraised him, the merest hint of a smile playing on her pale, pinched lips.

'So, this is the new meat.'

'Yes, ma'am,' said Daisy-May. Joe noted the deference in her tone. 'Not sure I've made a believer of him just yet.'

The Duchess raised her eyebrows. 'I did warn you.'

Joe looked from the girl to the elderly woman. 'Is this conversation going to take place without me?'

'Rude of me, I suppose,' said the woman, holding out a delicate, bony hand. 'They call me the Duchess.'

Joe shook it, instantly surprised at the force of her grip. 'Why do they call you that?'

''Cos she's a duchess,' piped up Daisy-May from the corner.

'At least I was soil-side,' said the Duchess, giving Joe's hand a final squeeze before releasing it. 'These titles seem to cling to one somehow. "Ma'am" is fine.'

She beckoned to the seat in front of her desk.

'I can only imagine the number of questions you have,' she continued as Joe sat. 'I warn you now, I won't have all the answers, and the ones I do have are unlikely to please you.'

Joe leaned back in the chair slightly, the reassuring creak of leather greeting him. 'If I'm dead, what is this place?'

'You accept, then, that you are dead?'

'I accept that I saw a body that looked a hell of a lot like mine bleeding all over a farmhouse floor.'

'An unsubtle way of getting the point across, I admit. Although by the sounds of it, one too subtle for you.'

'Joey thought someone had been mocked up to look like him,' said Daisy-May, smirking. 'Like you could ever get two blokes that ugly.'

'Any film make-up artist worth her salt could manage that,' said Joe defiantly. 'And it's *Joe*.' Then his head dipped, and the fight left him. 'Not the ARU copper walking through me, though. That I can't explain. So I'll put a pin in *I'm dead*, until I can stick it in *no I'm fucking not*.'

The Duchess nodded approvingly. 'That's what most of the souls entrapped here do.'

'Where's here?'

'It has many names soil-side,' she replied. 'Limbo. The In-between. Purgatory. Here, we call it simply the Pen, for that's what it is: a holding pen for an infinite number of, as we call them, the Dispossessed.'

'What are the Dispossessed being held for?' Joe asked

'A difficult question to answer,' said the Duchess.

'Only if you don't try.'

The old woman knitted her fingers together, forming a triangle of skin and bone. 'I knew you'd be feisty. It's a trait I don't loathe, within reason.'

'Reason seems in short supply here,' said Joe. 'I'm hoping you're the exception.'

'What are we, without hope? There's precious little of it in purgatory, Joe Lazarus, so we'll take all you have to give.'

Joe looked around at the fustily decorated room. 'I'm supposed to believe I'm in *purgatory*?'

'You *are* in purgatory, there's no supposing. A bland vanilla milkshake to those souls that end up in the Next Place or the Pit – heaven and hell to you – perhaps, but a necessary one. Our inhabitants may be too wicked for heaven and too pure for hell, but they are vital. They, and the Pen, are the ballast that keeps those two realms in check. It's not a glamorous job, but it's a necessary one.'

Sounds to me like it's a dumping ground for the fuck-ups, thought Joe. And if that's true, it makes me one of those fuck-ups. How can that be right?

He took a moment, trying to clear his mind. He needed to consider this like he would a case. Everything was a case, when you broke it down. A riddle to be solved. A hidden truth to unearth. You just needed to remember that logic was your friend, and to ask it the right questions.

'What determines if someone goes to the Pen, rather than heaven or hell?' he said, finally.

'A warden in a soil prison doesn't sentence the prisoners he receives, he merely processes and corrals them,' said the Duchess. 'Why would I be any different? Those sorts of decisions are made on a much higher level, Lazarus; my job is to run the place. Amongst other things.'

Joe leaned forward. 'If this is purgatory, why am I here? I was the easiest sketch of a good guy you could draw when I was breathing. Why aren't I in the Next Place, or whatever the hell you called it?'

'What do you remember?' said the Duchess. 'From before?'

Joe blinked, realising it was a question he hadn't asked himself; he just assumed he had the memories. What *did* he remember?

The ditch.

The farmhouse.

The murdered gang members.

The girl.

He tried to cast back beyond those things and couldn't; it was as if his memories were cordoned off. He felt panic rising in him as he tried to think of his parents, his family, anything of a life beyond this moment. Was he even married? Did he have kids?

The Duchess reached into her desk, withdrawing a bottle of Scotch, then poured him a glass. 'I find this helps. Not everything's different here.'

Joe took it, hand trembling, and brought it to his lips, gulping it down, the liquid burning reassuringly in his throat.

The Duchess quickly topped him back up. 'Your mind is, I assume, failing you.'

He sipped at the drink this time, still shaking. 'One minute it is, yeah. The next, I'm remembering what toys I loved as a kid, and the name of my wife. Know what that's like? How much of a head-fuck it is?'

'Of course I do,' said the Duchess. 'I'm here, aren't I?'

'So what's happening to our memories?'

'When one is born on the soil, one is a blank slate of bone and flesh. When born on this side, why would it be any different?'

'But I remember the farmhouse, and the murdered lads. My name. My job.'

That same small smile played on the old woman's lips. 'And that's why you're sitting in here with us and not thrashing around with the half-soul animals outside.'

She leaned forward, and it seemed to Joe that the room leaned with her. 'You're one of the lucky few to retain an awareness, a consciousness; those wretched Dispossessed souls, don't.'

'I don't feel lucky.' He looked away, trying to drag back more memories. 'How long was I waiting in that ditch?'

'Long enough for us to notice you. Normally, you would have simply passed on to the realm that your earthly behaviour warranted, but you've been chosen for something else, Lazarus, and to *do* that something else, it was important for you to see just how dead you really are.'

Joe raised the glass to his dry mouth, his jiggling hand sloshing the contents against his lips. 'Mission accomplished.'

The Duchess returned the bottle of whisky to her drawer.

'In time you'll remember more, as memories, some of them random, some of them not, are returned to you. This ability makes you of importance to us, and what we do here.'

Joe set the glass down on the table, noting the moisture that had gathered on it. 'Which is what, exactly?'

'Sounds like I'm up,' said Daisy-May, tapping him on the shoulder. 'Time for the tour: keep your soul inside the car at all times, at least if you want to keep it.'

1984, that was what the room they'd brought him to reminded him of.

Not the book, but the Apple advert, with its cast of shaven-headed, jumpsuit-wearing drones, all of them transfixed by the gigantic screen in front of them, the bespectacled face on screen intoning its edicts.

This memory – the realisation that it *was* a memory – surged through Joe, adrenalising him. It was like waking up on a Saturday morning and realising you didn't have to work that day, a blissful, unexpected present.

Books and old adverts are one thing, he thought. What's next? The wife I can barely remember? The children?

Who killed me?

The more he pawed for these memories, strained for them, the more the fluttering feeling of panic built in his chest. His head felt fragile, like someone had taken a hammer to his egg-shell skull, leaving his trauma brain mushy and dull.

Stop it, he commanded. The quicker you search for them, the faster the memories are running away. The Duchess said it will come gradually, if it comes at all. Focus on what you know.

I'm Joe Lazarus.

I'm a copper. A good one, I think.

I'm in a room that reminds me of an Apple advert.

There were key differences, though. There was a huge screen

at the front of the room, true, but also hundreds of smaller ones, which the men and women sitting behind them studied intently. These workers weren't dressed in monochrome jumpsuits as their on-screen brethren had been, but instead wore crisp black uniforms, all of them carrying a thin slit of red on the sleeve.

'So,' said the Duchess, motioning expansively. 'What do you think this is?'

Joe looked around at the workers hunched over their screens, a constant droning murmur of industry coming from them.

'A control room,' he said finally, 'though I can't fathom what for.'

The Duchess nodded towards the giant screen. 'Look closer.'

He did as he was told, or at least tried to; the images on the screen were snowy, with just the merest hint of images underneath the static. Then, gradually, like staring at a magic-eye picture, he began to pick images out.

A teenage girl, her body slumped in a blood-filled bathtub.

An elderly woman, beaten and blue, motionless on a bed.

A boat full of still-as-death men, women and children.

A deserted farmhouse, the body of a man – Joe's body – drained of lifeblood.

He felt memory cogs whir and something spark in his chest that wasn't panic or confusion. There was familiarity in these images, mixed in with the horror of what they portrayed. Something else, too.

Professional curiosity.

He knew what the images were. They were something to cling to, a part of his identity that death hadn't been able to power-wash away.

'These are crime scenes,' he said, fascinated.

'They are.' The Duchess smiled (and this was a smile, rather than a cruel smirk), and the effect was so alien to her it was as if someone had scraped her skin backwards with a comb. 'And as you can see, we have something of a full slate.'

'A full slate of what?'

'Cases, of course,' she said. 'I suppose you could say we're a purgatorial police force.'

'Daisy-May mentioned this before,' said Joe, glad something had stuck. 'I assumed she was joking.'

'Our official title is the Soul Extraction Agency,' said the Duchess. 'So as you can tell, we don't really do mirth.'

'Cool kids call it the Dying Squad,' said Daisy-May. 'I do, anyway.'

Joe looked to the heavens. 'Fucking hell.'

'Lot to take in,' said Daisy-May, nodding. 'Problem for you is, you need to and fast, 'cos the clock's ticking.'

'The girl puts it well,' said the Duchess. 'The purpose of this compound, of the team we belong to, is a simple one: we solve crimes.'

'Aren't there real, flesh-and-blood coppers around for that?'

The Duchess smiled like she'd heard something funny. 'You tell me. Apparently, you were one.'

Joe bristled. 'What's that supposed to mean?'

'Allow me to put it another way: what percentage of crimes end with the suspect being charged? That's if a suspect is found, of course.'

'Nine per cent.'

The figure was out of Joe's mouth before he had time to think about it. He hadn't needed to sift through his Swiss-cheese memories for it; it was hard-wired.

Because I'm police, and that's never going to change.

'Very good, Detective,' said the Duchess. 'On the soil, nine per cent of crimes end with the suspect being charged. A demographic, I might add, that is overwhelmingly weighted according to the victim's income and demographic. The poor and impoverished aren't the forgotten victims, because no one knew about them in the first place.'

Joe struggled to keep the incredulity from his face. 'So, what, God flags up the victims he knows won't be avenged and just sends you over a file?'

The Duchess looked at him as if he was barely toilet-trained. 'Yes.'

His eyes returned to his dead body. The dozens of screens around it showed gorier crimes, but he was willing to bet there weren't many other coppers amongst them. 'If that's true, then why am I here? I was police: you kill one of those, the whole force doesn't stop till you're avenged.'

'A valid point, but everybody answers to somebody, and I'm no exception,' said the Duchess. 'The word has come down from on high: I am to place every resource at your disposal to enable you to discover the identity of your murderer.'

'What's so special about me?'

'A good question,' she said coldly. 'Frankly, there are far more deserving cases worthy of my team's attention, including Daisy-May's own death. But orders are orders, and sometimes a death can be so brutal, so unjust, that it leaves a psychic wound in both the world of the living and that of the dead. Closing that wound takes priority over everything. Who better to do it than a real-life detective?'

Joe looked away, soaking up the Duchess's words. Maybe that's why I'm here, and not kicking back in heaven, he thought. My murder was too unjust.

Or maybe the Almighty saw a genuine plod going cheap and fast-tracked me.

'What if I can't close that wound? Can't solve my murder?'

The Duchess inspected a nail. 'Think of the Next Place – of paradise – as the ultimate promotion, Joseph. Cracking the case will show you are worthy of such a promotion. If you can't?

Well, I'm afraid the afterlife isn't a realm in which one can fail upwards. You'll be slung into the Pen with the other cattle.'

Joe shifted on his feet. 'I lock up bad guys for most of my working life, one or more of those bad guys murders me, and the reward's a do-or-die mission?'

'Nobody said the afterlife was fair,' said the Duchess.

'Fair or not, this still feels like an interview for a job I didn't apply for.'

'You applied for it when you entered that farmhouse,' said the Duchess. 'You just didn't know it. This is a chance for you to secure your place in heaven, Lazarus, by simply doing your job. Many of us – *most of us* – aren't offered that opportunity. Don't waste it.'

Chapter Six

When they'd exited the Duchess's office and returned to the surface of the Pen, Joe realised that his first instinct of comparing it to a refugee camp was on the money. The translucent hordes of ex-humanity within the walls had a desperate air to them, like they'd given up on the afterlife in the same way it had given up on them. They shambled aimlessly, their eyes devoid of understanding, seemingly oblivious to him.

Daisy-May was, he had to concede, different; or at least, the Dispossessed treated her differently. Whereas he was the invisible spectre at the feast, she seemed to be a Mother Teresa figure to the creatures; they flocked to her like seagulls stealing chips.

Like the white-haired girl we saw earlier, he thought. She's got that same connection with the people here. Daisy-May talks, and they listen. There's power in that.

He stood back, bemused, as the girl made her way down the ragged line of Dispossessed, distributing pieces of what looked like chewing gum as she went. 'What's that you're giving them?'

'Your new best friend, mate.'

'Why's it my new best friend?'

'You'll see, when we get to the soil.'

Joe frowned as an elderly woman placed a square onto her

39

tongue, then closed her eyes, chewing, her face visibly relaxing. 'What is it? A drug?'

Daisy-May plucked out the last few pieces from her bag. 'More of a sedative. It calms them, mellows them out. With what's about to happen, that can only be a good thing.'

'What is about to happen?'

'Something your eyes will explain better than my gob.'

She held her hands out apologetically to the horde, showing she was out, then turned to Joe. 'Pisses off the Duchess, me giving this stuff away. Says it's a waste, like feeding caviar to a donkey. I say that's bollocks. If we can give these people comfort, where's the fuckin' harm?'

Joe looked at the Dispossessed who had taken the gum. He suspected there was more to the substance than Daisy-May was saying. Maybe even more than she knew. They had slumped to the ground, a look of beatific contentment on their faces. There was something in that look that was familiar. He'd seen it before.

At work. On a case. I can't remember which, but I know the look, the effect.

'I appreciate you have the best of intentions,' he said, 'but it looks to me like you're feeding an addiction.'

'Nothing addictive about it,' said Daisy-May, 'which you should be grateful for, 'cos soon enough you're going to be popping it too.'

'I don't need it,' said Joe. 'I need to be sharp if I'm going to solve this thing, not wrapped in cotton wool.'

Daisy-May looked away into the distance, squinting at something Joe couldn't see. 'Told you. Gum works differently for us. Now stop fuckin' dawdling – we've got some shopping to do before we head back to the old country.'

Joe didn't know what he'd expected to see as he followed Daisy-May deeper into the Pen, but it certainly wasn't a market stall. There was a certain joy in seeing it, though, because it set off a ripple in his subconscious, prodding at buried childhood memories. One thing the Lincolnshire of his youth hadn't been short of was markets and their stalls of useful crap. None of them, he felt sure, had been quite like the one he faced now.

A selection of belts hung at the back, each one adorned with glass vials containing a vivid green liquid, along with several guns of varying sizes. A collection of masks rested on the table underneath, and Joe picked one up, noting the rubberised hose that went from the mask to the oxygen tank. Like the ones that dropped on a plane when the air got thin, he mused.

'You buying that, or what?'

The old woman behind the stall glared at him through blue-bottle glasses encrusted with grime, the whiskers on her face so faint it looked like a tug of wind would snatch them away. Joe studied her with interest. He could understand her, which meant she wasn't Dispossessed.

'Buying it with what?' he asked.

The woman whipped a shotgun out from under the stall, levelling it at him. 'Buy something,' she growled, 'or move on.'

Joe laughed. 'Why, what are you going to do if I don't? Kill me again?'

The woman's finger began to tighten on the trigger. 'You think you can't die in the Pen, boy? Believe me, you can. Death on the soil's got nothing on here, trust me.'

Daisy-May placed an arm in front of him. 'Don't mind him, Mabel. He's fresh off the boat. I'm setting him right.'

The elderly stallholder lowered her gun slightly, not taking an eyelash off Joe. 'He smells like shit.'

'That's his soil life, still on him. It'll be gone soon enough.'

Mabel grunted, returning the gun to underneath the table. 'You hope. I got my doubts.'

41

Joe smiled sweetly back at her. 'Why do we need this charmer, exactly?'

''Cos going soil-side's like going to the moon,' said Daisy-May, 'only twice as hard, and ten times more dangerous.'

'Who's going to be after us there? The ghostbusters?'

'You'll know when you need to know,' said Daisy-May. 'Don't want to pickle your brain. You've only just accepted you're dead.'

Mabel whistled through her teeth. 'You're going soil-diving? With *him*?'

'New boy needs his water wings,' Daisy-May said. 'Word's come from the top: me and Joey here have to work out who had him gatted.'

Mabel looked at him disdainfully. 'Should be getting a medal, whoever did that, not getting chased by the Squad.'

'What's your problem?' said Joe, looking at her curiously.

'Time's ticking, Mabel,' said Daisy-May.

'When ain't it?' Mabel replied, still eyeing Joe with contempt. She turned, pulling a backpack down from the wall. 'Be needing a couple of tanks, I suppose?'

'Yep,' Daisy-May replied, 'plus as much gum as you can spare.'

'Not much.' The woman placed her hands on her hips. 'You been giving it away again?'

Daisy-May shrugged. 'Know you think I'm mental.'

Mabel reached under the table once more, bringing out two ancient cigarette-pack-sized tins. Their metal skins were rusted, pockmarked with dents. A nuclear mushroom cloud had been emblazoned onto each one, the phrase 'ATOMIC FIRE GUM' crowning it. They look like something from the fifties, Joe thought. Standard issue for Middle America baby boomers.

'Know why you help the Dispossessed in the way you do,' said Mabel. '*Respect* why you do it. Just worried you don't understand where kindness'll get you in the Pen.'

Daisy-May shoved the oxygen tank into Joe's hands, then pocketed the tins of gum. 'Same place it'll get me on the soil, when the reckoning comes. You think things are bad here, you should visit Nottingham. Besides, there's the wrong thing to do, and the right thing. I'll always shoot for right.'

Mabel nodded, and Joe couldn't decide if it was in agreement, resignation or worry.

'Need one more thing for the trip,' said Daisy-May. 'Well, two.'

Mabel frowned. 'Shooters?'

Daisy-May nodded.

'All take, take, *take* with you, girl.'

The woman kneeled down, rummaging around before bringing out two pistols. At least, that was the closest thing Joe could liken to them; they had handles and a thin, cigarette-shaped barrel, looking both futuristic and dated at the same time. Exposed cogs whirled and clicked, seemingly of their own accord, and a vial of green liquid jutted out from the back in lieu of a gun hammer.

Daisy-May took them with a grateful nod. 'I'll keep hold of these for now. Could do with a couple of holsters, though.'

'Leaving me with nothing but scraps,' Mabel grumbled, reaching back and hooking a bandolier. 'That everything?'

The girl smiled at her. 'Got any spare prayers lying around?'

Mabel snorted. 'If there's one thing that don't work in a place like this, girl, it's prayers. You haven't learned that yet, then you're in more trouble than you know.'

Daisy-May passed her a piece of crumpled paper. 'Here's the paperwork for the gear. Requested by big dog herself.'

Mabel scanned the document, then stuffed it into her pocket. 'Spose we have to trust that your Duchess knows what she's doing, don't we?'

Her attention went back to Joe, and she clicked her tongue disapprovingly. 'One more thing.' She took a glass jar from the shelf behind her, its thin membrane of dirt failing to disguise the contents: a hundred or so coloured discs, none of them bigger than a chocolate Smartie. The old woman's hands rooted around in the jar, pulling out a bright orange disc and handing it to Daisy-May.

'This a snack?' the girl said, looking at it curiously.

'It's a last resort,' said Mabel, 'in case you get trapped behind enemy lines. If you do, chew it, and it'll be over quick.' She nodded at Joe. 'Or slip it into this lunk's tea after he lets you down. 'Cos my gut tells me he will.'

Whether it was a trick of the mind or of the eyes, there was one fact that Joe couldn't deny: no matter how long they seemed to walk – or how fast – the wall in the distance never came any closer. They had to be getting somewhere, though, because the longer they'd walked, the more the herd of Dispossessed had thinned out, and the smaller the ragged stall they'd just left became.

'So where are we now?' said Joe. 'The Pen, or limbo?'

'The Pen *is* limbo,' said Daisy-May. 'Keep up, mate.'

'What's beyond the walls, then? The one's we're supposedly getting closer to?'

'Dunno.'

'You don't know?'

'I doubt the Duchess knows. You know everything about the living world when you were in it?'

'I knew when I was getting closer to something.'

They walked in silence for a moment.

Joe coughed.

'You ask if we're nearly there again, I'll make you wish you were dead.'

'I *am* dead,' said Joe.

'Deader.'

'And despite being dead, we still need guns,' he noted. 'Why is that? What could possibly pose a threat to us in the living world? You can't shoot a ghost up there. Can't even see one.'

'You heard Mabel,' Daisy-May replied. 'Death on the soil's got nothing on here. Believe me, you can be hurt. The shooters are protection.'

'Protection from what?' Joe pressed.

'Newbie spirits with a thousand questions.'

'Better than a smug one with zero answers.'

'Travelling to the living world, it's no joke,' said Daisy-May quietly. 'When you see it, you'll understand.'

'I doubt it.'

She was silent for a moment.

'There's something in the living world that *can* hurt us, trust me. Something that polices us, makes sure we don't physically interfere or interact. It's why you need me there, to make sure you don't get its attention.'

'This "it" got a name?' said Joe.

'The Xylophone Man.'

He laughed.

'You won't be taking the piss if you ever meet him. That fucker'll take you straight to hell. Word is, that's what happened to Mabel.'

'That'd explain her personality,' said Joe. 'One more question.'

'If you ask if we're nearly there again, I'll shoot you. We're closer than you think. It's an illusion – keeps the Dispossessed from getting too close to the wall.'

Joe cast a glance behind him again, the stall and woman now little more a smudge on the horizon. 'What was Mabel's problem with me?'

'Mabel's a Dying Squad legend. Any problems she's got, she's earned fair and square.'

'Not with me, she hasn't. I met her all of ten minutes ago.'

'She's cranky around noobs,' said Daisy-May. 'Knows what the job entails, so worries when she sees a new recruit on their first mission. You should show her some respect, mate. She has the record for solved cases on the soil. She's a legit OG.'

Joe tilted his head up, his nose twitching. The sky was darkening, like God had dumped a bag of grit into it. The Dispossessed scattered all around them seemed to know this, somehow. Like they could sense something was about to happen.

'Why isn't she coming with us then, if she's so badass?' he said.

'She's retired. Lost her taste for it, I think, after the whole hell thing.'

'I can see how it'd make you fall out of love with the job.'

Daisy-May looked up at the sky too, and scowled. She started to walk even faster, driving up their pace, easing past the distracted Dispossessed. 'Word is – if you believe the word – she saved the life of a mouth-breather on the soil. Broke the barrier between the living and the dead to do it. Know how badass that makes her?'

'We can do that?' said Joe, watching fascinated as the hairs on the back of his hand waved in response to something in the atmosphere he could feel but not see.

'A few of us can, but none of us should,' said Daisy-May, shooting another look at the sky and beginning to jog. 'Breaking the barrier between the living and the dead's the big no-no of the afterlife. That's the shit that'll bring the Xylophone Man running.'

Joe massaged his jaw, teeth singing. 'Right. Understood. Sort of.'

A guttural horn sounded, its base growl vibrating through the landscape. The buzz from the Dispossessed died down immediately, an expectant silence draping itself over them, their eyes wandering, searching for something unseen.

Joe felt Daisy-May's fingers wrap around his wrist.

'You see that red mark painted on the wall over there?' she said.

He followed her finger, squinting. 'Yeah.'

'When I say so, you run to it and you don't stop for anything. Understand?'

'That a trick question?'

'Do you *understand*?'

Joe nodded. 'I do.'

The horn fell silent.

A flash of silver light appeared in the sky, followed by a moan from the crowd.

'*Run*,' whispered Daisy-May, and Joe did, keeping pace with her as she drove towards the wall, the mob ignoring them as they gawped at the sliver of silver in the sky, one that quickly became a full-on tear, like someone had slashed it with a knife. A roar went up from the crowd, moths to the light that scarred the volcanic clouds.

Daisy-May veered off to the right and Joe matched her, ducking as she ducked, weaving when she weaved, the girl ready for the crush and able, it seemed, to predict where the crowd would surge and where it would ebb, the wall getting closer and further away at the same time.

'Hurry up,' she called, her usual slouchy insolence replaced by a tone of desperation. 'We don't have much time.'

Then there was another change in the air – electricity crackling, a chemical reaction that served only to drive the crowd into even more of a frenzy. Daisy-May stumbled, falling into the fine, powdery earth that was not quite sand but not quite soil either, and Joe slowed just enough to haul her up, what passed for breath fighting to get into his lungs.

He risked a look behind him and saw wave upon wave of men, women and children scrabbling towards the silver tear in the sky, bodies forming in a gigantic human tower, those that fell instantly replaced by others, the mob fighting, falling and grasping to get within touching distance of the light.

'Come on,' said Daisy-May, sprinting again for the wall. 'Not much time before it closes.'

'What is it?' Joe called out, his arms pumping, legs burning.

'You ever . . . play the lottery . . . when you were soil-side?' panted Daisy-May at full pelt.

'No . . .' he said certainly. 'I had better ways . . . of wasting . . . my money.'

'Well, these poor fuckers . . . don't. Once a day . . . this split appears . . . and it's the only chance . . . they've got . . . of getting to the Next Place.'

Joe slowed, chest on fire, and looked over his shoulder, watching as a girl not much older than Daisy-May slipped between two barrel-chested men and hurled herself towards the light. At the last second someone collided with her, knocking her away, and a boy, eight at the most, stole a march on them all, clambering over the shoulders of a middle-aged woman and leaping desperately for the rip in the sky.

It took him.

The light blinked out of existence, plunging the square back into the same twilight gloom it had suffered before.

A cry of anguish from the crowd behind them sounded, one that was quickly followed by screams of rage. Joe risked a glance back. The crowd began to turn on itself, child fighting with adult, adult warring with pensioner, a sort of frazzled, ragged violence infecting them all.

Then he collided with the wall.

He slumped to the floor, shaking his head at the zombie-style apocalypse at their back. Daisy-May was running her fingers over the implacable concrete hide, inching to the right, step by step, her face a picture of stress and panic.

'Did that thing really lead to the Next Place?'

She tapped a part of the wall and nodded to herself. 'Who fucking knows,' she said, looking back at the frenzied mob, then helping Joe to his feet. 'All I know is, this is the only time that we can safely cross over to soil-side, 'cos the Dispossessed are so busy tearing themselves apart they don't have time to notice us leaving. Toss me that backpack.'

He did as he was told, and his young mentor quickly withdrew a rusty spike, measuring out three steps from the wall then bending down, grinding its still-sharp tip into the powdery, moon-like surface.

'What if they did notice?'

Daisy-May pulled out a thick orange rope from the backpack. With one eye closed, she stuck her tongue out in concentration, forehead sweating as she carefully threaded the rope through the spike's eye, then tossed the end to Joe. 'Two missions ago, I passed through the wall here only to find I'd got ten Dispossessed tagging along for the ride. That's bad.'

'Why?'

'It's about balance, mate. If everything rushes out from the middle, the whole of existence topples over. That's what the Duchess says, anyway.'

Now there was a terrifying thought. He felt off balance enough as it was.

He looked down at the length of rope in his hand. 'We going mountain-climbing?'

'Sort of,' said Daisy-May distractedly, looking past him at the riot. 'Wrap that shit tight, like your afterlife depends on it, 'cos where we're going, it does.'

Joe did, Daisy-May taking the rope and hooking it onto her

gun belt bandolier, then feeding the other side around Joe's midriff, tying it taut around his waist.

She pointed to the two oxygen canisters next to the backpack. 'We'll need those for the Gloop.'

He thought about asking what the Gloop was, then decided against it. He'd find out soon enough, and it was sure to be terrifying. Better he horror-delay it.

Daisy-May yanked one of the tanks onto her back, then fixed the mask dangling from it over her mouth, intimating that Joe should do the same. He saw her frown at a small clump of Dispossessed a hundred feet away. At their centre was the white-haired teenage girl they'd noticed before, the one Daisy-May had christened June. She seemed to be calming them, like Daisy-May had done with the gum.

'That girl again,' he said, his voice muffled.

'That girl again,' Daisy-May replied grimly.

She paused, like she was weighing up whether to say something else, fingering one of the holstered guns subconsciously, then thought better of it. 'Remember, where we're going, always look forward, never look back, and one step at a time, every time. Concentrate on that, and you'll be all right. And we're not on Platform 9¾ here; touch nothing, because believe me, it'll touch back.'

She adjusted the oxygen mask covering her mouth. 'One more thing. There isn't any air in the Gloop. If this respirator comes out, you're fucked.'

With that, she stepped into the wall and disappeared.

Chapter Seven

Joe didn't know how to explain it, other than that Daisy-May was there, and then she wasn't.

As he wondered when the impossible had become the mundane, the rope snapped taut, pulling him towards the sheer face of concrete and wall. There was a sound like a startled animal snared in a trap, and he turned, fighting the pull of the rope to see the white-haired girl, the seemingly self-appointed leader of the Dispossessed, pointing at him. She let out a rebel yell, the other half-souls around her screaming in response.

So much for calm.

He was jerked backwards, the wall swallowing him, giving him that same sense of displacement he'd experienced in the farmhouse, the Dispossessed stumbling towards him the last thing he saw before he was yanked to the other side. He couldn't decide whether the look in their eyes was one of hate, fear, desperation, or a combination of all three.

Within seconds – or whatever counted for seconds in the living nightmare he found himself in – Joe saw why Daisy-May had christened it 'the Gloop'.

It was as if he'd been deposited within a living, pulsing membrane, the pink hurricane of congealed jelly all around him suffocating, like he was being bear-hugged by it. Diving – that was what Mabel on the stall had called it – and Joe reckoned she had that right; it was like deep-sea diving into some ancient mariners' trench.

Daisy-May hadn't turned as he'd been pulled into the Gloop, and in fact Joe could only just see her. The razor-taut rope that connected them was dragging him onwards, and was the only real sign she was moving at all. She'd told him to never look back, but she'd said nothing about looking up. As he did, it only furthered the impression of being dropped into a living organism.

A brain, perhaps, because as he looked closer, he saw thin, indistinct images, like memories being projected onto the matter. Transfixed, he reached out to a scene of a couple arguing, snatching a hand back when he remembered Daisy-May's command not to touch anything. He yanked his eyes away, only to find that she had disappeared from view.

Then, instead of being pulled towards her, he was tugged backwards, the rope around his stomach going taut. Something was dragging him back towards the Pen. Slowly, slowly he tumbled away from the girl he could no longer see, his backside crunching into a floor that looked like trifle but felt like concrete.

He cried out, his voice soundless and smothered.

I can feel pain then. Daisy-May wasn't just trying to scare me.

It wasn't a particularly comforting realisation.

He lumbered clumsily to his feet, the pressure of the place crushing him along with the panic at being, for the first time, completely alone. Silence pressed against his ears. He was about to tug the part of the rope that was still attached, somewhere, to Daisy-May when the rope behind him snapped taut again. Twirling around in a helpless half-speed ragdoll limbo, he saw what was doing the pulling.

Crawling towards him was a Dispossessed, getting handful by handful of rope ever closer.

Fighting against the crushing Gloop, Joe looked desperately around, because only *desperately around* would do now, his sense of *forwards* and *backwards* lost in this unimaginable strangeness. What would the Dispossessed do to him if it caught up? Probably not much – it didn't look the most switched-on of creatures – but that didn't mean he wanted to waltz with it, particularly with his oxygen mask feeling as flimsy as it did.

J
O
E

a voice from a half-dream said, its tone a bad connection swaddled in echo. He looked frantically for the source, every surface covered with images from times and places he didn't recognise. The rope bit tight, this time not from the direction of the Dispossessed and the Pen but from the opposite way, towards the space ahead of him that Daisy-May had inhabited. He caught it and yelped as it zipped through the palms of his hands.

A crude image of Daisy-May loomed large on the mass of matter in front of him, an animated cave-painting with a length of rope protruding from it, pulling him on to God only knew where.

Has to be better than here, Joe thought. If it's hell itself, it has to be better than here.

J
U
M
P

commanded the outline of Daisy-May, and Joe did, an undignified, lurching tumble-leap of blind faith, feeling – somehow – the girl's physical hand wrapping around his wrist, guiding him towards her image.

A grip of steel and bone tightened around his ankle, and he looked back at the waxy soul that had latched onto him. It yanked hard, pulling him away from Daisy-May and back into the crushing Gloop. The creature's other hand closed around the oxygen tank on his back, trying to use it as a ladder rung, the leather straps biting into Joe's shoulders. He tried to kick the thing off, achieving nothing more than yanking the straps tighter, the creature moaning with the slow-motion struggle of it all.

Daisy-May screamed, a lifetime away.

Y
O
U
R
M
A
S
K

Joe reached for his face, finding skin instead of rubber.

For a second, he thought he would be all right, that the breathing apparatus had been overkill, a placebo to ease him through this madness. Then he felt the tightness in his lungs, like a bicycle pump had been jammed into his soul, inflating it with every stroke, and appreciated that he was as far from all right as it was possible to be. Bony fingers dug into his scalp, and he knew he didn't have the energy to shake the creature off.

Was it like this the first time I died? Did it hurt like this? How many times does someone get to die?

Everything went black.

Then, it was as if he'd broken through the surface of an icy lake. Air rushed back into his lungs, his sight sprinting close behind.

The mask was back on his face.

Fingers were hooked around his collar.

Daisy-May – or the top half of her, at least – was in the Gloop, leaning past him, a gun in her fist, resolution on her face. The weapon kicked in her hand, a thin trail of neon exploding from the barrel in slow motion. Joe flinched as it arced towards the Dispossessed hitching a ride on his back, the bullet visible but translucent. It connected with the thing's head and exploded, tendrils splaying out from it, latching on to the Dispossessed like a parasite and ripping the creature away from him.

Organic was the word Joe couldn't shake. Gunpowder and fire had carved apart the boys in the farmhouse. There was no dignity in a gunshot wound, no beauty; it was an act of sledgehammer brutality. This was different. This looked like an autopsy of the creature's very being. The tendrils plunged themselves into the Dispossessed's body, twining deep into its core, stripping away the creature, layer by layer.

It won't stop until it's reached its soul, thought Joe. *And maybe not even then.*

He felt himself being yanked upwards. Sound began rushing into his ears, his last sight of the creature a floating, dissolving cluster of green particles that were already beginning to brown and crumble away.

Chapter Eight

Exiting the Gloop was like jumping out of a lake. Or into one, Joe couldn't quite decide which. He stayed crouching, a catastrophe of noise and colour all around him, his hands jammed over his ears, trying to shut everything out until he got his bearings. After the womb-like silence of the Gloop, this world's sensory tempest felt like drowning.

He opened his eyes slowly, letting the watery gloom bleed in, trying to process where he was.

Banks of woolly grey clouds overhead, pregnant with rain, and, if they put their minds to it, snow.

A sawdust-like sprinkling of frost.

A chorus of birdsong. A lawnmower chuntering in the distance.

A breeze full of life rather than nuclear winter death.

Metal hammering against metal.

'This is the living world,' said Joe. 'We're back.'

Daisy-May nodded as she worked.

A phalanx of stone tablets faced him, some of them crumbling at the edges.

'And we're in a graveyard.'

His companion continued to pound the metal spike into the grass next to her. Apparently satisfied, she took the rope that had tethered them together through the Gloop – the other end of which she'd pinned to the ground by the wall of the Pen – and fed it through the spike, tying it off. She gave the metal a final whack, then poked the rope, satisfied, apparently, with its tautness.

'This is how you get back,' she said, her back to Joe. 'Follow the rope.'

'It's how *we* get back,' said Joe. 'You're not planning on going anywhere, are you?'

He noticed that Daisy-May's shoulders, slim things that sloped away before they'd had a chance to get going, shook violently. He walked over to her and she shuffled around, not allowing him access to her face.

'Thanks,' he said, an inadequate opening but the best he had. 'For what you did back there.'

Daisy-May went still, and Joe heard her take a deep breath. She got to her feet and turned to him, her eyes teary and red. 'Didn't want to shoot that Dispossessed.'

'I'm glad you did,' said Joe, crouching down to rub his ankle. 'It had a hold of me. I'd be dead if it wasn't for you. Again.'

'It was just scared,' said Daisy-May. 'A Dispossessed in the Gloop's like a sheep wandering onto a motorway.'

'You did it a kindness, then. I don't think it was in pain,' lied Joe. It had, in fact, looked to be in plenty.

She slipped off her oxygen tank, dropping it next to the spike impaled in the ground, then ran her nails through her mane of pink hair. 'No coming back from what I just did. That man isn't dead like you and me are dead – he's *dead* dead. Every last cell of who he was, bleached away.'

'The way those things have to live, maybe it's for the best,' said Joe, placing a hand on her shoulder. 'Maybe it's a release.'

Daisy-May shrugged him off. 'Easy to say when you haven't been "released". You think your memory loss is bad?

At least you know who you are, what makes you you. There's no heaven, hell or purgatory for that Dispossessed. There's only consciousness. What's left won't remember where he is, or what he is, or who he was. He'll exist in a constant state of disorientation and terror for every second of every day – forever.'

She started pacing, retreading the same piece of grass, going back and forth, back and forth. 'You know the only difference between us and that bloke I just killed? An unseen fuckin' God deciding *we're* worthy of a second chance and *he* wasn't. Solve enough crimes and we get to go to paradise. What did he get? Oblivion. That sound fair to you? That sound *just*?'

They stood in silence, Daisy-May jabbing at her eyes like she was annoyed at them for letting her down, Joe shoving his hands in his pockets, unsure what it was he'd done wrong, but feeling guilty about it anyway.

'So you got the same deal, then? You solve who killed you, you get to go to heaven?'

Daisy-May nodded. 'Mostly.'

Joe frowned at the peg. 'What if you solve your murder before I solve mine?'

Finally, she smiled. 'Then I get to blow this gig. Another reason why you need to take notice of where that rope is, Joey. You may be taking that return trip alone.'

He cast a glance over the graveyard, realising it was familiar somehow. Soot-grey clouds patrolled the sky, the grass below them clipped short like a crew cut, a neatness in keeping with the place as a whole. There were no dissolving gravestones here, no sense of sloping decline; the graveyard was cup-final-day immaculate, and that inexplicably bothered him.

'Your name's Lazarus, right?'

He put the thought to one side. 'Last time I checked.'

Daisy-May was crouching in front of a marble headstone,

tracing her fingers along the name that had been etched on it. 'Grace Lazarus any relation?'

Was she?

Joe searched his memories; bruised, flighty things slippery to the touch. Whenever he did this, he had to fight hard against panic. What if he couldn't find the memory he was searching for?

What if he could, and he found it wasn't a memory he wanted to keep?

Then an image popped into his mind, short and sharp, like a blade between the ribs. 'Grace Lazarus was my mum. Still is, I guess.'

A slow-burn pain followed.

He kneeled next to Daisy-May, staring at the chiselled letters. 'She died when I was young. Can't remember how young, and not sure I want to. Happy to let that memory go.'

Daisy-May nodded like it made sense.

Joe scanned the place again. 'Why start here?'

'Because *here* is ground zero,' Daisy-May said, wiping her nose with the back of her hand. 'Wherever we go from here, this is where we return, 'cos it's the only way we have of getting back to the Pen.'

'That doesn't really answer my question,' said Joe.

'And *don't* you just have a lot of them.'

'Copper, remember?' he replied. 'This rope isn't how we got back the first time, from the farmhouse. You took my hand and there was the whole wall-of-light thing.'

'You get kid gloves on your first trip to the Pen,' said Daisy-May. 'You don't get given much in the afterlife, but you get that.'

'Good of them.' Joe looked at the spike in the ground doubtfully; it was hilariously fragile, considering what it was for. 'Why would we want to go back to the Pen?'

'Are you serious?'

'Seems to me that place is a barely upgraded version of hell,' said Joe. 'Why not just stay here, on the soil? There's fresh air, sunlight, no zombie legion of Dispossessed trying to eat you.'

'You are serious.'

'There or here, what's the difference? We're dead wherever we go, and at least this place doesn't look like a pound-shop apocalypse.'

Daisy-May perched herself on a gravestone, picking at her spindly wrist and staring at him fiercely. 'This place is poison to us. Like leaving uncooked meat in the sun. We ain't supposed to be here. It ain't natural but sometimes it's necessary, and that's why we have to find out who murdered you *fast*. Those that overstay their welcome, they're what you'd call ghosts. But not your average Caspers. Something happens to us if we're soil-side too long.'

'Worse than amnesia?'

'You don't what to know. Trust me when I say it's brutal, though.'

She reached into the pack she'd taken from Mabel at the stall. It looked military-issue to Joe, but World War Two era; a battered khaki canvas bag that reminded him of an old military knick-knack shop from his childhood.

And there it is, he thought, a smile blossoming. Another memory. A nice one this time.

Daisy-May took out the tin emblazoned with 'ATOMIC FIRE GUM' and tossed it to him. 'If you want to keep the few memories you've hoarded, you'll slap your gob round this.'

Inside were half a dozen ancient-looking sticks of gum, enclosed in a gold foil wrapper.

'This is the smack you gave to the Dispossessed back in the Pen. Sorry – the "sedative".'

'It's not a sedative to us,' said Daisy-May. 'It's protection. Keeps the amnesia at bay.'

'I've already got amnesia.'

'You've got *selective* amnesia; you still remember who the essential Joe Lazarus is. That's what makes you special – makes you Dying Squad – but without the help of this gum, special won't last. Only person in the Pen that can come here and not use the gum is the Duchess, and she's a badass demigod. You're just an above-average copper with a ropy-as-fuck memory.'

'Thanks. You really know how to make a bloke feel valued.'

He peeled the wrapper off, then looked at the vividly pink gum suspiciously. 'What's in it?'

'You remember the sky, back in the Pen?'

He thought back to the red-and-black limbo clouds, the ones that had reminded him of a nuclear winter with a stomach ache. 'Sure.'

'Well, whatever's in that sky, it fills up our dead lungs and gives us an afterlife. Same shit's baked into this gum.'

He popped the gum into his mouth and, as his jaw cycled it, it was as if his mind was an elastic band that someone had gently twanged. The mind-fog that lingered over both the memories he could remember and those he couldn't lifted. He felt energised, clear.

He felt like himself.

A car coughed behind them, gargling fumes. They both turned to see a group of mourners coming up the graveyard path, heads bowed, tones hushed. Behind them was a hearse, a few feet from the church gate, its engine idling. Two crisply dressed undertakers eased their way out of it, one adjusting his hat slightly, the other looking up at the sky as if daring the sun to show.

A priest exited last, his hands clasped together, his eyes blinking in the light.

I know that man, thought Joe. Is it through the police?

No, that's not right.

He swallowed hard. His stomach dropped, along with the penny.

That's my Dad. This is his church.

'Please tell me,' he said, 'that we're not at my funeral.'

Chapter Nine

'Mahogany coffin,' said Daisy-May, whistling in appreciation. 'Your old man's sending you off in style.'

They observed the funeral party from several feet away, four pall-bearers each taking a corner of the coffin, the oldest, at the front right, bowing slightly under the weight. Joe drew blanks for all of them.

Of all the trippy shit I've had to endure over the last few hours, he thought, this is the trippiest. Who imagines that they'll attend their own funeral? Follow their own stone-cold body, scanning a congregation for faces they recognise? Feel complete indifference when looking at those mourners? It doesn't feel like I'm at my own funeral. It feels like I'm a spectator at someone else's.

'Is it weird that I'm half tempted just to reach out and flip the lid off?' he said, falling into line behind the pall-bearers.

'That's a big no-no,' said Daisy-May. 'We cannot physically interact with the living world. Think I was clear on that rule.'

'Because of the Xylophone Man. Spooky.'

'Yes, Joey. The terrifying inhuman monster that will drag you to hell.'

'It's Joe. And I thought that punishment was for interfering with the living, not knocking over random objects.'

'It isn't worth the risk, trust me. Besides, most can't do it; I can't physically interact with the real world, so a newbie like you's got no chance.'

Joe wasn't really listening any more. Instead, he was staring at the vicar, who was watching the pall-bearers set down his casket. There was something about him, other than the fact that he was his father. Something that was causing a grip of rage in his chest, one that seemed to tighten by the minute.

'By the eyes you're making at the vicar,' Daisy-May said, 'I'm guessing you two have history.'

'Not much of a guess,' said Joe.

She was right, though. He felt the sting of years lost between them, and it wasn't some Technicolor saccharine highlight reel; it was a jet-black promo of pain and angst, one that it was difficult to pull any clear memories from.

His father's appearance was troubling. Joe couldn't remember what he'd looked like before, but he guessed it wasn't like this; it was like life's disappointments had withered the man's neck, something the dog collar encircling it couldn't hide. Time had peeled the skin of his skull backwards and pushed his eyeballs forwards, clerical robes dangling off his scrawny frame. Ineffectively dyed black hair jutted out, except for the crown of his head, which was bald, revealing a smattering of liver spots. He wasn't so much a man as a buzzard in a gown.

I look better, Joe thought, and I'm dead.

Daisy-May looked at him, a smirk on her face. 'Let me guess – strict religious upbringing, you rebelled against it, you two never made your peace?'

Was it that?

It wasn't.

There was truth in the girl's words, but it was more than that. It was something he'd done.

Except that's not right. It was something I was accused of doing.

64

Then it came to him, the thrill of the clawed-back memory fading as soon as he appreciated its magnitude.

'Stealing,' he said. 'He accused me of stealing from him.'

Daisy-May looked at him curiously. 'You remember that?'

He stopped. 'Yeah. Why?'

'Duchess said your memories would come back quickly. Mine didn't. Still haven't. Maybe you are hot shit, after all; that, or you're just making it up.'

'Who'd make that up?' said Joe.

'Good point.'

They took a seat off to the side as mourners continued to straggle in.

'Did you do it?' said Daisy-May.

'Did I what?'

'Steal from the church.'

Joe glared at her. 'No. I caught the thieves when I was alive, remember? It was literally my job.'

'When you were an adult, sure. Who knows what you did when you were a kid?'

'I do. Trust me.'

Daisy-May raised her eyebrows. 'So if it wasn't you, who did nick the money?'

'I don't remember,' said Joe.

Which was true enough. Truer, certainly, than what he'd said before, because he hadn't taken the memories of his innocence from the amnesia fog; he'd assumed it. Fatal, normally, for a copper worth his salt, but how could he do anything else? He had to believe that.

Daisy-May looked up to the heavens. 'You don't remember, 'cos despite the gum you dropped, the air here's already rotting those little grey cells.'

'What do *you* remember?' asked Joe. 'From before you died? About how you died?'

'Like I said, not much. More will come back to me. *Was* coming back to me, until you became my next assignment and I had to return here.'

She rose from the pew. 'Time to go: think I've made my point about the whole you're-really-dead thing.'

'A few minutes more,' Joe said, as his father coughed and turned to the collection of mourners, ready to begin.

'Your funeral,' said Daisy-May, shrugging resignedly.

It struck Joe that if youth was wasted on the young, funerals were certainly wasted on the dead. But he was here, and if he got lucky, his father's eulogy would be a breakdown of who he was as a person, and a visual who's-who of who loved him, and maybe a few who didn't. All valuable things when you were trying to piece together the end of your life.

Now, though, in a cold, quarter-empty church, all he could think was: was this what he was worth?

He'd dedicated his life to fighting crime, giving people closure, righting wrongs. His reward, apparently, was a drizzle of people so old that they were probably booked in for the funeral after his. There was a smattering of younger people, but were they his friends? It didn't feel like it; their faces didn't spark anything in him. They could be anyone.

Certainly, his dad seemed rattled. He was just standing there, soundlessly mouthing like a fish out of water. Maybe he's overcome with grief, Joe thought. Or maybe he's trying to imagine what grief would feel like.

'Turn-out could have been better.'

He bristled as Daisy-May slouched in the pew next to him. 'Yeah, well, it's probably a weekday. Difficult for people to get the time off work.'

'That's probably it.'

Joe frowned. His father, having dispensed with the greetings and platitudes, now paused, seemingly unsure how to proceed. He yanked on his dog collar, looking like he wanted to be anywhere else but the house of God, delivering a eulogy for his fallen son.

What happened to him? thought Joe. He's tugging on that dog collar like it's a fucking penance. He doesn't even look grief-stricken. He looks bored.

Bored, and uncomfortable.

The reverend toyed with a flamboyant ruby ring that barely clung to his bony, hooked finger. 'At this time, it would be traditional for the eulogy to be read. Traditional, me being Joe's father, that I read it. It is a tradition that I intend to break, to allow for some people who might be able to say it better.'

Jesus, thought Joe. Comes to something when you farm out your own son's eulogy.

Daisy-May whistled, poking his arm. 'You know, I'm no expert on churches, but this place is *mighty* fucking fancy.'

Joe tore his attention from his twitchy father and followed the girl's gaze to the high-vaulted ceiling. Just like that, memories began to flow. Whether these came from the gum, the familiarity of the surroundings, or something else, he had no way of knowing. There was joy in it, like drinking from a cool, clear glass of water, but also a little fear, because it was like he was gulping when he only wanted to sip.

Growing up, this pile of rocks had been a virtual second home to him, and a shabby one at that. The roof leaked, the heating clanked inefficiently, and the whole building gave the impression that a puff from the devil would bring the structure crashing down. His dad had been trying to build somewhere new. His sanctuary, he'd called it, for the needy. But donations weren't forthcoming. There's no money in religion, he would always say. People want salvation but are rarely willing to pay for it.

They'd paid for it now, though. Someone had, anyway:

brand-new seats, a rebuilt glass-ceilinged reception, an altogether unnecessary video screen with a crystal-clear sound system. A wealthy parishioner, perhaps, leaving a wildly generous bequest to the church? Whatever the source of the money, it proved something to Joe that he'd always known: the building – the legacy – was more important to his father than the people he was supposed to be saving.

'Is that your old man?'

Joe followed Daisy-May's finger: it was pointed at a large stained-glass window to their left. He hadn't noticed it before, but now that he squinted, he saw that she was right: weak daylight refracted through a coloured glass depiction of his father. He was looking beatifically towards the heavens, his arms outstretched.

Who does he think he is, thought Joe, Jesus?

The glass version also bore the fat ruby on his finger. It was an item of jewellery that brought another influx of memories: it was as if Joe was watching a slideshow of his childhood. The poverty he had grown up in, poverty that his father had embraced like a spiritual hair shirt. The cast-off school uniforms that had been a size too small, or too big.

His father had always had contempt for gaudy displays of wealth. When had that changed?

As his flesh-and-blood father welcomed a man and woman up to the pulpit, Joe was tipped out of his historical deep-dive. He knew this couple. More than just knew them.

'Who are they?' asked Daisy-May.

Names matched with faces that interlocked with memories.

A rush of joy, one he had feared beyond him. These two people were all that really mattered in his life. Why was that?

Claire. *My Claire.*

'That's my wife,' said Joe, his voice wobbling, eyes stinging. 'Claire.'

Daisy-May nodded approvingly. 'She's a fuckin' hottie. What was she doing with you?'

'Good question,' he said, swallowing. He couldn't remember how they'd met, not yet, but he knew how looking at her made him feel. Just the sight of her had always made him want to be a better person. There was a warmth to her that permeated even the grimness of this occasion. The rest of the mourners seemed to share his feelings; all of them smiling fondly at her.

Do we have kids? He couldn't picture them. *Surely that's something death can't wipe out. Did we choose not to? Or did we try, and couldn't?* It felt like he should at least remember that.

'What about the bloke next to her?' said Daisy-May. 'The one shaped like a meat wardrobe?'

Joe focused.

A memory popped up of a boy. This boy looked much like the rugby player standing next to Claire, same build, with the same tousled sandy hair and an us-against-the-world grin. They were playing together on a sun-dappled lawn.

Cops and robbers. We always used to play cops and robbers. Except we'd always fight over who got to be the robber. Ironic, considering what we'd go on to become.

Joe smiled. 'His name's Pete. He's my partner on the force.'

'*I'm* your partner on the force.'

'My real police partner, not this rent-a-ghost bullshit.'

Daisy-May slung an elbow into Joe's ribs. He rubbed them, watching as Pete stepped up to the lectern, Claire holding on to his arm for support. They came, he thought. If no one else did, at least Pete and Claire came.

Was it wishful thinking on his part to imagine that Claire knew he was there? That if she did, that knowledge would bring her some degree of comfort?

She knew. He was convinced of it. The way she was smiling. The grief in her eyes, but also the hope.

I could stay here, he thought. Fuck solving my own murder. Fuck the Dying Squad. I could stay here and be close to her. Watch over her. Be her guardian angel. I've got the gum. I'd never forget her again.

Except he would, because already that memory fog was starting to gather. How long had it been since he'd taken the gum? Fifteen minutes? Ten?

Pete nervously cleared his throat, almost as if calling for Joe's attention, his rugby player's physique stitched into his Sunday best, his hand yanking at the tie slung around his neck. Always looking like a squaddie who's spent the night in the cells, thought Joe fondly. Pete could never play anything but bad cop to my good with a face like that. A bit of a curse, and a gift.

An interview room formed in his mind, the two men inside it, questioning some no-doubt-nefarious criminal, a well-oiled tag team fuelled by brotherhood.

'It's a bit unusual, both of us being up here,' began Pete, half smiling at the small congregation then nodding at Claire. 'Not as unusual as it not being the *three* of us, though, because it was always the three of us, since the first day of primary school. Joe, me and Claire. We never seemed to need anyone else. I can't believe that's over.'

And there it was. Joe really was dead.

Some desperate part of him had hoped there would be some unlikely last-minute reprieve. It wasn't coming. If your best friend said you were dead, you were dead.

It was funny the rhetoric used when talking about those who had died; *they'll be looking down on you, watching over you* was the party line, and Joe supposed that was true enough. The tone of that rhetoric was way off, though. There was no whimsy here, no beatific fondness; there was only anger, regret. He'd never touch his wife's face again, or go for a drink with his mate. He'd never get the chance to put things right with his father.

Maybe I'm in hell already, he thought. How could it be worse than this?

The small scattering of mourners stood outside, watching as the coffin hovered over the freshly dug grave.

'We're still here,' said Daisy-May, shifting from foot to foot. 'How much more convincing do you need?'

'None,' said Joe, as he watched Pete and Claire break away from the main group. 'This is something else. Come on.'

Daisy-May matched Joe's stride as he followed the couple. 'He's got a steel trap of a mind, they said. A copper who knows how to get shit done, they said.'

Joe glared at her. 'I'm trying to listen.'

'I can't believe it,' Claire was saying, staring at the casket. 'He's really gone.'

'Doesn't seem real,' said Pete. 'He was a force of nature, Joe. Can't remember him having a cold before, and he's gone, just like that. It's not right.'

Claire took out a cigarette and tried to light it, the engraved silver lighter in her left hand wavering along with the flame.

I bought her that lighter, thought Joe, smiling at the sudden memory. It was a well-done-for-quitting-smoking present. She laughed. That was one of things I always loved about Claire: she laughed at things she shouldn't.

Pete reached out and steadied her hand, allowing his to linger.

'Got one of those for me?'

Joe turned to see his father approaching. The old man smiled at the couple, and Claire tried to smile back, offering him the pack of cigarettes.

The reverend dug one out and accepted the flame.

'Didn't take you for a smoker, Bill,' said Pete.

'Lapsed. My son always had a knack of bringing out my

71

worst habits.' He inhaled deeply, his eyes closed like he'd found his true calling. 'Any leads?'

'It's an ongoing investigation that I'm not at liberty to discuss, sir, but when I catch the bastard, you can be damn sure you'll be the first to know.' Pete held his hands up. 'Sorry for the blasphemy.'

Bill smirked like it was a joke only he was in on. 'My son's lying dead in the ground. Hard to think of what's more blasphemous than that, and you can tell God I said so.'

He looked at the cigarette as if seeing it for the first time, and let it drop to the floor, crushing it underfoot. 'I'll see you both at the wake?'

'Of course,' said Claire, kissing him on the cheek. 'Thank you for doing it in the evening for us. Gives us the time we need.'

'Joe always loved a party,' said Pete, shaking the reverend's hand. 'That lad was born a night owl. We'll send him off in style.'

The group broke up, Pete's hand lightly on Claire's back as he guided her away.

Joe felt a squeeze on his arm.

'We should watch that bloke,' said Daisy-May. 'These things are *always* one partner double-crossing the other. I'd say he's our prime suspect.'

'Fuck off,' said Joe, still watching them go.

Daisy-May flinched a little.

'I just mean—'

'Just . . . don't,' he said. 'Pete would die for me, and I for him. He's family. You might as well accuse my dad.'

Daisy-May held up her hands, placatory. 'Understood. What's next?'

What was next? A familiar tingle, the sense that the truth was there, waiting for him to uncover it.

This he knew how to do. This he was good at.

'I want to go back to the crime scene,' he said. 'We're going to work this back before we try to work it forward.' He looked at her expectantly. 'How do we get there? Is there some teleportation trick we can use?'

Daisy-May withered him with a glance.

'Yes, mate. It's called walking.'

Chapter Ten

Joe and Daisy-May stood where they'd first met. The farm-house was just as they'd left it, if you ignored the boarded-up front door and reams of police tape.

'How long is it since we were here?'

'A fortnight, in soil time,' Daisy-May said. 'Minutes in the Pen can be days on the soil. It's just one of the many fucked-up aspects of the afterlife.'

Joe watched as the yellow tape caught in a snag of wind. 'So can we turn back time somehow? Say, to a few minutes before I was killed?'

Daisy-May raised her eyes to the raw grey sky. 'Assume that to any high-concept questions you may have, the answer's no.'

'Right, because time travel would be the most ridiculous thing that's happened to me recently.'

Daisy-May rooted around in her backpack, taking out a roll of stickers and a felt-tip pen. She circled with her finger to him. 'Turn around.'

Joe frowned but did as he was told, Daisy-May leaning against his back, scribbling on a sticker then ripping it off, fixing it proudly to his chest.

'*I AM JOE!* Am I likely to forget?'

'Remember the whole the-air-here-rots-your-mind-and-gives-you-amnesia talk I gave you?'

'I did,' Joe said, deadpan, 'but then I forgot it again.'

'Funny fucker.'

Except she was right.

These memories are hard won, and I'm going to fight to keep them.

She reached into the backpack again, pulling out a notebook and handing it to him.

On the cover was a *Dragnet* insignia.

Joe felt his face light up as another memory bobbed to the surface. 'I used to watch this with my dad because he watched it with *his* dad. It's one of the few good memories of him I have. I think.'

'Yeah, that's kind of the point,' said Daisy-May. 'It's to write notes in as we go along – because you will forget, the longer we're here – and the whole *Dragnet* thing's a link to your past. You can thank the Duchess for this.'

'How does she have access to my memories? Does that mean she knows who killed me?'

'If she did, don't you think she'd save us some time? That's for the Almighty gaffer to know, and us to find out.'

'So she's nothing more than a branch manager, the Duchess.'

'If she is,' said Daisy-May, 'what does that make you?'

Joe tucked the notebook and pen into his trench coat, offering a thin smile. 'Thanks for the book.'

'It's not an engagement ring.' Daisy-May gestured towards the house. 'Shall we?'

Joe stood for a moment, considering the place, his eyes devouring every malnourished brick and neglected timber frame. There was a scent to crime scenes like this, one you didn't pick up with your nostrils but with your mind. The nuts and bolts of policing you could teach to anyone, given time. Investigative instinct you couldn't.

Finally, Joe nodded to himself, crossing the deserted road and ducking into the narrow sliver of alley that ran alongside the house.

'Want to include me in your thinking here, Joey?' called out Daisy-May, struggling to keep pace with him. 'Supposed to be a partnership, right?'

'We're not partners,' said Joe, instinctively avoiding the alley's pooled water. 'And my name's not Joey.'

The alley opened out onto a scorched-bare back garden and levelled-flat wide-screen fields. Stubborn trails of mist picked at sky and soil, an ocean of grey cloud above it all. Snow in those bastard clouds, thought Joe, with a flash of numb fingers and the steam rising from a thermos. A wintry night shift, perhaps? Or maybe a frozen-to-the-bone stake-out.

He stopped, hands on hips, drinking it in. 'There's something important about this back garden. Something that led me here originally.'

A couple of tyres, forlorn and forgotten.

The shell of a car, burned out and abused.

A collection of syringes ignored when his colleagues had swept the place. The rear of the farmhouse didn't give him much to go on either. There was no tape on the back door, primarily because there was no back door; whether the ARU had ripped it off when they stormed the house was unclear. A large slab of wood stood in its place, held there by a battalion of nails.

He turned to Daisy-May. 'I can walk through this?'

She nodded. 'One of the few perks of being dead.'

He faced it directly, stretching slightly, on his toes, taking in a lungful of air he didn't need to psych himself up. 'All right, then.'

As he stepped forward, the sensation was similar to when the ARU member had passed through him; like raindrops tinkling on his spine. Not as strongly as before, though, he thought, as the kitchen came into view. Either I'm getting used to it, or inanimate objects don't have as much of a kick as flesh-and-blood ones.

The room was in almost total darkness, the wall of wood that had been sutured to the outside blocking out any trace of natural light. There was a stillness to the place but a heavy one; it was as if the house knew that violence had been carried out within its four walls, and hadn't yet begun to heal.

Get a fucking grip, Joe thought. Houses don't bruise, they don't need to heal, and nothing haunts them.

Although that wasn't true, because the fact was – and facts were still his god, the life raft to cling to in the midst of the madness – he'd been killed in this house, and here he was, back at the scene of the crime, trying to find out who'd done it. If it wasn't an actual haunting, it was a solid homage to one.

'Here's what we need to do,' he said, grateful to be running a crime scene again. 'We need to light this place up, then trace the murder back. Start with the boys we found at the front door, examine blood splatter, work out the angle of the bullet's trajectory. Re-create the moments that led up to my death. The bodies might have been moved, but the evidence hasn't; it's still here, waiting for us.'

'That sounds great,' called out Daisy-May. 'Hit the lights for us, would you?'

Joe reached out instinctively, snatching his hand away at the last moment. He felt frustration building within him. How could he conduct a murder investigation if he couldn't even throw a light switch?

'I'm just pulling your leg, mate,' said Daisy-May, entering the room. 'Here's how being a dead copper has its advantages.'

A haze of light pulsed from her hands, soundtracked by the beating of tiny wings. Joe stared open-mouthed. She was holding a small, clear box containing three winged insects that, if pressed, he would have described as dung beetles. They threw themselves violently against the sides of their plastic prison, their eerie pallor growing brighter as they did so.

Daisy-May slid open the front of the box, releasing them, and Joe watched, fascinated, as the three beetles flew over his head, shadows spiking in their wake, the room's bleak gloom pierced by their unnatural light.

'What are those things?'

'Back in the day – and we're talking the OG pharaoh's day – these things were all the rage,' Daisy-May replied. 'Symbolised rebirth, regeneration, all that heavenly-cycle-of-renewal shit. Me, I just like the way you don't need to change their batteries. They beat a torch any day.'

The insects split up, one staying in the kitchen, frantically circling the dangling lampshade and giving the room waves of light, while the other two flew out of sight.

'So, what are we looking for?'

Joe ran a hand across the dining table, a neglected, woodlouse-nibbled thing splattered with a variety of fluids. 'Well, what do they teach you in the Dying Squad? Aren't you supposed to solve crimes?'

'Usually, yeah,' said Daisy-May. 'And I'm good at it; some would say better than good. But then I was seconded to babysit your dead arse, so now my job's keeping you safe, making sure you don't fuck up too badly, and keeping track of the clues, if you find any.'

Joe stopped at the wall, leaning in closer to what looked like a bullet hole. 'You retain memories better than me, then. Why?'

'Because I've been doing this longer than you.'

She clicked her fingers at the hovering beetle, then pointed at the wall. Joe looked on, amazed, as it obeyed the command, throwing a fierce shawl of light onto the pockmarked surface he'd been examining.

He squinted at the bullet hole. 'And you have the gum.'

'Gum that wears off, meaning we still need to work fast. You're a detective, aren't you? Detect.'

He gave the wall a final look, then went out into the hallway, one of the beetles already ahead of him, lighting the way. In the centre of the floor were two dried pools of blood.

'This is where I found the murdered gang members,' he said softly, crouching down to examine the stains, then looking back towards the kitchen. 'There's no trail of blood, nothing to indicate they did anything but die right here.'

He took a half-shuffle forward, pointing to a scar of dried blood next to the front door. 'One of them hears a knock at the front door and goes to open it. He's paranoid enough – or savvy enough – to realise that all may not be as it seems, so he has his mate to back him up. Then, when the door opens, who-ever's on the doorstep fires, and doesn't stop till he drops them.'

'He, or she,' said Daisy-May.

Joe nodded, jumping to his feet and pointing to the pepper-sprayed wall. 'Should rule nothing out until you can rule it in, that's true, but look at the distribution of gunfire. Whoever came blasting did so with something big and heavy. You ever fired a shotgun?'

Daisy-May held up her emaciated arms. 'With these?'

'Well those things buck like a bastard in arms bigger and meaner than mine. This wasn't a woman. I'd stake my career on it.'

'Your old one, or your new one?'

Ignoring that, Joe stood still, head tilted, like the house had a secret that it was dying to tell him.

'Let's go upstairs,' he said finally. 'I want to see where I died.'

'Of course you do,' said Daisy-May, wrapping her arms around her slight body, her usual bluster dimmed.

As they made their way up the stairs, the only sound that

could be heard was the pair of scarab beetles lending a staccato light to their ascent, shadows looming large all around them. Joe winced when they reached the landing, something deep in his core protesting.

'Know when they say it's like someone walked on your grave?' said Daisy-May. 'Being this close to where you died, well, it's like someone digging that grave up.'

Joe bent double as the feeling intensified. 'Is there anything you can give me for it?'

'The advice to make it snappy. That gum won't last forever, mate.'

He squeezed his fists together and stood up straight. There was no more putting it off.

'Then let's get this done.'

He turned from the room where he'd discovered his own body, towards the hallway. Three doors were peppered on each side, closed and concealing any secrets they might be hiding.

'Check those, would you?' he said, gesturing. He needed a moment alone. 'I want to poke around the crime scene.'

Daisy-May muttered something about being treated like a poor man's Scully, then headed for the first door on the left.

Joe stood in the room alone, glad of his own company, if not the surroundings. It was time to cut off the emotional attachment to the room, set aside the horror of it. This was just another crime scene.

There's something wrong with this picture, he told himself. What is it?

The crusted bloodstain his body had left was easy enough to find; he'd been shot here in this room, he was sure of it, and definitively enough to mean there was no crawling away, no raging against the dying of the light.

That wasn't what was bugging him, though.

He looked around, trying to work out what was, the beetle hovering close to a chunk of ceiling that was seemingly biding its time to fall, Pollock-like shadows splattered on the walls thanks to a chink in the window's boards.

The walls.

He moved quickly around them, searching for the bullet holes that had dug themselves into their downstairs brethren, finding none.

He hadn't been shot with the same weapon the gang members had. Hard to prove, admittedly, without access to the forensic evidence, but his eyes could be trusted when nothing else could; the room was clean. Unlike the carnage that had been wrought downstairs, whoever had executed him had done so cleanly and professionally. Did that mean he'd died before those boys, or afterwards? Had the same person pulled the trigger?

'Nothing in the other rooms,' said Daisy-May, appearing at the doorway. 'Unless you're after ciggie butts and rat shit.' She shivered, looking at the room as if it was a shifty stranger. 'Stank's bad in here, man. Never get used to the smell of killing.'

Joe frowned. 'You can smell this?'

'You can't?'

'Feels like the walls are closing in on me, if you can call that a smell.'

Daisy-May nodded. 'Closest the likes of us will get when we're on the soil. Some bad shit went down here, Joey.'

'Joe,' he said, automatically. 'And yeah, I'm the non-living proof of that.'

He went to the window, the wood that had been placed over it not as thick or regimented as it was on the others, allowing a crack of dusk in as a result.

'Something brought me here. A tip-off, maybe, but something else, something I can't remember. Something *in this room*.'

Daisy-May sat down on the corner of the bed, looking around her. 'There's nothing here, mate.'

'There is, we just haven't seen it,' said Joe, his vision beginning to drift.

She watched, concerned, as he reached into his jacket and popped a stick of gum into his mouth.

'When they're gone, they're gone. That's not me being tight, that's me saying that the quicker you use them, the quicker you'll become immune.'

'You don't need one yet?' said Joe, massaging his temple. 'Because my brain's getting mushier by the second.'

'I've learned to ration it. One every two hours. You feel your mind going, check your notes in your notepad, sound off what's important. You do that, you should be able to space the gum out more.'

He'd almost forgotten the notepad. Maybe it's like any drug, he thought. The more you use it, the less effective it is.

All he knew was, his vision was clearer and his mind wasn't far behind.

'Know why county-line drug gangs pick these farmhouses?' he said, because saying it out loud helped order his thoughts.

'County line?' asked Daisy-May.

'Drugs gangs. Ones based in cities that use kids in the country to funnel and sell their dope for them.'

She shook her head.

'Those gangs love places like this, because smugglers used them. They're right next to the coast, so perfect for shipments of fuck-knows-what coming through. This one – like most of the ones in Lincolnshire – was built in the 1700s, and used to store items like tea, cloth and wine. Custom duties were sky high at that time, so the black market was where it was at. Same goods, except cheaper. True during World War Two, too. The canny crook brought in by sea all the shit you couldn't get normally, and made a killing, keeping it in places like this.'

'Is there a point to this, or have you forgotten it?' said Daisy-May.

Joe gave a desperate laugh and slumped against the wall. 'I can't remember how I was killed, but I remember minor plot points from *Dad's Army* and fucking *Poldark*.'

'Life's a sick joke,' said Daisy-May, smiling at him. 'Whichever side of the astral plane you're on.'

He peeled himself off the wall. 'Point is, dealers in the big city, they're using places like this – and kids in places like this – for the same reason. Funnel the drugs from overseas, flood the countryside market, pluck children from council estates and broken-arse homes. All of them desperate and ready to earn some money.'

'All of which means what?' said Daisy-May, looking at him expectantly.

'All of which means that this is a stash house,' said Joe, 'and we haven't found where they keep the stash.'

He looked around him, glaring at the room, daring it to give up its secrets. It was naked and neglected, the only furniture being the bed Daisy-May was sitting on. Something sparked in his consciousness, some déjà vu.

'Can we move this?' he said, pointing at the bed.

'You been taking *we're dead* notes or not?' said Daisy-May.

'I need to check behind it,' said Joe, looking at the ragged wooden panelling on the wall.

'Then go through it,' said Daisy-May. 'For someone who thinks he's Sherlock, you're pretty thick.'

Joe ignored the barb as Daisy-May hopped off the bed. He took a breath, then ran towards it at full speed, jumping as he got to the edge, the wall of wood behind it rushing towards him as he overshot, his eyes involuntarily closing. He crashed though the wall, muscle memory telling him he felt pain that he didn't.

When he opened his eyes, he was in an enclosed jet-black room, the suggestion of the stooped ceiling enough for him to crouch down, despite the impossibility of him hitting his head on it.

'Kind of dramatic, weren't it?' said Daisy-May from the other side of the wall. 'Hang on, help coming.'

The sound of tiny beating wings could be heard, light flooding a room that Joe instantly saw was more of a dug-out corner of hell.

He took a step backwards, his mind refusing to accept what his eyes were showing him.

'Fucking hell,' said Daisy-May, behind him now.

Two girls lay on the floor, their eyes staring lifelessly into the void.

It was the girl at the back who drew Joe's attention, though. Her skin – or what was left of it – was warped and taut, clinging to the bones beneath, but that wasn't what made him stare. It was what the waxwork corpse was wearing: a stained white Nirvana T-shirt with a blizzard of marks on it, a mane of pink hair, its colour undimmed by death.

'Jesus Christ,' said Daisy-May, her voice cracking. 'It's *me*.'

Chapter Eleven

Even with the fragile memory of his training, it was difficult for Joe to say how long the bodies – how long Daisy-May's body – had been there. Judging by the state of them, it had been months.

'You didn't know about this?' he asked, turning to her.

Daisy-May shook her head.

'How can that be?'

'Do you know how *you* died?' she asked.

'You know I don't.'

'Well then, why would I? We don't all get to be like you, a single mission before you go to paradise. Until now, I've been solving other cases, told to be patient and wait my turn.' She kneeled down in front of her own decaying corpse, shaking her head. 'Would have liked a fuckin' heads-up, though.'

Joe placed a hand on her shoulder. 'This is a good thing.'

'I'm looking at my corpse,' said Daisy-May. 'Rats have eaten my ears off. Define good.'

'But this is us getting somewhere, because our deaths must be connected. We find out what happened to me, we find out what happened to you. We both move on.'

'How about we find out what happened to me, *then* we find out what happened to you?'

'Fine,' Joe said. 'None of this makes you doubt your Duchess? Because she had to have known about your body being here.'

'I never know how much she knows,' said Daisy-May. 'Have to figure not everything, or what would be the point of the Squad? Way I see it, we need to discover this shit for ourselves. Memories need to come back naturally so we can trust what we find out. Don't lead the witness: isn't that one of the first things they teach you in cop school?'

'More like don't beat the witness, but I take your point.' Joe bent down to the shell of Daisy-May, pursing his lips. 'I'm sorry you had to die this way.'

'Make it up to me by helping me find out who did it,' said Daisy-May. ''Cos chances are, they had a good part in killing you too.'

Joe tried to cast his mind back, a black nothing his reward.

'We have to keep backtracking,' he said, with a confidence he didn't feel. 'Doing that brought us to this, which is our first piece of the puzzle. How did you get here? Can you remember?'

'Think I'd need your help if I could?'

'What's the last thing you *can* remember?' said Joe.

'Plenty,' said Daisy-May. 'My last mission. Every conversation with the Duchess. The Dispossessed. Every memory, pretty much, that I've formed since dying.'

'So what's the problem?'

'The same as you have – I can't remember a fucking sausage from before then. Don't know who I was on the soil, or at least, the *details* of who I was. Know my name, and what makes me *me*. Anything else? It's Swiss cheese, mate.'

Joe smiled ruefully. 'Join the club. It's an exclusive one, but the membership's pretty flaky.'

'I never want to join a club that'll have me as a member,' said Daisy-May, returning the smile.

There was a moment of silence between them, and then Joe clicked his fingers, bringing the beetle to heel. He was impressed when it responded, and he pointed it towards Daisy-May's body. He didn't know what he was looking for, just that there had to be something, some clue, no matter how small, that would get him on track again. The insect, agitated in its small confines, twirled around the decomposing corpse, giving it even more of a ghoulish air.

A Rolodex of memories filled his head, other bodies from other cases. Had he solved those, when he'd been alive?

He took a half-shuffle back, taking in every inch of Daisy-May's corpse.

Nothing on the weather-beaten Converse trainers.

Nothing on the ragged jeans.

Nothing on the sunken upper torso.

Nothing on the arms except the suggestion of skin and scar tissue.

Nothing on the left hand except five talon-like nails.

Nothing on the—

'Wait,' he said.

In contrast to the long nails on the left hand, the ones on the right were barely there; it was like they'd been violently whittled away over a long period. There was crusted blood on the skinny fingertips, too.

Like she was trying to scrabble away from something, he thought, digging her escape. She must have known, though, that such an act was pointless; the wall separating the bedroom and the cubbyhole was almost a foot deep. She'd have needed a pickaxe, or better yet, a jackhammer to get through.

The detached way he'd considered this gave him pause. For all he knew, this was the way he'd always been when investigating a case, but the victim didn't usually accompany him to the autopsy. Daisy-May was standing right there.

'You don't have to see this.'

'Got nowhere better to be.'

He shrugged, then stepped closer. What was it about those nails?

The knowledge that he couldn't physically touch the body did little to take away his squeamishness at being so close to it.

'The fuckin' *face* on ya,' said Daisy-May. 'If you think this is bad for *you*, what do you think it's like for *me*?'

'Sorry,' said Joe. 'You're right.'

There.

On a floorboard next to her was a small pile of broken-off nails, and beside that, a message, one word that had been scraped into the ground in blood, fear and desperation.

'KEGS,' said Daisy-May, seeing it too. 'What's that mean?'

'You tell me,' said Joe. 'You wrote it.'

'KEGS? Like underwear?'

The word on its own made no sense.

But as initials? There was something there. Something from his past. His childhood.

He looked at the letters again.

It was there, so close, taunting him.

He reached into his pocket, withdrawing the tin of gum.

'That's too much, too soon,' said Daisy-May.

'This is important,' he said, taking out a stick, unwrapping it, then putting it on his tongue.

He chewed.

Synapses sparked, trying to reignite.

He tried to keep the look of triumph off his face.

'The local school. King . . . King Edward's Grammar School.'

'Then we head there?'

'Are you asking me or telling me?'

'This is your show, Joey.'

'We head there. And it's Joe.'

He looked at the crumbling body of his young guide. 'You're OK with your body just rotting here? No telling when it'll be discovered. Can't see this place going on the property market any time soon.'

Daisy-May sniffed. 'Some mook finding a load of old bones won't make me any less dead. My soil body means nothing any more. Finding out how I died's all that's important. Same should go for you.'

Joe kneeled down beside the second body, next to Daisy-May's. It had withered away to just a few flaps of skin, a surfeit of bone and a shock of vivid green hair. 'Is this girl familiar? The hair leaves an impression.'

Daisy-May screwed up her face in frustration, finally shaking her head. 'Nothing. Fuck.'

Joe found himself grateful he could turn away from the pair. 'Well then, we go to the school. Best be on your guard. I don't remember why, but KEGS gives off a bad vibe.'

'It looks like I died bound and gagged in a sex dungeon,' said Daisy-May. 'Can't be much worse than that, can it?'

Joe smiled like he remembered what sympathy was.

Chapter Twelve

If there was something the Duchess had become expert at during her one-hundred-and forty-eight-year reign, it was finessing the truth.

Or lying, if you insisted on being coarse.

It didn't mean she liked it, but in the Pen, truth was a commodity that needed to be rationed. Serve out too much of it, and the souls under her command got sick. Certainly, the truth would disagree with Joe Lazarus.

No, better he believed that solving the riddle of his own death was his primary aim, why she'd sent him back to the soil. Better, too, for the girl. She had plans for Daisy-May, and they had no chance of coming to fruition unless Lazarus did what she needed him to. Funny that lying was always portrayed as a sin in that fable, the Bible. It was often the only way of doing truly good things.

The Duchess leaned back in her chair, the leather creaking, the glass of Scotch in her hand reassuringly cold. Often, it was enough to pour the drink, to hold it in her hand, and deprive herself of the taste. It was something she'd been spectacularly unsuccessful at doing during her time on the soil, and she enjoyed the sense of power denial brought her now, the sense of being in control of her own destiny.

Hah. She could almost hear the Almighty's chuckle at that one.

A trilling crackle filled the air, like a 1970s telephone filtered through an echo chamber. The Duchess placed the glass down on her desk (ensuring its damp bottom was on the coaster, just so) and stared at the black-and-gold telephone in front of her. She tried to remember the last time she'd heard it ring.

She wasn't sure if she'd *ever* heard it ring.

Realising that glaring at it wasn't the same as answering it, she lifted the receiver from its cradle.

'Yes?'

'All right, your ladyship. How's the palace?'

Mabel.

It was a long time since she'd heard her voice, but that absence hadn't made the timbre – that affected West Country burr – any less irritating.

'Much as you left it. The afterlife keeps spinning.' The Duchess picked up her glass, swirling its contents around. 'How's civilising the savages going?'

'You ever showed your face down here, you'd know.'

The Duchess bared her teeth. 'That's what I have you for, amongst other things.' There was a swollen silence between the women. 'Daisy-May came to see you, I believe?'

Mabel grunted. 'She was with the new boy. Hope you know what you're doing there, Rachel.'

'I do,' said the Duchess, 'and I would ask you to remember my rank.'

Mabel muttered something unintelligible.

'Was there a purpose to this call?' said the Duchess. 'As delightful as it is.'

More crackled silence.

'I saw her today, in the Pen.'

'You saw who?'

An alarm sounded, deep in the bowels of the control centre. 'Our sister, Rachel. I saw our sister.'

The Jankie girls had made few friends during their time on the soil. Their parents had endorsed such solitude – in fact, they out-and-out dictated it – and that was fine, because the sisters had each other, and each other was all they really needed. This enforced isolation was never explained to the girls. Their grand-mother simply told them, 'You have been bred for greatness, my darlings, and those that have not will muddy that breeding.'

The sisters were all terrified of their grandmother – who never seemed to age, to the extent that they assumed she'd been born ancient – but that hadn't stopped the Duchess and Mabel being jealous when Hanna, the youngest sibling, was summoned to Oma's bedroom on her sixteenth birthday. They had hovered outside the door, their ears inches from the thin oak panelling, the city and its noises trying to drown out the conversation.

After an hour, the door handle turned, and the girls jumped backwards. Hanna exited the room, looking through her sisters as if they weren't there, as if she was already living in a future that had no place in them in it. They'd spent the rest of the day exchanging fevered whispers, desperately trying to discover what Oma Jankie had told her, but Hanna never said a word; instead, she smiled a smile that said, *I'm not really here any more*, picked at her modest birthday dinner, then announced that she was going to take a bath alone, a once-a-year privilege for the impoverished and puritanical Jankies.

It was Oma Jankie who broke down the bathroom door an hour later.

They found Hanna lying in the bath, the water the deepest red the Duchess had ever seen, dyeing the ends of her sister's white hair. Hanna's arms lay on either side of the simple metal tub, two slashes on each wrist. The Duchess never forgot the precision of those cuts; her younger sister had always been meticulously neat.

Mabel remembered it differently, but the Duchess was convinced that there had been a look of joy on Hanna's face.

One that said: *I'm free.*

One that said: *Here I come.*

Oma Jankie had screamed, dropping to her knees in the bloodied puddles that had formed underneath the bath, and sobbed one word with a fevered mania that the Duchess, all this time later, still heard with total clarity.

Bitch.

Bitch.

Bitch.

There had been no funeral, or at least if there had, the two remaining Jankie sisters hadn't been invited to attend. As the years tumbled by, and the scope of the duties that awaited her became clear, the Duchess had avoided thinking of her baby sister and the way she'd taken her life, a life that had already been promised to something – and someone – else.

It was difficult to avoid thinking of her now, though, because there she was on the screen, bright as day, standing at the entrance to the compound.

This isn't possible, thought the Duchess. It can't be her.

'This compound is supposed to be unfindable.'

'It is, ma'am, or at least it was. In all my centuries in the Pen, no one has ever discovered it before.'

The Duchess turned away from the monitor to consider her number two. Remus Grave wasn't the most assuming of fellows: cloud-white hair that straggled to his shoulders, a crisp, smartly pressed tunic (always spotlessly clean), the sort of constant half-smile that suggested he was in on the joke, or too polite to admit he wasn't.

Bloke looks like he shits lavender; that was what Mabel always said, and the Duchess approved of the meaning, if not the language.

What she approved of even more was the experience Remus brought with him. He'd served as the warden's right hand since the Pen's inception, and the knowledge he'd accumulated – and retained – had been invaluable to the Duchess. Never telling, always gently advising, Remus was a source of strength she knew she could always rely on.

He'd been wrong about the compound being unfindable, though.

'How could she have found it?'

'"She" being your sister?' said Remus.

'My sister's in hell.'

'With respect, ma'am, she *was* in hell. Now she's standing outside this compound.'

'How do we know for certain it's her?' said the Duchess.

'Her hair is somewhat memorable. There's also the matter of Mabel's report, as well as the dispatches of that little guttersnipe you're so fond of.'

The Duchess turned sharply. 'That *guttersnipe* has a name.'

'Of course,' said Remus. 'I meant no offence. Daisy-May is resourceful beyond her means, and has an affinity with the Dispossessed. Claims to speak their language. Claims this white-haired girl can speak it, too.'

'If that really is Hanna, she shouldn't be able to speak *any* language,' said the Duchess. 'Hell should have left her an addled zombie, more damaged than the Dispossessed.'

'Perhaps it has,' said Remus. 'Perhaps it's a coincidence she's found her way here.'

'Only idiots believe in coincidences.'

'Yes, ma'am.'

'She should be in hell,' the Duchess said again, almost to

herself. 'The only way to get out is to be released. Who'd sanction that?'

'The devil works in mysterious ways,' said Remus.

The Duchess didn't reply. Instead, she took a step closer to the screen, staring fiercely at the pixelated image on it.

'Dumb animals to be corralled. That's what I was always told. That's what *you* always taught me.'

'That's because it's true,' said Remus. 'It's what I've witnessed over a millennium.'

'Well what I'm witnessing now is my hell-imprisoned sister, at my unfindable compound, with a militia of Dispossessed at her side,' said the Duchess, 'and none of them look awfully keen on being corralled.'

Remus nodded. 'No, they don't. What are you going to do about it?'

The Duchess considered the question. How many souls had asked her that over the last century and a half? Too many. She was tired of the responsibility, weary of the weight of the crown. Always someone waiting for an order, always someone waiting to be told what to do, always someone wanting a piece of her.

Her relief was supposed to have arrived by now, the next warden shadowing her, ready to take over when her time was up. Where was he? Something had gone wrong, somewhere, and her entreaties to the Almighty had gone unanswered. With no warden to replace her, was she to go on forever? When would she have served her time?

Stop feeling sorry for yourself, snapped Oma Jankie, the ever-present critic in her mind. *Do you think your sister is?*

Oma was right. If that *was* her sister outside, she was bubbling with self-assurance. That would have been disturbing enough by itself – the Pit, with its multitude of horrors, should have flayed every last shred of decency, hope and life from her – but

95

that self-assurance seemed to have rubbed off on the fifty-strong group of half-souls flanking the girl.

They're following her, thought the Duchess. Like people follow me. Another impossibility to add to the pile.

'Ma'am. Look.' Remus's voice broke her reverie.

Hanna – if that was who the white-haired teenage girl truly was – was waving directly at the screen, a smile on her flickering face.

How does she know we can see her? She's spent the last couple of centuries in hell. She should be capable of little more than eating dirt.

The girl on the screen pointed to that dirt.

'Move the camera downwards,' commanded the Duchess.

The picture panned down obligingly.

A single word had been scratched into the soil.

'Zoom in on that.'

The camera did as it was told, struggling, then finding focus. There was an audible gasp in the control room as they saw the word.

Talk.

The Duchess strode away from the bank of monitors.

'Where are you going, ma'am?' called Remus.

'You asked what I intended to do. I *intend* to see just what it is my sister wants.'

She turned back to him.

'Open the doors. I'm going out.'

'You're going out?'

'There seems to be a troublesome echo in here.'

'It's been a long time since you've left the compound, ma'am.'

'No time like the present, then.'

Remus nodded. 'I'll put together a guard for you.'

'No,' said the Duchess. 'I'm going alone.'

Remus's face became pinched. 'You'll be unprotected. You have no idea what you're walking into.'

'I won't be unprotected,' said the Duchess.

There was a pause.

'You can't be serious, ma'am. Not the cannons.'

'Can't I? You forget your place, Remus.'

Remus bowed his head. 'I only mean that they're intended as a last resort.'

The Duchess took a step towards him. 'I'm the leader of this damned realm, and I'll use them as and when I see fit. If that *is* my sister, and she has a problem with it, well, I'll blast her straight back to hell.'

Chapter Thirteen

Blood and bleach, that was what school had meant to Joe. Why that was the case, he couldn't be sure. That memory hadn't been gifted back to him. It was a feeling he got, a phantom stench in his nostrils, as he stood looking up at the imposing Victorian pile of bricks.

Blood, bleach and broken dreams.

'Looks like fucking Hogwarts,' said Daisy-May, whistling appreciatively.

'Appearances can be deceiving.'

'How do you know? My school had metal detectors,' said Daisy-May, 'and a stabbing a week. This place has *Latin* above the entrance. Trust me, they're not that deceiving.'

'I know the same way you know that.'

She pulled a face. In truth, he couldn't really explain it. There was no single memory he could dredge up to illustrate the wrongness of the school, just the residue he'd carried over from his life. A wriggle in the gut, too, that part of the puzzle was here, the next link in the chain that would lead to his killer.

'It looks deserted,' he said. 'It must be the weekend.'

'Good work, Poirot. That's real detecting.'

'Come on,' he half ordered, passing through the entrance,

'and I'll show you why this won't be much of a nostalgia trip for me.'

Daisy-May did as she was told, and Joe heard himself gasp as he entered the building's main reception area.

'Déjà vu kicking your arse?' said Daisy-May.

'Something like that.'

And it was, because the simple act of walking through the door had been like hurtling through a kaleidoscope of images, all indistinct but no less painful for it. He couldn't remember why he'd hated school, what had happened here to leave such a ragged imprint on his psyche. Certainly, it wasn't the unre-markable reception area. The walls were wood-panelled and etched with the golden names of past students and long-dead teachers, the ceiling high but bowed in the middle, like it had tried to reach for heaven and failed.

'What are we looking for here?' said Daisy-May, wandering over to a collection of ancient dust-cloaked trophy cabinets, the floor-to-ceiling paintings of ancient headmasters forming an unlikely guard of honour around her.

'You tell me.'

'Head's full of what I don't know, instead of what I do,' she said, stopping at an unloved cabinet and kneeling down for a closer look. 'But this school ain't me. I'm pure Nottingham. Not a reason in the world I'd have known it even exists.'

'Yet you did,' said Joe, crouching down next to her, 'to the extent that you scraped its name in the ground next to you. Which leads to another question neither of us have asked yet.'

'Which is?'

'Just how did a "pure Nottingham girl" find herself eighty miles away in a Lincolnshire farmhouse?'

An uneasy silence settled over them.

Finally, Daisy-May nodded towards the trophy cabinet. 'That's you, right?'

Joe looked at the faded photograph resting against the copper-coloured trophy and saw that she was right. A beaming teenage version of him stood holding the same trophy. He was flanked by his old partner Pete, and his wife . . . what was her name? He started to panic, his brain fuzzy, the memory taunting him. He could see her face, the way she smiled, could hear the tone of her laugh. There was the notepad. He could look at the notepad.

Wouldn't that be an admission of defeat, though? He was just a few hours into this investigation; looking at his notes would be like sneaking a look at the answers to a test. He had to be able to remember on . . . *Claire*. That was her name. Claire.

With that memory came others.

'We were in the debating society together. Don't remember being much of a debater, but I must have been halfway decent, I suppose.'

'Makes sense, right?' said Daisy-May. 'Your boy Pete said as much at the funeral. You three were tight.'

'Apparently school-friend tight.'

Daisy-May jabbed at the photo. 'You and Pete, boy scouts from the start, man. Couple of squares like you would have got crucified in my school. Only debating society we had was gangsters trying to knock months off their juvie-detention sentences.' A smile lit up her thin face. 'That's the most I've re-membered about my past. Memory just popped in there, like a fucking stocking-filler. It's being around you, for some reason.'

Joe bared his teeth in frustration, slamming a formless fist straight through the cabinet. 'Not for me. This whole thing's like walking through someone else's memories. It means noth-ing to me until it does, and when it does, I wish that it didn't. And it's not like I own the memories; they're on lease. Only guarantee is, the longer I stay here, the less likely I am to keep them.'

'That's the afterlife, Joey. Sooner you accept it, happier you'll be.'

'How am I supposed to be happy about being dead? It makes the job ten times harder.'

'Only if you look at it with your old, soil eyes. We can go places the regular police can't. Do things they're not allowed to. We don't need search warrants or court orders. Think we'd have just been able to walk into a closed school if we were still breathing? Walk through walls back at the farmhouse?'

Joe let the words sink in. She was right. There were advantages to this whole deal; he just had to learn to appreciate them.

'No red tape to cut through, I suppose,' he said.

'That's the spirit.'

'All right then. Let's get to work.'

The school was a potpourri of smells, almost all of them unpleasant. Joe had got the faintest memory of blood and bleach standing outside the main entrance, but walking down the corridors of his youth was like mainlining the past: sweat, food, disinfectant and mustiness infected him with that same sense of unease, like something was happening in margins he couldn't yet see. It was new, his sense of smell. He supposed he should be grateful.

Bang.

'You hear that?' he said, whirling around.

'A door slamming in the silent-as-fuck school?' said Daisy-May. 'Yeah, I did.'

They doubled back on themselves, inching along the corridor, the muted green light spilling from the emergency exit signs just about sufficient to show the way; a crackle in the air like something was waiting for permission to explode.

There was another bang, louder this time.

'That came from the toilets,' said Joe, breaking into a run.

'How do you know?'

'Because I remember where the toilets are.'

'Some people in the Squad get posted to New York, you know that?' said Daisy-May as they rounded a corner, then staggered to a stop outside the boys' toilets, 'and we're traipsing around school pissers. This is a crock of *shit*.'

Joe ignored her, taking a step towards the toilet entrance. A mottled wooden doorstop was just about propping it open, and as he cautiously approached it, the hairs on the back of his neck stood to attention, like they knew something he didn't.

'Yeah, I feel it too,' whispered Daisy-May. 'Tread carefully.'

They inched closer to the door, Joe's gut writhing.

'Something's wrong here,' he whispered.

Daisy-May turned to quieten him.

They stood at the entrance.

They exchanged a look.

They walked through the door.

The emergency lighting flickered a staccato red, a slash of moonlight filtering through the window.

A boy stood with his back to them, bent over the sinks. He was dressed in a school uniform that had seen better days, his once white shirt greyed out with mould, his trousers ragged and half-mast.

Bit late to be walking around school corridors, thought Joe. Especially if it *is* the weekend.

The boy paused, as if he'd heard the thought.

He turned.

Joe would have put him at twelve years old. His skin porcelain white, his body twitching like a doll inexpertly massaged into life. His left eye looked them over, a feat beyond the right, because a tangle of brown vines grew from it, stretching up from his eye socket and crowning his ginger hair. His hands had been colonised in the same way; it was as if he'd slept, then stumbled out of a Brothers Grimm fable.

One of the scary ones, Joe thought.

The child opened his mouth, and Joe saw that his throat also contained a tangle of brown vines. He tried to speak, cracked vowels rising and falling from his veiny blue lips.

Joe felt Daisy-May's hand grab his arm. 'Poor kid's infected.'

'Infected with what?'

'You wanted to know what happens if we stay too long? That. Whatever killed this kid meant he hasn't been able to cross over.'

'How do you know he's dead?' whispered Joe.

'Because he's got a leaf growing out of his fucking eye.'

The boy held his hands up to them, and it seemed to Joe that the snaking brown vines tightened around them as he did so.

'Can't,' the boy croaked, pleading with his one good eye.

'Can't what, mate?' asked Daisy-May gently, taking a step towards him.

The boy covered his right hand with his left, rubbing them together, desperation etched onto his face, the veins in his neck bulging. 'Can't . . . get . . . it off.'

Daisy-May smiled sympathetically. 'Annoying stuff, right? You wait there. I might have something to help you with it.'

'So, what do we do?' said Joe.

'When they get like this, they're too far gone,' Daisy-May whispered back. 'Nothin' left but pain and confusion.' She reached into her pocket and pulled out two sticks of gum. 'Know what my orders are here? Your orders too, now that you're part of the Squad? We put poor bastards like this kid out of their misery. There's nothing that can be done for them, the Duchess says, except release them from their hell. That's what the orange discs Mabel gave us are for, amongst other things. Know what I said in reply?'

Joe shook his head.

'That we're not killers. That we're supposed to protect, to seek justice, not be a fuckin' death squad. Everything's important. Every*one*.' Her tough-as-nails tone broke a little. 'No one else dies because of us.'

She stitched on a smile, then walked slowly towards the boy, crouching in front of him, and holding out a stick of gum. 'It's OK, mate, you can trust me. This'll make you feel a lot better. Promise.'

The boy looked at the gum suspiciously, and Daisy-May nodded in encouragement. He reached out, his hand shaking slightly, and grabbed the stick, jamming it into his mouth.

The effect was almost instantaneous.

His good eye glazed over and he slumped slowly to the floor, his back resting against one of the toilet stall doors. He breathed a sigh of contentment, and some of the vines that had entwined themselves around his scalp began to fray and crumble.

'Like in the Pen, the gum calms them,' said Daisy-May. 'And like in the Pen, the Duchess is against it; thinks it's a waste of good resources, that they're too far gone.'

'How much of these "resources" do we have left?' Joe asked, watching as the boy's head began to nod.

'Enough,' said Daisy-May, patting the tin in her pocket. 'If you're as good at your job as the Duchess says you are.'

'So, what do we do with him?' said Joe, nodding at the boy. 'Just leave him here?'

'There's a bloke I know that will take him. Sort of like Mother Teresa, but works with needy spirits rather than starving kids. He works from close by to—'

The boy screamed, his head upright, his good eye flashing with fear, his pointing finger a divining rod pinging between the two of them.

He scrambled up, backing away from them, his gaze never leaving them.

'You,' he screamed, again and again. '*You.*'

Joe and Daisy-May exchanged a look.

'You know this lad?' said Joe.

'No. You?'

He shook his head.

'Yeah, well, he thinks he knows us.'

The boy gave them a final fearful look, then passed clean through the row of sinks behind him and disappeared.

They stood in shocked silence, which Joe finally broke. 'What was that all about?'

'I ain't got a hotline to God,' said Daisy-May, 'and my memories about my life are just as shithouse as yours. My guess, though, is that the lad didn't have the first clue that he was dead. May *never* have known it, depending on how long he's been here; not everyone gets a guide like me to show them the way.' She sighed. 'Chewing that gum was probably crueller in his case.'

Joe looked in the direction the boy had fled in. 'Should we go after him?'

'State he's in, we'd only make things worse,' said Daisy-May. 'And the clock's ticking. If we don't find what we're looking for here, we're going to end up like the poor lad.'

They finally found what they were looking for in the science labs.

A search of the ground floor had turned up little more than a collection of classrooms that were so old, Joe could have believed they were unchanged from his days there as a pupil. It was when they'd hit the first floor that the school's parched silence had been broken. The distant chatter of voices had become clear: a male voice, and a younger female one, making enough sense to suggest these weren't brain-damaged stranded ghosts but living, breathing human beings.

Joe couldn't decide if that was a good thing or not.

The voices were coming from an ancient-looking room, its mighty tan door firmly closed and muffling the sounds from within.

'Little clandestine for a parents' evening,' said Joe. 'Whoever's in that room isn't allowed to be, I'd bet my badge on it.'

'Always in a hurry to bet that thing,' said Daisy-May, 'but I reckon you're right.'

A sense of past lives, none of which he could truly remember, washed over Joe as he took in the classroom. There was a row of Bunsen burners idling at the back, and several long wooden benches ran down the guts of the room. At the back of the space, light peeked out from a half-open door.

Light, and the sounds of rhythmic, intense grunting.

'That people shagging?' said Daisy-May, half disgusted, half intrigued.

'It sounds like it,' said Joe, 'unless the act has changed significantly since I was killed.'

'It hasn't. Not sure how much it helps us, though.'

'When you're on the trail of a killer, things that *shouldn't* be on that trail are your friends. Whoever's in that back room shouldn't be. I'll go, though, you don't need to see it.'

She smirked. 'What a gentleman. After you.'

As they walked towards the room at the back (storeroom, thought Joe, the muscle memory of formaldehyde and row upon row of bottled insects rearing up in his subconscious), the panting seeming to grow louder and more rhythmic, until it reached a merciful conclusion as they arrived at the door.

The clink of a lighter firing into life.

The door opened.

A girl exited, rearranging her school uniform as she did so, a half-smile on her lips.

Sixteen, thought Joe. If that.

The glow of a cigarette tip flared in the darkness and a man emerged from the gloom. It was as if he had stepped out of a more glamorous life into this one. He was dressed in aspirational footballer clobber. A designer jacket, with jeans that were as well cut as they were expensive. The look said money, with just enough dyed-in-the-wool hooligan danger to give him an edge. Genetically, he could have been from central casting; his old-school Hollywood good looks contrasted sharply with the humble surroundings.

'That's fucking sick, man,' said Daisy-May. 'Girl's barely my age. Lad's gotta be five years older than her.'

'Welcome to Lincolnshire,' said Joe.

'Good-looking bastard, though, I'll give him that. Who wouldn't want a bit of him? Question is, what's he getting out of it?'

'Guess,' said Joe grimly.

'Got one of those for me, Ryan?' said the girl, walking clean through Joe as she did up her shirt.

The young man winked at her, taking a deep drag of his cigarette, offered her the box, then held it out of reach. 'What you got for me?'

The girl bit her lip, then gestured to a cabinet standing next to the desk at the front of the room.

Ryan smiled a thousand-watt grin that belonged anywhere else, then pointed his smouldering cigarette at the cabinet. 'You keep my drugs — the big man's drugs — next to the teacher's desk?'

She smiled uncertainly. 'Genius, right? Mr Sutts loves me. Pervert. And I'm a prefect. He gave me the only spare key for the cabinet, and I keep the dope near the hazardous shit. No one'll mess with it, trust me.'

Ryan nodded. 'I do trust you, love.'

He beckoned for her to come over, which she did all too willingly.

'I trust you with my life, 'cos that's what's at stake if somethin' happens to that gear. Same goes for your life too, right? Because if something happens to me, there'll be no one to protect you.'

The girl swallowed, as though battening down her fear. 'Course,' she said. 'It's the game, I get it.'

'I know you do,' said Ryan, kissing her tenderly on the cheek. 'Now go fetch my drugs.'

She beamed like she'd been given an A, then swaggered over to the cabinet, pulling out a set of keys.

'She's about as gangster as you,' said Daisy-May.

Joe nodded. 'A rich girl playing a game, and vulnerable because of it.'

The cabinet door swung open, and she reached down into the bottom, pulling out several glass vials of white powder.

'Not bad,' said Ryan, smirking. 'Risky as fuck, but method in your madness.'

She handed them over. He stored them safely in a cheap-looking canvas rucksack. She bit her lip again, shifting from foot to foot.

'She'd be a shit poker player,' said Daisy-May.

'Lots of chat in school about that copper at the farmhouse,' said the girl. 'The one that got killed.'

Ryan looked at her, the temperature in the room plunging. 'Not much for chatter, me.'

She glanced down as she asked, 'It wasn't you, was it?'

He grabbed her arm. 'What did you say to me?'

'You're hurting me.'

'That's not what you said.'

Tears pricked in the girl's eyes. 'I asked if it was you that killed the police— the copper. Don't care either way, just want to know.'

Ryan leaned into her, his bum-fluff inches from her face. 'Know what happens to people that ask questions like that, love?'

She shook her head. She'd begun to silently sob.

'They don't ask again. Understand?'

She nodded furiously.

He released her arm, raising his hand to brush away a lock of hair from her face. 'Course you do, because you're the smartest girl I've ever met.' He pulled her to him, gentle now. 'There's only you, Jen. You know that, right?'

She dabbed at her eyes. 'You want to hang out? Go for a drive?'

Ryan shook his head, shouldering the rucksack. 'Later. Keep your phone on. Got work now.'

'Trying not to get my hopes up,' said Daisy-May, 'but I think I'd class this fucker as a person of interest.'

'I think I would too,' said Joe. 'Let's find out what his *work* looks like.'

Chapter Fourteen

The Dispossessed had never found the main compound before – what Mabel jokingly called 'the palace' – because, visually, there was nothing to find. There were two entrances: the service hatch Daisy-May had favoured when escorting Joe for the first time, and a second one secreted in a cave to the west of the centre of the Pen.

Well hidden, for a place that was never supposed to be found.

It was in the cave that the gang of Dispossessed had gathered.

The Duchess walked down a seemingly endless bleached white corridor, the merest imprints of doorways either side of her, the ceiling so high as to be out of sight, and remembered when Daisy-May had walked down it for the first time. *It's like being inside God's intestines*, the girl had said wonderingly. *And not in a bad way, neither.*

If only she knew how accurate that was.

The Duchess reached the outer door and stopped.

What's your plan here, little Rachel? asked Oma Jankie. *To get to the Pen, Hanna will have crawled out of the bowels of hell itself. Think she'll be in the mood to talk about old times? Only thing that girl will want is revenge. You've got her title.*

'She can have it back,' said the Duchess, her voice echoing away into nothingness. 'I don't want it. I *never* wanted it.'

Liar, said the voice of her long-expired grandmother.

The Duchess waited, hovering at the gate. Despite what she'd said to Remus, venturing out of the compound alone – whether or not that was her sister – was a risk. If it *was* Hanna, and if she could communicate and co-opt the Dispossessed, then there was no telling what she was walking into.

But she had to know.

She leaned into the wall, whispering to it, and with a grinding sigh it heaved itself open, welcoming in rays from the fire-and-brimstone sky. The group of Dispossessed were right where she'd seen them on the monitor, silhouetted against the tumultuous clouds, the teenage girl a foot or so in front of them. The Duchess tried to think of the last time she'd felt nervous.

She couldn't.

The crunch of her boots fractured the silence as she walked outside. Back straight, chin out, she told herself. You're the ruler of a realm, for heaven's sake.

She'd hoped against all hope and reason that the girl wasn't Hanna, but as she stopped within a hundred yards of the group, she finally accepted the truth of it. It might have been over two hundred years since she'd last seen her, but no one looked like Hanna except Hanna. No denying, either, how she stood apart from the Dispossessed next to her. There was a solidity to her, a balance that the other creatures didn't have. But then, if this girl had fought her way out from hell, how could she be anything but solid? Anything but the fiercest sort of fighter?

The Duchess raised a hand in greeting.

Hanna raised one back.

The Duchess swallowed when she saw the neat scars across the girl's wrists, a flashback to the sight of her sister and a bath full of blood.

It's her, she thought. It can only be her.

Hanna smiled, then opened her mouth. A parched croak escaped, like her voice was bound in barbed wire. 'Rachel.'

The Duchess said nothing; just took a step forward.

The ranks of Dispossessed flanking Hanna bristled.

Hanna held a hand up, calming them. 'You look old,' she said, in words of glass and blood.

'You look the same,' said the Duchess.

'I'm not.'

I bet.

'Where have you been?'

'Where do you think?' asked Hanna, her words a bleeding graze on a winter's day.

'The Pit.'

'The Pit.' She nodded.

'How did you escape?' the Duchess asked.

'Do you really want to know?'

'No, frankly, I don't. What do you want, Hanna?'

Hanna tried to smile, and the Duchess realised the physical pain it cost her. 'To share what you have.' She gestured to the Dispossessed at either side of her. 'For all of us to share what you have.'

The Duchess felt unsteady, as if the world and everything she knew in it was crumbling. 'That's not the way things work here. You know that better than anyone.'

'It's the way . . . they *haven't* worked,' rasped Hanna, as if trying to catch her breath. 'It's time to change that.'

She probably hasn't spoken this much for centuries, thought the Duchess. It's like she's remembering as she goes along.

Or she had the capacity for speech tortured out of her.

The Dispossessed chittered around her, but Hanna's response to them was lost on the Duchess.

'How can you understand them?' she asked.

'We have something in common,' said Hanna. 'We are all outsiders, pushed to the margins by people like you.'

'You did this to yourself,' said the Duchess. 'You didn't need any help from me.' She looked at her sister – truly looked at her – for the first time. 'Hanna, I have to know.' She swallowed. It was a question that had been burning in her since that day. 'When you took your own life, was it because you didn't want the burden of it all?'

Hanna said nothing.

'Or . . . was it because you did?'

She held up her scarred wrists. 'Imagine being told you're a god. That you'll command a realm. That your lifetime on the soil – one of poverty, and cruelty, and anonymity – will come to an end as soon as you die. Imagine being told that, and then being expected to wait.'

'*I* was told that,' said the Duchess. '*I* was expected to wait. You were greedy. No wonder you ended up where you did.'

A flicker of something crossed Hanna's face. An old look of defiance that the Duchess couldn't have forgotten if she'd wanted to. Gone before she knew it, but it had been there all right.

'What does it matter now?' said Hanna. 'Neither of us can change the past. Will you help me change the future?'

'I'm not convinced the future needs to change,' said the Duchess.

'All I want to do is share,' said Hanna. 'We could rule together. Create a new order where everyone is treated equally. Surely you cannot object to that?'

It was difficult to, the Duchess conceded. Hanna had been destined to rule the Pen. Would it be so bad to share? There was no sign of her successor. He should have been here by now.

She should be preparing to hand over to him, yet she still had to shoulder the burden alone. Hanna could help her with that burden.

And she was so tired.

'You're my sister, and I'd welcome you here,' she said. 'Depending on your intentions with the Dispossessed.'

'All I ask is that they receive basic levels of respect. That they live here as equals. They're not so different from you and me. The Pen is so vast, yet the Dispossessed are shunted round it like cattle. Bring them into the fold.'

The Duchess went to reply, then stopped. She needed more time to consider.

It's not just sharing with her, she thought. It's the trillions like her, the ones she's leading, the one's she's giving hope to. It's against the natural order. This consciousness they're showing will be the end of everything. The Pen cannot support it. Existence cannot support it. That's what I was taught. That's all I know.

Hanna held out a hand to her, and once again the Duchess noted the neat scars decorating her sister's wrist. Hanna had always wanted a bracelet – had pleaded for one, in fact, for her sixteenth birthday – but Oma Jankie had simply laughed and rapped her fingers with her cane. *Trinkets are a distraction worn by soil-loving morons*, the old woman would say. *We're better than that. We must be.*

The Duchess raised her hand up high.

There was a whine, like a machine was stirring, gathering itself, winding itself up.

'I'm sorry, Hanna,' she said. 'For everything.'

She dropped her hand.

Endless voices – mostly male ones – had lectured the Duchess on the pointlessness of defences.

She'd been given a cursory look at them on her first day, Remus attempting to skirt over them. 'They'll never find the control centre, ma'am,' he'd said dismissively. 'And if they somehow do, well, they'll have no concept of what it is. They're animals, and animals can't pick a lock.'

'That may be true,' the Duchess had replied, 'but wolves can't pick a lock either, and that doesn't mean they're not dangerous. Why else would these defences have been erected, if not to guard against such a possibility?'

'There have been other perils over the years,' Remus had replied. 'Horrors the warden has had to face down. The Dispossessed have never been one of them.'

They were now, though. Consciousness was like a virus; fifty lucid Dispossessed today could be five hundred tomorrow, and where would that end? What would they do when they realised the true nature of their prison, that they would be trapped here for all eternity?

What would they do with her clever baby sister to lead them?

Ten cannons had been built into the side of the caves, five on each side, carefully concealed within the rock crags. They'd never been fired under the Duchess's reign, because to do so was a last resort – and what if they didn't work?

The only other option didn't bear thinking about. She wasn't some vengeful god; she was merely trying to do her job.

When her hand dropped, those cannons blazed into life, pumping out gallon upon gallon of unfiltered soil air into the banks of Dispossessed, knocking them clean off their feet and submerging them in a waterfall of green liquid. Soil-side, the atmosphere eradicated the memories of any ghostly souls that ventured there; this concentration was weaponised with a hundred times that potency.

The Duchess waited a moment longer than she needed to,

the guns screaming, then raised her arm again. The cannons slowed, their faint Gatling-gun whine finally dying away.

Her eyes hunted for Hanna, finding only a sea of green, the drenched Dispossessed lying motionless.

Was this victory? Turning the Pen's weapons upon these poor, simple people? Her own sister?

It didn't feel like it.

Finally, the first few Dispossessed got to their feet. There was no purpose to their movements, no control. Their body language was loose again, limbs floppy. They blinked, then began to amble away, stumbling over the people still lying on the ground, too dazed to even stand.

She felt something loosen inside her.

I haven't seen her yet, though, she thought. It won't be all right until I've seen her.

Minutes went by.

Then, movement.

A stick-thin figure sat up, looking around. There was a slackness to her, her aura. The purpose had gone. The confidence. Slowly, painfully, the girl got to her feet, a jerkiness in her movements, confusion. Whoever Hanna had been before the cannons had fired upon her, she was different now. Diminished.

It had worked.

So that's it, thought the Duchess, sagging. I've lobotomised my sister. She climbed out of hell, and I've rewarded her with oblivion. Just another zombie, doomed to shuffle around for eternity.

Hanna began to do just that, stumbling away from the compound.

Still, it was over. Whatever this insurrection was, the Duchess had smashed it.

Then Hanna's spine straightened and she stopped, turning back.

The two sisters stood watching each other.

Hanna dragged her fingers through her sodden hair, flicking it off her shoulder.

She winked at the Duchess, and walked away.

Chapter Fifteen

The air may have been rotting his memory by the second, but it didn't stop Joe from remembering the Sundown. He stood in the centre of the bar, the laughing, jeering patrons oblivious to his presence, and tried to work out what had changed.

Nothing was the quick answer. The same music played on the same jukebox, the same paint peeled in the same places, the same cigarette smoke hung in the same air, the same people sat in the same places, all of them talking frantically about the same things. Time hadn't touched Lincolnshire, and licensing laws certainly hadn't.

Strange, the things he was remembering. He wouldn't have given a second thought to these people in years, yet here they were, their names pinging and popping in his head.

Stranger still was the edge to the place. There were plenty of old faces, that was true, but there was a rash of new, younger ones too, familiar because they were obviously the progeny of the old guard. These kids contributed to the manic energy of the place, jarring in what would normally have been a quiet country pub. There was a strung-out-ness that couldn't be explained away by the passing of years, or the lateness of the hour.

As hard as it was to believe, a good proportion of the people here seemed to be spectacularly, unapologetically high.

Not everyone, admittedly – the old guard were eyeing the place and everyone in it with a boozy, barely concealed disgust – but the new lot, certainly. And this wasn't a dozy skunk high or rat-poison coke high, this was something different, something more frenzied.

Crack, thought Joe. The twitching, the fidgeting, the look in the eyes. This place is full of fucking tweakers.

Growing up, the worst the pub had indulged in was under-age drinking, a sin the local police had batted a knowing eye at. They figured it was better to have the local teenage rabble in one place causing minor problems than spread out on the streets causing large ones. It wasn't policing that would have gone down well in the big city, but small towns and smaller villages required smarter thinking.

This, though?

This was on a different scale. In London, this place would have been shut down so fast the battering ram wouldn't have touched the sides, yet here, lawlessness had been allowed to run amok. Where was the local bobby?

Where was . . .?

Joe frowned, the name eluding him, an amnesia backslide that stoked panic within him. He thought back to the farmhouse and tried to remember what they'd seen that had brought him here.

'Daisy-May,' he called out, looking around wildly, hating the desperation in his voice.

'Here,' she said, taking his hand. 'Don't lose it.'

'I can't remember,' he said.

'We've just been to the school,' she said, slow and kind. 'We found a dealer there, Ryan, and we've followed him here.' She nodded towards the dark-haired man with his charming smile.

Joe smiled shakily. 'Right,' he said. '*Right.*' He gestured around him at the tweaked-up throng. 'These people look normal to you?'

'These people look fucked up.'

'That's what I think too,' said Joe. 'And Ryan, our friendly neighbourhood drug dealer? The little shit's been doing it openly.'

'It's a country pub,' said Daisy-May. 'Dealers gonna deal.'

'Not to this extent. Not this blatantly. This place is flooded, and here's what worries me. Bloke in the other corner? My age, shorter, bald, holding court?'

Daisy-May followed his pointed finger to a portly man who was manically talking to whoever'd listen, or pretend to. 'What about him?'

'He's the local plod.' He dragged his name from the ether. 'Owens. Jim Owens.' He let out a relieved breath. 'Never the sharpest tool in the shed, but straight as a die. Policed by common sense, and not the rule book. Knew when a quiet word was needed to bring someone into line, and when it was time to use the law.'

'Something's changed, then, 'cos it's happening under his nose, and he's not shifted from his seat.'

'Pete would be fucking furious if he saw this. Something's rotten here, Daisy-May.'

'Turn it up then!' Jim called.

The bartender dutifully pointed a remote at an ancient television, its fat base resting on a flimsy-looking metal shelf.

'Talking of Pete,' said Daisy-May, nodding towards the screen.

His old partner was on the local news, standing in front of the farmhouse where Joe had been killed.

'. . . here with Detective Inspector Pete Burns, at the site where his partner, Joe Lazarus, was tragically killed in the line of duty. DI Burns, can you give us an update on the case?'

Pete always hated this shit, thought Joe. Another random memory, but a true one. Hated the forced formality of it. Hated how it stopped him from getting on with the job.

'I can say that we're following several lines of enquiry,' Pete replied to the interviewer. 'Vigorously.'

'There are reports that the murder was drug related and additional forces are stepping in to aid the investigation. Are you able to confirm that at this point?'

'Not during a live investigation,' said Pete shortly. He looked straight down the barrel of the camera. 'What I can confirm is this: whoever was responsible for the death of Joe Lazarus will be brought to justice. There is no rock you can crawl under, no corner of the country you can flee to. We will find you. We will arrest you. We are coming for you.' He blinked rapidly, then pulled his collar up and strode away.

'Sounds like your boy Pete means business,' said Daisy-May. 'Rate we're going, he'll solve this thing before we do.'

'He's one of the best,' said Joe. 'No bad thing, having him kicking over stones. Especially when the living can't see us looking under them.'

The news segment ended, and Jim stood to do a little bow. 'Taught him everything he knows,' he said, winking at the watching punters.

'Kind of disrespectful, don't you think?' said Daisy-May. 'A dude was just murdered.'

'So I heard.' Joe watched as Ryan, a few feet away from them, pocketed a thick slab of notes, then grabbed the peak of his baseball cap and winked at the seemingly uninterested local officer.

'So, what now?' said Daisy-May.

'Quickest way to catch a rat is to follow the trail of shit it leaves,' said Joe, watching the dealer roll through the door.

★

As they trailed Ryan down a harshly lit tan-brown corridor, Joe felt almost buoyant. He recognised that feeling. He was in control again. *Even if I'm really not.*

The folk ramblings of the jukebox in the bar gave way to the harsh bleep of the dance floor in the next room, or what passed for one in the Sundown. Bass reverberated around them, the muscle memory of it announcing itself to Joe even if he could no longer physically feel it, the volume increasing with every step he took.

Ryan ducked through a doorway off to the right, and as they followed, memories of a thousand drunken teenage nights out came crashing back. Darkened corners promising more than they could ever deliver, the same DJ even, a string bean of a man caught in a never-ending trap of trying to seem younger than he was.

And Ryan was headed straight for him.

'This bloke was kicking around when I used to come here,' shouted Joe above the techno racket. 'Few years above me at school. Started DJ'ing here fresh out of school. Even back then he was rough around the edges.'

'Our Ryan don't seem too happy with him,' said Daisy-May.

Joe took a step forward, realising she was right.

'Packing them in as ever,' yelled Ryan over the music. 'Not a single punter. Why do you keep doing it?'

The DJ smiled with everything but his eyes. 'Love it, man. It's my job.'

'Tragic, mate, is what it is. Everyone younger than you. Should give it up.'

The DJ, nervous now, nodded. 'You might be right.'

Ryan leaned in. 'Where's my money?'

The DJ put his hands up. 'Need twenty-four hours, Ryan. Twelve, if something comes off that should.'

'That's what you said last time. Always twelve hours with you, man.'

'Don't have it now,' yelled the DJ, his eyes taking solace in his decks. 'Will do soon. Don't know what else to tell you.'

Ryan grabbed him by the collar. 'Think that's what I want to hear?'

'Do you really want to do this now?' the man said, as much desperation in his voice as bluster. He glanced towards the corridor, clearly hoping some would-be dancers would appear.

A frown creased Ryan's good looks. He released the DJ and took a step backwards.

'No dealer on my estate would have that,' yelled Daisy-May. This one wouldn't either.

With quicksilver speed, Ryan whipped out a taser, jabbing it into the DJ's ribs. The man's body aggressively spasmed, then dropped to the floor. Ryan grabbed him and led him like a dog along the corridor and back into the main bar. Two pool players meekly abandoned their game as he shoved the DJ's twitching body onto the table, scattering the balls to all four corners, then calmly walked across to the jukebox and yanked out the plug, the pub's clientele all rubberneck gawps.

He jumped up onto the pool table, inches from the sprawled DJ's head. 'Evening. Is everybody enjoying themselves?'

If they were, they were forever holding their peace.

'No one? That's a shame. I love a party.'

He looked down at the DJ, who was coming to. Taking careful aim, like a golfer sizing up a difficult putt, he brought his foot sharply against the man's ribs, causing him to yelp in pain.

'This bloke likes a party, too. Difference between me and him is, I know when the party's over. There's an art to that, right? Knowing when to arrive, and when to leave. Pride myself on knowing it. When it's time to settle up and say goodnight.'

He swung his foot at the DJ again, eliciting another scream.

'This prick here, he forgot to settle up. Not for want of me reminding him. I'm reasonable. One of the good guys.'

He jumped down from the table, the room flinching in response.

Joe looked out amongst the faces, searching for someone who would put a stop to it. The local copper, Owens, surely? There was letting things go, then there was this. Owens stood at the back, though, craning over the woman in front of him, conspicuous by his stillness, his face a mask of apathy.

'A lot of you buy from me. Most of you are good for it. But the big man? He's worried. Worried there are coppers poking about now, after what went down at the farmhouse. Thinks people will be asking questions, and the only thing he hates more than people not paying is people talking. You get me?'

Joe had heard this plastic patois before, small men dressing up as big gangsters reciting bad dialogue from worse films, but not like this, not holding a roomful of people in the palm of their hand.

Ryan shook his head. 'Don't think you do. Think it'll take an example. Statement of intent, that's what the big man would call it.'

Deathly silence, Ryan searching for more attention he didn't need, but wanted anyway.

He drew out a knife.

A muffled cry from the back, silenced with a glare.

'We got a good thing going here,' said Ryan, 'and the big man, he says good things need to be protected, fought for.'

He placed the tip of the knife on the back of the DJ's neck.

'Shit,' said Daisy-May.

Joe stared at Owens, willing him into action. He'd stop this now, surely. There was a difference between relaxed policing, being able to read the room and knowing when the riot act needed to be read. This was zero policing. This was a man who didn't care, or one who was being paid not to.

The DJ stirred as the knife pressed against his neck, drawing a blood bead.

'Lad's all front,' said Daisy-May. No one had ever sounded less sure of anything in their life.

'This is a message,' said Ryan. 'Pilgrims run this town. Anyone who breaks one of our laws, like this fucker here, there are consequences.'

Owens wasn't going to do anything, Joe realised. He was either too scared, or too bent.

'We have to do something,' he said, as Ryan continued to glare at the punters.

'Like what?' asked Daisy-May. 'Haunt him into seeing the error of his ways?'

'We're police, or that's what you told me,' said Joe, as Ryan raised the knife, relishing the moment, the anticipation. 'We don't stand aside and just let things like this happen.'

'Tell that to him,' Daisy-May nodded at Owens. He was rooted to the spot.

She clocked Joe moving forward and shot him a warning glance. 'Know how you feel, mate, but trust me, interfering ain't worth the consequences.'

'You're wrong,' said Joe. 'It's up to us.'

Ryan began to bring the knife down.

'Fuck,' muttered Daisy-May.

Joe lurched at him, knowing it was futile, knowing he had to try anyway, his formless body passing through the pool table, the knife slicing through him, on a collision course with the stubby gristle of the DJ's neck.

Until Daisy-May dived forward, sticking out an emaciated arm, creating a barrier between neck and blade.

Ryan blinked in surprise as steel struck thin air.

He drew the blade back and plunged it down again, getting the same result.

'*Fuck*,' said Daisy-May, her fist clenched, her arm a bar of unbreakable iron as the knife hit it again and Ryan looked at it in slack-jawed wonder. Then she drew back both arms and shoved the dealer, sending him cartwheeling down onto the pool table and over the side.

Joe turned to the open-mouthed crowd, then back to Daisy-May.

'*Fuck*,' he said.

Chapter Sixteen

Countryside whipped past, formless as it was endless, a slim sliver of car window welcoming in night air neither Joe nor Daisy-May could feel. Ryan hunched in the driver's seat, his hands wandering over the steering wheel, neck twitching, eyes drifting constantly to the rear-view mirror, as if he was expecting to catch out his unseen passengers.

'This bloke'll kill us if he doesn't slow down,' said Daisy-May, reclining amongst a back seat of pizza boxes.

Joe looked back at her from the front passenger seat. 'I thought you said you couldn't do things like that. Are you a poltergeist?'

'You've been watching too many films.'

'Or not enough to know what just happened.'

'Poltergeists are just a ball of piss, confusion and rage,' said Daisy-May. 'What I've set on our arses by saving that bloke in the pub is a thousand times worse.'

'You did a good thing,' said Joe. 'No one gets punished for that.'

'Ain't a world where that's true,' said Daisy-May. 'Specially not this one. I broke the rules, all right? I crossed a line, and there're consequences for that. *We do not physically interfere.* That's Dying Squad 101.'

Ryan cursed as a bend presented itself at the last minute, tyres screaming in tarmac protest as he wrenched the steering wheel and hauled the car around it.

'What I did, it's like sneaking into the lion enclosure in the zoo, smearing yourself in raw meat, then banging on the bars with a baseball bat,' said Daisy-May. 'It'll have heard, and it'll be hungry.'

'The Xylophone Man,' said Joe, grateful to have plucked the name from the ether.

Daisy-May nodded.

'It was pretty badass, though. You stopped that knife dead. Pushed the fucker clean off the pool table. You couldn't have done that when you were alive, a girl of your size. How?'

She looked out of the window. 'I dunno.'

'You don't know?' said Joe, incredulous.

'It's not like someone taught me it,' said Daisy-May. 'Didn't think about it, just reacted. Mabel, the woman who sorted us out with the weapons back in the Pen? She said it can only happen if you're pure of heart and have righteous fury in your soul. Maybe that's why you just fell over when you tried.'

Joe snorted. 'So what can this Xylophone Man do to us? What's worse than dead?'

Daisy-May picked at the scabs on her arm. 'Hell.'

'Not while I'm around,' said Joe.

'You're better cutting me loose,' she said, looking anywhere but at him. 'I'm a danger to the investigation.'

'There *is* no investigation without you.'

'I'm telling you, it's over. You're not going to solve this thing with the Xylophone Man on your arse.'

'I'm not that easy to push away.'

'You're soft, you,' said Daisy-May. 'No place for that in the Dying Squad.'

'We're partners,' said Joe. 'That means something, whether you're alive or dead.'

A small smile flickered on Daisy-May's face. 'First time you called me a partner.'

'Yeah, well, don't let it go to your head.'

They sat in silence, Daisy-May looking around the car distastefully, like it reminded her of something.

'Why we in this car, Joey?'

Joe blinked, digging his fingernails into the seat, a futile gesture that somehow made him feel better. His mind was a sea shrouded in mist, endless waves forming then breaking.

'We . . .' he began. 'We . . .'

His hand reached for the tin of gum, then hovered there.

Think, he told himself. Facts. Facts are your friend. The gum's a crutch, nothing more. You can do this.

We were just in a pub.

We'd followed the drug dealer from the school there.

And?

And?

The dealer lost it in the pub. Daisy-May stopped him.

'We're following the dealer. Seeing if he leads us to his boss. Putting the pieces together.'

'That's good, Joey.'

'And my name's Joe, not Joey.'

Daisy-May winked at him. 'That's my boy.'

This, he remembered.

Family Kingdom, a barnacle of pallid neon, its roller-coaster peaks oozing into the night sky, the screams of families trying to hide their mutual loathing of both the place and each other. Row upon row of market stalls welded onto the back of the place, overflowing with counterfeit tat and authentic crap.

Multiple bars themed with despair, arcades offering short-term gain and long-term addiction.

Daisy-May stared wonderingly out of the window. 'Not seen this place in *forever*.'

'You've been here before?' Joe said.

'Few times with my family, when they still remembered what that meant,' she said, a look of half-wonder on her face as the light twinkled on it. 'Most exciting place in the world, Family Kingdom.'

'You know the area, then,' said Joe. 'You never said.'

'Never remembered, until now. Farmhouse and church didn't spark anything in me. Here does.'

'Well, if you *are* destined for hell, believe me, it'll look a lot like this.'

'You're such a snob, man,' said Daisy-May. 'Nothing worse than a dead bloke with false standards.'

Ryan brought the car to a stop, mounting the kerb outside Super Bucket, the theme park's main fast-food outlet. He sat there, hands still on the wheel, music still pumping, foot thumping on the floor.

'He's worried,' said Joe, studying his face. 'He didn't get the DJ's cash, and he got shown up in the pub.'

'You can tell that just by looking at him?'

Joe shrugged.

Ryan punched the wheel three times, the horn blasting in response.

He turned around, facing Joe directly. '*Come on!*' He screamed the words again and again, the veins in his neck bulging, his good looks curdled like aged milk, passers-by looking at him warily from the pavement, chivvying gawking children away.

'Can he see me?' Joe said to Daisy-May wonderingly. 'Sense me, somehow?'

Ryan, body shaking, yanked open the driver's door and jumped out.

'Guessing that's a no,' said Daisy-May.

They followed behind him, Joe's hand passing through the door handle as he briefly forgot his lack of physicality. Daisy-May observed the trickle of day trippers who had made the winter pilgrimage to the Kingdom.

'Hope this bloke's leading us to the promised land,' she said.

'This is police work,' said Joe. 'You follow a lead till it plays out.'

'We're fucked if this leads nowhere.'

'Listen to Negative Nancy.'

'Xylophone Man's on our tail now, as well as memory loss,' she reminded him. 'Time's short, mate.'

'This is the hand we've been dealt, so we play it,' said Joe, gesturing as Ryan shoved his way through Super Bucket's doors. 'And this is our lead, so we follow it.'

Like pretty much everything else in Family Kingdom, the fast-food place hadn't changed. Joe's certainty of this was like a reflex. Maybe memory really was his superpower, like the Duchess had said. Slowly but surely, it was returning.

Red bubbles of plastic masqueraded as tables, their rusting metal chairs buckling under the pressure of the diners on top of them. Luckily for the chairs, there were very few customers, the winter culling all but the hardiest tourists.

Ryan nodded at the bearded man behind the counter, then slid into a booth near the back. Joe and Daisy-May sat across from him.

'Is it wrong that I feel hungry?' said Joe, looking longingly at the counter, sniffing the air.

'You're dead,' said Daisy-May. 'You wanting shit isn't. Even death can't kill that instinct.' She drummed her fingers on the table impatiently. 'So, what, we just wait?'

'Work like this? Seventy per cent patience, thirty per cent luck, a hundred per cent facts.'

'Rank maths there.'

'Police work rests on facts,' said Joe certainly. 'The minute you move away from that, you slip. Every bent copper I ever knew forgot that.'

'Like the local plod back at the pub?' said Daisy-May.

'Exactly, like Owens. No idea what happened with him, but corruption's a malaise, not a big-bang event; it creeps in when you rush investigations, and massage evidence. We just need to be patient.'

Daisy-May looked out of the condensation-drenched window, watching a thin flurry of snow fall. 'Don't have the luxury of patience. Not with you-know-who on his way.'

Two boys, no older than seventeen, moved off from the counter, burger boxes in their hands. Joe glanced to see whether Ryan had moved – he hadn't, if you didn't count the fingers dancing over his phone's screen – and stood, beckoning for Daisy-May to follow him. 'So, what does he look like, this Xylophone Man?'

She slouched out of her seat and reluctantly followed. 'Never seen him, just heard the horror stories. Doesn't look like us. More monster than man.'

Joe felt a pantomime shiver ripple down his spine. Every time I think I understand this world, it changes, he thought. Can't get a foothold in it. People get scared of dying because they don't know what comes next. If they knew what did, they'd actually have a reason to.

'Who sends him?' he said, as a weathered, beaten woman who could have been anything between twenty and sixty entered the restaurant, looking around warily as she did. 'The Duchess? Does she decide the rules?'

'What does it matter?' said Daisy-May. 'There ain't a

high court here, there ain't a right of appeal. It's harsh, Old Testament shit that you either get out the way of or you don't.'

'So, how do we get out of his way?' asked Joe, edging closer to the woman and the man behind the counter.

'We do what we came here to do,' said the girl. 'Faster than we are doing. Speaking of which, Prince Charming's back that way.'

Joe beckoned her closer. 'Watch.'

Daisy-May obeyed, seeing instantly why Joe had been so interested in the silent exchange.

If you hadn't been up close, you'd have missed it. Some instinct had led him to the vantage point, his body half through the counter, half in the kitchen. He'd have had no chance if he'd still been a flesh-and-blood copper.

It wasn't burgers, fries or chicken nuggets the man behind the counter was slipping into the branded paper takeaway bag: it was drugs.

There were advantages to this whole Dying Squad thing after all.

'Well, fuck me,' said Daisy-May, peering over the man's shoulder. 'Bet that shit isn't on the menu.'

Joe smiled, despite himself. 'We had a working theory on this,' he recalled. 'Knew drugs were being dealt out of Family Kingdom, just couldn't work out where exactly they were funnelling them through. Thought it was the club here, for a while, but they closed that down because of all the fights. Didn't stop the flow, and so we knew wherever they were doing it through was still in play. Super Bucket is the last place we thought to look. Suppose that means it should have been the first.'

He watched as the woman slunk away.

'Poor cow,' said Daisy-May. 'Probably the highlight of her week.'

'No one makes her take it,' said Joe distractedly, eyes locked on the man behind the counter as he deserted his post, making a beeline for Ryan. 'Only person who makes an addict is an addict.'

Daisy-May shook her head at him. 'Middle-aged white bloke with money telling the poor and fuckin' desperate how to live. Colour me shocked.'

'Drugs are a nuclear bomb,' said Joe. 'Fatal for the person taking them, and worse still for the devastation they leave behind, devastation that can last decades.'

'You're wrong on this.'

'And you're a kid. I've got years of experience that say I'm right.'

'Fuck you. Those years of experience just mean you're bitter. Jaded. You compare drugs to a nuclear bomb. Know how desperate you have to be to inject a nuclear bomb?'

'You don't know what my job's like,' said Joe, walking towards Ryan's table. 'The things I've seen.'

And he was seeing things again, lots of them. Wasted bodies found in malnourished apartments with bone-dry needles. Skeletal heads with every drop of moisture sucked out of them, looking too large for the emaciated frames. Neglected children, as thin and wasted as their parents. Whittled away before their time. Each image worse than the last, a memory tap he couldn't turn off even now.

Memories he'd rather forget.

'You don't know what it's like to have the hope pulped out of you,' Daisy-May replied. 'That's if you had any in the first place. That woman was my mum, my mate, my aunt. Vicar's boy like you, what do you know of her life? You've had one of fuckin' privilege.'

The words stung like a wasp.

She was right, of course. He was making assumptions and

134

jumping to conclusions, two things a copper should never do – or a faintly decent human being, either. He knew nothing about the woman who'd bought the drugs, nothing about what had led her there. Nothing, come to that, about Daisy-May. You ended up dying in a dungeon, something bad had led you there.

'That privilege meant I bled to death in a farmhouse,' Joe said, offering half a smile.

Daisy-May played a tiny violin of sympathy.

'But I take your point. Me being a judgemental prick will get us nowhere.'

'Thanks,' said Daisy-May.

As the takeaway employee slid into the booth next to Ryan, (Joe noting the 'manager' title on his shirt) the dealer squirmed in his seat, clearly desperate to be anywhere except here.

'Hard to accept that a bloke with "Super Bucket" on his cap is going to be a drugs kingpin,' said Daisy-May.

Joe shushed her.

'How'd it go at the pub?' asked the manager, scratching at the hair spilling out from under his hat.

'Booming,' said Ryan.

'Any kickback about the farmhouse? Anyone asking questions?'

Here we go, thought Joe.

'No one's that stupid. What about here?'

The manager leaned back, hands behind his head, a king in his kingdom. 'People want their sweets. A dead body isn't going to change that.'

'About that,' said Ryan.

'I haven't asked the big man any questions,' said the manager, 'because what answer will either of us want to hear? What difference will it make?'

Ryan grabbed the peak of his cap, dragging it closer to his

skull. 'Feels like all bets are off. Like a line's been crossed.'

The manager smirked. 'What did you think this was, lad? This is the game. Bit late to be asking what the rules are now.'

'I'm cool,' said Ryan.

'Don't care what you are, as long as it's not loose-lipped.'

'Don't report to you, do I?' said Ryan, leaning closer. 'I report to the man, and you'll never be that.'

Shit. They were both just flunkies.

'Glad you brought him up. He wants to see you.'

Ryan blinked. 'Tonight?'

'Not going to be tomorrow, is it?'

'Where?'

'Where d'you think?'

Ryan sat back, his knee jiggling against the underside of the table. 'What's he want?'

The manager rose from his seat, the edge of the table clinging onto his gut. 'Think he'd tell me? Didn't look in a good mood, though.'

'When does he ever?'

'When collections get made and not missed,' said the manager.

Ryan winced. 'What've you heard?'

'Nothing that's my business. Might want to get your excuses ready, though.'

Joe and Daisy-May watched as the man strolled back to the counter. Ryan stayed where he was, his leg beating a rhythm of fear.

'Feels like we're getting somewhere, don't it?' said Daisy-May, when he finally slid out from the booth and headed for the exit.

Joe smiled at her. 'Almost makes me want to say, *Watson, the game is afoot.*'

Daisy-May wrinkled her nose. 'Fuck off with your Watson.'

★

The few hardy souls on the seafront wouldn't have noticed the man, even though he was mere feet away. Their attention was on the deluge of snow spat at them by the cauldron-black sky, and the general misery of their lives. *He* noticed *them*, though. Noticing people – and their transgressions – was part of his job.

Not his favourite part, admittedly. That came when it was time to punish those transgressions.

He was watching such a transgressor now, exiting the tawdry fast-food restaurant that was squatting a few feet away from him. The teenage girl wasn't much to look at – nor was the middle-aged policeman accompanying her – but looks could deceive when it came to the business of sin, and this girl had sinned more than most. It was his job to hold such individuals to account, and it was one he carried out with enthusiasm.

After all, there was no rule, written or otherwise, that said he couldn't enjoy his work. Or, indeed, indulge in the occasional moment of pleasure-denial.

The Xylophone Man – his favourite of the lurid names he'd been called over the centuries – watched as the girl and the man walked away into the snow-swamped night. He could take them now, of course, but where was the fun in that? No, better to track them, their stench humming in his nostrils, the girl's fear growing ever more deliciously pronounced as he closed in.

How did the saying go?

The game's afoot.

Chapter Seventeen

It was almost two hundred years ago that the Duchess had first learned of Das Purgatorium, and the role she had been bred to play in it. She had only to close her eyes and she was back in her grandmother's room, its walls a deep red, the carpet thick under her feet, that musk of incense that always seemed to hover around her.

'Come closer, child,' Oma Jankie had said, her hard German vowels unblemished by the thirty years she'd spent in America, 'and I will tell you of our ways.'

She'd done so reluctantly, and not just because she'd always been afraid of Oma Jankie, wary of the whiskers sprouting from her chin, and her black eyes. Her sister was not yet five days cold in whichever unmarked grave her parents had seen fit to dump her in. The Duchess was curious as to what Oma Jankie had said to Hanna, but also terrified; what words could have caused her spirited younger sister to take her own life?

Oma Jankie had twitched a bony, beckoning finger, and the Duchess had kneeled next to her bed.

'I'm dying, Rachel. Do you know why that is cause for celebration?'

The Duchess hadn't known, nor had she cared to guess. From experience, she knew her family had a low tolerance for flippancy, and a high tolerance for the amount of pain they were willing to inflict upon their children. Pain equalled strength. Strength equalled power.

'Our lineage dates back thousands of years. We have never been a rich family – such vapid trivialities don't concern us – but we have been perhaps the most important in history. What do you think of that, child?'

What she'd thought was that her grandmother was half senile and wholly raving, her tenuous grip on reality loosening by the second. What she knew, though, with unblinking certainty, was that her younger sister was dead and she didn't know why, so she kept her mouth firmly shut.

This lack of an answer didn't slow down Oma Jankie. 'Our family is bred to do one thing, and it's nothing earthly. When we pass on, it is to neither heaven nor hell, it is to purgatory. What do you know of this place?'

'Only what the Bible tells us,' the Duchess had answered dutifully.

Oma Jankie had laughed at that, the sound of a rook cawing. 'An instruction manual for idiots. We have other texts that you will learn in time. None will say anything as important as this: purgatory is the central axis that supports existence. My job, now that Hanna has effectively renounced her title, is to prepare *you* to rule it. You will recruit some of these lost souls to save others, to earn their place in heaven, but most are nothing but Dispossessed: dumb animals that must be corralled.'

'Like a farmer,' the Duchess had said, not believing a word of it but wanting to humour her.

That had raised half a smile from Oma. 'A farmer. I'd never thought of it like that, but yes, I suppose it is. And like a farmer, unless the herd is kept in check, the farm will descend into chaos. The fields will be overrun, the natural resources de-stroyed. There are untold trillions in the Pen – there will only be one of you, and a handful of your team – and if they are not kept cowed, these animals, the realm will fall into disarray and ruin. It will be your job, little Rachel, to make sure that *does not happen.*'

The Duchess had been curious at this, though not brave enough to voice that curiosity. If these creatures were so dumb, why did they need to be watched so intently? What was it you were watching for, exactly?

Oma Jankie had put a rough hand on the Duchess's soft cheek and smiled. 'Your sister, my Hanna, was born for this role. It was ordained. But upon learning of her destiny, she couldn't wait: she was so desperate to take up the mantle, she took her own life. It was a life that was not hers to take. God decides when it is your time to become warden. You cannot decide it for Him. Such an act is seen as a power grab, an open defiance of His will. It is seen as insurrection. You are now next in line, so when you depart this mortal coil, you will become the Warden of the Pen.'

'Where has Hanna gone?' asked the Duchess.

Oma Jankie glowered, then spat into the bedpan lurking to the left of her. 'To the bowels of hell. She has been cast into the Pit, never to return, and why should she? After today, her name will never be spoken of again. Simply know this: she will suffer more than any sane person would have believed possible.'

The old woman had shot out a hand and grabbed the Duchess's wrist, pulling her towards her with disconcerting strength. The Duchess looked into Oma Jankie's dark eyes.

'As the second youngest sister, you will now take on the role of warden. It is the highest of honours, and one you should thank your sister's eternally damned soul for. You're not who I hoped for, but you're who we have, so we must make the best of it. For the likes of us, my duchess, death is merely the beginning.'

That beginning had been equal parts thrilling and terrifying over the last century and a half. Now, after Hanna's defiant facing-down of the cannons, and with no immediate successor, all the Duchess was left with was clammy fear, and worse, uncertainty.

'Ma'am.'

She opened her eyes, taking in her jumble-of-memories office. Remus stood in the doorway, his hands behind his back, a serene expression on his face.

'Have you found Hanna yet?' she asked.

'Regrettably, no,' said Remus.

'Why not?'

'We have the cameras, but they've found nothing so far. Nothing from Mabel, on the ground. There's only one of Hanna, and an awful lot of Pen.'

'In all your time, have you ever seen anything like this before? Her immunity to the cannons? Her ability to rile up the Dispossessed?'

Remus shook his head. 'It's like she's getting help. An outside agent, perhaps?'

The Duchess looked away. It was a rabbit hole of paranoia she was reluctant to dive down.

'There was one other thing,' said Remus.

'There always is.'

'Daisy-May. She's run into some problems.'

The Duchess turned back to him. 'What kind of problems?'

'The musical kind.'

The Duchess clenched her fists. Her throat dried, constricting in panic. 'She knows better.'

'Apparently not.'

You stupid girl, she thought. How many times have I told you of the dangers of interfering?

'What happened?'

'We don't know for sure. There must have been physical interference, though, to have drawn the Xylophone Man's attention.'

The Duchess drummed her fingers on the table.

'You suspected she was special, did you not?' said Remus. 'Few can interfere in such a way. A pity that talent has marked her for hell; I know that girl meant a great deal to you.'

'*Means* a great deal to me,' said the Duchess. 'She's not lost yet. There's still Lazarus. If he does what's asked of him, the Xylophone Man won't be able to touch her.'

'A big if,' said Remus, bowing his head.

'Ifs always are,' said the Duchess. 'Checks and balances, that's all the Xylophone Man and his master are interested in. The girl's transgression demands a soul as sacrifice. Who's to say that has to be Daisy-May's? Joe Lazarus's would fit the bill.'

There was one place in the Pen that not even Remus knew about. Getting there wasn't easy, but that made it even more special, as did the view once you'd scaled it to the top. It was somewhere that the Duchess could decamp to with no interruptions, where only God could reach her. He never had yet, but she knew that meant very little; the Almighty sang to his own tune and was altogether ambivalent about handing out a lyric sheet.

Still, for now, she was alone, her domain and the stunted souls within it stretched out beneath her, the closest she'd get to gazing down on all of creation. Dumb animals, that was what she'd always dismissed the Dispossessed as, because of Oma. Because of Remus, too; her faithful number two had always been vociferous on the subject of their herd-like qualities, and his voice was one worth listening to. If you had been identified as a future warden of the Pen, there was no one more loyal than Remus. To serve the warden, and by extension the Pen, was the purpose of his existence. Sometimes, she wasn't sure he'd ever been alive.

As she watched the Dispossessed from her place in the clouds – it was, after all, the warden's job to watch them – it was becoming more and more difficult to believe they were harmless cattle, despite Remus's beliefs.

They'd worked out the walls.

Or at least, worked out the optical illusion hiding the walls.

This illusion – the one that made you believe they were unreachable, a constant speck in the distance you never got closer to – had apparently been shattered. She watched now, as significant clusters of half-souls bunched together, driving against the walls as one.

The odd straggler had often found their way to them by sheer luck, but this wasn't that.

It's almost like they're testing for weaknesses, she thought. Not that there are any.

That was true, wasn't it? She had been here for almost a century and a half, and it had been the case for as long as she was in charge. The Pen was no-man's-land, its walls a stopper between the soil world, the Pit and the Next Place. There were doors through those walls, of course, ones that led to the membrane separating the living and the dead known as the Gloop, but their locations were hidden. The odd stray wandering through them was of no great consequence.

But if the walls themselves came down? If the trillions of Dispossessed were somehow able to break through them? It shouldn't be possible. She'd been told it was impossible by Remus. By Oma. But if it were – and the Dispossessed grouping in this way had never happened before – then the whole of existence itself would be threatened.

There had never been this number of grey souls before, thousands more pouring in every day, their earthly existence neither bad enough for them to be flung down below, nor good enough to gain entrance to heaven.

The old rules don't work any more, the Duchess thought, and these creatures dance to a different beat. Maybe my ears have got too old to hear it. My sister's haven't, though, and somehow Hanna can communicate with the Dispossessed. Lead them.

Lead them *where*, though?

She frowned as a group of roughly thirty Dispossessed stopped clawing and scratching at the wall in front of them, then shuffled along several feet, transferring their efforts to a new section of masonry. A trickle of others joined them, pressing against those at the front.

Standing behind them, every inch the puppet-master, was her younger sister.

Hanna moved amongst them, clearly orchestrating their efforts, telling them which area of the wall to work on and when it was time to move on.

'Let her,' said the Duchess to no one, her voice imbued with a confidence she didn't feel. 'Let them claw at the walls and see where it gets them. Those walls were created by the Almighty Himself. They are indestructible. Unbreachable.'

Horns sounded, and the Dispossessed raised their heads expectantly.

The slit in the sky appeared, white light hazing from it, growing longer and wider by the second. A cry went up from the masses, countless bodies turning towards the light.

There. Still predictable. Poor bastards. Whatever they did in their soil lives, they deserve better than this.

They surged forward, ripping, screaming, clawing, biting their way towards imagined paradise, the sound repugnant to the Duchess even after all this time.

At least, most of them did.

The Duchess frowned, looking away from the light to the patch of wall the gang of Dispossessed had been trying to claw their way through. Not only had the group grown bigger – they were a hundred strong now, at least – they also shared a common trait: not a single one had paid the tear in the sky the slightest bit of notice. They, unlike the scores of their brethren grasping towards the light, had ignored it completely, resolutely, soundlessly and methodically, continuing their examination of the wall at Hanna's behest.

Despite the vast distance, the Duchess was convinced that her sister looked in her direction and smiled.

She didn't like that.

She didn't like that at all.

Chapter Eighteen

Joe knew there was a kind of beauty in what he was seeing. He also knew that his soul – or what was left of it – didn't have the imagination to appreciate that beauty. Caravans filled the landscape, their roofs of rounded bubbles shrouded in snow, scattered pinpricks of light giving the scene a look of cosy hibernation.

'Sort of looks like a Christmas card, right?' said Daisy-May.

'Yes, if the card manufacturer was Poundland,' Joe replied.

'No love for your home town. It's a fucking shame, mate.'

'The *shame* will be me being damned to wander here for eternity, believe me.'

They'd followed Ryan on foot, the dealer having eschewed his car for the short walk to Duckings Caravan Park. It was off season, the place virtually deserted; just a few dashes of light were visible, sturdy year-rounders taking advantage of the rock-bottom prices. Joe supposed it was just about preferable to sleeping on the beach, but it was toss-of-a-coin close.

The sound of the sea, just a few hundred feet away, was soothing at least, something of childhood to moor him. He found that the crash and rebirth of the surf helped him to order his thoughts, and the facts.

'You got a weird look on your face,' said Daisy-May, as they followed Ryan through the rabbit warren of caravans and mobile homes. 'Kind of like you're having a fit.'

'We're close, I can smell it. You've been doing this as long as I have, you get the scent.'

'Whatever happened to facts?' said Daisy-May, deepening her voice. *'Police work rests on facts. The minute you move away from that, you slip. Every bent copper I ever knew forgot that.'*

'Was that supposed to be me?'

'Shh,' she said. 'Shit's flaring up.'

She was right. Ryan had stopped, his wiry frame silhouetted by the light seeping from a caravan roughly a hundred feet away. Compared to the surrounding others, it was positively palatial, something the steps – and fake pillars either side of those steps – were at unsubtle pains to point out. They moved closer as the dealer hovered outside, his foot placed tentatively on the bottom rung.

'Looks like he's walking to his death,' said Daisy-May.

'Who's to say he isn't?' Joe replied.

A dog barked from inside the caravan, a ragged growl of rage and impatience.

'Should have warned you,' said Daisy-May, brow furrowed. 'Dogs got an awful hate for us. Can sense us, and some dumber ones can even see us. Don't ask me why, but it's the truth.'

'I hate dogs,' said Joe.

'Who hates dogs?'

'Someone who's been bitten on a dozen midnight raids.'

'That my boy Ryan out there?' called a man's voice.

The *boy* readjusted his cap, as if that would make the situation better somehow. 'Yep, just me, boss man.'

'Cold night to be dawdling on the doorstep,' called the man. 'Come on in.'

Ryan reluctantly did as he was told, pulling the collar of his jacket up as the tidal wave of snow continued to fall.

'You all right?' said Daisy-May, looking at Joe's ashen face. 'Your face looks fuckin' mardy.'

'That voice,' said Joe. 'It's familiar.'

'Familiar how?' said Daisy-May.

Joe didn't answer, instead following Ryan up the steps, the dog inside unleashing a flurry of barks as he reached the door.

It couldn't be him. It couldn't, because if it was, it meant that the little he knew, the little he thought he remembered, was a lie.

As he passed through the side of the caravan and saw the man on the other side of it, he realised just how large that lie really was.

Pete.

They'd suffered together, cracked heads together, come up through the ranks together, blue-blood brothers to the end, unimpeachable, unbribable, everything police officers should be, protect and serve, serve and protect. The bloke had even given the eulogy at his funeral, for Christ's sake. Pete was the last true thing he knew.

The last true thing he knew hurled an ashtray at the dog snarling at Joe's phantom ankles. 'Fucking quiet, Tigger. You *know* Ryan. He knows you, right, Ryan?'

Ryan confirmed that he did.

'Told you, man. Dogs *hate* us,' said Daisy-May.

She looked warily from the yapping canine to the middle-aged man. 'That's the dude from your funeral, right? The one with your wife?'

Was it? Suddenly, in this poisoned shell of steel and poverty, Joe wondered. How could this be Pete, the best copper he knew, the best *man*, one he'd tried to emulate? If that memory wasn't true, then what was? He suddenly craved soil-fuelled amnesia, but instead was rewarded with clarity of thought so pronounced it seemed almost cruel.

'Yeah, that's Pete,' he said. 'My partner.'

'Shit,' said Daisy-May. 'Sorry.'

'For what? He could be undercover.'

'Right,' said Daisy-May doubtfully.

The dog jumped at her, yelping in surprise as it passed clean through and collided with a table resting against the far wall, sending a small mound of handguns scattering.

'Fuck's *sake*,' said Pete, getting to his feet, grabbing the hound by the collar, then yanking open the caravan's flimsy front door and roughly manhandling it out into the ocean of white. He turned to Ryan, offering him a hangman's smile. 'Strange, Tigger acting like that. You know what they say about dogs?'

Ryan shook his head.

'That they're a good judge of character. They know, on a level they don't really understand, when something – or someone – isn't right. What do you think about that, Ryan?'

'Ryan's snitching for him,' said Joe. 'We've done it a hundred times. Identify the weakest link in the chain, break it, and it leads you to the next part of the chain.'

Daisy-May said nothing.

'Don't know what you've heard,' said Ryan. 'Did what you wanted at the Sundown.'

'Hmm,' said Pete. 'What was it I wanted?'

Ryan sat down on a seat that hadn't been offered. One look from Pete sent him leaping out of it.

'Put the fear out, after what happened at the farmhouse.'

'And did you do that, Ryan? Did you put the fear out?'

'DJ was pissing himself.'

Pete smiled. 'DJ Pissing Himself. Not sure he'll get many bookings with that name.'

Ryan relaxed a little at this imagined olive branch. 'He's flat-out shit anyway.'

'I'm sure.'

Pete stood up, frowning at the mess of guns the dog had caused. 'Please continue.'

Ryan shifted on his feet. 'Did my rounds, made my sales, collected my debts. Went like I was going to stab the DJ, so they know it's business as usual.' He looked at Pete, brazening it out. 'Why, what did you hear?'

Pete picked up a small handgun, slid back into his seat, beckoning Ryan to take a seat opposite him. He placed the weapon between them.

The dealer stared at it, beads of sweat erupting on his forehead.

'What did I hear? What do you think I heard?'

'What I just told you.'

Pete nodded. 'Yeah, that's about right. You threw your weight around in the bar, acted the tough lad. Made an impression when you hauled that cunt onto the pool table. Would you really have done him, in front of all those people?'

Ryan puffed his chest out, every inch the star pupil dying to please. 'Course. Said to send out a message, didn't you?'

Pete smiled, reaching for the opened packet of cigarettes on the shelf behind him, withdrawing one and lighting it.

Pete doesn't smoke, Joe thought. He quit. We both quit, last December; a joint resolution, before the rest of the poseurs in the squad jumped on the bandwagon a month later.

'He's still alive, though, right?' said Pete. 'The DJ, I mean. Still walking around, shitting out his bad song selection. Or have I heard wrong?'

Ryan bit at his lip. 'Something weird happened.'

Pete looked away, drenching the air with smoke. 'Something weird?'

Ryan squirmed in his seat. 'Yeah. Hard to explain.'

Pete looked at him sympathetically. 'Take your time.'

Tigger, the displaced dog, started barking aggressively outside.

Daisy-May squeezed Joe's arm. 'Something's not right.'

'I know,' he said, frowning at his old partner.

She nodded to the window. 'Out there. Can't place it, but something's off.'

'It's not too clever in here.' He's undercover, Joe told himself. This isn't what it looks like; he's undercover.

Ryan took off his cap, moving it from one hand to the other.

'Because the way I heard it, pretty boy,' said Pete gently, 'is that you had some sort of fit during the moment of truth. Is that right?'

Ryan puffed out his sparrow chest. 'Wasn't the way of it. I would have done him. Something stopped me. Something I couldn't see.'

Pete looked for the ashtray, then remembered he'd thrown it at the dog. He sighed, then tapped the cigarette ash casually onto the table. 'Something you couldn't see. Your conscience, you mean?'

'Wasn't that. Something properly physical literally stopped me.'

Pete smirked. 'An invisible vigilante?'

Ryan looked down.

'Or maybe it was a poltergeist.'

Daisy-May was at the window, peering out into the blizzard, the dog's shape just visible. Her hand hovered over the bandolier strapped around her chest.

Joe was too focused on his old friend to care.

'Know what I think?' said Pete, leaning forward. He beckoned for Ryan to come closer.

Ryan reluctantly obeyed.

With rattle-snake speed, Pete yanked him forward, his right hand grabbing Ryan's crown of sweaty hair, his left jabbing the lit cigarette into his eye.

No, thought Joe. No.

Ryan screamed in pain, bringing Daisy-May's attention back from the window.

'Fucking hell,' she said. 'Fucking *hell*.'

'Here's what I think,' said Pete, his face inches away from Ryan's, his finger grinding the flaming stub deeper, the sound of singe in the air. 'I think you've been sampling the product, which is the oldest mistake in the book. I think you were high off your arse, at a time when I'd gone to great lengths to explain you needed to be grounded and sharp. To be low-profile. To keep your head down.'

Ryan screamed for his mother and salvation that wouldn't come.

'I think you *didn't* think. Didn't think I was serious, and I'll be honest, Ryan, I just had my best mate in the whole world killed. If that isn't a statement of intent, then what is?'

Joe blinked.

That's not true.

I can believe everything else. That I'm dead, the Pen, the Dying Squad, all that fucking nonsense, but not this.

Not this.

Pete released Ryan, tossing the stub away, dropping Ryan to the floor with it as he howled pain.

'So that's it,' said Daisy-May. 'Sorry, Joe.'

Joe held his head in his hands. 'This is bullshit. I'd remember it. It would have come back. So it must be bullshit.'

The dog outside began to howl in anguish.

'You want to keep the other eye?' said Pete. 'Take your worthless arse outside and wait for me. We've got a house call to make.'

Daisy-May returned to the window, taking one of the guns from its holster. 'Don't like the noises that dog's making, man.'

Ryan held his head in his hands, whimpering as he stumbled towards, then through the door.

Daisy-May's face was inches from the glass, her forehead tying itself in knots. Without taking her eyes from the window, she reached for the other holster, removing the weapon.

'Joe.'

He looked up, punch-drunk.

'He's found us.'

Chapter Nineteen

Joe would say one thing for the Xylophone Man: its appearance put earthly sins such as betrayal and murder into perspective.

Roughly seven feet tall, dressed in a black trench coat, an elephant's skull sat where its head should have been, its tusks, one half-sheared off, one jutting upwards, clawing at the sky. The creature's hollowed-out eye sockets stared straight at them, the surrounding bones weak, like they were on the verge of collapse.

It was the mouth that shocked the most, though: wide open, endless, hundreds of misshapen black-and-white teeth sprouting from it like a diseased piano.

'Looks like a man, in a certain light,' said Joe.

'Not this light,' said Daisy-May.

'No,' said Joe. 'Not this light.'

The creature raised a bony limb in greeting.

Joe stifled a laugh, realising it was one half-step away from a scream. 'What do we do?'

Daisy-May looked down at her gun. 'We see what it wants.'

'I thought you knew what it wanted.'

'Thought this'd be over when you found out how you died, yet here you are. It's all wrong, mate. All of this.'

She retrieved the second gun from the holster on her chest and handed it to him.

Joe looked at it doubtfully. 'Is this thing going to work?'

'Probably not.'

'Then why give me it?'

'You fancy going to see that thing with just your wits?'

Joe looked at the bleak figure outside, the shadowy void of it contrasting with the freshly laid white snow. 'I don't.'

They both walked through the front of the caravan, a feat of mind-over-matter-over-structure that Joe was adapting to. His finger found the trigger of the gun, the glass vial shining in the moonlight, the green liquid within sloshing about.

Daisy-May raised her hand, whether in greeting or surrender, Joe wasn't sure.

Snow tumbled down, adding to the inches that had already gathered. The silence was funereal, utter and enveloping.

Joe tried to look the Xylophone Man in the eye, then became certain that to do so would unspool his mind completely. It opened its mouth, teeth glittering.

'You know why I'm here.'

Neither a question nor a statement, the voice harsh, as if it had scored the words into glass. Joe noticed Daisy-May's hand was shaking, then realised his were too.

'Didn't break the rules lightly,' she said, with colourless swagger. 'Stupid rule anyway.'

'It has existed longer than you and I,' said the creature, 'and will surely exist long after we're gone.'

Its voice is like death, thought Joe. Rotting, fetid death.

'So, what, you're my judge, jury and firing squad?' asked Daisy-May. 'Hate to use the "I got friends in high places" line, but you know, I do.'

This thing doesn't care about friends, Joe knew. And it certainly doesn't look scared of high places.

'I serve a power higher than you could know,' said the Xylophone Man.

'Didn't say otherwise. Just trying to get a little dialogue going, that's all.'

The creature took a step forward.

'What do you want?' said Joe, struggling to understand how he could negotiate with such a being. 'Because it always comes down to that, right?'

The Xylophone Man laughed, a sound like bleach poured into an open wound. 'The girl and her immortal soul.'

'Greedy fucker,' said Daisy-May.

'She had no choice,' said Joe. 'She saved a life, and where I'm from, that counts for something.'

The creature giggled, and Joe felt his nose start to bleed. He placed the back of his hand against it and saw black instead of red.

Daisy-May raised her gun.

Joe followed suit.

'They won't help you,' said the Xylophone Man.

'Hard to see how they'll hinder us, either,' said Joe, 'if you're set on not listening to reason.'

A car's engine burst to life.

Joe and Daisy-May threw the briefest of glances behind them and saw Ryan clambering into Pete's idling Range Rover.

They looked back to the Xylophone Man.

They fired.

The gun bit into Joe's hand, the noise deafening in the real world rather than the womb-like Gloop Daisy-May had fired it in before, and he watched, fascinated, as the bullets powered towards the creature.

They exploded, green tendrils extending as they had before, reaching out and tying themselves around the beast, slathering it in a parched green cocoon, obscuring it completely.

'Bogeyman my arse,' muttered Daisy-May. 'Now *move*.'

No way will it be that easy, thought Joe, following Daisy-May as she sprinted for the Range Rover. No way.

The vehicle began to reverse through the snowstorm and the pair jumped, passing through its door to collide with the back seat.

They looked out of the rear window as a whistling noise sounded, like wind screaming through a bone graveyard.

The green binding around the Xylophone Man faded, then crumbled into nothingness.

The creature stood there unharmed and unfazed.

'Why's it just standing there?' asked Joe.

'Because that thing's fucking destiny,' said Daisy-May, 'and you can't outrun destiny, no matter how fast you are, and no matter how hard you try. Not in the end.'

Chapter Twenty

The Range Rover inched forward, a mountaineer scaling Everest, or trying to, Pete swearing to himself as he push-me-pull-you'd the vehicle up the steep incline, swirls of snow all the time trying to impede them.

'What's the plan, Joe?'

'No "Joey"?' asked Joe, his eyes inches from the window as he scanned the horizon. 'No smart remarks?'

'Don't feel in much of a joking mood,' said Daisy-May.

'We slowed it down once,' said Joe gently. 'If it catches up with us, we can slow it down again.'

'Then what?' said Daisy-May. 'Whichever way I look at it, I'm properly fucked. Xylophone Man may stop you doing what you need to do, if the mood takes it. You're better off on your own.'

'We started this thing together, and we'll end it together,' said Joe, as Pete gunned the engine, gears grinding, wheels gasping for purchase. 'We're partners.'

'That guy Pete was your partner,' said Daisy-May. 'Look how that worked out for you.'

'Well, as long as you don't have me killed, you're one up on him.'

'I love a low bar,' said Daisy-May, smiling despite herself.

'Welcome to my life. Afterlife. Whatever.'

The car juddered to a halt.

'So, what's the plan?' said Daisy-May again. 'Other than trying to outrun the Grim fucking Reaper.'

Joe stepped through the car, the blizzard easing just enough to reveal where they'd ended up.

'You believe in destiny, Daisy-May?'

She stood next to him, looking at the concrete structure facing them. 'Only when it looks like the Elephant Man and it's chasing me. Why?'

Joe pointed at the plaque on the wall. 'Because when you're on the run and things look bleak, what else do you need but sanctuary?'

Of all the many sources of familial strife Joe had encountered throughout his childhood, his father's failure to open an outreach centre had been one of the most pronounced. The council's refusal to grant him the funds was parsimony his father saw as evil, preventing, as it did, his ability to help the area's poor and needy.

His mother had never shared her husband's enthusiasm for the project. *Empire-building*, he'd overheard her tell a friend once. *He wants to help people, but not as much as he wants his name on a plaque. The Reverend Narcissist.*

Joe stared at that plaque now. His father had gone for *The Sanctuary* in the end, the name etched in a bold, flowing font. It had clearly been built recently, when Joe was still alive. He should remember it.

Feels like whoever's feeding these memories back to me has an agenda, he thought. Wish I knew whether it was a favourable one.

'This more of your old man's work?' said Daisy-May, looking up at the squat blob of concrete, lights blazing from the thin slits of the centre's windows.

'How did you guess?'

'The Sanctuary. Not overburdened with imagination, is he, your dad?'

'Not a crime I'd attribute to him, no,' said Joe.

Daisy-May looked at the black waves that stretched out below them, the full moon giving them a pale-blue cast, the wind whipping at the craggy hill they stood on. 'What is this place? Any closer to the sea and it'd be a boat.'

'An early-warning base, originally,' said Joe. 'Army built it to sound the alarm if the Nazis were at the gates. In my day, it wasn't much more than a place for teenage boys to bring teenage girls to do teenage things. Looks like the old man finally got his wish to put it to a more spiritual use.'

'Renovations to the church, taking over this place. Sounds like the reverend's cash-rich,' said Daisy-May.

'What are you getting at?'

'Nothing that you haven't thought yourself. Knowing what you know about Pete, you don't think it's strange he's come to see your old man? That doesn't raise a red flag?'

Joe laughed. 'When I was ten years old, I found a five-pound note in the street. My dad was so straight, he made me hand it in to the police. When no one claimed it, it was finally returned to me, and he made me put it in the church collection basket. He's no drugs baron, believe me.'

Car doors opened, Pete and Ryan finally exiting the Range Rover.

'Hope you're not going to disappoint me here, boy,' said Pete.

'Put the word out that there'd be a bonus if they showed,' said Ryan, fidgeting with the dirty gauze now covering his eye. 'Plus free skag. Never yet met a junkie that'd turn down a handout, specially a yellow-belly junkie. We'll have a full house, boss, believe me.'

Pete nodded. 'You clear on what we're doing here?'

'Crystal,' said Ryan. 'No loose ends.'

'This whole tale's nothing but loose ends,' said Daisy-May. 'I'll say this, though, Joey, if this is my last stand, you've picked a prime spot for it.'

Just because he couldn't physically smell any more, it didn't mean Joe didn't keep the muscle memory of it. It flexed in him now as he looked out upon rows of people in metal cots laid out on a bleached-clean floor, bathed in yellow tungsten light, a mighty wooden cross overseeing it all at the front of the room. The room smelled of childhood and charity.

My father's home for the homeless. He always talked about it, and I thought talk was all it would ever be. A shitty father, maybe, but at least he's helping these people, and who needs help more than them, on a night like this?

His father was at the back, in conversation with a middle-aged woman. It was difficult to miss (although Joe supposed that was the idea) the tapestry that rested on the wall behind the good reverend. It depicted St Lazarus – how subtle – standing amongst a crowd of kneeling, grateful commoners, their hands outstretched, desperate to receive the sainted priest's favour.

The Reverend Narcissist thought Joe. Maybe Mum always had it right.

He turned as a woman laughed.

Claire.

His wife glided from one bed to another, talking, smiling, sympathising, comforting by the act of simply being herself. They were enraptured with her, men and women alike, and despite the grimness of the room, the bleakness of the snow-storm outside, she seemed to glow, an angel descended from heaven.

Except angels don't exist, thought Joe. As far as I can tell, there're only devils and washouts like me. Maybe that's why the world's such a fucked-up place.

He remembered how his father had shaken his head when he'd brought Claire to meet him for the first time, openly disbelieving that a woman like her could have ended up with his disappointment of a son. *She's special,* the reverend had said to him the next day. *Don't blow it.*

Had he? That was something Joe couldn't remember. All he had was his love for her, and his sense of not being worthy of her love in return. That, he could believe he'd *never* forget, no matter how much soil air he inhaled.

Except it didn't work like that, did it? There was no place for love-is-eternal idealism when you weren't breathing any more.

Joe took out a piece of gum – realising that after this, there was only one stick left – looked at it regretfully, then popped it into his mouth. He could almost hear the hooves of last-chance redemption thundering in the distance.

'She's like a fit Mother Teresa, your ex,' said Daisy-May.

'She's one of those rare people who isn't happy unless everyone else is,' said Joe, the gum twanging back his sense of self and hacking away the memory fog. 'Just the way she is.'

'I'm going to check out the back,' said Daisy-May. 'Don't like the no-show from the boys outside.'

Joe nodded, glad of a few moments alone.

He inched closer to Claire, unable to resist the chance to be near her again, to hear the timbre of her voice, to see how she carried herself with a calming grace, how she made you want to be better than you knew was possible but to try anyway. She was chatting to a young man whose sallow cheekbones were so pronounced it was as if they were trying to elbow their way out of his face. He was ragged, with a beard of scabs on his face.

There's still something behind his eyes, though, Joe observed. He's new to this life, or at least, relatively new.

The trainers on his feet were expensive, and still in pretty good nick. No way had he got those at a shelter.

The man scratched at his arm, agitated. 'Need to get out. No good for me here.'

Claire's smile was soft and kind. 'It's no good for you out there, either. There are several inches of snow already, and there's plenty more forecast. It's three below. You'll freeze to death.'

He plucked at his mange of beard. 'Walls are closing in here. Bad vibes, bad chemicals. Bad people.'

Claire placed a hand on his arm. 'What's your name?'

'Bobby,' said the man, almost as if he were embarrassed.

'Bobby,' said Claire 'Do you trust me?'

The question caused him to blink furiously, as if the caring tone and gesture were too much for him to comprehend. He looked over at Reverend Lazarus. 'Don't trust him. Fucken do-gooder.'

'But do you trust *me*?'

His cloudy eyes met hers. 'Spose.'

She's amazing, thought Joe. She's smiling like he's a film star. Poor fucker probably hasn't seen kindness like that his whole life.

'Well then, stay,' said Claire. 'I want you to stay, and be safe, and tomorrow's another day. That's what I tell myself these days.'

She took a breath, steadying herself. 'I . . . lost someone recently, and a lot of the time I look the world dead in the eye and spit in it. Question what it is I've done to deserve the pain I'm feeling. Resenting anyone who isn't feeling that pain themselves. Why should they be happy?

'Then something will happen that gives me a moment of joy – a song on the radio, a bad joke my husband always used to tell – and I'll realise this won't be forever. Tomorrow might bring something better. I'm not promising it'll be perfect – anyone who does would be lying – but at least there'll be the chance of something better. Go out there in this weather, and there won't be.'

She gently squeezed Bobby's arm, then got to her feet. 'Now, we're about to serve up. Why don't you hover near the front, so you're first in line?'

Bobby smiled, then nodded.

Grief like Joe had never known dug its nails into him.

I'm really dead. I believed it, but I didn't know what it meant, not really, because I still felt like me. But this is what I've lost, what's been taken from me. Claire. Our life together. What we had, what we should have had. There's no coming back.

He reached inside his coat, fingering his single stick of gum.

And if I don't get this case cracked, this might be as good as it gets.

Reverend Lazarus clapped his hands, nodding at the simmering saucepan in the centre of the room. 'Wonderful that so many of you could be here today,' he said. 'If ever there's a night that shows the importance of what we're trying to achieve, then surely it's this one. Knowing you'll all be here tonight, safe and warm, as the storm rages outside – well, if that's not God's work, I don't know what is.'

He moved behind the stove, picking up a ladle. 'Now, in a moment Claire and myself will start serving the food.'

A smile from Claire.

'But first,' continued the reverend, 'I hoped that you might all join me in a moment's prayer.'

A murmur from the flock, neither negative nor positive, more resigned.

'Heavenly Father,' began the reverend, 'thank you for the bounty you have bestowed upon us. We give you thanks . . .'

The sound of scraping metal could be heard, and Joe, along

with the rest of the room, turned towards the slowly opening front door.

'Good evening, everyone,' said Pete with a smile. 'I'm sorry to interrupt. Hell of a night.'

Joe watched the room watch Pete, the atmosphere crackling with unease. Glances were exchanged between the homeless men and women, fear traded like it was a precious mineral.

They're afraid of him, he realised. And it goes beyond the usual wariness of the police. That kind of fear is personal. It comes from having history. A bad one.

'Reverend Lazarus, Claire, if I could have a quick word,' said Pete jovially, throwing smiles like confetti as he walked through the room. 'It won't take long.'

Joe moved closer, grateful that for all of its disadvantages, at least death removed the need for a wiretap.

'We were just about to serve up,' said Joe's father, trying badly to hide his annoyance.

'The roads are closed, in and out of the town,' said Pete, leaning into them both. 'Unless you leave now, you won't get home in time.'

'I've been driving these roads all my life,' said the reverend, with a familiar pomposity. 'A little snow doesn't change that.'

'I barely got up here, and I'm in a Range Rover,' Pete replied, his voice beginning to crack. 'It's Joe's wake in two hours. It's going to gut-punch me if I can't be there, but there's no way I'm going to allow you to miss it. I'd never forgive myself.'

Crocodile tears, thought Joe. And they're both falling for them.

'Bill, I'd like you to take Claire and leave now, while you still can,' continued Pete. 'I'll stay here and serve up to these fine people.'

Claire placed a hand on Pete's. Joe took a pointless step forward, teeth bared as if he could warn her away. 'You're one of the good ones.'

Pete smiled. 'That's what the paycheques say. Doesn't always feel like it.'

I know that smile, thought Joe. That smile used to mean *just one more pint*, a joke no one else would get. Guess the joke was always on me.

The reverend tugged at his dog collar. 'It doesn't feel right just to abandon my post like this. I have a duty of care to these people.'

'And it's one I'm more than happy to discharge,' said Pete. 'I don't want to speak out of turn here, Bill, but you've got a duty to Joe, too. You need to send him off right, and you can't do that if you're snowed in here. Now go. Take Claire, and I'll see you soon.'

Claire smiled, taking her father-in-law's hand in hers. 'Pete's right, Bill. You're allowed a night off, and we owe it to Joe.'

The look on the reverend's face, it seemed to Joe, suggested that he didn't owe his son very much at all, but he nodded anyway.

'Detective Inspector Burns – Pete – will serve you,' he said, addressing the room. 'I trust you'll behave for him. The weather is extremely treacherous, so I'd ask that you stay here for the night, where it's warm and safe, and I'll be back in the morning to check on you.'

Not the most dutiful of shepherds, thought Joe. Fucking off his flock at the first opportunity. Just like he fucked off my eulogy.

The men and women looked at each other, shifting uncomfortably, awkward and unsettled.

They know something's up, thought Joe. Feels like they'd rather take their chances out there in the cold, rather than in the warm with Pete.

Claire gave Pete a peck on the cheek. 'It won't be the same without you. Do you think there's any chance you'll make it?'

166

'Just as soon as I finish up here,' said Pete with a smile. 'If there's any chance at all, I'll be there.'

Joe followed Pete as he accompanied them to the door, the reverend giving his flock a final look, and handing Pete the keys to the place, before Claire gently dragged him away. Pete watched them leave, then turned back to the expectant diners, sticking his fingers in his mouth and whistling sharply.

Ryan, brown masking tape now hiding his damaged left eye, emerged from a door at the back of the room.

'You cunts are in a lot of trouble,' said Pete.

'Deliveries: down. Sales: down. New customers: down. The worst week since we started. Why?'

Pete stood waiting, looking over the centre's guests.

'Because you shot a copper,' said Joe. 'One who just happened to be your partner and best mate.'

'Think there's more to it, pal,' said Daisy-May, returning to his side.

'Your lad promised us cash tonight if we came. Dope too,' called out a man from the back.

'Reverend Lazarus promised you salvation for your eternal soul,' said Pete, 'so we've all been guilty of telling fairy tales. I'll ask one more time: why are sales down?'

'It's gone bad,' said a woman at the back, hiding behind a friend. 'People are scared. Think there'll be police sniffing around now, after your partner got shot.'

'I'm the only copper you should worry about,' said Pete. 'This is my patch, and I control it. Thought you people knew that and understood it, as much as cloth-eared twats like you can understand anything. I bring the drugs in, you filter them out, where I say, and when I say. Local police know not to touch you. What's the problem?'

The problem is, you're a piece of shit, thought Joe. The

167

problem is, I'm dead because of you. The problem is, they're scared of you.

The man Claire had spoken to earlier raised his hand. Fancy trainers. *Bobby*.

Pete pointed at him. 'Scabby's here! What's up, Scabby?'

'The junk you've been giving us is crap,' said Bobby.

'Define *crap*.'

'Five of us dead from it, this month alone. Someone's cutting it with something.'

'Junkies dying from junk,' said Pete, waving a hand dismissively. 'Revelation.'

'You said we could keep some for ourselves,' said Bobby, looking around him for support. 'We know the risks, but this is something different. People dying's bad for business.'

With four steps, Pete was on him, towering over him and causing the younger man to cower. He raised a hand.

Bobby closed his eyes.

Pete smiled, and patted Bobby's face affectionately. He wiped his hand on Bobby's tattered coat.

'You've got a point there, Scabby,' he said. 'It *is* bad for business.' He looked over to Ryan. 'You have any thoughts on that, Cyclops?'

Ryan shrugged.

'Cyclops doesn't have any thoughts, and despite appearances, he's usually full of them. Might have only one eye, but opinions and teenage girls?' Pete sneered, disgusted. 'He's fucking *drowning* in them.' He jerked his head at his one-eyed henchman. On cue, Ryan slunk into the shadows.

'You've been good soldiers,' said Pete, smiling at the room. 'Don't think I don't appreciate that.'

He retreated to the front door, the throng watching him uneasily, like they'd expected the cane but gotten a certificate for good behaviour.

'Though it's now time,' he said, 'to bring our arrangement to a close.' He gave them a final wave, then backed out of the door.

A dozen voices murmured.

'Said it was a bad idea.'

'Never trusted him.'

'Dealing's bad news. Dealing for a copper? Forget it.'

'So, we're *not* getting money for coming here?'

Bobby looked around. 'Does this seem shady to anyone?'

'What do you mean?' asked an elderly woman at the back.

'The lad's right,' said Joe, scanning the room.

Bobby tried the front door, and it rattled stubbornly. 'It's locked.'

'I don't see Ryan,' said Joe.

'On it.' Daisy-May started running towards the back room.

'Joe,' she yelled. 'You need to get back here, *now*.'

Every inch of the room was covered in petrol. Ryan tossed a now-empty can into the corner and took out his lighter.

'They can't mean to burn these people alive?' said Daisy-May.

Ryan retreated towards the back door, flicking his lighter into life.

'I think that's exactly what they mean to do,' said Joe. 'And we have to stop them, even if it means damnation. Screw the Xylophone Man. We're damned anyway.'

Ryan opened the back door, raising his arm, the flame flickering in the wind.

'I'm damned,' said Daisy-May. 'You're not. The Xylophone Man doesn't give a flying shit about you, and that's the way we're going to keep it.'

'We can't just stand by and do nothing.'

'Any sort of *something* that we do is going to light us up even more, and we've already got enough heat on us. You must really love my company, mate, 'cos you do something here, you'll be joining me in hell forever.'

Ryan looked at the lighter like someone had planted it on him.

'Don't do it,' Joe said to him, knowing the futility of it. 'There's no crossing back over that line, lad.'

Click.

Click.

Click.

Ryan flicked the lighter again and again, birthing the flame into life, then letting it die. Uncertainty crawled over his face.

Finally, he turned, and walked towards the back door.

'Good lad,' said Joe.

Ryan stopped. The lighter flickered back to life.

No, thought Joe, as Ryan went to throw it. I can't do nothing. If that means hell, so be it.

He jabbed out a hand, trying to grab Ryan's wrist but doing nothing more than passing through him, losing his balance, Ryan shivering slightly as he did so.

'It'll go out,' said Daisy-May, as the lighter tumbled floorwards.

It didn't.

Instead, flame licked floor and an honest-to-goodness roar sounded, a lake of fire that quickly became an ocean surging across the room.

Ryan took a final look, then backed out of the room, leaving Joe and Daisy-May standing helplessly in the kitchen, surrounded by flames.

'How come I can't do what you did?' said Joe, looking wildly around him. 'You're barely an adult, and I'm a cynical old fucker so wedded to my job it killed me.'

'There's your first problem,' said Daisy-May. 'You're too old to learn new tricks.'

Joe dodged the verbal bait. 'Try using that trick of yours to find a fire extinguisher.'

He ran through the kitchen wall into the main room. The flames were stoking panic amongst the people trapped there; led by Bobby, several men were throwing themselves against the locked front door.

If the door was out, maybe they'd have more luck with the windows?

A quick look confirmed they were better off trying to head-butt their way through the door. When the army had built this place in the forties, they'd built it to last; no wider than a cigarette packet, the windows reminded Joe of those on a medieval castle. Enough space to fire an arrow through, but only just. No way was any human being getting out that way.

He lurched through the front door into the night air, and immediately saw the problem: as well as locking the door, Pete had also wedged a spade under the handle. He was sitting behind the wheel of his idling four-by-four, Ryan standing next to it, pulling at his cap agitatedly, looking up at the centre like his conscience was trying to make him do something that might save his soul, rather than eternally damn it.

'Fucked-up, this, boss. Who they gonna tell? Who's gonna believe them, even if they do?'

'They can ID both of us, tie us directly to the county line,' Pete said, gunning the engine. 'It's exactly the sort of evidence an outside police force would spot. It was good while it lasted, but it's done. Nothing left for me here but prison.'

'So, what?' said Ryan. 'You're going to go on the lam?'

'My plans are none of your business, boy.'

Ryan took his cap off, then put it back on; crusted blood was gathered around the masking tape on his eye. 'Burning them alive, though. Fuck.'

'You've got your orders. Fetch the stash from Josie's and meet me at the wake. I'm closing down the line. You'll get paid, we go our separate ways. And if you try to fuck me in any way, I'll take your other eye. Try pulling little girls then.'

Joe stared at his former partner, desperately searching for some sign of the man he'd believed Pete to be.

Pete gave the building a final look. 'Waste of skin in there, Ryan. We've done them a favour.'

Joe didn't find it.

'The back door's open,' shouted Bobby.

Joe had raced back inside to find Bobby standing at the threshold of the kitchen. Flames had colonised the old-fashioned cooker, the table and chairs, and engulfed the mustard-coloured tiles. The back door, though, stood ajar, and hope caught alight in Joe, just as fiercely as the flames.

Ryan left it open. Some part of the boy's conscience, maybe, giving his soul an out.

The other trapped men and women were oblivious to it. They continued to hammer desperately on the front door, screaming for help Joe knew wouldn't come.

Daisy-May stood in the kitchen doorway next to Bobby, rubbing her arms agitatedly. 'Open door won't help. Flames and smoke are too thick.'

Joe saw that she was right. The night air was fanning the flames, creating a vortex of oxygen and fire impossible to get through without burning to death. Screams of fear went up from the main hall as the flames began to creep in. Joe watched Bobby stumble back to where the group crowded the front door. Thick smoke advanced upon them as they clawed, scraped and screamed at it, anything to escape the advancing flames.

'It's going to be all right,' Bobby called out to them.

Joe closed his eyes, wishing he was smarter, that his afterlife wasn't such a curse, and that there was someone who could help.

There was no choice.

Asking her would be a death penalty, a red flag to announce her location to the Xylophone Man. But if they didn't help the living, what right did the Dying Squad have to seek justice for the dead?

Daisy-May and Joe stood outside the Sanctuary's front entrance, snow surging through their weightless forms, the screams of the men and women on the other side of the door bruising the night.

'You can save your speeches,' said Daisy-May, glaring at the spade wedged under the door handle like it was a personal insult. 'I'll do it.'

Joe nodded. 'I could try again.'

'Could do with the laugh, but it'll be a waste of time.'

She steadied herself, and kicked at the spade with the heel of her moth-eaten trainer.

A *clang* whispered back.

She shook her head. 'To be honest, I wondered whether that was going to work. Thought it might be a once-only deal.'

A chill trembled through Joe, and he looked behind him.

'Daisy-May.'

'I know,' she said, kicking out at the spade again. 'I felt it too.'

Joe squinted into the darkness. A white smudge was coming up the hill, perfectly unhurried.

'It's here,' he said.

'I *know*,' she repeated, refusing to look, frowning at the billows of smoke exiting the window slits, muttering to herself, sizing up the spade once again.

This time, the *clang* was loud and clear. Daisy–May called out in triumph as the spade fell limply to the ground, then risked a look behind her. The Xylophone Man continued to stroll up the hill, just a regular demon out for an evening soul.

'The door isn't opening.'

She whirled around to find her partner was right. 'That's because your prick of an ex-partner locked it.'

Another glance.

The creature drew ever closer.

'What are we going to do?' said Joe, desperation in his words.

Daisy–May reached into her bandolier, withdrew the two pistols, then shoved them into Joe's hands.

'You're going to hold it off,' she said, taking a step towards the front door. 'I'm going to jimmy the lock.'

Joe nodded, swallowing hard.

But it was as though Daisy–May had already forgotten him.

The shrieking crack of the pistols ruptured the night sky, meshing with the screams from inside the centre.

Don't look behind you, Daisy–May told herself, because there's nothing there that you want to see.

She tried to steady her arm, her right hand inside the locking mechanism, or what she hoped was the locking mechanism.

Joe gasped, then choked.

Don't look, thought Daisy–May. Concentrate.

She closed her eyes as she heard her partner gargle out a scream, focusing solely on her hand and willing it to solidify, crying out as metal meshed with solid matter. She grasped the gears of the lock, massaging the pins, then yanked them clear out with a scream of triumph and pain.

The front door swung open, smoke billowing from within, ceiling-high flames framing the hysterical men and women inside as they tumbled out, passing through and round her.

At last, she turned.

Joe was suspended in mid-air, his back rigid, paralysed, like a fly caught in a web, the Xylophone Man observing him, detached, bored.

'Put him down,' said Daisy-May. 'It's me you want.'

'What do you know of what I want?' said the Xylophone Man.

'He's salad dressing, I'm prime rib. The Duchess's favourite daughter, aren't I?'

There was a long moment, and the creature nodded. Joe slumped to the ground, gasping.

Phantom air rushed from Daisy-May's lungs, her body snapping to attention like someone had poured cement down her spine. She rose several feet off the ground and began to float towards the beast, its jaws opening wider and wider.

'Mussel Shoals,' she gasped. 'Get . . . to Mussel Shoals.'

Joe's face contorted in horror as the rows of xylophone teeth enveloped her.

There was the scream of teeth on flesh.

Then there was nothing.

Part Two

There are two ways of seeing: with the body and with the soul. The body's sight can sometimes forget, but the soul remembers forever.

Alexandre Dumas, *The Count of Monte Cristo*

Chapter Twenty-One

My name's Joe Lazarus, and I think I'm dead.

I'm running, and I don't know why. I'm covered in snow – though it's more like drenched – and the blizzard's all around me, like nature's making a point I've missed. I don't know how long I've been running for, but I'm not out of breath or even sweating, so it can't have been for long. The night's as black as I've ever seen it, without so much as the blink of a cat's eye to light my way.

There's a white Range Rover in front of me with a coughing exhaust and a throaty grumble, one that hints it's straining to go faster – and would be if it wasn't for the weather. Is the Range Rover the reason why I'm sprinting down a country road in the middle of a snowstorm?

The car slows slightly, its two red slabs of brake light burning into the haze of white, then torturously navigates a sharp left-hand bend. I don't slow my pace – in fact, I double down, speeding up, making up some yards, and have precious seconds to think.

What's the last thing I can remember?

Nothing.

A voice tells me I'm a detective, but I don't know whether I can trust it.

Something in its tone rings true, though, or true enough. I go with it, consider it a placeholder till something more solid come along.

The bend's kink straightens out and the car roars in appreciation.

I don't know why I can't let it get away, why it — and whoever's driving it — is so important, only that it is.

Then, a thought comes from nowhere, wrapped with a bow.

There was a woman.

A young woman, and she was helping me.

She warned me about forgetting. Said it would happen — that I could delay it — but it would come for me eventually. Ironic that the only thing I can actually remember is the promise of amnesia.

The snow slows for a second, and I think back to an old primary school teacher, Mr Jennings. All snow is, Joe, *he'd say, is the Almighty running his fingers through his hair. God's dandruff.* About as useful, too.

I laugh, a hollow sound carved out further by the featureless landscape. How can I remember that, but not who am I, where I am, or why I'm chasing a car down the road?

Except that's not quite right.

Joe.

That's what Mr Jennings called me.

Joe.

There's a name badge on my coat to back up the fact.

I AM JOE!

Joe Lazarus.

The car accelerates, and although I'm not tired (not even sweating, and how can that possibly be?), I can't keep up.

It rounds the corner and it's gone, its exhaust smoke taunting me.

I stand in the middle of the road, totally alone.

I don't see the other car until it's too late.

It's quieter than the Range Rover — its purr is electric — but that doesn't excuse me having missed it. I turn, too late, its lights dazzling, and it's like it hasn't seen me, because there's no squeal of tyres, no change in direction, just an onward plough straight towards me.

The second before the car hits, a final night terror stitches itself back into my subconscious. A misshapen figure stalks towards me, its bones

*twisted like a Dalí nightmare. There's a skull where its face should be,
and when it opens its mouth, all I see is an endless helter-skelter of
black and white teeth and an ocean of blood.*

*It speaks without speaking, its voice poison in my head. As it whis-
pers its name, I almost welcome the car hitting me.*

Except it doesn't.

*It passes clean through me, and I scream a scream that's unearned,
because there's no pain.*

That's because you're dead, you dumb fuck, *a girl's voice says.*
You're dead, and you'll forget things. It's why you've got the
notebook.

The notebook.

I pat my coat, a reassuring bulge my reward.

I take it out, running a finger over the embossed insignia.

Dragnet. Dragnet, *because of my dad.*

I open it and begin to read.

'So, I am a detective,' said Joe aloud, just to hear his own voice.
'Just not a very good one.'

It had done its job, though, the notebook. It had helped
bring him back.

He was dead and his memories, what made him *him*, were
being eradicated by the world, rotting away by the second.

He remembered the outreach centre. It burned still in the
distance.

He remembered the creature that had taken the girl.

He remembered the guilt he'd felt at not being able to save
her.

He remembered that grasping back this knowledge was getting more difficult by the moment, and pretty soon, it would
be impossible.

He remembered the gum.

He put a hand into his pocket and dug out the wrapper,

his thumb pressing down on nothing. It was gone. He'd used it all.

He'd used it all, his memories were fragile and dissolving, and he was no closer to discovering who had killed him.

He looked around, taking in his surroundings properly for the first time. Snow-covered fields as far as the eye could see, and the sea whispered somewhere off in the distance. There wasn't a single visual landmark he could use to tether himself. All there was was snow.

He took out the notebook and opened it again. Based on what was written here, Pete his ex-partner, had confessed to his murder.

I just had my best mate in the whole world killed. If that isn't a statement of intent, then what is?

He could see Pete boasting to Ryan. If he was still a breathing, flesh-and-blood copper, he'd be typing up that confession and clearing a space on the shelf for his next commendation. So why was he standing in this freezing field, utterly alone, with the trail cold?

On the next page, two words had been written. Both were a little smudged, like they'd been written in haste. A name. One he didn't immediately recognise.

Terry Groves.

He knew that name. How?

An image of a man popped into his head. Short, like a jockey.

Terry Groves, aka the Jockey.

Joe massaged the memory.

The Jockey had been a big-time heroin dealer. He owned a couple of racecourses, but that wasn't why they called him the Jockey. The exact reason escaped Joe, but he was fairly sure it involved riding crops and strangulation.

Why did I write this name? What's the relevance?

He remembered an interview room. He and Pete had finally linked the Jockey to a drug line out of Marseille, and Pete was warming him up. Talking to him about his tough-guy reputation. Stoking his ego.

There'd been an enforcer the Jockey had taken down early in his career. The kill had made him, reputation-wise.

The Jockey had laughed when Pete had mentioned that. 'I never touched the bloke. Was going to, but he was already dead when I got to his place. Overdose. All I had to do was cut the throat of a dead man. Put out I'd taken care of him. Get yourself that sort of rep, gangsters give you credit for plenty of other shit you never did. Your rep snowballs. Christ, by the end they said I took out Al Capone and Don Corleone.'

Pete had taken note of this, Joe remembered. Maybe he'd done more than take note of it.

Maybe he'd used it as a mission statement.

Because something about Pete's admission had felt off. In Joe's experience – no matter how unreliable a narrator that experience was – people copped to a crime for two reasons: they were so crushed by guilt they had to drain it off their soul, or they were taking gangster credit where it wasn't due.

Pete had never been one to waste time with feeling guilty about things, a truth Joe had known before learning of his true nature; which suggested his former partner was appropriating the crime. Ruling by the threat of violence was one thing; ruling when that threat had become reality quite another. Better for his lackeys to believe that the cost of crossing him was death, that Joe's death was all part of his master plan, than the alternative: that someone else got there first. And in one of Pete's own safe houses, too.

Conjecture, thought Joe, mixed in with reaching, bullshit and flat-out guessing. Which doesn't mean I'm wrong, because the one concrete fact is this: I'm still here, walking around like the littlest undead hobo, trying to uncover the truth. If I had, I wouldn't be here any more.

The Duchess had been pretty clear about that, if not much else.

He flicked through the notebook, trying to find further clues. Two more words had been written at the back, and judging by their spidery, smudgy scrawl, they'd been written in haste.

Mussel Shoals.

It had been the last thing Daisy-May had said to him before she was taken.

I couldn't help her, he thought. Daisy-May's first thought was always to help me, and when she needed help in return, I failed her. I don't have the first idea where she was taken, or how to get there.

All I have left is the case. If I can solve that, her sacrifice will have meant something.

He read the name again. Mussel Shoals was familiar, somehow. Not from his police past, though. Further back than that.

Chimes tickled the air, just audible on the breeze, the sound of the sea washing beneath him.

This was the coastal path. The one that led to Mussel Shoals.

And if Daisy-May said he needed to go to Mussel Shoals, that was good enough for him.

After all, he had a murder to solve.

Alabama's Mussel Shoals was a recording studio not so much steeped in swampy, sawdust soul and blues as submerged in it. A rock-and-roll institution, the humble dollop of concrete had hosted the Rolling Stones, Lynyrd Skynyrd and many other musicians keen to tap into its fault line of R&B magic.

Skegness's Mussel Shoals was an abscess of concrete located just under the crumbling pier, a place where kids came to talk tall and fumble, and the lost came to get high and OD. Built in the 1950s to house a dainty collection of gift shops, it now represented a visual tribute to the town's faded glory.

Or maybe I'm just a snob like Daisy-May said, thought Joe. Maybe it is a damn shame most of my memories of my home town are bad ones.

At least such long-term memory grasp had its uses. Mussel Shoals, Joe knew, had long been a resource that Pete and he had used, its collection of addicts and informants providing tip-offs and intel for a twenty-pound note or the threat of a prison cell. *This* was where he'd first learned about the farmhouse. Though when you considered that that information had led to his murder, perhaps it wasn't a good thing.

Still, old habits died harder than dead-already coppers, and there were worse spots to stake out and eavesdrop. Something as big as his murder would send ripples through the area's criminal community, a community that called Mussel Shoals their home. So, he'd wait, and he'd listen, and he'd see what he could find out.

Chimes sounded again, from an EU-funded art installation erected to improve the area, one that had suffered constant vandalisation by the EU-hating locals. They meant he was close. Voices sounded below him. Raised, desperate and laced with fight.

Scrambling to the edge of the tarmac seafront, Joe dropped to the concrete ramp that led to Mussel Shoals. The wind picked up, kicking up a flurry of snow. A bleak underpass faced him, the shops that had once nestled there long gone, leaving a group of emaciated men and women squatting in their skeletons.

A blazing fire separated the group. An elderly man and woman sat on one side, screaming expletives at teenagers on the other, harsh Slavic tones Joe would have identified as Bulgarian if his life had depended on it, or Romanian if it hadn't.

Standing aside from them, watching peacefully, was a man

whose long white hair and longer, whiter beard made it look like he'd come to a fancy-dress party as God.

Maybe it's the big dog himself, thought Joe. Maybe that's why Daisy-May said to come here. Wouldn't be the craziest thing that's happened today.

The man bent over double, racked with a coughing fit, turned slightly, and Joe saw that not only was he younger than he'd first looked, but that his left sleeve was baggy, empty and pinned to his shoulder.

Probably safe to shelve the God theory, he thought. Unless the Almighty's missing an arm.

He crept forward, unable to shake a lifetime's habit, although he could be neither seen nor heard.

'You know, there's really no need to creep and crawl,' said the one-armed man, keeping his back to Joe. 'When they get agitated like this, the likes of you are the last thing they worry about.'

Joe's jaw dropped.

'Yes, I can see you, and no, I'm not dead,' said the man, turning towards him and smiling warmly. 'I'm Elias.'

Joe stared from Elias to the squabble by the fireside. The elderly couple had shambled away, and Joe yelped in surprise as one teen walked straight through the fire after them.

Elias nodded in their direction. 'Just because I'm not dead, it doesn't mean they're alive.'

He yelled, instantly drawing the group's attention. They turned as one, and as Elias spoke to them, Joe understood the placatory meaning, if not the tongue it was delivered in. The group, chastised, bowed their heads.

'What did you say to them?' asked Joe.

'I told them that if they didn't behave, I'd confiscate the few drugs they have left.'

'How do they have any drugs at all?'

'Because it's my job to bring peace to these souls,' said Elias. 'Like the gum you use to retain your memory.'

Like Daisy-May did in the Pen, thought Joe. 'They look normal,' he said, staring intently at the group. 'No vines. Is that your doing too?'

'It is,' said Elias, smiling at him. 'I'll settle the natives, then you can explain what it is the Duchess has sent you here to do.'

Joe squatted on the syringe-ridden concrete floor, chewing on a piece of gum that Elias had provided. The one-armed man was moving around the kneeling malnourished ghosts, distributing further pieces of the memory aid. It's almost like he's a priest, thought Joe, and they're his faithful disciples. He wasn't sure how he felt about that.

As they jammed gum into their mouths, a peace descended upon the group. Satisfied, Elias pulled a forlorn wooden chair across the concrete and placed it opposite Joe. Reaching into an artfully battered black briefcase, he withdrew a tartan thermos flask, slowly rotating the top off and pouring himself a cup of something steaming.

'I'd offer you some,' he said, 'but you're dead.'

'How can you see me?' said Joe. 'See them?'

'You don't seem particularly surprised that I can,' Elias replied, blowing on his drink and inhaling deeply.

'I just watched an elephant man eat a teenage girl whole,' said Joe. 'Surprise fucked off long ago.'

'The Xylophone Man,' said Elias. 'At least, that's what I know him as; he goes by many names.'

'You didn't answer my question.'

Elias took a sip of his drink, his breath ragged and misting in the winter air. Joe closed his mouth, self-conscious, but if his lack of breath bothered Elias, he didn't show it. 'You're a member of the Dying Squad, I assume. A greenback, if you're asking me those questions.'

Joe sighed at his evasiveness. 'You know the Duchess.'

'I do.' Elias took another sip and winced, throwing the contents of the cup onto the snow that encircled their makeshift camp. It melted through it like acid. 'She's the reason I'm here.'

The group of souls opposite them slumped down, a dazed look on their faces, the battle they'd been fighting earlier apparently forgotten.

'They'll be peaceful for a while,' said Elias. 'The gum works as a sedative for them rather than a memory prompt.'

'Apparently so. Why?'

'They've been on the soil too long. Deprive a brain of oxygen and that brain becomes irreparably damaged. The opposite is true for the likes of you. And them.'

'Are they like the Dispossessed back in the Pen?'

'Some would say yes, some would say no. It depends on how far gone you consider those stranded on the soil are.'

'And how developed the Dispossessed are,' said Joe.

'Quite.'

'How do you know about all this?' Joe asked. 'About the Duchess?'

'The Pen's reach goes much further than just the afterlife. There are many servants like myself whose purpose it is to continue its mission on the soil.'

'You make it sound like a cult,' said Joe.

'More like an offshoot of a religion,' said Elias. 'We're a type of Salvation Army. I'm here to give solace to those souls who died on the soil and couldn't pass over. This group, for instance, have been here so long that every ounce of themselves has been scorched away. There was no Dying Squad to avenge them; a travesty when you consider the brutality of their deaths.'

Joe frowned, troubled by something he couldn't quite place.

He got to his feet and walked towards the dozing group, stopping when he was a couple of feet away. 'I know these people.'

Elias coughed, taking out a handkerchief and catching the worst of it. Once he had the fit under control, he looked doubtfully at Joe. 'How could you possibly know them?'

A trickle of recollection began in Joe's mind, one that quickly became an invigorating flood. He paced, collecting the memories, trying not to drink down too many at once. 'Are you from around here?'

Elias shook his head. 'I was sent here on a pilgrimage.'

Joe took a final look at the dosed-up group, then returned to his seat on the floor. 'Well, I am, and it used to be different. More insular. Then, a few years ago, it gets a huge influx of Europeans. Poles, Romanians, they come to work in the fields, the warehouses, whatever; the point is, they come to work. And the locals have their noses put out of joint, because suddenly, those jobs they didn't want before are the most attractive jobs in the world, now that someone else wants them. There's tension between the groups, barriers, and not just language. Kind of ground where prejudice breeds. A gang of locals start attacking the foreign workers – the Romanians, in particular, got it bad – and little old me, just three months in service and green as it gets, is parachuted in as the local boy to broker some sort of peace.'

Elias snapped the flask back together and returned it to his satchel. 'How did the locals react to that?'

'Not well,' said Joe, 'I'd been there less than twenty-four hours when they firebombed a houseful of immigrants. Thirteen of them, packed into a two-bed house, burned to death.' He nodded over to the group. 'I recognise their faces. Some of them were in that house.'

Elias smiled like he'd passed a test. 'The Duchess said that if you found your way here and if you remembered those poor souls, well, there was still hope.'

'Hope of what?'

'Hope that your memory wasn't too far gone. That you'd still be able to crack the case.'

'You can talk to the Duchess?' said Joe. 'How?'

Elias convulsed again, his cough barking, and quickly brought the handkerchief to his mouth. Joe noted the dots of blood.

Elias noted the noting. 'You're a detective. I'm sure you can work it out.'

Joe looked at him closely. The man's skin was waxy – not at the level of the Duchess's, but not far off – and stretched back, accentuating the bulge of his eyeballs. The dancing flames did their best to hide the grooves under his eyes, but they could only do so much.

'You're dying.'

Elias nodded, looking down to his empty sleeve. 'Admirably blunt, Detective, but you're quite right. Cancer's taken my arm and will take a good deal more before I pass.'

'I'm sorry,' said Joe.

Elias smiled. 'I'm not. It's a gift. Some of the terminally ill can see traces of the afterlife, and when you have one foot in the door like I have, a great deal more. It's often put down to hallucinations from painkillers, the rantings of the dying, but it's not. It's a glimpse of what comes next.'

Joe rubbed his face, trying to knead some logic into it. 'So how does the Pen come into all this?'

Elias smiled, revealing his shrunken gums. 'I was lucky enough to be born into a very particular chapter of the Church, one whose life's work is to help souls like those over there. Our time on the soil may be short, but while we're here, it is our job to help those souls who cannot pass on. It's a blessing.'

It's a cult, thought Joe, and one of the truly fucking insane ones.

Still, perhaps it was a cult that could be of some use.

'There's a soul at the school, a young boy. He's like these people here, but worse, somehow. Would you be able to help him?'

'I'm sure I could,' said Elias, 'and positive that I will.'

Joe got to his feet, smiling at the one-armed man. 'Thank you.'

'Where will you go?'

'I was a detective on the soil. A real detective, not this phantom crap. I'll work it out.'

Elias nodded, looking through Joe like he was wrestling with something. 'You know, they sent me to this area because of the spike in deaths. Souls of homeless men – and a few women – dying from drug overdoses.'

Joe nodded grimly. 'Always a problem round here.'

'Yes, but the interesting thing about these deaths was that they were recovering from their addictions. They'd kicked the habit yet wound up dead anyway.'

'People relapse,' said Joe. *Daisy-May taught me that. Both that they relapse, and that they're people.*

'Not to this extent,' said Elias, 'or in this number.'

Curiosity stirred in Joe, the scent of something. 'How do you know?'

'Because it's my business to know,' Elias replied. 'I need to understand how the souls in my care died, so I can best help them.' He picked absent-mindedly at the arm that wasn't there, weighing something up. 'Josie's Beach Shack. Do you know it?'

A sliver of a childhood memory twinged. 'Yes, I think I do.'

Elias placed a single stick of gum on the floor next to Joe. 'It's a drop-off and pick-up point for moving drugs. The people moving those drugs – many who ended up dead, and under my care – were all homeless men and women who had been, at one time, members of the outreach homeless shelter. That's a piece of information a "real" detective should be able to do something with, is it not?'

Chapter Twenty-Two

The Xylophone Man enjoyed the power he wielded more than he should. He was the first to admit it, and the last to feel guilty about it.

The looks he received, the cowed, furtive glances, the way the souls around him seemed to dim in his mere presence, these were signs that he was doing his job, honouring his true calling. That they brought him such pleasure was, he supposed, the reason he'd fallen in the way he had, cast out of the Next Place, never to return.

Not that returning was something he had much interest in doing. Here – unlike in that other place – he was respected. Here, he was the Infernal Serpent, the Babbling Wretch, the Culler of Men, the Xylophone Man – so many names through the ages, all carrying the same outcome for those who transgressed the rules of the unnatural order.

He watched, with neither amusement nor regret, as the shambling half-souls he walked amongst veered away from him, knowing on some animal level that he was something to be feared. The Dispossessed. Laughable creatures. Even the Almighty must have been tempted to wipe them out. He didn't consider them clean enough for heaven, after all.

Slowly, the Xylophone Man began to ascend the hill he

needed to ascend, stopping for a moment to gaze upon the scene below. Very different in appearance to his usual dwelling, but not without its poetic beauty; the blood-red sky, black and grey clouds billowing across it, appealed, as did the wall stretching as far as the eye could see.

The Pen.

A smile formed on the Xylophone Man's face as he heard the roar of horns, then watched as a crack appeared in the sky. He had timed his ascent for this very reason, to see the dumb animals scratch and grab at their chance to escape the damnable place. Their heads snapped to attention, turning as one to the split in the sky, flocking towards it.

What kind of God allows the cruelty of hope? he wondered. At least in the Pit, the damned know their place in the scheme of things. These pitiful bastards know just enough to be damned by such knowledge. Who, really, is the evil one?

The crack closed, and as the Dispossessed laid into each other, the Xylophone Man's attention began to wander. Really, it was poor sport, and not worthy of his time, or his talents.

But wait.

Wait.

Now, wasn't that interesting?

A small group of Dispossessed – if you considered two hundred half-souls a small group – were ignoring the split in the sky completely, instead pressing as one against the wall of the Pen.

The Jankie girl, Hanna, was orchestrating their efforts.

If he'd been capable of it, the Xylophone Man would have smiled.

He had doubted his master's orders when he'd received them (those doubts had, of course, been left unvoiced), but they had been brutally clear: Hanna Jankie was to be released from the Pit and shown the way to the Pen. His master hadn't explained the reason for this – he wasn't in the business of explanations – he had merely commanded it be so, with a final edict: the Xylophone Man, his faithful servant, was to teach her a long-forgotten tongue.

Not forgotten by his master, though. Like the most demonic elephant, the master of the Pit never forgot. So, the Xylophone Man had followed orders, and taught the girl the language of the lost, and the Duchess's younger sister had learned quickly, and she'd learned well.

Watching her draw the shambling half-souls towards her, the Xylophone Man understood the method behind his master's madness.

He's trying to spark a revolt, he thought. She's been released here to rile up the troops. She may not believe that – she may believe that she's trying to liberate them – but the end result will be the same. Chaos in the Pen, which my master will look to exploit. To what end, who can say?

One thing he could say, and with a great deal of certainty, was how delicious the Duchess's favourite had been.

What fun he'd had with her, and what fun there still was to come. There was goodness in her, a purity he rarely had access to in the Pit, and the taste of her was all the sweeter for it.

Yes, Daisy-May Braithwaite was the choicest of delicacies, and one he intended to feast on for eternity. And if the Duchess didn't like it?

Well, he'd reserve a place in hell for her too.

The ascent took him longer than he expected. It always did. The ripples of fear he generated almost made up for it; it was rare for one of his kind – and there was, really, only one of his kind – to come above ground, to inhabit *these* grounds, and he enjoyed the macabre celebrity this afforded him.

It was about the only thing he did enjoy, because

the Duchess's meeting request had been troubling. The Xylophone Man wasn't in the habit of being invited to places; he never usually required one. The Pen, though, was different – you just didn't wander in; you were invited, or deposited there.

He knew her by reputation, of course. Everyone in the Pit did. The Duchess's merry little band (what had the girl called them? The Dying Squad? Laughable) were virtually untouchable. Only the gravest violations of the law made them vulnerable to the likes of him, and sometimes not even then. The girl had broken the ancient laws, though, shattered the link between their world and the soil world, and such transgressions could lead to the end of existence itself. There had to be repercussions. Surely the Duchess could understand that?

'Come.'

He did as he was told, feeling small compared to the huge concrete door, appreciating that that was the point. It was a psychological ploy that would have worked on many, but he was the Xylophone Man; he was a force of nature beyond intimidation.

The Duchess looked up at him, frowning slightly. 'Really, Oliver, it's a little early in the morning for fancy dress.'

The Xylophone Man – whose soil name had been the rather less flamboyant Oliver Pipe – bristled.

'You have your methods, and I have mine.'

'Your methods aren't needed here, though, are they? Kindly remove that ridiculous mask. My house, my rules.'

He scowled, the elephant skull on his head shimmering, then disappearing altogether.

'There, now, isn't that better? Such startling features, why not let them shine through?'

Where others would see a compliment, the Xylophone Man unearthed the insult in the rough. With his greasy, lank hair, sharply pointed nose, and dishwater eyes, he was all too aware of how unassuming he looked, how starkly average, how shorn of authority and fear.

'I usually take the trouble to offer my guests a drink,' said the Duchess, a hint of playfulness in her voice.

He bristled, never having looked, or felt, smaller. 'You know well enough that I cannot imbibe.'

She gave a sketch of a smile. 'Rather an inventively cruel punishment. Your master is not without his bleakly poetic imagination, I'll grant him that.'

The Xylophone Man snorted. 'As is yours. I was lucky enough to witness the light show on my way here.'

The Duchess beckoned for him to sit.

His coat creaked as he did so, its leather sighing as he positioned himself primly in the seat. 'I assume this is about the girl?'

'She's one of my best, Oliver.'

He laughed, the sound of glass breaking in a bag. 'Then I will no doubt soon be seeing many of your worst. There are rules that must be adhered to, Rachel, or have you forgotten?'

The Duchess smiled hate. 'Hardly, but if the girl interfered, as you claim, physically crossing the divide, there must have been a good reason.'

The Xylophone Man was warming to his task. He crossed his legs, knotted his hands in front of his right knee and smiled smugly, revealing a film of blood that had settled between his teeth. 'A good reason carries as much weight as a bad one. Your girl crossed the line; the reason for doing so is irrelevant.'

'Where do you have her?' asked the Duchess.

'Where do you think?'

Her hands grasped the table, her knuckles turning milky white. 'If I knew the answer to that, I wouldn't need to ask.'

He smiled, not the xylophone smile he saved for his victims, but one laced with smug malice. 'Why not save her? Your term of office allows you to grant clemency to a soul destined for the Pit, does it not? Why, it's a veritable get-out-of-jail-free card. Say the word, and I'll release her.' He leaned forward, grinning. 'Oh, that's right, you've already used it. On your sweaty sow of a sister Mabel, if I remember correctly.'

Later, when she considered it, the Duchess knew she'd stepped over the line. Emissaries of the Pit (and the Xylophone Man was much more than that) were not to be touched. Only his master could do that, dealing out whatever punishments – and rewards – he saw fit. Daisy-May had taken a sledgehammer to their fragile ecosystem, and there had to be consequences.

That didn't mean that snapping the toad's neck wasn't worth it.

With a flick of her finger, she sent him flying from his chair, propelling him through the air into the wall opposite, the delicious crunch of bone filling the cramped confines of her office. He screamed in surprise, trying to slump down, the Duchess keeping her finger – and his body – raised.

Not fatal, of course; you couldn't kill what was already dead. Human bodies didn't forget the sensation of pain, though, the sounds of it, no matter how hard they tried to. And more than anything, it was the sheer indignity: one who stalked this realm and the old one, feared by all he crossed, reduced to a powerless, broken puppet in her presence. His master wouldn't like that.

Fuck him.

The Duchess released the Xylophone Man, watching him slump to the ground.

He coughed, reaching for his misshapen, lolling neck. 'You'll regret that.'

She smiled ingratiatingly. 'Unlikely.'

She reached into her desk, withdrawing an ancient piece of paper, pushing it across.

Shakily, the Xylophone Man took his seat again and picked it up. 'What's this?'

'I suppose you'd call it another get-out clause.'

He snapped his neck back into shape, bone wobbling against bone, then peered at the document.

He laughed.

'This is your great white hope? Really, Rachel.'

'It's not my anything. It's His.'

The Xylophone Man turned his nose up, as if the parchment could infect him somehow.

'Read it aloud,' said the Duchess. 'You seem slavishly loyal to the rules, and that one's set in stone.'

He brought the paper closer. '"A soul in the devil's custody may be released if another agrees to take its place. This soul must do so willingly, and of its own volition."'

He placed the parchment back on the table, grinning. 'In all your infinite, sprawling time here, have you ever known a soul go willingly to the Pit?'

The Duchess leaned forward. 'No. But that doesn't mean that one won't.'

The Xylophone Man sneered, and there was almost pity in it. 'Lazarus? Joe Lazarus is to be your shining white knight?'

'He will be what he is destined to be, and that will either be to the girl's aid, or to her detriment.'

The Xylophone Man rose, regaining his courage by the second. 'Why does she mean so much to you?'

The Duchess looked down, unsettled, feeling unpleasantly human. 'What she means to me is irrelevant. Where did you put her, Oliver?'

He tried to choke down his glee.

He failed.

'Where you found her.'

His elephant fright mask shimmered back into place, the face beneath it leering. 'Trapped in the rotting remains of her body, reliving every bad thing she ever did and remembering every fetid secret she ever hid.'

Chapter Twenty-Three

Blackness is never really black, that's what Grandma used to say. I mean, it seems it, right? At first, it seems pretty non-negotiable, a bleak maw of eternal fucking nothingness. It's only after several moments of letting your eyes adjust – settle, my grandma would have said – that you see the truth: that darkness is just as colourful as the brightest summer day.

It was during summer holidays at my grandma's that I sussed this. The old woman hated that title (*already feel old*, she'd say, *no call for you to make it official*), so June, her Christian name, it was. Suited me; my mum never liked me using her title either. Always assumed it was because she knew how fuckin' useless she was, and that she didn't deserve it.

The trip to June's was the highlight of my year. Compared to my inner-city, concrete life, the rolling countryside, no matter how flat, blew my fucking mind. My mum never came with me on these trips; she wasn't close to June. Barely even distant, as far as I could see.

I loved everything about those long summer months, except for the night-time. For as long as I could remember, I'd gone to sleep with a blanket of noise and confusion, whether it was Mum holding an after-the-pub party, or one of the street scraps that always seemed to happen right underneath my bedroom window, the street light opposite flickering, like it was leading them on. Hell to most people, but just life to me, and the silent-as-fuck countryside, well, it just wouldn't let me sleep. I needed the breaking of the bottle, the scream of the piss-head, the wail of someone too far gone to care. What I got was the occasional dog bark, the odd owl fart, and fuck-all besides.

It was the darkness that was the worst, though. When June flicked the light switch, it swallowed the room whole. Sensory isolation poured paraffin on my oil-slick imagination, oxygenating bad vibe flames and ensuring nights of zero sleep. On the third night of this, with shadows carved under my eyes, June sat on the corner of my bed and took my hand in her weathered, sandpapered palms.

'What's the matter, Daisy-May? You look older than me.'

'It's the dark, June. I close my eyes and it's dark, I open them and it's darker. Like I'm trapped. Could I have a light?'

She snorted at that, like I'd asked permission to go on a three-day smack binge. 'Your problem is, you've been trained to *see* the dark and *miss* the light.'

Grandma was full of these cryptic asides, and me, being unencumbered by manners or fucking tact, told her so.

She bustled over to the wall and flicked the switch, plunging the room into darkness. 'Now,' she said, 'what do you see?'

'Nowt, that's what's the matter.'

'That's your memory talking, not your eyes.'

'My eyes can't talk neither.'

'Don't get smart with me, girl, get smart with yourself. *Look.*'

I did, and after a minute, I realised Grandma was right. There were different shades of black; once my mind got the message not to panic, it began to pick out shapes, outlines, smudges of suggestions of objects. A corner table here, a chair leg there. The longer I looked, the more I could make them out.

'See?' said June, who was now hazily visible by the side of

my bed. 'You're like me in that you think too much and feel too little. Your mother, well, she's the opposite. Don't know which is worse, but I do know that you need to switch that big brain of yours off when the lights go down. *Feel* more, Daisy-May, and life will see you right.'

She was right, my grandma, my June, and those summers in Anderby Creek, in Lincolnshire, saved me.

Wait.

Wait.

Why did I tell Joe that I didn't know the area, when I did? The theme park, I remembered that, but not June. Not the summers here. And she wasn't right about the darkness, either, because the darkness I'm staring at now, right this moment? Well, that hasn't revealed itself to me. Quite the fucking opposite.

'What's going on?' I say to the dark, not expecting a reply. 'Where am I? Why am I only just remembering my past?'

'Because you've been doing too much thinking,' explains Grandma's voice from the tomb-black gloom, 'and not enough feeling.'

I know it can't be her, but that doesn't stop me from saying, 'Grandma?'

'June. You know I like to be called June, love.'

I ask what's wrong with her voice, knowing mine is pregnant with fear.

My eyes desperately search the darkness until an outline appears from the black.

A body, a *something*, moving, shuffling, snuffling, wearing my Grandma June like a shawl.

'Why did you do it, love?' she asks, her words wet with blood.

I try to back away and can't, because there's no backing away from this reckoning, no escape. 'Why did I do what?'

June smiles, the chunks of vomit in her teeth smiling with her.

'Kill me, Daisy-May. Why did you kill me?'

A scream and a tumble of sound and vision, and I'm booted from darkness to light. More specifically, a railway station platform.

It's raining. June's supposed to be here to collect me, but like the summer weather, she hasn't shown up. A small pink suitcase sits at my feet, puddles forming either side of it.

I'm thirteen.

I look along a platform that's deserted and distorted in that abandonment. The angles are wrong, too exaggerated, too sharp. A bird flies in front of me, and something's wrong with that bird because it moves in slow motion, like things did in the Pen but also completely differently.

This is the past.

Like June in the bedroom, I'm being shown something from *before*.

I'm afraid now because I was afraid then, and I was afraid then because I didn't think she was coming. I'd travelled from Nottingham for the summer, I didn't have a phone, I didn't have her number, and she didn't show up when she was supposed to. I'd been for the three summers before, and June had always been waiting for me on the platform, but not this time.

Then, I see her. She is at the ticket barrier, red-faced, her hair as messy as her eyes, confusion in them but fear as well. She shambles up the platform towards me, and I'm grateful. I'll be able to hug her again, get swallowed up by her smell, and her love. That's what the Next Place must be like.

Her hand slams into my face. The shock of it hurts a lot more than the slap.

'Why did you kill me, Daisy-May?'

Except that wasn't what she said, not then. She hit me not out of anger but out of fear, and that was what scared me the most. I was used to being knocked around, but not by June, and I knew, somehow, that this wasn't *my* June, that something else had got hold of her mind, was already breaking it apart and keeping the pieces for itself.

'Why did you kill me, Daisy-May?'

The station platform revolves like a West End set, and I'm in my grandmother's pantry, its shelves buckling under the dozens of jars of spreads and jams and other impossible-to-identify ingredients, its smell one of childhood. Dozens of photographs are carefully stuck to the wall, all of them with Post-its stuck beneath them, words scrawled on them in black felt-tip.

Fridge.

Car.

House.

Daisy-May.

My eyes prickle with tears as I look at the photo June took of me the previous year, on a visit to a nearby theme park. She couldn't remember me. Not enough to trust that she didn't need a reminder, anyway.

Why did you kill me, Daisy-May?

I turn to see June, her face blue and bloated, traces of dried blood on her lips.

That wasn't what you said. You said, *Found them*, and there was relief in your voice. You sat me down, explained that it had started six months ago, like a thief coming when you least expected it, stealing memories, faces, names, and only grudgingly returning them. The photos and Post-its were the only way you had of trying to keep a degree of control. You told me there was no coming back from it. You leaned closer, like you were afraid the dementia was eavesdropping.

You asked me to do something.

Why did you kill me, Daisy-May?

Because you asked me to, Grandma June.

Because you came straight out and asked me to.

Time lurches like a spilled drink, and I sit facing June in the kitchen. Judging by the light, it's later that same night. A radio play burbles in the background while two mugs of Ovaltine steam on the table in front of us. Whatever this is – a flashback, a psychic re-enactment, sadistic time travel – the June sitting opposite me isn't the monstrous, blood-gushing figure from earlier. This is Grandma how I remember her: warm, comforting, stable.

Because that's the cruellest way to do this.

'I have a glass of Ovaltine every night,' she says. 'Memory hasn't got so bad that I can't remember that. It helps me sleep when not much else will, but I take comfort in the routine more than the beverage, to be honest.'

And you were being honest, all right. Too honest for both of us.

She reaches down, fishing around in her ancient, chapped leather handbag, and digs out a piece of paper.

'There's a lad's number on this. Want to think of a fancy name for *drug dealer*, but I can't. Tried to buy the stuff myself, but he's not having it. God knows what he thinks a seventy-five-year-old's going to do to him – not exactly the most likely candidate for an undercover copper – but he won't sell to me.'

I ask what she wants me to buy, except I already know because this has already happened, and I'm nothing more than a dummy with a ventriloquist's hand up my arse, relearning and redoing things I've already done.

'Called OxyContin,' said June. 'Read about it on the internet, didn't I? All you do is grind up the tablets and slip them into my Ovaltine, and I drift away, peaceful like. And you know what the best thing is? My memory's such a bleedin' sieve, I won't even remember I asked you.'

She laughs at that and I cry, not at the suggestion itself, although that was awful enough, but at the knowledge that I've already lost my grandma, because that woman would never have asked her granddaughter to carry out such a task.

A blur of vision and a wave of nausea, like I'm inside a viciously shaken snow globe, and the kitchen becomes a squawking, stuffy, shrieking bowling alley.

This is where I came to buy the drugs I needed to kill my grandmother.

The alley's full of kids my age, all of them sucking the life out of the summer holidays. I notice an older lad standing apart from the main group, his back to me, his lanky frame slumped over a slot machine, and I know, somehow, he's who I've come to see. He's got a vibe like a prefect on a school trip.

I walk towards him, an unwilling actor in a play I didn't audition for, the carpet sticky under my feet, the second-hand smoke its own type of ghost, co-haunting the place with me. The lad has a baseball cap on, an NYC logo on the back of it.

'All right?'

I wasn't. I was about as far from all right as it was possible to get. Couldn't let it show, though.

'In this shithole with a bunch of kids,' he replies. 'Why wouldn't I be?'

He doesn't turn as he says this. I try to see his face in the arcade screen, but all I get is a baseball cap and shadows.

I say the words – *Heard you might help me out with something. Lady called June asked for the same help, but you said no* – and then the bloke turns.

No.

No, it can't be.

I know this lad.

I've seen him before, without realising I'd seen him before. It's the dealer from the pub, the one I stopped from killing the DJ.

This is punishment for my intervention in the pub, in the Sanctuary. I'm trapped here, in this sick rerun of my past sins.

The drug dealer Grandma June sent me to was Ryan.

I didn't remember him when I was with Joe. Would I have acted differently if I had? Was it something other than the desire to do the right thing that made me lash out at him in that pub, damning me to the Xylophone Man?

'Here to buy,' my mouth says to Ryan, 'not to chat.'

He liked that, that insolence. He likes it now. He hasn't said it, but his eyes say it for him. I liked those eyes, that look. Still do.

'Your nan asked for forty tabs. That's a ten-year stretch if you're the filth.'

'Do I look like the filth to you? Think I'm some educated basic bitch slumming it undercover?'

That smirk back on his face. 'Proper undercover. You can still see the price tags sticking out of their trackies.'

'Cheeky fucker.' There was fire in my chest as I warmed to it. 'I'm legit, mate.'

'All right, legit. I'll sell you ten, for a hundred.'

'You're mental if you think I'll pay more than seventy.'

He liked the bartering, the negotiation, when he was used to nothing more than cowed acceptance.

I hated how much I liked it. This was my mum, this situation. Bartering with a dealer. I was destined for something different, something better. Grandma June had betrayed me. I hated myself for thinking it, but it was true.

'You're tapped if I'll do 'em for any less than eighty.'

I smiled, and we shook on it. It sealed a pact neither of us really understood then, or later.

I fall for him because I need to fall for something.

No mother worthy of that title, and the grandmother that was wanting nothing more than to die. I didn't have anyone left to believe in, and Ryan's old-before-his-years swagger was easy to throw my hopes into. Pound-shop Bonnie and Clyde, that was what his mates called us. *Like that's a bad thing*, he always replied. *I fucking love the pound shop.*

It's a relationship that's crept up on me, inching forward every day with criminal purpose and whispered sweet nothings. I know he's no white knight, but what am I?

Days slid into weeks, the end of the summer holidays lurking at the corner of our eyeline, Grandma's memory slipping the leash with ever more regularity. She never forgot to ask, though. She never forgot to do that.

Tonight, love?

That hopeful tone in her voice, that pleading, when she'd spent her lifetime doing anything but.

Tonight, love?

That whimper, that tremor, that desperation for it to be over, for me to take the drugs and grind them into powder, slipping them into her mug so she could drink the poison deeply, let it soak into her veins, her soul, her brain.

Tonight, love?

But even though she's an imposter, I can't. I'm still waiting for my Grandma June to come home.

The world shakes and burns again, time lurching forward, and I'm in Ryan's ratty Ford Fiesta, the same one that Joe and I followed him to the theme park in.

When had that been? Hours ago?

Days?

Years?

He puts a rough hand on my cheek and tilts my face towards

his. 'I'll do it. Quick, painless, when she's asleep.'

I look at Ryan, really look at him. A spliff in his left hand, steering wheel in his right, the gangster prince of all he surveys – all he surveys being the bank holiday tourists streaming across Skegness high street, the air fire-hot clammy.

'Say the word, and it's done.'

This is the night. I've been brought back to the night that I kill her.

'Up to me,' I hear myself saying, and the dead me of now curses this younger counterpart of then, rages against her foolishness for not seeing this red flag of wrongness, a man untold years older than her casually offering to commit murder on her behalf, a Valentine's rose dipped in the blood of her grandmother.

Suddenly, we're outside June's house.

Ryan's parked a hundred yards away, because I asked him to, because I knew that obeying June's wishes would leave a mark and I didn't want that mark on Ryan, or that stain on *us*, because if I didn't have *us* any more, then I had nothing.

I walk to the front door, visualising the pills, where I've hidden them, under the third floorboard to the left of her bed.

My grandma, my June, stands stock still in the middle of the living room, blinking in confusion.

She screams when she sees me, fear and confusion in her eyes.

Who are you? she asks. *Who are you, and what are you doing in my house?*

It should have made it easier, but it didn't. Nothing could have made it easier.

Time slips again and I'm retrieving the pills, grinding them into a fine powder as I've been instructed to, then pouring them into a steaming cup of Ovaltine. I knock the last dregs in, and immediately they float to the surface, because not everything goes down, not everything sinks to the bottom.

Not the really bad stuff, anyway. That pokes around at the edges, no matter how hard you try to flush it down.

I put one foot in front of the other, the stairs sighing, like the house knows what we've cooked up and is voicing its distaste.

On the landing now, some play squawking on the radio, one June will never get to finish.

I thought it would be easier because she couldn't remember me. Like, if it was just killing a stranger, that was absolving me somehow. But when I got to the room, I realised it was a lie. June *could* remember. She pretended she couldn't, but you can't make your eyes pretend, no matter how hard you try. They were shiny with tears when I walked into her bedroom. It was almost a relief to see her guilt at what she was making me do.

She still made me do it, though.

Three gulps, that was all it took. Three gulps to end a life.

'Careful,' I said. 'Drink it slower, or you'll burn yourself.'

That almost made us laugh.

Almost.

Another cocktail-shake of time and place and I'm back in Ryan's car. 'Smells Like Teen Spirit' plays on the radio as Ryan drums his fingers on the steering wheel, sweat lingering, like the day hasn't got the message it's night yet.

I don't want to see this. I don't deserve to live through this again.

I look at Ryan, and know I'm going to say something bad. Something that will change things forever. Something Ryan's offered before, and that I've always refused.

Something puppets my mouth open. 'I'm thinking things,' I say, staring out the window. 'Help me to stop thinking things, mate.'

Ryan smiles like I've delivered the punchline before hearing the joke. 'Course. Got just the thing.'

★

We're at a beach hut. The sun's setting over churning waves.

'Where are we?' I say.

'Moggs Eye,' Ryan replies, a flame dancing over the syringe he's holding.

The name of the place makes me smile.

There's still time to stop this before it starts.

I try to scream the word, but my mind catches it before it can get out.

Ryan inches the needle tip towards my arm.

I'm about to become something I always swore I wouldn't.

My mother.

Heroin floods my veins. This isn't a dream I can wake from, or a mistake from the past I can put right. This is my reality, my hell.

And the really bad stuff is yet to come.

Chapter Twenty-Four

The screens in the control room were really just a prop. They worked, in as much as they displayed the images from locations around the world that they were supposed to, but those images, if the Duchess wished, could have been shown on anything: rocks, the infinitely endless grainy floor, the sky-kissing Pen wall. People, though, she had discovered, needed a touchstone to their old life. Seventy years ago, it had been called the war room, banks of flickering, low-quality black-and-white screens doing the same job the finger-nail-thin screens attached to the wall were doing now. Seventy years before that, they'd been the briefing chambers, rows of charts displaying their soul-saving sorties across the soil globe.

Dying – the what came after – was enough of a head-spinner. *Got to give the fuckers what they know. Madness is a lot easier to drink down if you recognise the brand.* That was what Daisy-May had observed when she'd seen the room, and she'd been right, about that and a good few other things. Those good few other things were why the Duchess wasn't prepared to let her be condemned to the hell she was currently stuck in.

She stood on the gantry at the top of the control room, her bony hands gripping its cool steel, letting it take the strain. She could help the girl. It meant taking a person away from doing good things and putting them in a bad place, but it was worth the risk.

A crooked smile sneaked onto her face, one that said: *easy to say, when you're not the one risking anything.*

She was, though. They all were, all the souls under her command. Those in the Pit and the Next Place saw them as neutral peacemakers, souls with nothing at stake and so nothing to lose. What those in the Pit and the Next Place didn't understand — with the exception of the overlords of those two domains — was that without the middle of *anything*, the top and bottom collapsed into one another, ending *everything*. The Pen was the ballast, keeping the two extremes in check. It was a job without glamour and reward, but no less important for that.

The Duchess closed her eyes.

How can the dead get tired? Daisy-May had asked her once. *Don't need stamina when there's no air to breathe, mate.*

That's when you need it most, girl, had been the Duchess's reply. *If you don't know that yet, you will.*

She'd know it now, all right. Trapped in with forgotten nightmares freshly remembered, all of them feeding on the last dregs of her sanity.

It was a hard truth that brought the Duchess back to her screens. Her eyes flicked between them, two in particular, separated by thousands of soil miles but bound by invisible tendrils that fed each other, even if the concerned parties didn't know it yet.

On one screen, a Lincolnshire-based Joe Lazarus, trekking along a snow-covered beach. On the other, an old woman, sitting on a park bench, bathing in the sort of winter sun New York roused itself to on occasion. To look at her, you'd think she was doing little more than reading a copy of the *Post* without a care in the world, or rather, with nothing more than the cares the paper was informing her she should have. Appearances were never more deceptive than in the afterlife, though, particularly when you were a member of the Soul Extraction Agency.

The Dying Squad, bitch, corrected Daisy-May's voice. *For life.*

The Duchess smiled. *Dying Squad it is, girl. Let's see what I can do about the life bit.*

Venturing soil-side. It had been a while.

The Duchess disliked going to the old country, because the older *she* got, the more the journey drained her of the little afterlife force she had. The lights, the sounds, the colours, all of them jarred when you were used to the cloak of purgatory. Under normal circumstances she would have left the trip to an underling, but when you were trying to beat the word of God on a legal technicality, it was best if you showed up to the courthouse to defend yourself.

She picked her way warily through the mass of Dispossessed, keeping her head down and trying to disappear into the crowd. Whereas a few hours before, dozens had been grouped around certain sections of the wall (disturbing enough), now there were hundreds, in concentrated pockets, straining against it.

It wasn't just that, though. It was the focus on their faces. They were more aware of their surroundings, of each other.

Of *her.*

As she moved past them, they noticed her, normally glassy eyes following her, a flicker of intelligence there. And she hadn't seen Hanna yet, which worried her more than if she had.

How was her sister doing it? They were the Dispossessed, failed souls with their very essence panel-beaten from them. All Hanna's flowery talk of pulling them up wouldn't be enough. She was communicating with them, changing them, making them self-aware.

The Duchess flinched as one of those self-aware hands grazed her shoulder.

A space opened up in front of her, the stall she was heading towards revealing itself, an unlikely sanctuary and, fortunately, a fair distance from the walls the Dispossessed were paying such attention to.

She quickened her pace as more heads turned in her direction. She wouldn't run, because if she ran, she'd be admitting that something was happening here, something she didn't understand, and didn't want to.

Who she was trying not to hurry *to* made that lack of urgency more palatable. Mabel was a purgatory veteran who'd been around for almost as long as the Duchess had, fulfilling a role that, if not as important, was certainly in the same ballpark. The Dying Squad's very own woman-at-arms, who only a few hours ago had supplied Daisy-May and Joe with the tools they needed for the soil world.

The old woman, poured into a shapeless, battered smock that was wearing her rather than the other way around, scratched distractedly at her backside and gave the Duchess a smile stripped of sincerity.

'Did you see her?' she said.

'See who?' said the Duchess, instantly annoyed at the defensiveness in her voice, and at how her elder sister had instantly put her on the back foot.

A laugh from the armourer, one the Duchess had detested for the longest time. 'How many recently-returned-from-hell sisters do we have?'

The Duchess bared her teeth. 'Yes, I saw her.'

'What's she want? Only spied her from afar. Couldn't mistake that hair, though, nor that walk.'

'She wanted to share,' said the Duchess.

'Share what?'

'The Pen. Everything that comes with it.'

Mabel grunted knowingly. 'Did she now. And how did you respond to that?

215

'I let her know I didn't think it was a particularly good idea,' said the Duchess.

Mabel laughed patronisingly. 'Funny way of saying you shot her with a cannon.' She leaned forward. 'Hanna's communicating with them, ain't she? I seen 'em working the walls, looking for weaknesses.'

'There aren't any,' said the Duchess defiantly.

'Hope you're right,' said Mabel. 'What if you're not? Where's that leave us, Rachel? Where's that leave the Pen?'

'I didn't come here for this,' said the Duchess. 'I need a few things.'

Mabel looked at her doubtfully. 'You're going soil-side?'

The Duchess looked up at the cauldron of blackening, tumbling clouds. 'I'm hardly here to take the air.'

'That girl you're daft on.'

She nodded.

Something reluctantly softened in Mabel's face, like it had almost forgotten how. 'No one else you can send?'

'You?' said the Duchess, mirroring the slight thaw.

'I'm too old and fat to be stomping around on the soil,' said Mabel. 'If you've got your mind set on it, though, I best bring out the big guns.'

She reached under the stall, the starched tarpaulin overhead tugged by the stirring wind.

The Duchess frowned. 'Better hurry. The split will make an appearance soon, and I was rather hoping to cross over when it does.'

Mabel grunted, hefting a rusted chunk of metal onto the wooden counter separating them. 'Not that you're worried 'bout the Dispossessed.'

The Duchess bit her tongue, poking the gauntlet her sister had produced. 'Overkill, don't you think?'

'I don't,' said Mabel, spitting on the hem of her dress and

wiping the surface of the gauntlet. 'Things are bad down here, Rachel, and they're getting worse. More and more of 'em are wandering into the Gloop . . .'

'We don't call it that,' said the Duchess irritably.

'. . . and it's not just that. It's the air. Somethin's in the air, and you can pretend not to smell it all you like, but change is afoot. Somethin's coming.'

The Duchess eased her arm into the gauntlet, which despite Mabel's spit and polish remained more spit than polish, and it snapped shut around her arm, fine stripes of previously unrevealed steel twining themselves around the rusty outer shell.

When the thoroughly satisfyingly *clunk* sounded, she raised her arm, then waved it around, the metal now seemingly no heavier than the lightest blouse.

Mabel grunted. 'Always looked better on you than me.'

You didn't just merrily stroll through the Gloop and drop out the other side into the soil-world spot you wanted to be in. Passing from one side to the other was like catching a flight; if you didn't pick the right one, you could end up anywhere.

The knowledge of these pressure points along the Pen wall were known only to the Duchess, who disseminated the information to Dying Squad members as and when they needed it, clawing back those memories once their missions had been completed. Daisy-May had asked her once why only she was trusted with this information.

'Because when you're at war, you don't give the battle plans to the cleaner. You keep it need-to-know, and only I do.'

'What if something happens to you, though?' the girl had asked, a dog with a bone. 'We're fucked.'

'There are safeguards in place if that were to happen,' the Duchess had told her, an answer that would have been a rebuke if anyone else had asked. 'No one goes on forever in this job, not even me. Everything ends, even death.'

Never had been she surer – or gladder – of that irrefutable truth than right now, standing next to an endless stone wall, trying to remember where she'd put New York.

She inched her way along the wall, ignoring the prickle down her spine that told her she was being watched, her fingers dancing along the cold stone surface. She turned. The massed group of Dispossessed were staring at her, all of them silent, all of them still. There was no denying that, no matter how much she wanted to.

She would have to be quick.

Her fingers caressed the wall, the gauntlet on her right hand glinting in the volcanic clouds that had formed above her.

No, she thought, that's Mexico City. Closer, though.

San Diego.

Los Angeles.

Her fingers edged to the right.

She turned around again.

The Dispossessed had edged forwards, silently cutting the distance between them and her clean in half.

Colorado.

Kansas.

Kentucky.

Another turn of the head, the herd inches from her now.

I can't risk going through with this many, this close, she thought. Because I can't blast them all, even if I wanted to.

There.

New York.

Horns heralded the split in the sky.

A snap of heads in that direction, the glassy eyes of the surrounding bodies illuminated by white light, the daily green card from heaven appearing.

Saved by the horns, thought the Duchess. Even if it doesn't pull all of them away from here, it will pull away most.

It didn't.

The crowd circling her – too many to count – didn't move an inch, their heads rotating back into position, a parlour trick that had worked for an aeon discarded.

Show a magic trick to the dumbest rube enough times, Mabel had once said to her, *and they'll work out how it's done eventually*. It was a statement the Duchess had laughed off. Now, with a swarm of those rubes in front of her, it didn't seem as funny.

Her left hand reached out to the wall, passing through it.

The gauntlet on her right arm began to hum.

'I'm sorry,' she said, and she meant it.

She fired.

Green light gushed out from the gauntlet, impure, poisoned soil air hitting the bank of bodies in front of her. They spasmed, green vines erupting from limbs and eye sockets and orifices and joints, dragging their jerking bodies to the ground.

The Dispossessed screamed, the sound a croaked garble.

The pack still standing dispersed and backed away.

'Are you happy now, little sister?' the Duchess yelled, looking for Hanna amongst the clump of withered bodies. 'Was mass murder part of your plan to share?'

When no reply was offered, she gave the devastation a final look, then stepped back into the wall.

Chapter Twenty-Five

Joe gazed out at the sea, watching fascinated as snow fell on the beach guarding it, enthusiastically adding to the inches that had already accumulated. *Maybe death won't be so bad if I get sights like this from time to time*, he thought. *Maybe it'll be the start of something rather than the end of everything.*

Then he remembered Daisy-May.

Guilt came with the memory of the girl. She was God only knew where, undergoing tortures he couldn't begin to imagine, and he'd done nothing to help her. Didn't even have the first clue *how* to help her.

I'll come for you after this is over. If that means breaking into hell itself, then so be it, but I'll come for you.

He took a breath. He was missing something, because he was still here, soil-side, and the Duchess had told him he couldn't pass over properly until he'd discovered the truth behind his death. A piece of the puzzle was still eluding him.

Pulling himself up a nearby dune, he searched the horizon, trying to spy a sign to the beach shop Elias had told him about. If his memory could be trusted – and it couldn't – he should be getting closer to it. He squinted at a pinprick of light tacked onto the night sky. Roughly a mile away, by the looks of it. Hardly a beacon of hope, but something, at least, to aim for.

And if it was free of demonic elephant men, he'd still be ahead of the game.

Josie's Beach Shack was something of a local institution, and like many institutions, it came with a public information warning: *You don't have to be mad to work here, BUT IT HELPS!*

There was so much in the statement that had boiled Joe's teenage piss. The exclamation mark, the capitalisation of the second part of the sentence, the fact that the second part of the sentence existed at all. Despite the tackiness of the poster, he had to admit that the messaging was pretty much on point; He hadn't been mad when he worked there – more skint and bored – but galloping insanity would have taken the edge off.

The shack wasn't quite boarded up – the window, with its dusty collection of knick-knacks, buckets and spades and windmills, was just about visible in the moonlight – but it might well have been. Other than the odd local walking a dog, visitors didn't come to this square inch of coastland much past October, and this was some way past that.

At least, he thought it was.

The red-and-white awning (faded, and just tatty enough to make him believe it was the same one from his day) billowed in the wind, the shack giving the impression that a goodly tug would send it spinning out into the sea.

People said that twenty years ago, Joe thought. Place'll see me into the ground.

He winced when he realised it already had.

Glass broke.

He whirled round, his eyes hunting for the culprit. The shopfront was unaffected; someone smashing the back window, perhaps? He strode forward, smiling a little as he passed through the window. I could get used to this, he thought. Think of it as a superpower, rather than a punishment.

As he stepped into the shop, ripples of déjà vu surged through him. The place wore the sleepiness of the off-season well, like this was its natural state and the occasionally fevered exertions of the summer were the aberration. His ears pricked at the sound of shoe heel on glass. It had come from the back.

He crept forward, unable to shake a lifetime's habit despite the fact that he could be neither seen nor heard, remembering the lie of this, that Daisy-May had been both seen and heard by the Xylophone Man, and had paid the price for it. She'd been nothing but kind to him – rude, maybe, but a kind rude – and he'd been unable to protect her. Was that what he'd been trying to do when he was alive? Was that why she'd ended up rotting in a back room and he'd died bleeding out on the ground?

'Focus, Joe,' he told himself. 'Focus, while you still can.'

He stooped at the doorway, bead curtains limply hanging down over it, familiar voices coming from the other side.

'It's sexy.'

'Part of the job.'

'Should get an eyepatch. Like a fuckin' pirate. No one'll mess then.'

Ryan, and a girl. Young. The rich girl they'd seen him with at the school, playing poor man's gangster moll. The prefect.

Joe stepped through the curtain into the restaurant that was sutured onto the shop, still expecting to feel the beads hit his face, the noise of them being swatted aside. Like an amputee who felt the twinges of a phantom limb, he supposed he always would.

'Restaurant' was a generous description at the best of times, but here, in the dead of winter, hosting a one-eyed gangster and his child accomplice, it seemed particularly generous. Joe wished Daisy-May could have seen it; her takedown would have no doubt been even more brutal.

The patio door hung open behind them, the pane of glass next to the handle broken and jagged. The wind ragdolled it back and forth, the bang echoing through the shop.

Ryan was crouched behind the counter. Joe saw him prising up a floorboard, then reaching down. He lifted up a battered leather holdall from the darkness, placing it reverentially on the unbroken floorboards, and then slumped with his back to the counter. 'Place gives me the creeps, Jen,' he said, closing his eye. 'Prefer it full of tourists.'

'Pussy,' Jen said, play-punching him on the arm. 'Nothing here but you and me.'

Ryan looked around, his gaze alighting on Joe. 'Something off about it, I'm telling you. Bad vibes. Like the air's full of something.'

Joe stared back, fascinated. *He can't see me, but he feels me. Feels something, anyway. Did Daisy-May's interference do that? Fuck, I wish I could ask her.*

'Bullshit,' said Jen. 'You cooking up for us, or what?'

Younger than Daisy-May. County line in full effect. Before you blink, they'll be using eight-year-olds.

Ryan nodded, reaching for the bag, and unzipping it. Within it was a bed of pharmaceuticals. Clear bags throttled with zip ties, bulging with powders and pills.

Fuck, thought Joe, that's a shitload of drugs. No wonder Pete wanted Ryan to collect them, if he's planning to get out. Hell of a retirement package, that lot.

Ryan took out a leather pouch from the bag, unfurling it to reveal a small bag of rocks, a simple glass pipe and a lighter. His hands shook.

Sampling the goods. Good looks gone. You're losing control, aren't you, mate? You're used to the world bending to you, but it's started pushing back, and you don't like it.

'Need it. Bad things afoot. That Joe, getting gatted?

223

Ain't going to end well.' Ryan's hand went towards his ruined eyehole. 'Thinking of splitting.'

'Are you fuck.'

Ryan nodded, the flame from his lighter dancing under the base of the glass pipe, the rocks within browning. He took a hit, sighed, and then sat back. 'Done here. That's why I'm collecting this shit. Too much heat, especially after what we did tonight.'

'Can't tie you to the homeless shelter, can they?' said Jen.

'Me and Pete are quits,' said Ryan, not hearing her, or simply ignoring her. 'He's on the move.'

'He tell you that?' asked the girl, taking the pipe from Ryan's trembling fingers.

'Doesn't need to. You kill a fed, you bring all of his fed mates.'

'But Pete's police, right?'

'Dirty police. There're other forces sniffing around. They root that shit out.'

Jen inhaled, smiling as the smoke filled her lungs.

'Come with me, back to Notts,' said Ryan.

She leaned against the bar, closing her eyes. 'This is home. Besides, we haven't got any money.'

Smart answer, thought Joe. You're in this up to your knees at the moment. Any deeper, and you might not be able to get out at all.

'Working on that. Plans fermenting.'

The girl's eyes snapped open. 'Fermenting,' she repeated.

Ryan missed the scepticism. Eyes like saucers, he leaned forward, a crooked smile plastered on his face. It didn't look as charming with the masking tape. 'Can't tell you. All you need to know is, after tonight, money's no problem.'

The girl began to pass out, and Ryan kicked her leg, jerking her awake.

'How much we talking?' she said dozily.

'Life-changing amount. Have to help Pete do something before I can get it, though.'

'You going to tell me what?'

Of course he is, thought Joe. He's dying to. It's why you're here. The Ryans of this world always need an audience to witness their genius.

'Tie up loose ends. The loose end ain't gonna like it, but he'll be too dead to complain.'

Jen, spacey and stoned but engaged, leaned forward. 'Told you – you're a bad-ass fuckin' pirate. Who's the unlucky dead bloke going to be?'

'Best you don't know the details, but you've got a part to play, if you want.' Ryan tugged at the rim of his cap. 'On second thoughts, forget it. You're too clean for work this dirty.'

The girl stuck out her chin. 'Bollocks. Just tell me what you need.'

Ryan looked away, like he was considering the proposal rather than admiring how he'd manipulated it.

'All right, I'll give you a shot. All you got to do is deliver a bad-news message to a bad man.'

'Man got a name?' asked Jen.

Here we go, thought Joe. The next piece of the puzzle, on a platter.

'Lazarus,' said Ryan. 'His name is Reverend Bill Lazarus.'

Chapter Twenty-Six

Fucking a guy for money – or a girl, for that matter – was no big thing, that was what I found out. When smack became your God – and it became my Father, Son and Holy fucking Ghost – everything else fell in line to service Him.

That first hit had been the answer to a question I didn't know I'd asked. The clawing anxiety, the guilt at the part I'd played in my grandma's death, losing that one sure thing in my life – all of those made sense when the heroin flooded my veins. The junk was a blood bond between my conscience and my need for peace. Took away the pain, at least for a little while. Made me wonder about what pain my mother had.

It was a good month before Ryan – who I never saw so much as pick up a needle, unless it was to inject me or another of his groupies – had suggested hooking. He didn't threaten, or intimidate, or even plead. Watching this back, you can see his genius. He made it seem like it was my idea in the first place.

'Girl I know? Raquel? You know, skinny, big tits, but a six when you're a straight nine? Jawing my ear off this morning, 'bout how she's making a grand a week.'

This was a fucking travesty, and I told him so.

Ryan, all affected boredom at a topic of conversation that he had not only started but actively fucking propagated, shrugged. 'Says she just hangs out with blokes.'

'You mean *they* hang out of *her*,' I said.

'Nah, not the way it goes down. It's just lonely old blokes looking for a bit of company. Innocent, like visiting an old people's home. What's it called? Help the Aged. It's like Help the fucking Aged.'

'How much does she get for it?'

Ryan shrugged. 'Depends how long she does it for. Got four hundred quid for a day last week. Get on that. Figure I might give it a bash myself.'

I'd snorted at that. Told him he hadn't got the patience to run a bath, let alone chat to a granny about her dead dog.

I scratched distractedly at my arm.

I said: 'You got any?'

'Any what?' he'd asked innocently.

'You know what.'

He looked away. 'You're after the stuff again.'

'Don't make it sound like that.'

'Make it sound like what?'

'Like I'm another lost cause.'

He looked back, like he was a doctor, like all he knew was compassion.

'You need it 'cos life's too hard without it, I get it. Always have, and I'll never judge you for it.'

'But?'

'But that shit costs, and I ain't an all-you-can-eat pharmacy.'

I said I'd get a job.

'Working the arcades? Pub? Mug's game, Daisy-May. Not where the smart money is.'

Ryan talked about the 'smart money' a lot, like it was a hidden stash only he had the map to, rather than a trust fund from abusing the weak and the desperate. I hadn't seen that then.

Now, rotting in the corpse of a farmhouse, force-fed memories, I see it in high definition.

So I went after the smart money, and to begin with, they *were* just dates. Friendless labourers, lonely widowers, rootless divorcees, men who had been set back by life and didn't know how to get back on track. I didn't see any money – Ryan was holding it for me because he knew how to keep it safe, he said, safer than any bank, who would take their cut in charges and fuck knows what else – but I saw plenty of heroin. That, my love kept coming, and I didn't have to ask any more, he somehow knew just when I needed it, because when I needed it was all the time.

I never questioned why adult men – some with a fifty-year head start on me – would want to hang out, why they liked that I looked young, because some questions you already know the answer to and don't need to hear it. I barely remember the first time I did more than hang out, but the man – four times my size, with bleeding gums, yellow teeth and the constant hum of sour milk – must have been a particularly difficult memory for the Duchess to scrub clean.

Because that's what she must have done. This was no truth waiting for me to discover when I found out how I'd died. The more I see here, the more it becomes clear that the Duchess interfered. Why would she do that?

I'm outside a caravan.

Ryan's on the steps, rapping on the door.

This is Pete's caravan. We've come to see Joe's partner, Pete.

I saw him at the churchyard, when I was with Joe, and didn't recognise so much as a nostril hair on the fucker. How can that be? How could I have gone to this caravan with Joe – the caravan we tailed Ryan to – and not remembered a thing?

It's undeniable. The Duchess must have taken the memory

from me. Why? It's cruel or a kindness, depending on how you look at it, and the Duchess has never had much time for either. There's an agenda there, involving me, and it's taken hell to show me that.

I disliked Pete from the start. His easy-going charm reeked of hard work and bad acting. It was the tone hiding behind the words and the anger hiding behind his eyes I hated the most. Plus, Ryan was scared of him, and that scared me.

Bent coppers got everything to lose, Ryan had said on the car journey over. *Which means he'll kill to keep it.*

'Why don't you set up on your own, then?' I'd asked. 'You got the contacts.'

He'd laughed at that, as if I was a seven-year-old who still believed in the Easter Bunny. ''Cos he'd kill me, without a blink of his fucking eye. I set up on my own, I become his competition, and his competition don't breathe round here any more.'

We step into the caravan and it seems bigger this time, somehow, despite the extra bodies. A party's in its death throes, strung-out, glassy-eyed fuckers fighting the good fight, the best of them jabbering incessantly, the others slurring occasionally, all of them with one thing in common: they're kids, just like me. Some older, some younger, but all of them in their teens. The only adults there were Pete and, at a big push, Ryan.

Pete looks up from the sofa, and winks at me. 'Hear a lot of good things about you, Daisy-May. Ryan says you're a woman who gets things done. A woman who can be trusted.'

I liked that, being called a woman. Made me feel different, more adult.

Pete hands me a beer, and I take it because I'm nothing more than a powerless puppet controlled by forces I can't understand, then or now. I also take it because I want to. It gave me a thrill, an adult – an adult copper, no less – offering me a beer, and treating me like a colleague at a high-level meeting.

'Give us a minute, will you, Ryan?' says Pete. 'Got business to discuss with the lady.'

I liked being called a lady even more than I liked being called a woman.

Pete clasps his hands together and leans towards me, a serious man with serious things to discuss, adult to adult. 'What do you know about what we do here, Daisy-May? What's Ryan told you?'

I try to think of a dignified way of saying drug-dealing, but can't.

'Lots of people will say that what we do's wrong,' Pete continues, seemingly not needing an answer to his question, 'but what we do is provide a service in a safe way, when others do it unsafely. Does that make any sense?'

It didn't then and doesn't now.

'Yeah,' I say.

'Now, I have people working for me, taking goods from one place – that place is Nottingham, usually – to another place, or places, namely the fine county we sit in now, Lincolnshire. We call it running the lines. Does that make sense?'

It was beginning to.

'You see, I've got a run coming up, and I think you'd be the perfect woman to oversee it. You'll be working with one of my other employees, so you wouldn't be going in alone, and you wouldn't be doing anything illegal.'

I look around for Ryan, and he nods at me like this is my big chance.

'What would I be doing?'

I knew what I'd be doing, but it seemed better not to admit it.

Pete smiles. 'Just delivering a bag, that's all. One train to

Nottingham, and a colleague will meet you at the other end. You give her the bag, you walk away five grand richer.'

Five grand bought a lot of smack.

It was the easiest *yes* I ever uttered.

Chapter Twenty-Seven

The Duchess had forgotten how much she loved the place.

It wasn't the New York she knew from her time on the soil, although technology notwithstanding, there were fewer differences between the Gotham of the 1850s and its 2019 incarnation than she would care to admit. And Central Park was Central Park; there was only so much modernising you could inflict upon trees and grass. Strawberry Fields, though, *was* relatively new, the circular mosaic within it asking any Lennon pilgrim who ventured there to *imagine*.

The Duchess didn't need to; she knew exactly what the slain Beatle thought about the memorial.

'Lovely, isn't it?' said the old woman sitting at its centre, a shroud of roses encircling her. 'Sacrilegious to sit here, I know, but it brings me peace.'

The Duchess snorted, taking a seat on the bench opposite the black-and-white memorial. 'I wouldn't call it lovely, so much as tasteless; the poor bastard was only murdered a hundred yards away. You always were an old hippy, Grace.'

Grace turned to look at the imposing Dakota building looming over the park. 'I'm sure John would love it.'

The Duchess snorted. 'I believe the expression he used was *maudlin as fuck.*'

Grace laughed, her rusty red hair bouncing, every inch the grand Viking dame. 'You little name-dropper.'

'The stories I could tell you,' the Duchess said, letting Grace's warmth infect her. 'If you think Elvis was bad on the soil, you should see what he gets up to in the afterlife.'

They turned back to the park, watching as a family booted a football around, the youngest son stopping play every few seconds when the action unfolded in a way he didn't want or expect. The Duchess watched, a small smile on her face, and allowed herself a moment of believing that everything would be all right.

'I always love this exact time,' said Grace, closing her eyes against the winter sun. 'Fresh from – what's the name Daisy-May uses? – the Gloop, and with the knowledge that the soil air hasn't yet begun rotting away one's sense of self. It's beautiful.'

The Duchess rolled her eyes. 'You're in a poetic mood.'

Grace smiled. 'Maybe it's the time of year. The promise of spring, but with the full lustre of what makes the winter so special. Rebirth. That's what you're here to talk about, isn't it?'

'Amongst other things. Has he been past yet?'

Grace got to her feet, stretching into the sunlight. 'Once, but it's not his time. Next lap should do it.'

She looked down at the Duchess and inspected her disapprovingly.

'You look tired, ma'am, in a way I didn't think it was possible that the likes of us could.'

'There's a difference between tired and weary.'

'Which is what?'

'Lord only knows,' said the Duchess. 'What I do know is that I've done this job for one hundred and forty-eight years, and I'm still not sure whether I'm any good at it.'

Grace turned away, watching a robin perched on a branch

opposite them as it twitched its head this way and that. 'Imposter syndrome. That's probably a fairly good indicator that you are, then. In my experience, those convinced of their own greatness are usually the most mediocre.'

The Duchess tried and failed to take the compliment as a couple ran past, jogging and talking, their eyes alive with love and mischief.

'That look never gets old,' said Grace.

'It never got young for me,' the Duchess replied. 'Did I ever tell you about my time on the soil?'

Grace gave a little wave to the robin as it flew off. 'You never told me very much about anything, ma'am.'

'Call me Rachel,' said the Duchess. 'What I'm about to ask you grants you that debatable privilege.'

'Rachel,' said Grace, trying it out. 'I like the warmth of that.'

'Precisely the reason I discarded the name when taking this position. Warmth only goes so far in our line of work, particularly when you're the boss.'

The Duchess smoothed down her tartan skirt, staring at the curving footbridge in front of them, a family walking under it, utterly oblivious to them.

'Certain families through the ages have been bred for one specific task, and I was no different. I, like my relatives before me, was groomed to be Warden of the Pen.'

Grace looked at her doubtfully. 'You always knew there was an afterlife, then?'

'I was certainly told there was, as well as what my role in it would be. Spectral royalty-in-waiting, an afterlife of service to be enacted for a term of one hundred and fifty years.'

'What happens after one hundred and fifty years?' asked Grace.

'Other than the abdication of my post? I don't know. The Next Place? Maybe even the Pit, if I'm judged not to have come up to scratch.'

Grace placed a hand on her knee. 'I think you'll be all right.'

The Duchess shrugged. 'I either will or I won't. What's of greater concern to me is my successor.'

The sun dipped behind a cloud, like it was trying to give them some privacy.

'Do you have a say in that?' Grace asked, looking back from the tunnel under the bridge. 'Who takes over?'

'Symbolically, yes,' the Duchess said. 'It's a little like the Queen of England – she's a figurative head of state, rather than an actual one. It's expected that I will rubber-stamp whoever comes to succeed me.'

'But that person hasn't arrived.'

'Exactly,' said the Duchess. 'He was supposed to have taken on the mantle of warden, and yet there's no sign of him. I have to assume at this point that something's happened to him. Something I'm not supposed to know about it. That being the case, it falls to me to choose my own successor.'

'Why?' said Grace.

'Because there's one who would take my title from me. A younger sister I believed lost forever, one driven by madness. Who knows? Perhaps she's driven by righteousness. All *I* know is, there have been enough duchesses of the Pen. My family has had long enough at the helm. Purgatory needs new blood if it – and civilisation – is to survive.'

'The girl,' said Grace. 'You're talking about the girl.'

The Duchess nodded. 'Daisy-May is untainted by the place. She saw the way the Dispossessed were changing – a fact I can no longer deny, even to myself – and she has a compassion that's been bred out of the likes of me. She's as worthy as any who has taken the role.'

'Will she do it?' said Grace. 'She's on the verge of graduating from the Dying Squad, isn't she?'

'There's a rather more pressing concern,' the Duchess replied. 'It's why I'm here.'

'Hold that thought,' said Grace, as a man in a grey jogging suit ran from underneath the lip of the tunnel. 'This is our man.'

The Duchess rose, following Grace as she began walking towards the runner, the loop of a waltz whirling around in her head, a long-forgotten dance on a long-forgotten night in a long-forgotten century. The man slowed, a hand clutching at his chest, grasping at his baggy hooded top as if it could steady him somehow.

He dropped to his knees, displacing the thin layer of snow that had gathered on the pack-ice beneath it.

I'd forgotten that look, thought the Duchess. That mix of outrage and disbelief that such a thing could happen to them. It's a good thing I came here today, because that look defines us. It shows that when push comes to shove and we fly above the soil, we're all the same really.

Grace bent down next to him, taking his hand. 'It's all right, Sean. It's going to be all right.'

The man's eyes bulged, taking in the kindly woman with the flame-red hair and the older, starched-straight woman hovering behind her.

'Ambulance,' he gasped.

'It's a bit late for that,' said Grace, stroking his hand. 'Besides, we're something much better.' She turned her head towards the Duchess. 'What is it you need me to do? I have a feeling it's not on-boarding Sean here.'

The Duchess took in Central Park, knowing that this, in all likelihood, would be the last time she ever saw it.

'I want you to save Daisy-May. And unfortunately for you, that means damning your son first.'

Chapter Twenty-Eight

'Cold in here.'

'Winter, innit? Turn the heating up.'

'It *is* up. This ain't like normal cold.'

Ryan sniffed, breathing out, his breath lingering in front of him. 'Normal cold, she says. Like it comes in flavours.'

Windscreen wipers swayed left and right, just about winning the war with the snow, the car's wheels less certain on the icy road beneath it.

'Grab the wheel, yeah?' Ryan said, taking his hands off the steering wheel and rubbing them together quickly. 'You ain't wrong, though. Baltic in here. Like cold's following us around.'

The girl, all saucer eyes, gripped the steering wheel angrily, white dots showing on her knuckles. 'Know what my mum says that is? Ghosts.'

Ryan cackled, grabbing back the steering wheel, the drugs in his bloodstream racing. 'Your mum's a dumb bitch. No such things as ghosts. 'Sides, why'd anyone haunt us?'

The girl looked out of the window. '*You* done plenty of bad shit. Sounds of it, you'll do plenty more. Spirits, man. They get restless, I believe that. Like kicking a wasps' nest.'

'I done nothing but just enough to get by,' said Ryan defensively. 'Ain't no ghosts interested in me. 'Sides, they haunt *places*, right? Like castles, crypts and shit. What's a ghost going to be doing in a banged-up Fiesta?'

There's the sixty-four-million-dollar question, Joe thought. What am I doing here?

He reached into his coat, withdrawing the notepad and pen Daisy-May had given him earlier, smiling, despite himself, at the *Dragnet* logo, running a finger over it, enjoying the sensation of being able to touch something.

Peeling back the cover, he removed the pen from his pocket, knocking it against his teeth. *Just think of yourself as a ghost-writer*, Daisy-May had said when she'd given it him, taking a good thirty seconds to laugh at her own joke.

He'd liked the girl. She'd had a fire, one that shouldn't have been extinguished.

He had to believe that an opportunity to help her would present itself. If there was a Next Place, and an Almighty with any vague sense of lingering justice, that would turn out to be true.

He blinked Daisy-May away for now, praying she wouldn't be added to the pile of things he could do nothing about but would spend the rest of eternity lamenting anyway.

Focus, he told himself one again. Focus.

He read through the log.

He instantly wished he hadn't.

My name is Joe Lazarus. I'm a detective with a murder to solve.
My own.

I was killed in a Lincolnshire farmhouse by my partner, Pete. I think.

In that farmhouse, I later discovered the bodies of two young girls. One of those girls – Daisy-May – is a ghost now, and she's here to help me. At least she was. She saved a man's life and got taken to hell by a creature with an elephant skull for a head. And I could do nothing to stop it.

He rubbed his eyes. If he lost his mind then read through this, the last thing he was going to want to do was find it again. If he did, he'd end up arresting himself.

The Xylophone Man, that was what the thing had been called.

I'll get you out of there, Daisy-May, I promise.

Somehow.

Though he had some real-life monsters to deal with first.

He began to read again.

Pete's running the county line operation. At least, I think he is. I think I'd discovered that, which is why he had me killed. I believe he lured me to the farmhouse, but one of his gang pulled the trigger.

He flipped over a page, pausing. That almost felt right, but not quite, because it wasn't just *his* body he'd found at the farm-house; there'd also been the gang members. Had Pete killed them too? If so, why?

I'm tailing one of his henchmen, Ryan, because he's planning something on Pete's orders, and it's to do with my dad. Maybe Dad knows something that he shouldn't, maybe he's the loose end the boy mentioned, but I'm getting closer, I can feel it.

Was that true? It had to be, because he didn't have much time left, and only a single piece of memory gum. And if it wasn't Pete who'd killed him – if his admission had been false – then who had?

Joe looked up from his scrawled handwriting as the car slowed. Blobs of lights twinkled in the distance and something stirred in him, something that wasn't quite nostalgia and wasn't quite dread.

The rectory. He was home.

One crime Joe could definitely attribute to his father was that of waste: light burned from the four-storey structure, a virtual lighthouse calling its prodigal son home. The house was many things to him, but what those things were stayed out of his grasp, and that wasn't just down to his rotting memories. It was the best part of two decades since he'd set his amnesia-lidded eyes on the place, and that had been the way he'd wanted it.

Hadn't it?

Ryan brought the car to a stop a few hundred yards from the entrance, the car's tyres slipping slightly on the icy tarmac before they settled. The gates were closed, but they weren't high enough to conceal the building's roof and the light spilling from the top floor.

'Run it through again,' said Ryan.

Jen rubbed her nose with the back of her hand. 'Fuck's sake.'

'Do it,' said Ryan, his gaze cool and impatient.

'I knock on the door of the rectory. I tell the vicar there's a fire at the outreach centre, and . . . You're *sure* he won't know already?'

She's jumpy, Joe thought. She should be. Get out, love. Run, and don't look back. While you still can.

'No chance the vicar'll know about the fire, 'cos if he did, he'd already be on his way there.' Ryan reached across, opening her door for her. 'Pete'll be at the wake too, and he'll offer to drive the vicar. Don't go with them.'

'Why not?' said Jen.

'Because anyone who gets in that car won't be getting out of it alive.'

Joe missed the crunch.

It had been his favourite thing about the rectory when he'd been a boy: the *crunch, crunch, crunch* of the gravel underfoot, the toe of his trainer scouring patterns and furrows in the surface. His mother had hated the way it scuffed up his footwear, but not enough to stop him doing it. There was no crunch for him now, though, just a silent, weightless trudge as he followed the girl to the front door. He was a ghost in his own existence, and there was a part of him that still refused to accept that, to see that this was anything but a temporary blip, that solving the riddle of his murder wouldn't somehow gift him back into reality.

Still, it felt like things were coming to a head. You got that in cases; you worked the angles till there were no angles left to work and then the investigation took on its own energy and momentum, propelling you towards the truth. It wasn't always the truth you wanted, but it was rarely one that was undeserved.

Whatever Joe was now – a ghost, a spiritual photocopy of the man he'd once been, neither of those things – he realised he could still feel. He almost wished he couldn't, because when he stepped into the hallway, the door answered by a woman he didn't recognise, Ryan's teenage assistant walking confidently inside, a torrent of regret hit him. Every missed Christmas, birthday and phone call with his father crashed down on him, soaking through his clothes and seeping into his bones.

This is what it'll be like, he thought, scrunching his eyelids shut. If I don't solve this thing before my memory goes, this is what it'll be like. Every second of every minute of every day for eternity, drowning in good times I can't remember and mistakes I can't forget.

And I've only got one stick of gum left.

He opened his eyes, disappointed to find the hallway right where he'd left it. Lingering for a moment, he allowed the girl to drift off towards the living room. He wanted – and needed – to look at the pictures on the wall more closely.

His mother and father on their wedding day, the age and worry shaved off them, smiling with a love they knew was untouchable.

His three-year-old self in a pair of yellow pants and not much besides, hanging off his father's neck.

His red-haired mother, young, fierce, indomitable, looking straight at the camera, almost as if she was daring it to capture her image, like she knew her life force could burn through the film itself.

All three of them on his first day at secondary school. His mother beaming at the camera, Joe and his father's eyes cast down, like they'd seen the men they'd become and couldn't bear the sight of it.

Fuck that, he thought. I'm nothing like my father. I was a good man, and I did good things. I still am. I still can.

If disconcertion had been present at the funeral, it was high on amphetamines and hanging from the ceiling at the wake. It was the pub all over again: the music too loud (music, in his father's house – he had no frame of reference for such a thing), the voices manic, drug hysteria bubbling under it all.

Joe stood at the back of the living room, next to the grandfather clock that was always exactly thirty-eight minutes slow, and watched. Ryan's girl, Jen, was twitchy, hovering at the back, not sure whether to approach the reverend as he called for quiet. Claire stood next to him, a glass of wine in hand, attentive, respectful. Pete, behind them both, nodded imperceptibly at the girl.

His father tugged on his dog collar – he wears it like a noose, thought Joe. What happened to him? – then clapped his hands together. 'If we could have a little quiet for a moment, please.'

Jen, hovering in the doorway, raised a hand. 'Got something to tell you, Vicar.'

The reverend scowled at her. 'I'm sure it can wait.'

'It's important,' said Jen, uncomfortable in her own drug-addled skin.

'Not as important as what the woman beside me has to say,' said the reverend, 'as she honours her dead husband and my son.'

The guests gave an awkward shiver as the girl looked down and took a step back.

Claire smiled at the room, lighting it up at will. 'Thank you, Bill, for letting me give the toast tonight. I'm not much for public speaking; that was more Joe's department.'

She looked down, a sad smile on her face. 'He'd have loved tonight. There was never a party he'd knowingly miss. "Wasted on the dead, funerals," he said to me once. "When I die, I'm going to make damn sure I'm there." I like to think he is.'

Joe laughed. It cut like a knife through his soul, but what else was there to do? If you couldn't snigger at the utter gallows-humour absurdity of the situation, then things truly were lost.

'I just want to share one story I have about Joe – how he proposed to me. Most of you will have known him well, so you'll know he was never the most romantic of guys. Practical, logical, absolutely – it's what made him such a great detective – but romantic? No. Is that unfair, Bill?'

The slightest of looks at Claire, then the reverend's gaze found the floor. 'It is not.'

A small chuckle.

This time, Joe didn't join in.

'But when it came to proposing, he surprised me,' said Claire. 'He had a graphic novel written for us; can you believe it? My Joe had a local guy draw a comic book for us. It had all the high points of our life together so far, and the final few pages were of us getting married and settling down. The very last picture on the very last page was of Joe and myself in front of a house, and I was pregnant.'

Tears filled her eyes, the reverend placing a hand on her shoulder. She squeezed it, smiling at him, and then seemed to draw fresh strength from somewhere.

She raised her glass. 'He was the best man I knew, and the best man I ever will know. To Joe.'

The guests raised their glasses in response. 'To Joe.'

Joe looked at Pete. He seemed genuinely upset.

Never knew you had such acting chops, mate. The stage was robbed of your talents.

Pete nodded at Jen again.

She moved through the crowd, heading for Joe's father.

'Lovely speech, Claire,' said Pete, hovering behind them, wiping a hand down his face. 'Never knew Joe was such a soppy bastard.'

Claire smiled sadly. 'He was full of surprises.'

'That he was,' said Pete.

'Vicar?' said Jen, with her saucer eyes.

'It's Reverend,' said Bill, scowling at her. 'Who are you, and what do you want?'

'There's a fire at the outreach centre.'

Joe searched his father's face. For shock. For horror. For fear. For grief. For anything and everything he'd failed to receive from his cold-as-ice dad.

Nothing. It's like his empathy's been carjacked.

'My God,' said the reverend, looking from the girl to Pete. 'The people got out, though?'

The girl shrugged her shoulders. 'The flames were high. Real high and fierce, even with the snow. I called it in, but I heard you'd be here and thought you should know.'

Pete put an arm around the reverend's shoulders. 'I'll drive you. Going'll be tough, the weather being what it is, but we'll make it.'

'Don't get in that car, Dad,' Joe told him.

'Of course,' said the reverend. 'Are the fire service on their way?'

'No way a fire engine's getting up that hill,' said Pete. 'We

244

might be the only chance those people have, Bill.'

Joe wasn't sure if he should be glad that his father finally seemed concerned about the homeless people, or pissed off that he was leaving his only son's wake.

Pete leaned in closer, whispering something to the reverend that Joe couldn't hear.

His father's face changed, became pinched, like he was trying to push down anger and fear at the same time.

What's he got on you? thought Joe. And why do I need to know so badly?

The Range Rover chugged through the blizzard, its white shell blending in with its surroundings, the beams of light shooting from its front showing the road as almost impassable.

Joe sat in the back, unease inching its way up his spine. Why get Dad out to the centre? he asked himself. What's Pete expecting him to do, confirm the place is on fire? A witness, maybe, to corroborate that he was there at the wake? Or like the homeless people at the outreach centre, is Dad a loose end?

'Good turnout at the wake,' said Pete, his hands gripping the steering wheel, his knuckles milky white. 'You did Joe proud. He would have loved it.'

'He would have hated it,' the reverend replied. 'Hated the hypocrisy of it, anyway.'

'No need to be like that. Everything happens for a reason, Bill. You should know that better than anyone.'

The reverend laughed. 'You're reciting lines I've delivered hundreds of times over the years, and that's what I've come to realise they are. Just lines.'

Pete kept his smirk pointing towards the road. 'Sounds to me like you've lost your faith, Bill.'

'Shouldn't you be more concerned with the people at the outreach centre?'

'Shouldn't *you*?' replied Pete. 'Anything you want to confess, Reverend?'

'Wrong religion.' Bill shook his head, looking at Pete with disgust. 'Where's your respect?'

'With your self-respect, I imagine. You weren't so high-and-mighty when you were taking my money.'

Joe leaned forward. *Now we get to it.*

'I didn't take your money,' said Bill, two dots of red appearing on his cheeks. 'I used it for good. On the renovations to the church, on the outreach shelter. Your blood money came in bad and I ensured it went out good.'

Pious bastard, thought Joe. Deluded, hypocritical one, too.

Pete winked at the older man. 'Doing good work, eh, Reverend? Nice ring. Love that tacky-as-fuck stained-glass window, too. Quite a selfie, that. Saving souls is tough work, though, right? Even the ones you farm out for drug running. Can't save everyone, I suppose. And why shouldn't you keep a little back for yourself?'

Joe froze. His father was supplying Pete with vulnerable people? Maybe Pete had leaned on him, maybe this had begun with threats, but the results were the same. His father was little more than a pimp, selling on the souls of the helpless.

Bill toyed with his ruby ring. 'This was a gift.'

Joe and Pete both laughed at that. 'Course it was,' said Pete. 'Charity begins at home. Wish your son had shared your progressive views. It would have made things a lot easier.'

Before Joe could wonder at that, the car swerved, the snow and ice beneath it tugging at the wheels as Pete steered the car against the drag.

The reverend struck the windscreen in frustration. 'You took the wrong road. This takes us away from the outreach centre.'

'We're not going to the centre,' said Pete. 'We're—'

Joe was jerked from the back seat as something smashed into

them from behind, spinning the car like a ice hockey puck, pirouetting it around and around before gravity took a hand and whipped it from the road altogether, glass breaking, steel crunching, men screaming, the car turning, everything ending.

Chapter Twenty-Nine

I'm back on the platform, a prisoner in my own body, a helpless puppet watching history brutally repeat itself. I remember this day. So fucking hot, it was like sweat had its tongue between my shoulder blades.

'Fighting weather,' the Ryan of the rerun in front of me said, a wink in his eye. 'Fighting and fucking. Now, you know what to do?'

I did, because the plan was simple and we'd been over it ten times already.

'Need to hear you say it,' Ryan said. 'I'll feel better if I hear how easy it's going to be from your own lips, love.'

'I hold onto the bag like my life depends on it, which it does.' Lines I've already said. This is the shittest play I've ever seen.

'Why does your life depend on it?'

My dry throat clawed for moisture.

'Because there's a shit-ton of money in it. For the next supply of drugs. Mostly heroin.'

'Correctamundo,' said Ryan. 'Continue.'

'When I get to Nottingham, there's a sandwich shop outside the main station entrance. I'm to go there, buy myself what I want, then take a seat outside. Precisely ten minutes after I've sat down, a girl'll come and sit next to me. She'll be carrying exactly the same bag, which she'll put down next to my bag. She'll swap them. We'll both smoke a cigarette – maybe even two – because that's what mates do after enjoying lunch together, particularly in Shottingham. Then she'll get up, my bag in hand, and walk off.

'I take her bag, and I have a mooch around the city for a couple of hours, because if anyone is watching me – and they won't be – that'll look less suspicious than jumping on the next train back to Skegness. Her bag is just as important as the one I exchanged, and it's one I'm not to look in, under any circumstances. I get the 3.55 p.m. train back to Skegness, and you'll be waiting for me at the other end. Didn't miss anything, did I?'

'Only the bit where you get a smacker from me at the end of it,' said Ryan, 'along with a clean five grand and a ton of the good stuff.'

I felt so adult, so gangster, like things were finally starting to happen. This day felt like the first day of the rest of my life. I didn't know that it'd be my last.

'Last stop,' says the conductor. 'We're in Nottingham, love.'

I'm jerked awake. I'm on a train, the carriage a furnace, like it knows I need ferrying to hell. I'm strung out, because two days before, Ryan took the needle from my hand and said, *Game face, love. Can't have you smacked up running the lines, can I? Important job you can't get wrong, 'cos if you do, it's not just you that has to deal with the consequences.*

Which is all fine and fucking dandy, but the thing with being strung out is it makes you want to sleep the sleep of the dead. So I sat in my seat, clutching the bag to my chest, and told myself I'd just close my eyes for a couple of minutes, because I knew I'd feel better for it, more alert. As tired as I was, in that cauldron of heat, I'd be no good to anyone.

After I'm woken by the conductor, it only takes a couple of seconds for panic to dig itself in.

There's nothing on my chest. That lack of pressure is the single most terrifying thing I've ever experienced.

'My bag,' I say desperately to the conductor, in this reprise of my darkest hour. 'Where's my bag?'

He didn't know then, and he doesn't know now.

Fear like I hadn't known was possible gnawed at my insides, teasing me, one minute letting me think I'd dreamt that I'd lost my bag, that all I needed to do was reach down and grab the frayed leather handles, that the peeling Head insignia was within a fingernail touch; the next dropping my stomach, reminding me of the truth of it, ripples of desperation that meant I'd never felt colder in my life, despite the Indian summer's kiss.

I'd lost the money. All of it.

I wanted a hit so bad.

Wanted it to take it all away, just like I do now.

A tilt-shift of time and space, and I'm outside a Nottingham café. Heat escapes like waves from the tarmac, the smell one of a city roasting in its own filth.

A girl walks over. She's the girl I'm supposed to swap bags with. She's carrying an identical bag to the one I've just lost. She's stringy, with blazing green hair, a short skirt and a long face, piercings haphazardly stung across it, like they were done while she slept.

She sits down opposite me, looking at the space where the bag should be.

She asks me where it is.

I introduce myself like that's an answer.

'Don't give a fuck who you are. Where's the bag?'

Bile rises in my throat, and it takes everything in my power to push it back down. How do I say I've lost it? How do I ask to be killed?

The stringy girl drags nails through peroxide so cheap it looks like it'll come off in her fingers. 'You've fucking lost it.'

I nod, an act so small it barely counts as a twitch.

'Fucking hell,' Stringy says. 'Fucking *hell*.'

I cease to exist to her, because she's already thinking of the best way of keeping herself out of the shallow grave that'll be dug for me. She takes out her mobile phone – a clam-shell Samsung so old it virtually screams drug-deal burner – and punches in a number she doesn't need to look up.

I get to my feet.

'Sit down,' Stringy orders. 'Sit down now, or it'll be worse.'

Legs buckling, I do as I'm told. Sweat slides down my legs, and I half wonder whether it's piss.

'Don't puke,' Stringy says. 'Act normal.'

'What are we going to do?' I ask, my voice against me, angry that I've given it a forum.

'Sit here and wait,' she says, taking out a pack of Marlboro reds and not offering me one.

'Wait here for what?'

Flame licks the cigarette, burning like the sun on my neck, and Stringy says nothing.

Five minutes that could have been fifty pass, and for every sliver of every second, I consider running.

My knee jiggles underneath the table as we wait.

Stringy demands I chill the fuck out.

I don't.

Maybe she's right. Maybe there's still a chance. Ryan will make it right with them, whoever they are. He knows I wouldn't try and rip them off. He won't leave me here.

A car pulls up.

Stringy sucks in a deep breath, grinding out her cigarette into the ashtray. She says she hopes I have a story ready.

I follow her to the car, twenty steps that feel like two hundred. The sun's in my eyes, obscuring the car's driver, if not the vehicle itself.

A tinted window lowers.

No.

This is a trick.

A devil's trick.

A Xylophone Man trick.

'Get in,' Joe Lazarus says, looking at me with his copper face, in his unmarked copper car, his copper hands reaching across and opening the passenger door. 'Get in, and let's have a little chat.'

Joe lay on his back, looking up at the shawl of stars draped across the night sky.

One of his mother's sayings cycled in his head like a burrowing ear worm:

Every time a bell rings, an angel gets its wings.

Every time a bell rings, an angel gets its wings.

Every time a bell rings, an angel gets its wings.

Except it wasn't a bell but a car horn he could hear, blaring insistently, and he was no angel, winged or otherwise. No amount of purgatory stardust would change that fact. He levered himself up with his elbow, looking across at Pete's car. A sprinkling of snow had already gathered on its exposed chassis, the car having landed on its roof.

Like a beetle flicked over by an angry God, thought Joe. Maybe it was. Maybe He is.

He got to his feet, a collage of glass encircling him, and heard a groan come from the car. The passenger-side door jerked open to reveal his father hanging upside down, restrained only by his seat belt. Bill yelped as he released it, gravity dropping him onto the upturned roof. Groaning, he flopped out onto the snow-covered ground.

He doesn't look good, thought Joe, and that's not just the cut on his head, it's the way he moved. It was like breathing hurt.

An engine spluttered, then died altogether, and Joe turned to see a battered Fiesta, its left side dented and mashed, Ryan in the driver's seat. He got out of the car, and, looking left and right, limped across the snow-covered road towards the scene, a ragged tear in the left leg of his tracksuit, sprinkling blood on the snow like confetti. He ignored the now unconscious reverend in favour of Pete, who was lying twenty feet away from the car, half buried in a womb of bloodied snow.

Ryan took one look at Pete, then spat square in his face. 'Don't take it personal, boss. You'd have done the same to me if I'd have given you a chance.'

He hobbled back to the unconscious priest, staring at the blood streaming down his forehead, weighing up his options.

Mercy, or the belief that the reverend would be dead soon anyway, tipped the scales. Ryan left him, limping back to his car, sliding into the driver's seat and trying to gun it back to life. When he couldn't – when he'd exhausted his apparently healthy supply of expletives – he reached into the back and pulled out the leather bag he'd taken from the beach shack.

Then, without looking back, he clambered painfully over the slate brick wall in front of him, landing in the snow-covered field beyond.

I need to follow him, thought Joe, but I need to see if my dad's OK first. Even if he is a weapons-grade arsehole.

He moved towards his father, a familiar fugue of amnesia he knew would deliver blanket unfamiliarity gathering in his mind with each step.

He reached into his pocket for the last stick of gum.

It wasn't there.

He must have lost it in the crash.

One look at Pete revealed that his old friend had lost more.

The left side of his face had been torn away, leaving a mush of flesh and gristle, his left eye snaking away from its socket, his jawbone jutting out, soundlessly moving up and down. Joe felt a wave of disgust shot through with pity for the friend he thought he'd known but hadn't. He crouched down next to him, aware that it was a futile gesture, that Pete couldn't see him, but doing it anyway.

'Why d'you do it, Pete? Why d'you sell out?'

Something sparked in his former friend's remaining eye, a glimmer of recognition flaming in the engorged pupil.

'Joe.' A blood-gargled word, but an understandable one.

'Bad news for you if you can see me,' said Joe. 'Means you don't have much time left.'

'What's . . . it like?' croaked Pete.

Joe frowned. 'What's *what* like?'

'Hell.'

A pulse began beating in Joe's head, unasked for and unwanted. 'I wouldn't know. Some of us remembered the oath we swore.'

Pete laughed, blood and mucus leaking from his bone-mouth. 'That . . . what you remember?'

'I remember it was our job to catch villains, not become them.'

Pete smiled with what was left of his face, his eye unfocused and filmy. 'That what . . . death is? Forgetting what we are? Maybe it won't . . . be so bad.'

Joe felt truth get his scent. Panic surged within him, a tribal beat he couldn't silence. 'I tried to bring the gang down. That's why you had me killed.'

'I . . . didn't kill . . . you,' said Pete.

'I tried to bring the gang down,' Joe repeated, the words failing to gain purchase.

Pete's eye cleared for a second, as it focused directly on Joe.

'You didn't . . . bring down . . . the gang,' he choked out. 'You . . . ran it.'

Part Three

They had their faces twisted toward their haunches
and found it necessary to walk backward,
because they could not see ahead of them.

Dante Alighieri, *The Divine Comedy: Inferno*

Chapter Thirty

Being Joe Lazarus's mother had never been the easiest of jobs. Grace was the first to admit it, and the last to apologise for that admission.

Not that the boy was without charm – he'd been born with an abundance of it, holding court from an early age with admirable flamboyance, young and old alike pulled into his magnetic field. *Trust me*, that had been his catchphrase. *Gather round and just trust me, people.* And people had, willingly, with one noticeable exception.

Her husband, the venerable Reverend Bill Lazarus, had always been uncertain about the boy. 'Trust no one that keeps asking you to,' he'd say, a wary bristle in his eye and a lack of Christian charity in his soul, 'because no one trustworthy ever has to ask.' She didn't like the sentiment, but she loved her husband for his conviction, and his incorruptibility, and his passion for his calling, so she nodded along, and gave Joe twice the love, taking up the slack for her husband.

Bill always watched his son warily, as if he was expecting to catch him brokering a deal with the devil; that he never did seemed to disappoint him almost more than if he had. Bill didn't understand his son, and because he didn't understand him, he could never truly trust him, and because he could never truly trust him, he could never truly love him, either. The two men in Grace's life ran on different lines of the same track, sometimes crossing each other but mostly keeping their distance, Joe flirting with trouble but smiling his way out of it, the reverend making angry peace with the fact that one of his lost flock was never likely to rejoin it.

Then, the day came when her husband's worst fears were realised, and Grace could never decide whether it was a good thing or a bad thing that he wasn't around to witness it. Money had started going missing from the church collection box. The amounts weren't large, but enough to cause a ripple of distrust amongst the congregation. It was some time before she admitted to herself that it could be Joe. It had been her husband's suspicion from the off – the thefts had begun to happen right around the time that Joe had begun attending church again, a rediscovery of faith Bill had been suspicious of – but she'd fiercely defended her son's corner.

I'm no thief, he would have said, if she'd had the courage to ask him outright. *I'm no thief, Mum, trust me.*

She didn't trust him, despite what she told Bill to placate him. Not this time. Instead, she deliberately let slip that there'd been a particularly generous donation at that week's Sunday service, and then lay in wait in the deserted church.

Nothing on the first day. Nothing on the second. Then, three days after she'd baited the trap, Joe set it off.

When she saw him taking the money – and he saw her – there was a look between them, one lasting several seconds, where neither of them blinked, or spoke, or moved. He gave her an excuse. Said he'd found some cash and wanted to contribute to the collection anonymously. It seemed to Grace, looking back at this moment in time – which was something she did almost constantly – that this was where she'd failed as a mother, because instead of questioning him, or punishing him, or chastising him, she instead smiled and said she trusted him.

I bottled it. Can't dress it up any other way. Instead of facing the truth about my son and trying to make him change, I swept it under the carpet, and nothing was ever really the same again. I lied to my husband by not telling him the truth, and I lied to myself by not facing that truth down.

A week before the cancer finally took her, Grace had sat Joe down for a pep talk masquerading as a casual coffee, taking his hands and looking into his eyes with the sort of courage that only facing the end of your life can bring.

'Life comes easily to you, love, but it isn't easy, it's hard. Anything worthwhile always is. You'll get choices in your life, forks in the road that'll take you right and left, and the easy road? It's rarely the right one.'

Joe had granted her a nod that said he wasn't a moron, but that she was for stating something so bleedingly obvious. 'I'll be all right, Mum,' he said, winking at her. 'Trust me.'

She'd nodded, because even at the end, it was easier than telling him the truth: that she'd lost her faith in him.

Half an hour into her return to the old country – a good ten minutes of which was spent marvelling at the sheer snow-capped beauty of the place – Grace had heard a car in distress, its horn beginning as an apologetic burp and quickly becoming an insistent belch, the same blast repeating.

Either the driver's calling for help, she thought, or his car's begging to die.

A brisk jog towards the sound had revealed it was the latter; a white Range Rover, upended, showing its steaming underside to the star-speckled night sky. The car had ploughed through an old stone wall and into a field housing three horses, all of them keeping a wary distance, whinnying at the noisy metal gatecrasher.

Around thirty feet from the wreck, a bleeding man could be seen, his arms twisted out in front of him, like an angel ripped from heaven then broken over the devil's knee.

Should have worn your seat belt, especially on these roads, and in this weather, Grace thought. Must be an out-of-towner, one with the common sense knocked out of him.

As she got closer, the snow stirring itself once again, she realised that this wasn't the case; that the man bleeding to death in the snow was as local as it got.

Pete. Perfectly still, the little face he had left pointing towards the sky, like he was in a staring contest with God.

'You'll lose, darling,' Grace told him. 'Not that I imagine you'll be seeing Him any time soon.'

Pete had been the childhood friend that every mother disapproved of but could never quite place why. To fall into the religious language of her husband, it was as if the boy had been born caked in sin; you could see it in his eyes, hear it in the words he didn't say and in the tone of the ones he did.

He coughed, scarlet spilling from his mouth along with a powerless sob, and suddenly he wasn't the man Grace blamed for corrupting her son, but the little boy she'd first met at the primary school gates, the one with aggrieved anger in his eyes but also a fire she'd liked, and she remembered that her role in the afterlife wasn't to judge, but to help.

She kneeled down next to him and saw a flicker of recognition. One foot in the old world, one in the new, she thought.

'Mrs Lazarus?' he croaked.

'Grace to my friends,' she said, taking his hand. 'It's going to be all right, Pete.'

'Grace. Amazing Grace, that's what we always used to call you.'

'I know, love. You always thought I *didn't* know, but I did.'

Another cough, more blood.

Can't be much of that left, Grace thought. Blood, or life.

'Saw Joe,' Pete said. 'He's dead, but I saw him.' He blinked in surprise. 'You're dead, too.'

'That's right,' she said soothingly. 'Where did he go, love?'

'Am *I* dead?'

'Almost,' she said, impatience yapping at her heels. 'But that's not as bad as it sounds. Where's Joe, Peter? Where did he go?'

Pete's eye twitched, death freeing his grip on life one finger at a time. He raised a hand towards the field opposite them.

Grace smiled and meant it, and then he was gone.

She got to her feet, already weary of the death she'd seen, and looked across at the field. A second body was visible, one she'd missed. A man, his black robe contrasting sharply with the white bed of snow he was lying in.

No, she thought, her already dead heart stopping in her chest. It can't be.

'Grace?'

She stiffened at the sound of her name, her back straightening, her body tensing. It had been many years since she'd heard the voice of the man who stood behind her. She'd assumed she'd never hear it again.

'Bill.'

She turned to see her husband, fear and confusion carved onto his face. She didn't blame him. She'd met the sculptor.

She supposed she should feel sympathy for him. Death was never easy to accept, especially when it was forced upon you suddenly. She couldn't, though. All she felt was red-hot rage. Not at his piousness, or his intolerance, or his lack of empathy, although the perspective of death made it possible for her to see all of those things clearly. No, it was his hypocrisy. He'd decried dishonesty in others – including their son – yet he'd been the biggest, most dishonest hypocrite of all. Taking drug money with his nose pinched and both eyes open. Burning to the ground the legacy they'd both spent a lifetime creating.

'How are you here?' Reverend Lazarus asked, already looking like he didn't want to hear the answer.

'I think you can work that out,' said Grace.

He looked down at his hands and then at the upended Range Rover. 'There was a crash.'

Grace nodded.

'Someone rear-ended us. We were driving to the outreach centre, and someone crashed into us.'

'Where's Joe, Bill?'

The reverend looked at his wife sympathetically. 'Joe's dead, love.'

'He's in good company.'

He recoiled at her tone. 'How are you here?' he asked again.

'All that God stuff you professed to believe when I was alive?' said Grace. 'It's all true. The problem you've got is, you may still believe in God, but he doesn't believe in you. Not any more.'

'That's a lie,' said Reverend Lazarus, tugging at his dog collar. 'That's blasphemy.'

Grace found curiosity encroaching on her rage.

'You took drug money,' she reminded him, almost gentle. 'What happened to you? What happened to the man I loved? What happened to our son?'

She remembered the posturing her husband was capable of, his chest puffing out; his inability to take responsibility for his faults. 'Joe was always a law unto himself,' he said. 'When he became an enforcer of that law, he only became worse.'

'Which you blame me for.'

'You were always too soft on him,' said the reverend, 'and look where that's brought us.'

Grace took a step forward. 'Did you know what he was doing? While you were bathing in blood money, did you have

264

any clue, any clue at all, what he was capable of?'

The reverend said nothing.

'Of course you didn't. Because it's easier not to see, isn't it, Bill? Easier to have your little fiefdom, the pious lord of all he surveys, and let the world around you burn – a world it's your duty to guide and protect.'

Her husband said nothing, his mouth puckering shut.

Take a moment, Grace told herself. Gather yourself. You still need him.

'Where's Joe, love?' she said, smiling. 'It's really important that I find him.'

Bill went to speak, but there was a rustle on the air.

Grace flinched when she saw what had come for her husband.

She held out a hand to him, trying to remember what it was she'd loved about him, settling for the compassion she knew he deserved considering what came next.

Or, more accurately, who.

A creature with a skull for a head, and a whiny buzz-saw giggle.

The Xylophone Man.

The reverend took her hand, then followed her gaze behind him, crying out in fear when he saw what Grace had been looking at.

'I'm a good man,' he said, turning back to his wife, pleading in his voice. 'I'm a good man, and I've done good things.'

Grace smiled and meant it. She only stopped holding her husband's hand when there was nothing left to hold.

Grace allowed herself a moment of grief.

Bill had fallen into temptation, making a mockery of the life they'd built together. The sacrifices she'd made had, at the time, seemed worth it. She'd believed in her husband's mission, his calling.

If only he'd believed in it, too.

But still, she paused. He wasn't the first man to fall prey to his weaknesses, and he wouldn't be the last.

Good luck, Bill, she thought. I forgive you, for what that's worth.

Now, she just needed to be able to forgive herself. That was what the mission the Duchess had given her would entail. She'd be damning her son for all eternity. Could she do it? Had Joe's crimes been so bad? Were they really worthy of the punishment that would be inflicted upon him?

How did you sentence your own son to hell?

She wiped her face clear of tears, and put her doubts aside.

You did it because it was the right thing to do.

You did it because there was no other choice.

She focused on the scene in front of her. There was no way of telling how long ago they'd crashed, but judging by Bill and Pete's wounds, it couldn't have been long; she'd seen enough car crashes in her afterlife to tell that. She could probably just about catch Joe on foot if he was going where she thought he was going.

A horse stood several feet away, breath flaring from its nostrils in the frozen night, its foot stamping impatiently on the floor.

Grace smiled at it. 'Now you're talking.'

If Joe had needed breadcrumbs to follow Ryan – and he hadn't – the blood trail he'd left would have done nicely. The boy's tracksuit leg flapped at the night, the snow hungrily drinking the blood flowing from it.

Seat belt couldn't prevent that, thought Joe. He'll barely make it.

He stopped, confused.

Where? Where would he barely make it to?

Who was the man he was following?

What had he just been told? It was something important.

Memories glowed like dying embers in a grate. He raked a poker into them, trying to draw out a last flicker of heat.

There was a journal containing something important.

He patted his coat, looking for the shape he hoped would be reassuring.

Nothing. If it had ever been there, it wasn't any more.

A crash, his subconscious mouthed. You must have lost it in the crash. Like the gum.

He looked behind him at the trail in the snow he hadn't left.

I'm dead, he told himself. I don't remember much, but I remember that. I'm dead, and I have to work something out.

He looked down at the name badge on his coat, which proudly declared: *I AM JOE!*

Joe. As good a name as any.

The lad ahead of him screamed in frustration, elbowing his way back into his attention. Facing him was a steeply inclining hill.

Ryan. Lad's name's Ryan. Another memory back, thought Joe. Might as well be a mountain with a fucked leg and several inches of snow, Ryan. No way you're making it up there.

It seemed like he intended to try, though.

Am I supposed to help him? wondered Joe. Is that what I'm supposed to do?

It didn't sound right – didn't feel right, either – but not much felt right when you were dead, with no memory, in the middle of a snow-drenched field.

A Lincolnshire field. He was in Lincolnshire.

He tensed himself then sprinted up the hill, gritting his teeth and passing the boy. When he reached the brow, he saw what Ryan had been so keen to get to.

The church, he remembered. I need to follow Ryan because I need to find out how I died, and he's the key, somehow.

He's heading there for a reason, and the feeling in my gut is that that reason involves me. Sometimes, gut instinct is as good as a fact.

Yep, said a voice in his head, *and this is the last time you'll be able to drag that information back. That fire? It's out now, bud. No more poking it back to life. Don't know how much longer you've got left, but it's not long. You need to get there, now.*

Joe decided that the voice in his head had a point – a good one – and started to run.

The Duchess hadn't expected the journey back to the Pen to be easy, because crossing from one realm to another wasn't supposed to be. She hadn't expected this, though.

The odd member of the Dispossessed getting trapped in the Gloop was par for the course; any flock had its wanderers, sheep that got themselves caught up in barbed wire by mistake. This, though, was the flock itself. Hundreds, possibly thousands of Dispossessed, their innate greyness magnified, somehow, by the glowing pink membrane that enclosed them, all moving in slow motion through the Gloop towards her.

Although that wasn't quite true, because they weren't so much moving as swimming, using their arms to propel themselves forwards. How can they do that? thought the Duchess. How can they even *think* to do that?

Then she saw how.

Hanna.

Her younger sister was performing a perfect breaststroke, heading away from the Duchess and dragging some of the Dispossessed with her.

She's trying to get back home.

The thought popped into her head unprompted, and although she tried to dismiss it, it refused to be sent on its way. If she and the Dispossessed couldn't share purgatory, they'd just

268

go back to the soil. And why not let them? Back there, they'd have no more impact than a gust of wind. They'd be brain-damaged lame animals, the humans they'd wander amongst none the wiser.

That was true, wasn't it?

Suddenly, the Duchess wasn't so sure, because every hour seemed to bring a new first, an old certainty made uncertain. That number of them all crossing over at the same time? There was no telling the damage they could do, because such a migration had never happened before.

You know what that means. What you need to do.

She did. She knew there was a nuclear option, and knew, too, the devastation that it would bring about, thousands of half-souls slaughtered as a result.

Including her sister.

It's not just that, though, she thought. It's Daisy-May. If Joe and his mother free her, she won't be able to get back. None of them will. They'll be trapped soil-side for decades. Maybe longer. Daisy-May was her chosen one, the one who would break the chain of inbred entitlement and herald a fresh period of purgatory rule. There was no coming back from what she was about to do.

As she watched a squad of Dispossessed push through the Gloop, struggling through to the living world on the other side, her hand instinctively went to the metal gauntlet around her right arm. *Not powerful enough. If the savages are at the gates of the temple, you either fight them off or you bring the temple down on top of them.*

She'd tried fighting them off, before this latest trip to the soil. It hadn't worked.

Then, she saw her. Hanna. Around fifty feet away from the outer wall of the Gloop.

She turned, as if she could sense the Duchess's eyes on her.

She smiled.

Don't smile just yet.

The Duchess reached for the pendant hanging around her neck, the thin gold chain breaking easily in her hand.

Her sister's expression went blank.

She mouthed: *No.*

Every Jankie sister had been thoroughly briefed on when to use their nuclear option – namely, never.

Taking the metal pendant in her hands, the Duchess separated the discs, tossing the left, dark side in Hanna's direction. The light side she kept for herself as she began to swim, a breaststroke motion through gallons of treacle, but one that nevertheless propelled her forward.

Stroke.

Stroke.

Stroke.

She felt a hand grasp her ankle, pulling her backward, the Dispossessed mouthing something to her.

It's trying to talk, she thought desperately. That's impossible.

Like the swimming was impossible.

Like the hunting in packs was impossible.

Like the charging the walls was impossible.

I need to wake up. I need to put a stop to this, now.

She grunted, kicking herself free from her attacker, the second half of the pendant still grasped in her hand, the wall she needed to pass through to return to the Pen a few feet away.

Stroke.

Stroke.

Stroke.

She risked a look behind her. She'd wondered whether Hanna would swim back to stop her, but her younger sister had doubled down, going for the exit to the soil world rather than retreat back to the Pen.

The Duchess kicked off again, the sisters swimming in opposite directions, both of them aware of what was about to happen, but only one having the ability to stop it.

Stroke.

Stroke.

Stroke.

I didn't want it to be like this, the Duchess thought, as she reached the barrier, her fingers plunging into it, a wobble of nausea hitting her as they did so.

She squeezed the pendant in her hand, and its twin, fifty feet away and buried amongst a clump of half-souls, began to whine. The Duchess knew she should push on through to the other side, that to dawdle in this nether world was fatal, but she couldn't help herself.

After all, it wasn't every day you blew up a realm.

The pendant she'd thrown exploded, a soundless green cloud erupting from it. A second grew from that one, bigger this time, which sprouted into a third and a fourth and a fifth, a living, breathing tumour growing in size and scope.

The Dispossessed that had been within its immediate blast radius were instantly ensnared, green tendrils shooting out of them, entwining themselves around jutting grey limbs and soundless screaming mouths. Multiplying and dividing and enlarging, the green forest of explosions grew again and again and again, the Dispossessed turning away, desperately trying to avoid it, failing utterly to do so.

Within five minutes this realm will be an irradiated wasteland, thought the Duchess, as mushroom clouds of pure, unfiltered soil-side atmosphere poisoned everything in sight, bleaching the Gloop of its throbbing pink hue and turning it a sickly radiation green.

I'd say God forgive me, but I know he won't.

★

I'm no longer observing. I'm in Joe's car. I'm in Joe's car, and he won't wind the windows down.

That would have been bad enough because of the heat – all of our stink mashed together, the stringy girl and my fear, something primal from Joe – but also because he's smoked pretty much from the moment he picked us up, chain-puffing one cancer stick into another, a mountain of stubs gathering in the car's ashtray.

This is the drive to the farmhouse I'm reliving.

'What's your name, love?' Joe asks, and I tell him, saying it like I'm ashamed of it.

'Daisy-May,' he says. 'So stupid, they named you twice.'

How could I have not known about Joe? How could I have not remembered what he was? How could the Duchess have not told me?

'Tell me what happened,' he says. 'From the beginning.'

I do. It's a short story with a fast end.

'Someone pinched the bag of money when you were asleep,' he says. 'That's what you're telling me.'

It was the only thing I had to tell. 'Must have been watching me. I only dozed off for a couple of minutes, and it was gone,' my mouth says.

It sounded weak then, and it sounds even weaker now, in this am-dram re-creation of the end of my life.

The stringy girl tries to snigger. Joe kills it dead with a look.

'*Who* must have been watching you?' he asks.

'Whoever nicked the bag.'

Joe curses as he slows the car, the clog of traffic up ahead stalling us.

'I'd heard you were an up-and-comer. Old head on young shoulders. Did I hear wrong, Daisy-May?'

I said nothing then. I say nothing now.

'I asked you whether I heard wrong.'

I tell him he didn't. He did, though. I was just a dumb teen-ager, in the way that all teenagers *should* be dumb.

'You're telling me you fell asleep and lost my money. That means two things. The first is, you're the type of stupid that needs a handler when she goes out in public. Are you that type of stupid, Daisy-May?'

They were the questions it was impossible for me to answer correctly. All I could do was keep him talking and try to think of a way out of it.

'No, I'm not stupid.'

Joe nodded, slipping the car into fifth gear, opening up the throttle, yelling above the engine roar. 'No, I don't think you're stupid either. I know stupid – come across it in my line of work every day – and you're not that. Which leads me to possibility number two.'

His eyes flicked up to the motorway sign that pointed to Boston, and he eased the car into that lane.

'Possibility number two is, you're clever but stupid with it, because you think you're smarter than us. You've made a deal with someone – maybe Ryan, maybe someone else. You pretend to be asleep, someone lifts the money on your say-so, and you sail off into the sunset. How does that sound, Daisy-May? Am I getting closer?'

'I'd never do that. Never betray you like that. 'Cos I know you'd kill me for it.'

Joe smiled, pointing his cigarette at me. 'I knew you were a bright girl. Doesn't change the fact that my drugs are gone, though, does it? You do your job, so she can do hers.' He indicated Stringy with his thumb. 'Otherwise it might seem you're both working against me.'

Stringy sobbed. Dryness caught in my throat, threatening to choke me, making me ask a question I didn't want to know the answer to.

273

'What are you going to do to us?'

Joe stubbed the cigarette out, tightness forming around his mouth, silence its own answer.

Time tumbles forward, and I'm back at the farmhouse. No matter how far I go, I always seem to end up back here.

Joe opens the back door and beckons us through.

'So rare to find a murderer with manners,' I say, passing by him. It's a half-joke he doesn't kill me for. I look to Stringy, gifting her the faintest of smiles, but it isn't returned.

It doesn't take long to see that the farmhouse is more of a doss house aspiring to be a crack house. If it ever contained furniture, it's been cleared out; there's a plasma screen in the corner of the room, propped against the far wall, and a makeshift sofa constructed from its box, two grooves made by two arses.

Joe points to the cardboard box, and Stringy and me sit down on it. He puts his finger to his lips in a *shush* and we obey, the room sweltering, thick curtains drawn, a stray ray of light sneaking past them, cutting the room down the middle, crumbling wallpaper heaving itself off the walls, FIFA on the TV, two controllers discarded, the game paused, Joe watching us impassively, the lad who let us in out of sight, mumble-talking to someone we haven't met yet.

A car pulls up outside. A door slams, followed by the sound of feet on gravel.

Three raps.

A muttered greeting on the doorstep, loud enough to reveal its cowed nature.

Joe folds his arms, not taking his eyes off us.

Ten steps, each one louder.

Pete, the guy I met in the caravan, in the doorway. I wonder which one's going to play bad cop, and then realise it'll be both of them.

Pete walks up to us, takes out a gun, points it at Stringy and pulls the trigger. No show, no spiel, no gloss, no hype, just a man pulling a trigger and a girl's head exploding.

A thin sliver of brain lands on my bare, shaking leg.

Brain on my leg, I think. It's a Wednesday afternoon, and there's brain on my leg.

It's an observation I make coldly, as if it's a ladybird or a blob of ketchup.

Pete smiles at me while Joe stands at the back. He's unhappy, something hidden beneath his impassive face. I don't know whether it's because his mate just killed a girl, or because he didn't shoot me as well.

'That was what's known as a statement of intent,' Pete says calmly, kneeling down in front of me. 'It's to save everyone time, because the older I get – and Joe will back me up here – the more valuable time becomes. Never have enough of it, and it's the one thing money can't buy. So, I'm going to ask you a simple question, and you're going to answer it. We go from there.'

He gets to his feet, the gun still in his hand, smoke leaking from its barrel.

'Where's our money?'

I reach out to my trembling knee, steadying it.

I realise I need to be braver than I thought possible.

'I fell asleep. When I woke up, the bag was gone. That's the truth.'

He can't kill me for the truth. That's honestly what I think.

He nods. 'I believe you,' he says, smiling. 'Thank you for your honesty.'

He raises the gun quickly, pointing it at my head.

This is how it happens. This is how I die.

'Wait,' a female voice says, clear and firm. 'Wait, Pete.'

There was a certain silence that set in before short, sharp bursts of violence erupted. Joe had learned to recognise it. It was as if the world had been briefed on what was about to take place, and held its breath in preparation. He had that feeling now, watching the seemingly empty church, a single flame dancing deep within it, casting inconclusive shadows on the walls inside.

I was too late to see anyone go in, he thought, but that doesn't mean they haven't.

Why had he been too late? He'd been on someone's – Ryan's – limping tail, and then, suddenly, he hadn't.

That's not true, he told himself. I saw him go in, I just mind-blanked again.

It was happening more often, and for longer.

I've got minutes left to solve this thing; any longer than that and it won't get solved, because any longer than that, and I won't remember.

He started jogging towards the church, picking up pace as he neared the refurbished front door, closing his eyes as he passed through it into the glass-roofed reception. Was it just hours since he'd been here with . . .

With who?

A girl.

The girl he hadn't been able to save. The girl he'd let down. Daisy-May.

I've wasted too much time, he thought. Treated it like an investigation I've got all the time in the world to solve, rather than mere minutes.

A scrape of metal off to the left, deep in the nave of the church.

Joe walked towards it.

This couldn't be happening.

It was a hallucination punishment from some demon he hadn't met yet. It had to be, because of all the betrayals he'd learned of – Pete, his father – this was the greatest.

Claire was here.

His Claire – *his wife* – was kissing Ryan.

Joe dropped to one knee, his vision swimming but his mind never clearer.

It's the pain of it, he realised. It's like a red-hot poker lancing a boil. It gives me clarity.

Just when oblivion would have been kinder.

Claire pulled away. 'You have it?'

Ryan nodded, lifting up the leather bag. 'Gear's all here, missus. We'll need to sell it quick, and for less than it's worth, but it'll be enough for us to set up fresh.'

Claire touched his face, covering the parcel tape shielding his eye socket, so he looked like his old self. 'That's what I – what *we* – need. A fresh start. Pete?'

Ryan smirked. 'Roads are bad round here, especially in this weather. You don't drive careful, you're likely to have an accident.'

'You've done such an incredible job,' said Claire, smiling at him like he was her star pupil. She stepped aside, and Joe saw that she had taken several candles from the church's altar and placed them around an ice bucket. A bottle of champagne poked out of it. She reached down, picking up two full glasses, and handed one to Ryan.

'Posh as fuck,' said Ryan, bashful. 'What we celebrating, angel?'

Claire winked at him. 'Success. Freedom. A new start together.'

Ryan drank deeply. 'Like the sound of those things.'

'I guess that just leaves the reverend. You took care of that, too?'

Took care of *that*? thought Joe. Who the fuck is this woman, and what's she done to my Claire?

Ryan shifted on his feet, suddenly uncomfortable. 'He was in the crash. In a bad way. Won't survive.'

'But you made sure,' Claire said, her smile slipping a little.

'Got blood coming out of his forehead, and he was turning blue,' said Ryan, wiping an arm across his forehead, beads of sweat catching against it. 'Bloke was dead, his body just hadn't caught up yet.'

Claire sighed, her kind face creasing sadly. 'That's disappointing. You were supposed to do all the killing.'

Ryan blinked rapidly, a look of surprise on his face. He put his hands to his throat, gagging, stumbling down onto his knees.

Claire threw away her untouched drink. '*I* only had to kill you.'

The first thing Claire does is smile.

There's no agenda behind it, no falseness, just a pure, simple beaming smile. I'm desperate to return it, because it's a smile of hope. A smile that suggests I might get out of this thing alive.

She turns to Pete and says *leave now*. A pout from Pete but no word of protest. He squares his shoulders, snaps off a nod and does as he's told. I realise she's in charge, that they're scared of her, almost.

The hope dies. That fear can't mean anything good for me.

'It's roasting in here,' Claire says to Joe. 'Could you get us a cold glass of something?'

Joe smirks like a try-hard schoolboy. 'Alcoholic, or something stronger?'

'There's a bottle of water in the fridge. If you grab that, and three clean glasses, if such a thing exists in this dump, then we can get started.'

Joe nods like Pete did, a foot soldier given his orders.

Maybe it's desperation – maybe it's because she's a woman, and she isn't pointing a gun at me – but I like Claire. She is kind but in charge, like you hear other people's mums are. I'm so fucking scared, and she's so fucking not, I've half-convinced myself she cares. There's a dead girl with half her face blown off lying next to me, and Claire hasn't batted an eyelash at her, yet I want her to be my fucking mother.

That's what desperation does to you.

Claire winks at me and takes my hand. Like we are the same. Like it is me and her against the world.

'You're dragged into a strange man's car, driven all the way here, frogmarched into this shit-hole in the middle of nowhere, and a girl gets shot right beside you. I might have only just met you, Daisy-May, but I'm guessing you're scared.'

'Yeah, I am.'

'That's what I thought. Pete, Joe? They're good when you need a sledgehammer, but they're not who you call upon when a scalpel's required. But then, what man is?'

Joe comes back with an icy bottle of water and hands it to Claire. 'Should my ears be burning?'

'They should be char-grilled, darling,' Claire says, smiling that smile again.

'No glasses,' Joe says. 'Casa del Farmhouse doesn't extend that far, apparently.'

This is just a normal conversation between normal adults; that's what I tell myself. Take the girl with the shot-off face out of the equation, and you could almost imagine we're a family.

Claire dismisses Joe and unscrews the bottle, passing it to me. 'Your need's greater than mine.'

I drink deeply, and no drink has ever tasted better.

'Looks like you needed that.'

'I had nothing to do with the bag being taken,' I stutter, between gulps. 'I might look dumb, but I'm smart as fuck. Smart enough to know that ripping off a drug dealer's just about the dumbest thing a girl could do.'

Claire sits back, placing her hands on her lap, and I mirror her. I read about that, somewhere, how it builds trust.

'Pete told me about you a couple of months ago,' Claire says. '*Whip-smart*, he said, and Pete's wrong about a lot, but not when it comes to people. He also told me you've had a hard road of a life, and I know a little something about that. I was excited for you when he told me you were doing your first run.'

She laughs when she sees the look of surprise on my face. 'You thought I was the pretty lady on the arm of one of the boys, am I right? The bookkeeper at best?'

I don't know what to say, so I just nod and take another drink, the water sliding out of the corners of my mouth. Claire frowns, agitated. It's almost like she's worried that she's putting me out, somehow.

'I won't say I'm in charge,' she says, 'because it's all an ecosystem we feed into. I will say that there's far too many swinging dicks in this operation, which is why I was glad to rubber-stamp you coming on board.'

She smiles apologetically.

'Sorry, I know this is a bit management-dresses-down-the-workers. The truth of it is, this is a business like any other. There's a demand for our goods, and we supply them. The goods may be classified as illegal, but goods they undoubtedly are. We provide a service, and I pride myself that it's a good one.'

She smiles stoically, like she's a doctor delivering bad news that's outside of her control.

'That's what makes today so problematic, Daisy-May. Those drugs had been bought and paid for, and we've got customers relying on us to supply them. It's what upsets me the most, the letting people down.'

'I don't want to let anyone down,' I say.

'That's so good to hear, Daisy-May. Let's see if you can help.

We'll start at the beginning: tell me what happened on the train.'

The problem with the beginning is its proximity to the end. Doesn't take long to tell Claire how I fell asleep, then woke to find the bag gone.

'I believe you,' she says finally, then looks over to Joe, who's been hovering on the other side of the doorway. 'I believe her.'

She gets up and places a hand on my cheek.

'Does that mean I'm free to go?' I ask.

She kisses me on the forehead, then walks over to Joe, leaning in to whisper something to him, and he nods like he's known all along. As she leaves, she doesn't so much as cast a glance back at me. I'm not worthy of it. Not in her eyes.

Joe's shoulders sigh. He glances away from me, like I'm painful to look at. I see then than he doesn't want to do it. It doesn't mean he won't, but he doesn't want to do it.

He takes out a gun.

'Let's get this over with,' he says.

Chapter Thirty-One

Animals didn't count.

Why that was the case had never been explained to Grace; it was just one of the irrefutable rules of the realm she now existed in. In almost all cases, interaction with the living soil carried with it the harshest of penalties – Daisy-May was testament to that – but animals were different. They were a loophole in the Xylophone Man's punishment plan.

Perhaps it's because they can see us, Grace thought. Horror films always have that right, because the dog barking usually means something supernatural is afoot.

And that was why she could mount a horse and ride it like Boadicea herself.

She let go a cry of pure joy as the horse vaulted the crumbling stone wall in front of it, eating up the distance to the church hoof by galloping hoof. Like anything, getting an animal to obey you took no little knowledge and practice, but Grace had spent her time in the afterlife doing plenty of both. Animals had been a link back to her old life, a source of comfort in a strange new world.

She leaned down, whispering in the horse's ear, its nostrils flaring, steam rising from its body, moonlight illuminating the blanket of white covering the landscape around her.

What a world this is, she thought. It's wasted on the living.

A scream sounded in the distance, demented, desperate, an animal roar coming from the snowy wasteland ahead of her.

'Easy, girl,' said Grace, patting the horse firmly, tugging on its mane to slow it. 'Easy.'

There was something about that scream, she knew. It hadn't sounded human, and if it wasn't human, it meant that something from the other side was here.

She eased the horse into a trot, then a full stop at the bottom of the hill. The scream sounded again, so violent Grace could believe it would have shredded the skin from the back of the poor woman's throat. And it was a woman – that much was clear now – the sound coming from the left of her when she needed to go right towards the farmhouse.

Wind picked up from nowhere, whipping snow from the ground, the horse protesting with a snort.

I don't have time to help her, Grace thought, patting the horse absent-mindedly, but it's my job, so I have to.

She kicked her heels, guiding her mount away from the brow of the hill and towards the area where the scream had come from, yelling encouragement to the horse, knowing that time was against her and that every second she didn't race towards Joe was one that brought him closer to being lost forever.

He's made his bed, and who's to say he shouldn't lie in it? she asked herself.

Because it's not just his bed, the Duchess replied, her voice unprompted in Grace's head. *If it was, you wouldn't be here. It's why you haven't got time for screaming women.*

Grace ignored her, urging the horse onto the narrow country lane shooting off from the field, snow spraying up in its wake.

Suddenly the animal bucked, rearing up, and Grace was flung through the air, the odd laws of gravity that she was still expected to adhere to working against her, beckoning her on to the snow, muscle memory tweaking her, making her think she'd been winded.

She rolled several times, coming to a stop at the feet of a girl. Or at least, what used to be a girl.

Around fifteen, with a shock of bright green hair, shivering and stone-cold naked, she was more of a child than a girl on the brink of womanhood. As Grace got to her feet, she saw the free-form madness in her face.

What was left of it, anyway; there was a gunshot wound where her left eye should have been. In her right was the glimmer of recognition.

'You can see me,' said Grace.

The girl squeezed her fists together, took a step closer, and then let out a primal scream, like she was trying to expel every abuse and wrong she'd ever suffered.

'Such pain,' said Grace. 'Perhaps more than anyone I've ever met soil-side.'

She reached out a hand, letting it dangle in the air, not wanting to force the issue. The agony is almost sweating from her skin, she thought. What happened to this girl? Why hasn't she passed through?

Terror in the child's remaining eye, though she was at least looking down to the hand Grace was offering.

'I can help, love,' Grace said. 'I can help you find the way.'

She removed her shawl and placed it around the girl's shoulders. 'I can't turn time back and change what happened to you. I wish I could, but I can't. What I can do, though, is show you the way to the next place. It's no paradise, but it's no hell, either. There's a peace to the Pen, one that's hard to explain but easy to experience. I can show you the way, then you can see what I mean.'

Another yell from the girl, some of its rawness stripped out.

She looked down at Grace's hand again, then took it.

A spasm went through the older woman, the girl's memories presented to her, their pain and horror.

Nottingham.

A car journey.

A girl called Daisy-May in the passenger seat.

Grace's son driving.

A farmhouse.

My God, thought Grace. *My God*.

'I'm sorry,' she said, drawing the girl to her, every gesture too small, too inadequate. 'I'm so, so sorry.'

She whistled, and the horse trotted over.

Peace clouded the girl's eyes momentarily, and Grace took her hand and laid it against the animal's mane.

The girl didn't smile, but she didn't scream either.

Grace leaned into the horse's ear, whispering, and it kneeled down on his hind legs. Carefully, slowly, she guided the girl onto its back. She whimpered, faint panic in her expression as the horse got back to its feet.

'It'll take you where you need to go,' said Grace, smiling at her. 'I'll make this right, or as right as it's possible for me to.'

She patted the horse, and it began to trot towards a clump of trees fifty yards away.

And if that means damning my son to hell, she thought, turning away, well then, so be it.

'The Pen is creaking, ma'am,' said Remus. 'Purgatory is on the brink of falling. All is lost.'

'Thank you for that summary,' the Duchess intoned, staring at the chaos all around her.

Half-souls piled on each other's shoulders, a hundred wide, a thousand tall, all of them scaling the walls of the Pen and hammering on the very walls of existence. Thousands grouped together as inhuman battering rams, colliding with the walls

285

again and again and again. Hairline cracks had appeared as a result, the sky above them a cauldron of blood-red and soot-black.

This isn't happening, the Duchess thought.

'If they keep pounding the walls like that,' said Remus, 'what comes next . . .'

'What comes next is unthinkable,' said the Duchess. 'What comes next involves the barriers between the soil and the after-life tumbling.' She frowned at Remus. 'Things must be bad for you to have left the compound.'

'They're worse than bad, ma'am.'

'Were we wrong? I was taught that I was a custodian of the afterlife, a cog that made everything work. I was taught that these half-souls were barely worth that description. You, Remus, taught me that I was a zookeeper, and a benevolent one at that.'

'I taught you what I taught all the other wardens. What was taught to me. It has worked for thousands of years. More.'

A tower of Dispossessed slammed into the walls once again, crumbs of masonry spilling in response.

'Well,' said the Duchess, 'it's not working now.'

'There's always the soil, ma'am,' said Remus. 'We could flee there.'

'And abandon my post? Are you mad?' She stared at him until he bowed his head deferentially. 'Besides, I blew up the Gloop.'

He turned to her, open-mouthed.

'I had no choice,' said the Duchess. 'Thousands of Dispossessed were in there. Hanna was in there. They'd have made it through to the soil.'

'It makes escape impossible, though,' said Remus, a hint of desperation in his voice.

'I thought that killing Hanna would end this insurrection,'

said the Duchess, looking hopelessly on. 'That without their leader, the Dispossessed would return to their rootless ways. I was wrong. About that, and a good many other things.'

'What are you going to do?' asked Remus.

'What Daisy-May always said I should do. Talk to them.'

The Duchess ordered Remus to return to the compound. She had to do this alone. She just hoped the Dispossessed didn't know what she'd done in the Gloop. Committing genocide against their kin wasn't the strongest peace offering.

A clump of Dispossessed stood a few feet from her, and she approached them slowly, her hands raised in conciliation. For as long as she'd known, the Dispossessed had a shambling gait, and a sheep-like instinct to follow. She had to hope some of that obedience was still there, that her natural authority would still make some sort of difference.

She called out in greeting.

The group turned to her.

They're considering me, she thought. Judging me.

Their mouths moved soundlessly. Life and intelligence flickered in their eyes.

Do they believe I was simply a good caretaker? she wondered. Or do they consider me something worse?

There were several seconds of silence, then, as one, they let out a high-pitched primal scream, pointing grey, gnarled accusatory fingers in her direction. It felt to the Duchess like existence itself had turned to look at her.

Existence began to stampede.

With the sound of countless charging feet answering her, she realised she couldn't go back into the newly irradiated wasteland of the Gloop, nor could she go forward into the wall of bodies facing her. She closed her eyes, remembering when her time on the soil had ended. Then, as now, it hadn't been her life that had flashed before her eyes, but the life she hadn't lived, and the things she hadn't been granted.

A job.

A life untethered to what came next.

Children.

Sophia, dead in the womb in her fourth month.

Elizabeth, stillborn in a hospital ward so primitive it was virtually medieval.

Cassandra, four days young before the soil world sent her back.

Several other miscarriages, each one a thorn in her blood, a reminder of what she had lost and what she was failing to provide in the future: a successor.

That was the legacy she'd left on the soil, one she had abdicated through biology and fate. There was no daughter – no son, come to that – to replace her. The boy that had been anointed to follow her hadn't done so. What better time, then, to raze such a tradition to the ground? Daisy-May was her chosen one, fresh blood where the old had congealed. It was why she couldn't just abandon her to a life of damnation, and why she'd need Joe's mother to convince him to do the unthinkable when he learned the truth about his death, and his true nature.

All of which meant nothing now that the Pen had fallen and untold thousands of its inmates were racing towards her, wanting their pound of flesh.

An explosion sounded above her. Her eyes snapped open, and she looked up – the legion of half-souls that had been stopped in their tracks looking up with her – to see the sky bleeding green. Quickly, she dug into the pocket of her trousers, taking out the nose plugs she'd used to traverse the Gloop, fixing them firmly into her nostrils.

Back on the soil, they'd have called it a dirty bomb.

Akin to mustard gas used in the First World War, a mix of

conventional explosive and radiation wept from the sky, a blanket of green mist falling upon the Dispossessed like rain. The potency was far less nuclear than that which she'd used to lay waste to the Gloop (she could tell that by its pale, almost yellow hue), and dispersed over such a wide area that it wouldn't cause permanent damage to the Dispossessed. It would distract them, though, and, when they got a lungful, slow them down.

The sky spat out a ladder, a thing of wicker and pine rungs, and the Duchess caught it, looking up to see a hot-air balloon emerge from amongst the grumbling clouds of green fog. There was only one other person in the Pen she knew with access to such firepower.

'Get a shift on,' Mabel yelled, reaching over the side to steady the ladder. 'I'm on the bloody clock, love.'

The Duchess allowed herself a smile, then did as she was told, her hands grabbing rung after rung, the balloon sagging slightly, despite her wiry, almost weightless frame.

'Faster,' Mabel called out. 'Faster, 'cos they know.'

The Duchess looked down and saw that her sister was right. The bomb may have momentarily distracted the Dispossessed – a title that seemed less and less appropriate by the second – may have slowed them down, even, but not enough. They began to grab upwards, their hands mere inches from her feet.

She climbed faster and faster, her sister working the flame, gaining them precious altitude from the rampaging horde.

Above her, Mabel cursed and reached down, bringing up a thick steel pipe.

'Might want to keep your head down, Rach,' she called out. 'Fire in the fookin' hole.'

The Duchess looked down and instantly saw the reason for her sister's request.

Much as they had done with the wall, the Dispossessed were forming an inhuman tower of half-souls, one clambering onto the shoulders of another, piling onto the back of the next, a discarded sketch from a poor man's *Inferno*, the whole thing looking like it could topple at any moment.

It won't, thought the Duchess. Not unless Mabel gives it a shove first.

A shrill whistle pierced the air, and a streak of light flashed past her.

Her hand found the next rung, and the next and the next, her head snapping back sporadically to see the tower collapse in a blitz of green fire and brimstone.

Mabel took a handful of her dress and unceremoniously hauled her into the basket.

The two sisters looked at each other, and for a brief second the weight of existence wasn't on them, and they were simply two little girls who had grown up in the poor-ass part of Brooklyn, girls who hadn't known about purgatory, or heaven, or hell, who hadn't slipped on the persona of a refined member of the English gentry or a tough-talking West Country lass to make a brave, quick-witted girl feel at home.

Mabel squeezed her hand, and then it passed. 'Well then, Duchess, what's the plan? 'Cos this was the extent of mine.'

The Duchess rose to her feet and got her bearings. She pointed a bony finger at a point in the distance, a part of the Pen wall that hadn't been attacked yet. 'Aim for there.'

Mabel nodded, reaching for the burner. 'What's there?'

The Duchess looked down at the sea of bodies, all, as one, beginning their assault on the Pen walls once again. 'The place where I go to think.'

The film of my life nears its final reel, my last minutes on the soil regurgitated then force-fed down my gullet.

I stare up at Joe and his endlessly dark gun barrel.

His forehead's sweaty.

His hand's shaking.

He can't do it. This will cross a line he can't come back from.

His gun arm falls away, and he slaps himself on the arse, gee-ing himself up, bringing the gun back up to cover me.

'I'm sorry.'

I ask what for. He doesn't answer.

He closes his eyes.

He tenses the trigger.

'Run,' he says, his voice the scrapings of a whisper.

I try to move but can't.

I realise I've pissed myself.

He fires, putting a bullet a foot away from me.

I flinch, the blowback from the bullet hammering my ear-drum.

'Run,' Joe says. 'Run and don't look back.'

I try to, try to get to my feet, but my feet don't get to me. Something's stopping them.

A burning in my throat, molten cauldron in my stomach.

'I'm sorry,' Joe says, but he's not talking to me.

'It doesn't matter,' Claire says softly.

I topple over onto my back, and I see the water bottle Claire gave me lying on its side.

'You poisoned her,' Joe says, clearly stunned.

I throw up.

Vision and consciousness keep slipping through my fingers.

I black out.

When I come to, I see a hidden door in the wall that isn't hidden any more. Joe is dragging Stringy's dead body into it.

I black out again.

I come to, and this time, I'm the one being dragged. It feels like there's acid inside me, eating anything it can see.

Joe won't look at me.

I lose more seconds, and then I'm inside the hidden room.

I know I'll die here.

My eyes flutter.

The bag.

The bag Ryan gave me to take, the one that was stolen when I fell asleep on the train. It's inside the hidden room.

Claire gives it a final check, then looks at me and says, 'Life? People? They'll fuck you if you let them. You let them. I didn't.'

She zips it up, then closes the door.

She doesn't look back.

The tape of Daisy-May's life ending ended, and she felt her consciousness returned to her.

There was pitch darkness, just as there had been at the beginning.

Her eyes began to adjust.

Her mind screamed.

Opposite her was Stringy, the girl who had been executed in front of her in the farmhouse. A rat picked at the little remaining flesh around her ruptured eye socket.

He put me back here, thought Daisy-May. The Xylophone Man took my soul and shoved it back inside my rotting-into-the-ground body.

The movie of her life – of her death – began to play again, and Daisy-May found she couldn't so much as scream in anger.

Joe watched as fresh horror fed upon fresh horror.

Ryan lay on the floor, unconscious in front of the altar, perhaps dead from whatever Claire had slipped into his drink. Claire was on to her third can of petrol, dousing everything in sight – the reupholstered pews, the drapes bearing his father's face hanging from the ceiling, the plush desert of carpet – all with a snarl on her face that Joe hadn't known she was capable

292

of. A girl – Jen – was lying unconscious next to the altar, the last loose end, ready to be snipped off by Claire.

She's going to make it look like a suicide pact, thought Joe. Star-crossed lovers ending it all in the house of God.

Could it be true? Could Claire have been behind the whole operation?

It didn't seem possible, but then what was impossible when the dead walked the earth unseen at the behest of gods and monsters?

A flame caught, the lighter in Claire's hand spraying the room with shadows, the petrol shimmering in the half-light.

Burning away the last pieces of evidence, thought Joe. I almost admire the thoroughness of it all.

'Angel.'

Claire and Joe turned as one to see Ryan standing in front of the altar, moonlight filtering through the stained-glass windows. He was distinctly unpoisoned and pointing a gun in her direction.

'Put the lighter down,' he said, 'and let's talk.'

'I saw you drink it,' said Claire, the flame in her hand dancing to an unheard tune.

'Spat it out when you weren't looking. Bitter as fuck for champagne. Plus, you've got form; it's how you did Daisy-May. Figured I'd play dead. If you hadn't spiked it, worst I'd look was silly. Better look than dead any day.'

Claire took a step backwards, the lighter wobbling a foot or so above an ocean of petrol. 'How did you know?'

'Woman like you'd never be interested in scum like me.'

She nodded. 'It was a worry, your feelings for that silly little bitch. I underestimated your sentimental side, obviously.'

That's not Claire, thought Joe. That's not my Claire.

'I loved that girl,' Ryan said, the gun wavering slightly.

'You got her addicted to heroin and pimped her out,' said Claire. 'That's an elastic definition of love.'

Ryan nodded at Jen's unconscious form. 'She'd have been no problem for you. Why kill her?'

'She's sleeping it off. When this place goes up, she won't feel a thing. No loose ends, Ryan. Joe taught me that. At least, until he became one.'

Joe's gut clenched.

'What's all this matter now anyway?' said Ryan, his eyes locked on Claire's. 'No need for us to fall out. We split the stash, then go our merry way.'

Claire looked around her, the flame from her lighter casting her shadow on the wall behind her. 'Anything about this situation strike you as merry?'

'It don't, but that doesn't mean it couldn't be. Where d'you put it, Claire? The money Daisy-May was bringing?'

'Where no one'll ever find it.'

Ryan looked past her into the gloom. 'I like a challenge.'

'You won't like this one,' said Claire, lowering the flame a fraction.

'You burn us to death, who wins there?' said Ryan, jabbing the gun at her like an outraged finger.

Don't like how that flame's dancing, thought Joe. Claire looks just about ready to drop that thing, and if she does, no one gets anything they want, least of all the bloke holding the gun like he saw in a film once.

'Walk away, Claire,' he said, knowing the futility of it, that his wife couldn't hear his words, let alone heed his advice, but saying it anyway. Whatever she'd done, he'd forgive her. Nothing was worth her dying. 'Walk away,' he pleaded again.

Claire and Ryan frowned at each other.

'You hear that?' said Ryan.

'I heard something,' said Claire, taking her eye off him for a second.

It was all he needed.

He fired, a hollow echo that ricocheted around the church. Claire screamed, the lighter jerked from her hand. Joe watched as it seemed to drift through the air in slow motion.

The flame'll die before it hits the floor, he thought.

It didn't.

Instead, it tongued the floorboards, a burst of fire flaring in response, digging a burning barrier between Ryan and Claire. The flames spread quickly, colonising the carpeted floors, the drapes, everything his wife had doused in petrol.

Curses of frustration from Ryan, cries of terror from Claire. Joe stood amongst it all, powerless.

'Why am I here?' he yelled at the sky. 'What am I supposed to do?'

'Joe?'

He looked back down to see Claire staring straight at him.

'Joe,' she said disbelievingly, cradling her bleeding arm, 'is that you?'

Chapter Thirty-Two

Something was wrong, Grace realised, and it wasn't just the flames dancing in the church's stained-glass windows. It was a shift in – for want of a more accurate description – *everything*. She stood perfectly still, trying to understand what had changed.

It was the air. She could smell it. It was a change she'd only experienced once before, when she'd had one foot in her soil life and one in her afterlife, the discombobulation that came from two worlds colliding. How was it possible that it was happening here, in a Lincolnshire village, in the dead of winter?

Above my pay grade, she thought, looking up at the silver shards of light that had appeared in the sky. I'll leave the nature of existence to the gods and the monsters. Wayward sons and fallen daughters are more my department.

She stuck two fingers in her mouth and whistled, the distant clomp of the horse's hooves becoming louder.

It was time to find out how much of her son the devil had left her.

Joe watched on helplessly as the fire raged, surging through the vestry like it intended to wash away its sins.

Claire held her arm against her mouth, coughing out smoke, her eyes streaming. Despite that, she could see him. Joe didn't know how, couldn't explain how she was staring into the whites of his dead eyes, only that she was.

'Joe?' she said, bookending the word with coughing fits.

'Claire? You can see me?'

She frowned, looking through him again, doubt clouding her face.

'You saw that too?' Ryan choked. 'Fucking Joe, man. Fucking *ghosts*.'

Joe took a step forward, blinking as the flames passed through him, and held out a hand to his wife. Maybe this is what I'm here to do, he thought. Save her. Redeem her. She was good, once. My memory's sketchy as fuck, but I know that to be true.

Claire screamed, pushing herself away with her feet, the supporting wooden beams above them creaking ominously as he moved closer to her.

'Stay away,' she implored. 'Whatever you are, please stay away.'

'Fuck this,' said Ryan, staring slack-jawed at Joe. 'Fuck this up its *arse*.'

He began to run towards the doorway.

He didn't make it.

There was a crack so sharp it was as if God had broken off a piece of existence and hurled it at the boy. That, and a flaming wooden beam; it fell from the ceiling, pinning Ryan to the floor by his legs. Flames reached out, grabbing the edge of the beam and crawling their way towards him.

Ryan looked at Claire, extending an arm.

She'll help him, Joe thought. Wasn't a broken-winged bird my Claire could ever walk past.

She was making no move to, though.

Because I remembered what I wanted to remember, he realised, and it was all a lie. Claire's no more an angel than I am. We're both bad people who do bad things.

Their gazes met for a second, and Claire laughed, a tone alien to Joe. 'Fumes in this place, stirred up by the fire, that's all it was. There's no Joe.'

'Don't fuck around, *angel*,' Ryan said, panting, the flames inching closer to him. 'Need help.'

'It's not coming, lad,' Joe muttered. 'Breaks my heart, but that's the truth of it.'

Ryan looked up, his eyes widening as he saw Joe again, and he began to scream:

The devil.

The devil.

The devil.

Joe reached out, their fingertips touching as the flames took Ryan, fear and incredulity carved onto the boy's face.

'It'll be all right, lad,' he said, though he didn't know if that was true. 'It'll be all right.'

He winced, turning away as Ryan screamed his last.

Claire was gone.

The rapidly disintegrating vestry was empty. Flames danced over the walls and consumed the huge projector screen hanging from the ceiling. Another slab of wood from the ceiling passed through him and exploded into fiery pieces, the world ending one lick of flame at a time.

There. A trail of fresh blood that could only be Claire's.

Joe followed it, a bloodhound amongst the flames as it snaked through the body of the church and up the wooden stairs to the bell tower. He took the steps two at a time, smoke billowing up them, racing him to the top.

He found Claire cornered, her back to a floor-to-ceiling stained-glass window.

Outside, jagged cracks of white light were scored into the heavens, casting the graveyard below in an unnatural bleached light.

Jesus, thought Joe. Even the sky's on fire. No way is that anything earthly. It's like someone's opened a shutter onto the afterlife.

On any other day, that would have been the most notable feature of the scene.

This was not that day. On this day, the detail seeking most attention involved his mother, thundering towards them on the back of a horse, looking like the fate of existence was resting on her shoulders.

The Duchess looked down at the sea of bodies below. It wouldn't take the Dispossessed long to find their way up to them, but for now, they were safe.

Safe. How laughable, she thought, as another crack appeared in the Pen wall, thousands of half-souls charging against it. The savages are at the gates. There's no such thing as safe any more, for anyone here or on the soil. Not if they break through that wall.

'What's the plan, Rach? What's your thinking place telling you?'

The Duchess turned to her sister, glad of the distraction. 'Do you remember Oma Jankie's stories of the ancient Egyptians?'

Mabel snorted. 'Not likely to forget. Those stories gave my *nightmares* nightmares.'

The Duchess smiled at that. 'Yes, our grandmother had a vivid turn of phrase, particularly when it came to the business of scaring her heirs. You'll remember the story of Ange-Tet?'

Mabel frowned, flicking through hundreds of years' worth of memories. 'She missed me out of that one.'

'Lucky you. Ange-Tet ruled his Egyptian subjects as foolishly as he did cruelly, driving the most cowed servants in history into a state of fevered rebellion. Only a small coterie of guards remained loyal, and when the people revolted, these men were driven back to the gates of Tet's temple. With the savages at the gates, Tet thought the only way to preserve his rule in the afterlife was to destroy himself in the living world, burying his mistakes with him.'

'Old bat rarely wasted a story,' said Mabel. 'She was preparing us for this day.'

'Perhaps,' said the Duchess. 'What if we're giving Hanna too much credit? What if this is God's doing, His way of wiping the slate clean? A reboot, that's what Daisy-May would call it. Purgatory 2.0. He's done it before, but we only ever heard of the flood on the soil, rather than the deep clean in the afterlife.'

'There's still Daisy-May,' said Mabel, placing a hand on her sister's shoulder. 'Game isn't up yet. If she gets back here, she can talk them down. A different voice in their ear to our Hanna, sure, but one they still might listen to.'

'It's a long shot, to say the very least.'

'Easiest decision you'll ever have to make,' said Mabel, "cos it's the only decision you *can* make.'

'If she doesn't get back soon, I might not even have that,' said the Duchess.

'Daisy-May's the only one that could ever talk to them,' said Mabel. 'You've always had faith in the girl. Don't lose it now.'

Chapter Thirty-Three

I'll get to my dead mother in a moment, Joe thought, turning away from the sight of her – and her horse – vaulting the churchyard fence. Right now, I'm more interested in my alive-for-now wife.

Claire was bending down, precariously perched on the edge of the bell tower, the colossal steel bell to the right of her, its bottom glowing red from the flames below. She picked up the aged leather bag that had been stolen from Daisy-May and slung it over her left shoulder, the bag of drugs Ryan had taken from the beach shack on her right.

'Claire,' Joe said.

Claire turned.

She screamed.

'You're not real. You're dead, and I don't believe in ghosts.'

'That doesn't stop them being real,' Joe replied.

Claire yelped, putting a hand to her mouth.

'I'm sorry,' she said. 'It was all Pete's idea.'

A rumble from outside, pure white light spilling into the room.

The sky's got worse, thought Joe. What the hell is causing it?

He took a step forward, knowing the wrongness of this conversation, how it violated the natural order, how the Xylophone

Man might be listening, but nevertheless unable to help himself. 'What was Pete's idea?'

'Killing you.'

Liar.

He didn't know how he knew she was lying, only that she was.

A dread certainty, buried in his gut.

Then, finally, everything clicked into place.

Memories of the man he'd been hit him, sledgehammer swings that kept coming.

The things he'd done.

The people he'd hurt.

The mistakes he'd made.

The crimes he'd committed.

Each one, each remembrance, a fresh razor-wire slash against his flesh.

'Joseph.'

He turned to his mother, who was apparently a hippy now.

'It's all right, love. I'm here to help.'

He was beyond help, beyond salvation, he knew that now, because he finally understood what type of person he'd been on the soil. A weak, low waster of a man, one who didn't have the courage or backbone to be good. His villainy was no outlaw raging against conformity, no rebel yell against his dipped-in-piety upbringing.

It was pitiful.

I'm not that person any more, though, he told himself. *The Dying Squad's changed me.*

Daisy-May's changed me.

There was a sigh from the church like it reluctantly agreed, and then a knee-snapping crunch, the bell tower floor giving up its right to an existence, dissolving under their feet. They fell, the flames from beneath reaching for them, Claire landing

302

a few feet away, hitting perhaps the only square foot of ground the fire hadn't yet taken.

Lucky, Joe thought. If anything about this can be considered lucky. Claire isn't who I thought she was. Who I remembered her to be. If she was ever good, she killed that version of herself long ago. Maybe I helped.

He felt an arm on his shoulder and turned to see his mother.

'You can't interfere, Joseph,' said Grace, a look of fierce determination on her face. 'You know what the consequences are if you do.'

He squeezed her hand. 'I know what the consequences are if I don't.'

He pulled free from her, walking through the flames.

'Don't do it, Joe,' Grace called out. 'If the Xylophone Man takes you now, it means the end of everything.'

'I can't put the past right,' he said, 'but I can make sure I don't get the present wrong.'

He walked through the flames, appreciating how he must look to Claire, an avenging angel untouched by earthly fire.

She reached out a hand and he ignored it, instead walking past her.

What was it Daisy-May had said? he wondered, staring at the chair in front of him.

You can only interact with the living world if you're *pure of heart and have righteous fury in your soul.*

He reached out a hand, letting it hover over the flame-riddled chair.

'Joe,' Grace begged.

Not going to pretend my heart's vaguely pure, but you better believe my soul's on fire with righteous fury. Fury at the person I was. Fury at the things I did. Fury that I've left it so long to put things right.

He felt a calmness come over him.

303

His hand closed on the back of the chair. Flames danced over his hands as he raised it above his head.

He looked around, settled on a spot, smiled, then flung it, one of the legs striking the window above Claire's head, the stained-glass impression of his father's face cracking. The heat did the rest, ripping it into the outside world, a wind tunnel of flame escaping as it did so.

That's not interfering, he thought. That's just working through my daddy issues.

'Jump,' he said to Claire. 'It's a couple of feet, at the most. The fall will hurt, but it won't kill you. The flames will.'

Claire looked at him. 'Thank you.' She raced towards the open window.

She almost made it.

Flames caught hold of the bag on her back, its cheap material encouraging their spread, emboldening them to grab at her hair and neck. Joe's hand passed through her as he tried to pat them out.

'Drop the bag,' he yelled. 'It's just money.'

Claire howled as fire spread over her like a fungus, her whole body consumed in a matter of seconds. She screamed, grasping at the burning bag as if it could support her, and fell head-first through the window.

The crunch when she hit the ground outside was sickening.

As Joe looked down at the broken, flaming ragdoll body of his wife, he felt a hand on his shoulder and allowed himself to be pulled away.

'You tried,' Grace said softly, the wail of sirens in the distance, 'but there's some that the fates don't want helped.'

She looked around her, as her husband's blood-money legacy crumbled where they stood. 'Let's find somewhere a little quieter. We need to talk.'

★

Total silence, unlike any Joe had experienced in years, blanketed the rolling hills beneath them, the day's first light offering the several feet of snow a red hue. It was as if God had reserved the spot just for them, an oasis of earthly calm.

'Never thought I'd see the Wolds again, but they're just as beautiful as I remember them, especially in this snow,' said Grace. 'Do you remember when we came up here one winter? I drove, because your dad refused to, said it was too dangerous. We brought sledges and stayed up here for hours.'

'Always thought that was a bad-ass thing to do, defying Dad in that way. We did almost die on the way home, though.'

Grace laughed again. '*Almost* doesn't count. The afterlife teaches you that, if nothing else.'

Silence between them, shifting in its seat.

'You know what I keep thinking?' asked Joe. 'I keep thinking about that talk you had with me, a week before you died. It was like you knew, or something.'

Grace held her hand up to the encroaching rays of sun on the snow beneath them. 'Maybe I did.'

'You asked me if I thought I was a good person, and I told you I tried to be.'

'You remember it all then,' said Grace, warily.

'I didn't give a flying fuck about the afterlife, and I certainly didn't believe in it. But now, remembering the things I did? The person I was? All I can think is, you were watching. Every dodgy deal, every broken bone, every abused girl I turned a blind eye to.' *Like Daisy-May, like all the other Daisy-Mays*. 'You were watching.'

'Yes,' said Grace. 'I was.'

Joe looked down at his feet. 'You were never one to telegraph a punch, Mum.'

'And you were never one to lead with anything but your chin. I won't pretend that a lot of what you've done over the years has brought me great shame. Now, the shame's on me; it's a petty, selfish emotion, and there were reasons it went the way it did. Your dad, for instance. The way you've wasted your life, though? That's on you.' She squeezed his hand. 'That doesn't mean it's not too late to make it right.'

'We get to it,' said Joe.

'We get to it,' agreed Grace.

They let the silence linger, not wanting to disturb it, Joe finally sending it on its way. 'Before we do, answer me something. You led a life as blameless as it's possible to lead; how come you ended up with all the other Dying Squad fuck-ups? I thought you'd be kicking back in paradise. God knows, you earned it, spawning me. Why are you here?'

The dawn broke properly, flooding them with light. Grace stood up, holding her arms out, embracing it. 'Long time since I've seen a sunrise like this. Like anything.'

'Not much of an answer, Mum.'

She closed her eyes, blocking the sun out. 'Because I hadn't earned it. Because I saw what a mess you were making of your life and thought I was to blame. Not all the way, but enough. Because I saw what your father was becoming, the things he failed to stand against that he should have, the depths he's fallen to since I died and left you both. Because we all have amends to make and penance to fulfil, and I haven't done either of those things yet.'

Joe rose from the log they'd been perched on, stretching out. 'Is that why you're here? To persuade me to dedicate my after-life to making amends?'

'I haven't got much longer,' said Grace, looking warily at the shards of light in the sky. 'Neither have you. I have a simple question: do you want to make things right? To make up for the crimes you committed on the soil?'

Joe swallowed, a razor blade of guilt in his stomach.

306

Daisy-May was dead because of him. She was suffering now because of him.

He couldn't let that stand.

'Yes, I do. Whatever it takes.'

Grace nodded sadly. 'Your answer might be different when I tell you what that is.'

She toyed with the bangle around her wrist, one that Joe knew she'd never have been seen dead wearing when she was alive. I reinvented myself as a good guy, he thought. If I can go to that extreme, my mum can become an undead kook.

'You asked me earlier why I ended up in purgatory when my behaviour marked me out for somewhere else. Did you ever think to ask yourself that same question?'

Joe frowned. 'I am now.'

'What did the Duchess tell you about your mission here?' said Grace. 'What was the exact thing she sent you to do?'

'Solve my own murder.'

'Right. Accompanied by a girl you were indirectly guilty of killing.'

'I didn't know that then, though. That memory had been taken from me. Now, I can taste it, the memory's so clear. Driving Daisy-May to the farmhouse. Claire poisoning her. I might not have pulled the trigger, but I'm just as responsible as either Pete or Claire. I've got just as much blood on my hands.'

Grace nodded. 'Now you have that memory back, I can tell you that the Duchess was entirely ambivalent about any closure you might get from solving the mystery.'

'Good job, since I didn't. Why tell me the opposite, though?'

'Because she is anything but ambivalent about the girl, and *she* needed to discover the truth, one way or the other. The Duchess sees Daisy-May as her successor, someone who will bring balance where she has failed to.'

'*Daisy-May* Daisy-May? Really?'

'Really,' Grace replied, 'and she couldn't accept such a position until she learned the truth behind her death. Learned the truth of your part in it, too.'

'Why?' asked Joe. 'Why's that so important?'

'Because by anointing Daisy-May, the Duchess is taking an axe to a millennium-old tradition. To abdicate in the way she intends to, well, it's simply never been done before. The role of Pen warden carries with it a tremendous psychological toll, one the anointed person has had a lifetime to prepare for. That's not to mention certain members of the Duchess's family, who will be furious at her decision. To deal with all that without the psychic healing that comes with discovering the truth about her past? It would be too much for anyone to bear.'

'And the Duchess believes Daisy-May's up to it? Despite all that?' asked Joe.

'She does.' Grace sighed. 'You've got a decision to make, and the Duchess reckons the question's best coming from me.'

'Must be bad then.'

'It is,' said Grace. 'About as bad a question as a mother can ask her son.'

Thunder rumbled, cracks of light appearing in the sky, mixing with the red rays of early-morning light.

'It's to do with that, isn't it?' said Joe. 'Something's happening at the Pen.'

Grace nodded. 'It was the reason Claire could see you at the farmhouse, communicate with you. The Dispossessed are storming the walls of the Pen, and if those walls fall, the realms of the living and the dead will concertina into each other. For whatever reason, Daisy-May has a connection with the half-souls. She can speak to them, talk them down. The way things are going there, the whole of existence will topple if she doesn't.'

Joe shook his head. 'What difference can a girl from the wrong side of Nottingham make to all that madness?'

Grace smiled. 'You always were a hopeless student of history, Joe. One person can make all the difference in the world.' She took a breath, like courage was mixed up with the oxygen she no longer breathed. 'Which brings me to you.'

'I thought it might.'

'When Daisy-May intervened at the bar, and then again at the outreach centre, she damned herself,' said Grace. 'That she did it for selfless reasons was neither here nor there; the laws are older than time, and just as unbreakable. She's rotting in the Pit now, every mistake she ever made, every wrong she ever committed replayed for her again and again, an eternal torment there's no escape from. Or almost no escape.'

'I had no idea,' said Joe. 'I'd do anything to change places with her.'

Grace sighed. 'I'm glad you feel like that.' She leaned in closer. 'An individual responsible for a person's death – who is willing to *take* responsibility – can, as a means of absolution, offer to change places with that soul in hell. It would mean an eternity of pain, suffering and unimaginable hardship, but she would be freed from the Pit.'

'You're really selling it to me.'

'It's beyond selling, and I'm not going to lecture you on absolution. It goes way beyond that, beyond any earthly crimes committed on the soil. It's a spiritual loophole left open because, frankly, no one's ever been good enough, or perhaps insane enough, to agree to it.'

She doesn't think I will, thought Joe. She's wondering whether my good-guy act is just that. She's wondering whether someone like me can actually change.

I'm wondering that myself.

'And if I *don't* agree to it,' he said, 'what then? If hell is door A, what's door B? Because I can't exactly see me picking the lock of heaven.'

Grace placed a hand on his shoulder. 'You'd remain in the Pen, Dying Squad until the end. How long that would be for, with the Dispossessed breaking down the walls, is difficult to say.'

He laughed grimly, realising something. 'Back there in the church, you said "if the Xylophone Man takes you *now*". You just didn't want him to pip you to the post.'

He looked down at the name badge Daisy-May had given him, a kind gesture from a foul-mouthed girl with a pure heart, one who had been wronged all through her short life, by him and many like him. She'd had opportunities ripped from her when she'd been alive, and now her selflessness in death had ensured the same thing.

He tore the badge off his coat, scrunched it up and tossed it on the floor.

Somewhere, a bird began to sing.

Grace waited.

Joe sighed.

'I'll do it.'

She found his eyes with hers. 'There's no coming back from it.'

'There's no coming back from the things I did, either, so why not double down? The girl's suffered enough.' He winked. 'Besides, I'll be helping to re-stitch the very fabric of existence. Who can top that? Not even Gandhi, the slack bastard.'

Grace placed her hands on his face and leaned forward, kissing his forehead. 'My little Joey.'

She recoiled a little when she saw who had appeared.

'He's behind me, isn't he?' Joe said, his voice unsteady.

Grace nodded.

Joe clenched his fists, the knuckles turning white. 'The Xylophone Man. Stupid fucking name.' He smiled for a final time at his mother.

'I'll be OK,' he said. 'Trust me.'

Chapter Thirty-Four

Daisy-May knew she'd finally lost her mind, because she could hear horses outside.

That didn't change the fact that she could hear them, their hooves thundering in the distance, their whispered whinnies getting louder by the hoofbeat.

Friend or foe? she wondered. Is there even a difference any more? Because the Duchess kept Joe's identity from me – scrubbed my memory clean somehow, to make that so – and if I can't trust her, who can I trust? She'll say she had her reasons, but that's what everyone says when you find out they've fucked you over.

A horse called out from a few feet away as if agreeing with her, then an old hippy walked through the wall, because, well, why wouldn't she?

'Hello, love,' she said, crouching down in front of Daisy-May. 'I'm Grace.'

She can see me, thought Daisy-May. The real me, not the soil-corpse me.

'You can talk now,' Grace said. 'You've been released.'

'Well fuck me,' said Daisy-May, 'so I can.' She took the old woman's hand and pulled herself up, looking down at the unmoving corpse that had contained her so effectively. 'What did I miss?'

Grace smiled sadly. 'Sacrifice. Death. The end of existence as we know it.'

Daisy-May snorted. 'That all?'

Daisy-May tried to fight the urge to holler a scream of pure joy, then gave in to it. Five minutes ago, she'd believed she would be trapped in the hell of her own mind forever; now she was on the back of a horse that was galloping like the hounds of hell were at its heels, as free as a soul could be.

'Should have done this a long time ago,' she called out to Grace, who was keeping pace with her roughly three feet away. 'Animals? I'll take them over humans any day.'

'Is that why you have a connection with the Dispossessed?' Grace shouted back.

'Think I have that connection 'cos I don't think of them like animals,' said Daisy-May, patting the horse's neck as it thundered forward. 'If more of you had done the same, maybe there wouldn't be all those cracks of light in the sky.' She looked up at the ever-more-ragged heavens. 'I don't know what you people are expecting me to do; could be that they're too far gone.'

'It could be,' said Grace, steering the horse towards the tumble-down brick wall that separated field from road, 'but we have to try. Too many people have given up too much for us not to try.'

'God loves 'em,' said Daisy-May.

If there'd been any locals around to watch – and the hour was sufficiently early to ensure that there weren't – they'd have been treated to the sight of two seemingly out-of-control rider-less horses careering down the village's main road, heading desperately for, of all places, the graveyard, its burning church lighting the way.

Daisy-May looked up at it wonderingly. 'You people have been busy.'

Grace nodded. 'I never thought I'd be pleased to see that building burn, but it seems fitting somehow. It was no longer a house of God.'

'You see two oxygen tanks kicking round here?' Daisy-May asked, pulling firmly at the horse's mane to slow its progress. 'We left 'em in the graveyard when we crossed through the Gloop. Going to need them, even if they are half a tank down. Should still be enough to get us across.'

Grace nodded. 'They're still here. A good job, as mine's out.'

'You came from the Pen?'

'New York.'

Daisy-May whistled. 'Never been that far from home. How come you get the glamour shit, whereas I'm traipsing around grief holes like this?'

Grace slowed her horse to a trot, then smiled at the girl. 'The Duchess moves in mysterious ways.'

She vaulted off the animal with an athleticism that belied her years, cupping its muzzle affectionately, then turned to a clump of gravestones. The rope that would lead them back through the Gloop, and back to the Pen was tethered to it. 'We have to hurry.'

Daisy-May nodded, jumping down from her own horse, and taking a last look around her. 'Could lie and say I'll miss this place,' she said, 'but I've seen where sinning gets you.'

They stood at the unseen mouth of the Gloop, oxygen tanks strapped to their backs, straggly mouthpieces attached to their faces, hands squeezing the still taut rope, and knew something was wrong without knowing what that something was. It was an instinct, enough to give them pause, their muffled breathing the only sound in the silent graveyard, the look between them searching.

Daisy-May craned her head backwards, checking the reading on her tank. There was roughly half left, plenty to get her to

313

where she needed to go. What was it, then, the thing that had crawled across her brain, warning her of danger? Whatever it was had had a nibble at Grace, too. Some instinct that they were about to make a mistake.

'Let's do this,' said the older woman, her voice swaddled in distortion. 'Let's go home.'

Whatever *this* is, thought Daisy-May, and whatever home is any more.

Grace passed through first, and Daisy-May was halfway through when something made her turn back to the dawn-speckled graveyard. Her eyes searched the surroundings, then she saw it: another figure had appeared out of thin air, passing through from the Gloop.

It was the teenage girl from the Pen.

The white-haired ringleader.

They exchanged the briefest of glances before Daisy-May was pulled through from the living world to the next.

Daisy-May didn't remember much about school, because an attendance record as spotty as hers didn't leave a great deal to remember. One memory that had burned itself into her consciousness, though, was a film she'd seen in Year 7.

When the Wind Blows, with its *The Snowman*-aping animation, was a classic case of bait and switch. There had been hoots and hollers from the class to begin with, then, as the film played, each child had fallen silent at the tale of a simple couple going about their daily lives, dying from the nuclear war that had occurred off-screen. It had given her nightmares for months. Despite its get-in-your-blood power, though, she'd never imagined she'd ever have to experience such a thing in real life.

Three seconds in the Gloop told her the lie of that.

Whereas the last time it had been a pulsing, organic thing of pink punk beauty, now it was a desecrated wasteland, every surface and texture poisoned with a sickly green hue. Thousands of Dispossessed lay motionless, tendrils entwining themselves around them.

She blew the place up, thought Daisy-May, turning her masked face towards Grace, whose eyes had the same desperate, haunted look. How bad must things have got for her to do that?

They stayed there for seconds that felt like minutes that felt like hours, floating uselessly in the cancerous, scorched-earth womb, knowing that every second they did, they were risking the contamination that had infected the Dispossessed.

Can't go back, thought Daisy-May, can't go forwards. She busted me out of hell just so I can rot away on the earth.

Daisy-May ripped her mask off, turning to see Grace on her haunches, clutching for churchyard air.

'Bad news, coming back to the soil that quickly,' gasped Grace. 'Kind of thing that'll give us the bends.'

Daisy-May lay on her back, looking up at a sky peppered with light slashes. There were more of them, even in the short time they'd been in the Gloop. Whatever was happening was happening fast.

She sat up, breathing air she knew was just as poisonous, if more slow-burn, her eyes searching the graveyard. There was no sign of the white-haired teenage girl. Had she imagined it? Had the Gloop worked its dark, hallucinatory magic even before she'd been fully immersed in it?

Grace dropped her tank at Daisy-May's feet.

'What are you doing?'

'What needs to be done,' said Grace. 'That sounds glib, doesn't it?'

'Sounds mental,' said Daisy-May, ''cos no way can you stay here.'

'The Gloop is a poisoned ruin. Half a tank won't be enough

315

to get through that much irradiation.'

'It will if we go fast,' said Daisy-May, uncertainty polluting her words.

'*Fast* will eat up the supply at an unsustainable rate,' said Grace, 'and you know it.'

She dragged Daisy-May's oxygen tank closer, disconnecting the thin rubber tube on her own and feeding it into her younger companion's. 'You're the Pen's only chance. I'm not.'

'You stay here much longer, there'll be nothing left of you,' said Daisy-May, making no move to stop the oxygen transfer.

'If *you* stay here, there'll be nothing left of anything,' said Grace. 'It's the easiest decision either of us will ever have to make.' She closed the valve on Daisy-May's tank, the dial hovering in the green. 'Let's just hope it's not the last one.'

The Gloop, again.

This time Daisy-May was prepared for the devastation, but that didn't make her progress any easier. Before, moving through it had been like swimming through treacle; now, it was like trying to slalom through a maze of rose bushes. As she moved forward, inch by inch, invisible tendrils grasped at her, slashing at her clothes and leaving their bloody marks on her.

The rope joining the living world and the dead was the worst of all: it was as if someone had secreted shards of glass in it, each pull further bloodying her hands. Bleeding when I'm dead, she thought, the sound of the rapidly dwindling oxygen ticking behind her, a metronome to soundtrack the end of days. The afterlife has so many ways to fuck you over.

She pushed through the tumbledown corpses, their sheer number unfathomable. Jaundice-yellow shoots had already done a good job of colonising them. It was like the Dispossessed she'd shot earlier had multiplied thousands of times over, a wasteland of afterbirth.

Monsters, that's what we are. We've been running a concentration camp all along, and saying I told you so *won't change a fucking thing.*

Nausea rocked her, and she felt bile rising in her stomach. She pressed on, knowing that a mouthpiece of vomit wouldn't get her to the other side any quicker, knowing too that removing that same mouthpiece wasn't an option, unless she wanted to be poisoned within seconds.

Except I'm already being poisoned. This concentration, the minute I stepped into the Gloop, it was infecting me. Whether that turns out to be temporary or permanent remains to be seen.

Growling to herself, urging herself on, she pushed forward, the door that would take her back to the Pen in sight, just, through the mush of green and decay, the fear of what could be waiting for her on the other side growing by the rope pull.

It was with around fifty feet to go that she saw the girl.

Chestnut, who she'd introduced Joe to just after he'd entered the Pen. The one she'd gifted the flower to. She was floating alone, apart from the mass graves of the other Dispossessed, fighting to free herself from a wild tangle of green vines.

Daisy-May knew that she didn't have time to stop, knew that doing so increased the risk of her own infection, but she knew, too, that if she didn't, the effort to break through to the other side was worthless anyway.

Groaning in pain, her every unliving cell burning, she yanked herself around, releasing the rope and kicking her legs like a frog, powering her way through the irradiation to where the child was floating. Fighting back another wave of nausea, she reached out, grappling with the thicket of vines wrapped around the girl's ankle.

There was a second between them, their eyes locking; fear in Chestnut's, grim determination in Daisy-May's.

The girl mouthed: *help me.*

In English, thought Daisy-May. Not the usual Dispossessed

language. She learned English. Dumb cattle, my arse. They feel the way we do. Joy, pain, fear, hope; they're no different.

I wasn't wrong.

Chestnut's eyes flashed with pleading.

The Duchess would leave this girl here. At best, slip her an orange suicide disc so she'd die quickly. That was why the Dispossessed were rioting, though. *They're the same as us,* Daisy-May told herself. *Have the same right to live. The same right to die.*

She grunted in triumph as she freed Chestnut's ankle from the vines.

Trouble is, she won't survive unless I give her the oxygen, and there's no guarantee I'll survive without it.

She jammed her thumbs under the oxygen tank's leather straps, shrugging it off her back, the mask remaining on her face for now. As quickly as she could, she eased the tank onto Chestnut's back.

Hope this doesn't kill us both, she thought.

Taking a final mouthful of air, she yanked off the mask and hurriedly shoved it onto the girl's face.

Breath instantly clouded it. Chestnut's eyes regained some of their focus.

Hauling her onto her back, Daisy-May felt Chestnut's hands tighten around her neck. The breath in her lungs dissipating like a punctured balloon, she kicked away, the girl a sack-of-coal dead weight, Daisy-May breaststroking desperately towards the rope that would take them both back to the Pen, her vision beginning to swim.

Fuck dying here.

Fuck Chestnut dying here.

Fuck either of us dying here.

If hell couldn't kill me, the fucking Gloop won't.

Get ready for me, bitches, I'm coming home.

Chapter Thirty-Five

When falling through to the other side, the first thing Daisy-May wanted to do was look up. Instead, her rapidly emptying stomach forced her head down.

The girl still clinging to her, she lay on her side, pain she hadn't felt for months – pain she hadn't believed it was still possible to feel – racking her body.

No way to tell whether the damage is permanent, she thought, as another convulsion tugged at her. Or even what that means if it is.

When her system had expelled every drop of poison, she reached up, prising Chestnut's arms from her throat. Quickly she tore away the girl's oxygen mask. Chestnut's eyelids fluttered, her mouth opening and closing like a goldfish, tugging the Pen's air into her lungs.

Still alive, then. Or as alive as you get in the Pen.

Shakily, her body peppered in bleeding slashes, Daisy-May got to her feet, slowly becoming aware of something strange.

There wasn't any noise.

In all her time in the Pen, the one constant had been the din, its cocktail of groans, moans and screams all-encompassing. You could no more quieten the Dispossessed than you could the wind, yet something had; there was a nothingness now that terrified her. It was like she was the last living soul in existence.

Nothing louder than silence, love. Grandma June had said that to her more than once, loving the noise and confusion that her granddaughter had brought to the place. *Plenty of silence in the grave, so you scream your bloody lungs out if you want.*

Daisy-May felt like doing just that now. The deathly quiet was terrifying. She'd assumed she'd dropped back into the Pen, but really, who was to say?

Plunging her hand into the ground, she drew up a clump of gritty earth. The same texture as that of her adopted home, but dirt was dirt wherever you were. It was hardly what Joe would have called a fact. Not that she would think back on many of his musings, now she knew that he was part of the gang that had killed her.

The nausea receding, she pricked up her ears, waiting for a sign of she didn't know what.

'She's just standing there,' said Mabel.

'Yes, I can see that,' the Duchess replied.

'Why's she just standing there?'

'I imagine she's curious about where the Dispossessed have gone.'

Mabel scratched at her backside, looking down at Daisy-May's pinprick form far below them. 'Girl's a scrapper. Made it back through the Gloop, and picked up a stray along the way. Could be you're right about her.'

The Duchess smiled. 'I enjoy being right. It means the world won't end.'

'Best hold your horses on that one, your ladyship.'

The Duchess looked up at the hot-air balloon above them, lashed to the wall and pulling against its leash. 'How much fuel does that thing have left in it?'

Mabel put her hands on her hips, appraising it. 'Depends what you have in mind.'

'Well, I thought we might save existence,' said the Duchess, reaching for the tether rope. 'Though first we need to collect the girl who's going to help us do it.'

Not that many would consider the strident voice of Mabel as salvation.

'I said, *grab it*,' the woman screamed down, the wicker ladder dangling underneath the balloon the lolling tongue of a panting dog. 'You bloody deaf, girl?'

Daisy-May reached upwards, pawing for the ladder. 'Half blind, since swimming through that radiation bath. Got you two to thank for that, I suppose?'

The Duchess winced.

'Who's that with yer?' called out Mabel.

Daisy-May reached down, dragging Chestnut to her feet. 'Someone who needs your help.'

The balloon's basket swayed in the wind, tugging at its occupants. Mabel shook her head, fishing in the pockets of her overall and pulling out a rag. She bent down, dabbing at the cuts on Daisy-May's face. 'State of you, girl.'

Daisy-May yelped in pain. 'Lovely bedside manner you've got. Who taught you, Adolf fucking Hitler?'

'You'll live,' said Mabel, getting to her feet. 'Probably best you fill her in on what you've got in mind, Rach, and let her decide whether it's a good thing or a bad thing.'

The Duchess began to speak, but Daisy-May held up a hand. 'Chestnut first. She's in a bad way.'

Mabel bent down to the girl, placing two fingers against her neck. She was conscious, but barely. 'You rescued this one from the Gloop?'

'Yeah.'

'Then she should be fully dead, rather than just halfway there.'

'What can you do for her?'

Mabel frowned, reaching for a leather bag next to the Duchess's feet. 'What I always do. My best.'

'I've asked more of you than I ever should,' said the Duchess, placing a hand on Daisy-May's shoulder, 'and more than I ever wanted to.'

'Why do I get the feeling that you haven't finished asking?'

'A little help,' said Mabel. 'I need you to hold her.'

Daisy-May did as she was told, crouching next to Chestnut and placing her hands firmly on the child's flimsy shoulders, smiling at her.

Chestnut's eyes fluttered open. 'What . . . are you going to do?' she croaked.

The Duchess's mouth dropped open.

'She spoke,' said Mabel, unbelieving.

'*English*,' said the Duchess.

'Not quite as dumb as you thought, eh?' said Daisy-May. 'I've been trying to tell you that for months.'

'Needle . . . looks sharp,' gasped the girl.

'It's full of adrenalin,' said Mabel, flicking the plastic housing. 'Same stuff as we give the Dying Squad on the soil, but purer.'

'Will it make . . . me better?' said Chestnut.

'Yep,' said Mabel. 'Well, that or kill you.'

'Fuck's sake, Florence Nightingale,' said Daisy-May, shaking her head.

She stared deeply into Chestnut's eyes. 'Do you trust me?'

The girl didn't respond, then finally nodded.

'You should, because I'm not going to let you die.'

She ripped open Chestnut's grubby grey tunic, then turned to Mabel. 'Do it.'

Mabel did, plunging the syringe into the girl's chest with

uncommon speed. Chestnut's back arched and she let out a startled scream, her eyes wide in outraged surprise.

Those eyes closed.

'Mabel,' said Daisy-May, panic in her voice.

'She's got enough medicine in her system to slay an elephant. In five minutes, we'll know if it's killed her, or cured her. She's got a fifty-fifty chance either way.'

'In the meantime,' said the Duchess, 'there's the little matter of the fall of the Pen to deal with.'

Daisy-May grasped the side of the basket, staring down on a tableau of anarchy.

'Christ,' she said. 'Think I preferred being in hell.'

'It's quite a sight, I grant you,' said the Duchess, the slightest quaver in her voice. 'One I never thought I'd see.'

'No one's ever seen anything like this,' said Mabel, her voice shorn of its usual bluster. 'If they had, it'd be more famous than the Last bloody Supper.'

It was a scene that no photograph could have captured, because the hundreds of thousands – possibly millions – of bodies they were looking down upon spilled out of their peripheral vision, charging as one against the endless brick structure.

'What's made them act like this?' Daisy-May asked.

'The white-haired girl you tried to warn me about. You.'

She turned to the Duchess. 'Me? How are you pinning this on me, exactly?'

The Duchess sighed. 'It's not a criticism; quite the contrary. It's my belief, Daisy-May, that they're like this because of the kindness you've showed them. Where I and my predecessors viewed them as the dumbest of animals waiting impatiently in line for the abattoir, you saw the human in them. You spoke to them, treated them as equals.'

'Thanks,' said Daisy-May. 'I think. What about that

323

white-haired girl, though? She was the one they were listening to, following, not me.'

The Duchess nodded at Mabel. 'She's our cross to bear, but it's my belief she couldn't have led the Dispossessed in the way she did without you. Her success was the product of your kindness.'

'I only wanted to make their lives easier,' said Daisy-May.

'And you did,' said the Duchess. 'Hanna abused that kindness.'

'I saw her, you know,' said Daisy-May. 'Just as I was passing from the graveyard to the Gloop.'

The Duchess's already waxy pallor lost another shade of colour. 'Hanna got through? That's impossible. Everything in the Gloop was destroyed.'

'Girl at your feet who may or may not be dying is the proof that that's bollocks,' said Daisy-May.

'Hardly our biggest priority if she did get through,' said Mabel firmly. 'The Dispossessed listen to you, girl, they always have. You've got their ear, and you need to whisper into it, or everything ends.'

'They cannot break through that wall,' said the Duchess, as the mass of non-humanity piled into it once again, a spider's web of hairline fractures growing. 'If they do, the whole Jenga-pile of existence will come tumbling down.'

The lights in the graveyard, thought Daisy-May. The carnage here was causing them.

'The boss wouldn't let that happen, though, right?' she said. 'He's still the top boy, the one with the finger on the button.'

'That's precisely what we're afraid of,' said the Duchess, 'because you're right, He *won't* allow that to happen. When a hard drive becomes corrupted, you wipe it clean and start again.'

Daisy-May turned away, leaning on the basket and staring coldly as the wall was hammered into once again.

'You lied to me, both of you. You knew what Joe did to me, yet you partnered me up with him and didn't say a fuckin' word. All my life I've been lied to, and I thought you were different.'

The Duchess looked down. 'You're right to be angry, but to free yourself – to prove yourself worthy of that freedom – you have to be the one to discover the nature of your death, or you won't believe it. Didn't you say the very same thing to Joe?'

'Don't mention that piece of shit's name,' spat Daisy-May. 'He's the reason I'm dead.'

'He weren't the one that killed you,' said Mabel quietly. She looked at her sister, who gave a curt nod. 'And the fact that you're here? He took your place in the Pit. Know how many people have done that in the history of everything?'

Daisy-May looked away, her fingers gripping the edge of the basket, her shoulders sagging slightly. Hell of a thing, that, she thought. He might be a murdering shitbag, but he tried to make it right. That doesn't help my rotting corpse much, though.

'Still stretching,' she said finally, 'if you expect me to join in the circle jerk of appreciation for the bloke.'

'I expect nothing more from you than the fulfilment of your duties,' said the Duchess, placing a hand on her shoulder.

Daisy-May shrugged it off. 'Thought I'd done that, by find-ing out how I died. I'm free now that I have, right? To go to the Next Place?'

'I'm talking about your *new* duties.'

Mabel frowned at her younger sister. 'What are you doing, Rachel?'

'The only thing left that I can.'

The Duchess removed a small circular metal pin from her starched white shirt. 'There will be a more formal ceremony when, and if, circumstances allow,' she said, fixing the pin to

Daisy-May's grimy, bloodied T-shirt, 'but this will do for now. I hereby abdicate command of the Pen and pass that command to you.'

Daisy-May's jaw dropped. 'What the fuck?'

'Been more regal acceptance speeches,' said Mabel, glaring at her sister. '*The Duchess*. Never suited you less, that title.'

A chunk of masonry fell from the wall below them, the eerily silent press of bodies stopping for a moment to gaze upon the light spilling from it.

'What if I don't want it?' said Daisy-May quickly. 'What if I just want to go on to the Next Place?'

'You don't have a say, isn't that right, Rachel?' said Mabel. 'Might as well be honest with the lass.'

The newly dethroned Duchess nodded her head. 'The title is binding. One doesn't just turn it down.'

'Why me? What's so special about me?'

'The fact that you ask that question at all.' The Duchess looked down upon the mass of bodies below, all of them tensed and preparing to charge into the light. 'You're the only one who can talk to them.'

'All of you could have talked to them,' said Daisy-May, resignation already seeping into her bones. 'Only thing stopping you was your inability to fucking listen.'

She peered over the edge of the basket. 'There's so many. What do I say?'

The Duchess leaned in close. 'You tell them how things would be different for them, under your watch. How things would change for the better. How you'll always fight for them. The truth, basically.'

Chestnut began to stir, her eyelids stuttering.

Mabel leaned down to her and checked her pulse again. 'Stable. Don't know how long for, but she'll be conscious soon enough.'

Daisy-May looked back to the Duchess.

'You serious about this whole making-me-warden thing?'

'It's hardly something I'd joke about,' said the Duchess.

Daisy-May looked thoughtfully at Chestnut's unconscious form. 'All right, then,' she said. 'When she wakes up, this is what I want you to do.'

All the horror that's happened, and all the horror yet to come, thought Daisy-May, doesn't change the fact that this is fuckin' bad-ass.

She hung over the sea of Dispossessed, left arm wrapped around the middle rung of the hot air balloon's ladder, right hand holding a flaming green torch, endless sets of eyes looking up at her, silent and expectant.

Speaking to a group like they're a group doesn't work. You have to speak to them like they're individuals, like the person they once were. That was what she'd told the Duchess, but now, faced with such masses, her statement seemed fanciful. And the words wouldn't come. They stuck in the back of her throat, her mouth unable to force them out. She looked up to the Duchess and Mabel, who were craning over the basket, waiting.

This isn't going to work, Daisy-May thought. I look too much like the Duchess, royalty lording it over her slaves. It's that shit that got us into this trouble in the first place.

She looked back down at the bodies below her.

I hope I'm right about this.

She closed her eyes and let go of the ladder.

'What's she doing?' cried Mabel, grasping the edge of the basket as Daisy-May's tiny body tumbled in the infinite sky. 'Girl's bloody topped herself.'

'Have a little faith,' the Duchess replied, with a voice shorn of it. '*She* clearly does.'

I hope, she didn't say. *I hope they catch her. I hope they don't tear her apart like she's a piece of meat if they do.*

Daisy-May had felt like this once before.

It had been seconds after Claire's poison had finally killed her, one of those odd sensations similar to when your consciousness is on the verge of sleep but your body rebels, jerking you awake by making you believe you're falling.

For a few seconds, that was what she let herself believe: that the farmhouse and the woman she'd thought was kind but who had in fact been a killer were just a mashed-up drug-induced nightmare.

Then, she realised she couldn't be awake, because the falling sensation ended, and *awake* rarely involved looking at your own dead body. That was when, so long ago now, the Duchess had appeared, announcing her presence with a discreet, rarefied cough. There'd been no sympathy from her, no attempt to soften the circumstances; just a matriarchal sergeant-major bustle, outlining the circumstances and her part in them.

She'd felt rage at that moment with the Duchess, but now, as the wind whipped her hair and she readied herself for impact – either from outstretched hands or tearing ones – Daisy-May decided that forgiveness was the way to go.

Because really, what was more important than forgiveness when it came down to it?

Forgiveness for her mother and her dereliction of those duties.

Forgiveness for her grandmother and the euthanasia she'd guilted her into committing.

Forgiveness for Ryan, and the advantages he'd taken of her.

Forgiveness for the Duchess, and for the prison sentence masquerading as honour that the old woman had inflicted upon her.

And finally, forgiveness for Joe, the man who'd helped kill her but who hadn't, at the moment of truth, pulled the trigger. The man who'd swapped places with her so she could be free, and so that existence had a chance.

I forgive you, mate, she thought. You and your facts. Hope you're OK.

She closed her eyes, and waited for the impact.

Mabel yelped.

They caught her, thought the Duchess. They could have let her hit the ground, but they caught her.

She watched as Daisy-May was passed along the heads of the Dispossessed. A hole in the tightly packed masses appeared, and she dropped down into it.

'Hope she knows what she's doing,' said Mabel.

'So do I,' said the Duchess.

Chestnut's eyes popped open. She rose unsteadily to her feet, then looked over the side of the basket, wide-eyed, at the massed ranks of her Dispossessed brethren below.

The Duchess stared at her. 'Land us.'

'You lost your bleeding mind?' spat Mabel. 'They'll tear us apart.'

'You heard me,' said the Duchess. 'Land us, right now.'

'What are you hoping to achieve by doing that?'

'It's not what I'm going to achieve,' said the Duchess, nodding towards Chestnut. 'It's what she is.'

Mabel shook her head, but nevertheless reached up towards the burner. 'Hell of a risk, this plan of Daisy-May's, and there's no coming back from it. You know that, I suppose?'

'You suppose right,' said the Duchess, smiling at her sister.

Daisy-May dropped to her feet. A three-hundred-and-sixty-degree circle of Dispossessed faced her. The attacks on the wall had stopped, at least momentarily, but for how long?

Don't try to flim-flam them, she told herself. Don't try to charm them. These are my people. We're the forgotten.

We're the Dispossessed.

I'm the Dispossessed.

She swallowed.

She held her head up high.

'Can you understand me?' she shouted, in the Dispossessed's native tongue.

A murmur of assent went up from the crowd.

'What about now?' she said, in English.

Blank faces. Some with recognition on them too, though.

'There you go. The warden? She'd tell you that was impossible. Me being able to talk to you. You being able to understand. To her, you're nothing but animals. Worse than animals, 'cos animals, they get love, at least some of the time. No one's ever loved you in the Pen. Respected you, except for me.'

'Hanna did,' shouted a voice from the back.

Murmurs of agreement.

'She listened to you, I get it. Not enough of us have done that. All I can say is, from now on, more will.'

'Just a girl, you,' came another voice. 'A girl that talks big. What can you do?'

'Help you. Make sure you're treated equal. Make sure the Pen's for everyone, not just the Duchesses of this world.'

'How?' A woman's voice this time. 'How will you do that?'

Daisy-May pointed to the metal pin on her chest. 'Because I'm the new warden – not that I'm big on titles like that. Call me DM. Call me what you like, as long as you help me change the place.'

Grumbles, mumbles and whispers all around her. Daisy-May could feel the crowd's energy, its pulse and flow; feel how the whole thing was on a knife edge, how the slightest push could bring it crashing down.

'Hanna says we have to take our freedom, not be given it,' a voice said.

Their speech is getting better all the time, thought Daisy-May. Feels like I'm getting schooled by a debating society.

'Hanna was wrong. All that's going to get you is wiped out.'

'Sounds like a threat.'

She was losing them. 'Where's Hanna now?' she said defiantly. 'She's run. Left you. I'm the one here now, trying to help you. Only place Hanna led you to was a massacre in the Gloop.'

'Just words,' came the reply. 'Where's the proof?'

'It's right here,' a voice called out.

The mass of Dispossessed looked up as one.

Daisy-May joined them to see the balloon containing Mabel, the Duchess and Chestnut descending. The crowd instinctively pushed back, creating a space for it to land.

Least that's something, she thought. They could just have stormed it.

They still might.

The balloon landed with a thud, Mabel catching Chestnut as she fell backwards.

The Duchess didn't so much as flinch at the impact.

'You all know who I am,' she said haughtily. 'This madness must stop immediately.'

A treasonous grumble went up from the crowd.

'We do everything for you people,' she cried, 'and this is how you repay us.'

A stronger murmur this time. Daisy-May looked uneasily around her.

'This girl, for instance.' The Duchess reached for Chestnut's arm, and helped her stand on the lip of the balloon's basket.

'Rescued from death by one of my own.' She pointed at Daisy-May. 'Where's the gratitude, you savages?'

'That true?' came a voice from the crowd. 'She rescue you?'

Chestnut nodded. 'I'd have died if it wasn't for Daisy-May. Almost did anyway. She cares.'

Daisy-May felt the energy in the crowd shift slightly. *Have to press it.*

'That's right, I do. That's where I'm different from the Duchess. How can you expect anyone called the Duchess to understand you? No offence, Duchess. I didn't grow up in a castle. I'm not royalty. I'm the same as you. Grew up poor. Died poorer. No one ever gave me anything. The likes of her can't understand. They'll never understand. I will. I do.'

'She's telling the truth,' Chestnut called out. 'Daisy-May's one of us. Why'd she save me if she wasn't?'

'I'm going to change things,' said Daisy-May. 'Build you somewhere to live. Give you purpose. But first, we have to sweep away the old ways.' She pointed at the Duchess. 'She's the old ways. That's why she needs to be banished.'

Excitement from the crowd.

'You ungrateful little *bitch*,' spat the Duchess. 'You had nothing, and I gave you everything.'

'You didn't give me anything that wasn't mine already,' Daisy-May replied. 'You can't hand someone their freedom. It's not something to ration out.'

The Duchess stood shaking, her nostrils flaring. 'The Pen is mine.'

'I'm the warden of the Pen now,' Daisy-May said defiantly. 'I can do anything I want, especially if it helps its people. I banish you.' She appealed to the crowd. '*Banish*.'

Banish.

The word was taken up and picked over by a few in the crowd.

Banish.

More seized the chant.

Banish.

The Duchess looks around her wildly, defiance in her eyes, but fear as well.

Banish.

Daisy-May held her arm aloft, pointing off into the distance.

Banish.

A thin path appeared amongst the mass of humanity.

Banish.

The Duchess looked hopelessly at Mabel.

Banish.

'*Banish*,' shouted Daisy-May. '*Banish.*'

The Duchess began to walk down the path the Dispossessed had created. Her head was bowed. Her eyes found nothing but the floor. A god, cast out from her fiefdom.

Banish.

Banish.

Banish.

Chapter Thirty-Six

Today is going to be the best day of my life.

The weather doesn't agree, but that's the thing about Lincolnshire winters: they'll start a punch-up in an empty room, then bill you personally for the damage. I don't care about the thicket of clouds or the walloped-flat landscapes. They can do their thing and I'll do mine, because Lincolnshire and I are going to have a long-overdue unconscious coupling. They can keep the house and the CD collection. All I want is Claire.

I ease my foot down on the accelerator, because there's no way I can get to her too quickly, and I'm late already. Leaving everything behind is never as quick or as clean as you'd think, but I'm on my way.

I look in the rear-view mirror, hoping to see nothing but an ocean of endless tarmac. Instead, I see the girl.

I see Daisy-May.

Of course, I know she's not really there – ghosts are no more real than good intentions or happy endings – but some part of my guilty conscience has begun to try and convince me that they are, because lately, I see her everywhere.

In the car.

In a restaurant.

When I try and sleep at night.

She never says anything; she never smiles, or laughs, or cries, or screams for mercy. She just stands there, watching me. A girl four months dead – a girl my wife poisoned, and I stuck in a stash room to die – is stalking me, and I don't know what to do about it.

I've tried to talk to Claire, to see if she's experienced the same thing, but of course she hasn't, and she shuts me down quickly. It's impressive how she can compartmentalise the different areas of her life, put murder in a sealed container and not have to break it out until she really needs to.

We do what we do now so that we never have to do it again in the future, that's what Claire says. *People like us don't play by society's rules, because society's rules don't play with us. Or at least, they don't play fairly.*

I agreed with her. I always agree with her.

At least, I did until the girl.

Daisy-May – whose presence I spent all of three hours in – has broken something in me. What we *did* to her has broken something in me. And Claire knows. She knows I'm different, and I don't mean in the seeing-dead-girls-everywhere sense. My heart's just not in the business any more. Not like Pete's. Not even like Claire's.

That's why I was so pleased when she agreed to stop. Leave this shit-hole and move to Carmel, like we'd always planned. Enjoy the good life and put all the filth behind us.

We've got enough money to last at least two lifetimes, and Pete will continue to run the lines himself. Or abandon them; it makes no difference to me. He has to make his own peace, and I have to make mine. I just think that'll be much easier to do in the California sunshine than the Lincolnshire drizzle.

The farmhouse looms on the horizon.

I look in the rear-view mirror and Daisy-May's no longer there. Maybe that means she's at peace.

She lay poisoned and dying in a locked room, darling, Claire's voice says in my head. *That doesn't sound very peaceful, does it?*

I bat the voice away, because it belongs to no Claire that I know.

I indicate, easing the car onto the grass verge a hundred feet or so away from the farmhouse. There's no earthly reason for a copper to be out here, and parking in the front garden of a crack house is the sort of thing that brings attention, every last eyeball of it unwanted.

I walk casually towards the place, when all I want to do is sprint, to get to Claire, to collect the money and drive off into the sunset. To Carmel.

Clint Eastwood, that's what people say when you say Carmel, if they say anything at all. The lethal enforcer used to be the mayor there when he wasn't busting celluloid heads. Claire and I always understood why he wanted the job: endless beaches, vast swathes of sun and hope; even the name sounded warm and welcoming.

Caramel, she used to say to me at school. *When you and I are older, Joe, we're going to live in Caramel. That's what I'm renaming it, and that's where I'm going to live. There are proper beaches there, not these windswept dumps. No one will know who we are, or where we came from, or what we've done.*

That bit was always important to Claire, even before we started running the lines. More than it was to me, anyway, but I got it. My childhood may have been dull, but dull meant safe; Claire's was neither. Claire's was abusive stepfathers and violence and broken bones and misery and abuse. So when she told me her dream of moving there, with the battered pages from a battered travel brochure, who was I not to humour her? I never thought it would happen, but that didn't mean I didn't want it to.

I guess that's what they mean when they say *better half*:

someone who sees possibilities you can barely dream of. Claire dreamed of Carmel and we're a day away from it. There's no point dwelling on how we made it possible; we're not those people any more. Or at least, we won't be when we get there.

I hear a chuckle behind me like I've said something funny, and I whirl around.

Nothing. Just a deserted country road robbed of its colour by the winter. Just guilt, trying to rob me of my nerve.

Fuck guilt. Fuck remorse. They're dead emotions that won't change a damn thing.

I knock on the farmhouse's front door three times, and after a moment, it opens. Two of Pete's boys lurk in the doorway. I don't recognise them – they're new muscle – but that's fine. Pete has been taking a more active role in the day-to-day running of the lines since that day in the farmhouse, and I've been happy to cede control. Let him deal with the fuck-ups, and the danger, and the guilt. I've done my shift.

I nod and walk past them, and then I see Claire.

She's in the kitchen, and despite how sordid the room is, she lights it with her mere presence. She looks up and smiles at me like we're the only two beings in existence. As far as I'm concerned, we are.

I go to her, taking her face in my hands, kissing her deeply.

'What did I do to deserve you?' I ask, as I step back from her.

'Maim, butcher, extort and murder,' she says with a laugh, taking my hand and leading me towards the stairs. 'All the greatest hits.'

A chill runs down my spine as we take the stairs two at a time, because we don't do this, we don't mention business or the things we've done. Not like that, not so nakedly.

She turns to face me, placing her palm on my cheek, and my heart is in her hand, so intense is her gaze. 'Close your eyes.'

I ask her why, and she says it's a surprise. I'm not in the mood for a surprise – all I want to do is get the money and get on the road – but I've never been able to say no to Claire, and I don't start now.

I jam my eyes shut.

Feet shuffle and floorboards creak as her hand guides me.

'Stop.'

Her hand falls away, and I hear her take several steps away from me.

'Open your eyes.' Playfulness in her voice. 'Trust me.'

I do.

There's a leather bag on the floor in front of me.

It's the one we gave to Daisy-May to run the lines with, the one she said had been stolen. It looks like she was right.

Claire stole it.

I try to speak, but the words won't come, will barely form on my lips.

The world speaks for me, and it's an angry yowl of gunfire rage.

I'm lifted off my feet, pain so ridiculous as not to be recognisable as such flooding my body, because pain is stubbing your nail or bashing your finger with a hammer, not this excavation of sense and sound. I land on my back, every gasp of air pumped out of me, and see nothing but ceiling. The ceiling stares back at me, almost like it's bored, like it's seen it all before.

It has. All this house really knows is murder.

I turn my head towards the door. Claire's not there, but the dead girl is. Daisy-May stands in the corner of the room, watching. If she's happy, she's not showing it.

There are two more roars of sound from downstairs, followed by two clumps of body hitting the floor.

Claire's a busy girl.

Footsteps on the stairs.

My wife – my killer – at the door.

She wipes down the gun's handle like they do in the movies, then breaks it over her knee, tossing it down next to me.

She kneels and takes out a phone. It's a burner, the type we give the kids to use.

'Police, please.'

I croak a nothing word, and she puts her finger to her lips to shush me.

'I just heard gunshots coming from Greenleaf, Church Lane, Manby. Please come quickly.'

She ends the call and snaps the phone in two, pocketing its entrails. 'Nothing worse than a bent copper who develops a conscience; that's what you said to me in the beginning, Joe, and you were right. You commit to the path, or you don't start walking down it.'

She looks at me with pity that feels like hate. 'We were months from getting out. A few more runs and we were clear. But you bottled it, didn't you? Started getting squeamish about how we were using kids, when it was your idea in the first place. Second-guessed yourself all the time, ducked opportunities we'd spent months setting up. That conscience was going to bring us all down, and for what? We own this town. You get jumpy just because some of the product was tainted? What did you think, that the junkies were going to complain to Citizens Advice?

I flinch at her coldness. *Junkies* sounds like a venomous, un-feeling curse when it's passed through her lips.

'We knew we were going to hell for what we'd done. I just wanted to go to Carmel first.'

She gets to her feet, and I suddenly don't feel anything any more, which is worse than the pain, somehow.

'You know, Pete was the one who wanted you killed. I told him no. I told him to let me give you one more chance, with the girl.'

The girl – Daisy-May – takes one step forward, lurching into vision again.

'Whatever excuse she came up with, the money had gone, and so she had to go too. *If Joe does it, we'll know he's still on board*; that's what I said to Pete. *Let me give him one last chance.* And what did you do with that chance? How did you repay me?'

I can't reply. What would I say if I could?

'We were so close, and you had to ruin it.'

Claire walks to the door, then stops, looking back at me. 'In a month's time, Pete will be gone too. This was never about Pete; it was about you and me. Killing you breaks my heart, but you would have got us caught.'

She lowers her head, like the conscience she doesn't have is bothering her. 'You know, in a way, I've done you a favour. When the ARU get here, you'll be the hero cop you always wanted to be, slain in the line of duty. If you'd carried on living, with that conscience of yours, you'd have been a disgrace, as well as disgraced. And you'd have taken me down with you.'

It was Claire all along, I think, as my vision begins to darken. How could I not have seen that, remembered it?

Life dims.

There's the sound of an army on the stairs, and my vision pings back into focus. Claire steps back into the room, and somehow I realise that this isn't the past any more.

This is the well-earned hell of the present.

My wife stands aside, and there's something different about her.

'I thought it would be nice to have a little reunion,' she says. 'These are the children we recruited over the years. My, how busy we were, husband of mine.'

She smiles fondly at the two dozen children who file into the room, handing out knives and forks to them. 'They're hungry,' she says, in a voice that is no longer her own. 'Starving, in fact.'

The children shuffle forward, scraping their cutlery together, all of them smiling, all of them intent on taking their pound of flesh, and I see that Claire's not Claire any more, that she's never been Claire, not really. In her place stands a monster, one with an elephant's skull for a head and a subliminal whine of a giggle.

'Dig in, children,' the Xylophone Man says, his long pink tongue flicking in and out. 'There's plenty to go around.'

As metal slashes into flesh and I scream in ways I couldn't have believed possible, my eyes meet Daisy-May's – or what passes for her in this version of hell. Then I remember.

This isn't the first time this has happened. It isn't even the thousandth.

'I deserve this,' I say, and mean it.

Epilogue

The Sea of Trees is thirteen and a half square miles of forest, ripped from the most terrifying horror movie you've never seen.

Sitting north-west of the imperious Mount Fuji, the forest's trees twist and turn as if they're in pain, their root entrails contorted in a permanent state of agony. The ground is uneven, as if it's trying to escape the horror of the place, but it's the isolation that terrifies the most; the trees, packed as tightly as a Tokyo commuter train, form a barrier against even the merest wisp of wind, creating a vacuum of emptiness where a breath sounds like a roar and a roar sounds like a jet engine.

Any hiker fool enough to enter the forest risks getting lost, so vast is its size, and if he did, well, that poor soul would be unable to call for help; drenched in magnetic iron, the soil of the Sea of Trees thwarts cell phones, GPS and even compasses. Those who enter often struggle to leave.

Of course, local folklore puts this down to the forest being haunted, because the Sea of Trees also goes by the name of the Suicide Forest, its lush isolation encouraging the desperate and the lost to commit the most final of acts. Untold numbers of Japanese have made the pilgrimage there over the centuries, to uphold their *seppuku* heritage. It is said that legions of their spirits haunt the woods.

Hanna Jankie, the white-haired, eternally teenage sister of the Duchess, was absolutely counting that they did.

She moved through the forest, ten members of the Dispossessed alongside her, their steps soundless in the ocean of trees around them. She had gone through oceans of fire, stormed the walls of the Pen itself, then travelled thousands of soil miles to get here, but they were the smallest hardships in the grand scheme of things. Especially when you considered that her scheme was grander than most.

Hanna stopped suddenly, sensing something, raising her arm to halt the group, then staring intently at the trees. Her followers matched her, their filmy, inquisitive eyes devouring the darkened forest.

Hanna smiled as a man stepped out from behind a tree.

She beckoned for him to come closer.

A sea of faces appeared in the Sea of Trees.

Men, women. Some children.

The legend went that these souls, these ghosts, were vengeful, intent on tormenting those who entered the forest.

They're not vengeful, Hanna thought. They're just unfocused.

She smiled as she walked towards them.

I'm going to do something about that. And when I have, when I've shown them the light, they'll discover just what vengeance is.

They'll discover, too, that there's a whole world out there to wreak it on.

The Pen's rulers past and present gazed out upon their domain. Where before there had been a landscape scraped clean of features and personality, now there were smatterings of settlements, roofs pointing towards the volcanic sky. The Dispossessed, looking a little less so, grouped together for comfort, their clicking chatter audible even from several hundred feet away at the Pen wall.

The Duchess shook her head. 'When they're not trying to tear down the walls of existence itself, they look half civilised.'

'You put me in charge so I could change things,' said Daisy-May, 'so I'm changing things. And they've stopped rioting, haven't they?'

'They have,' said the Duchess. 'I've made many bad decisions in my time, but making you warden isn't going to be one of them.'

'Sorry it had to go down the way it did,' said Daisy-May. 'Making a sacrifice of you, and all.'

'Don't be sorry,' said the Duchess. 'It worked. You had to make a clean break from the old ways, the old regime. Banishing me was an impressively Machiavellian way of doing that. Worthy, if I may be so bold, of me.'

'You played your part. Calling me a bitch. You were proper lairy. Think I even saw your nostrils flare at one point.'

'The frustrated actor in me seeping out,' said the Duchess, with half a smile.

'You're not worried about your legacy?'

She gave a cold laugh. 'Only insecure men with no way of living in the present obsess about legacy. The rest of us are too busy doing our jobs.'

She stared down at the people below. 'The Dispossessed now trust you in a way they never trusted me.'

'Have to work hard to keep that trust now,' said Daisy-May. 'Can't drop out of the sky every time with a girl rescued from the Gloop. Went big early on that score. Hard to beat as a statement of intent.'

The Duchess nodded. 'It worked, but for how long?

The Dispossessed have the trappings of civilisation, I grant you, but they *are* just trappings. The crack will still appear in the sky, and it will remain their only chance of getting to the Next Place. How long do you think a few mud huts will draw the fire from that anger?'

Daisy-May bit her lip. 'People need a purpose. That's true whether they're teenagers on the soil or half-souls in purgatory. I'm gonna give it to them.'

The Duchess looked at her warily. 'You're planning some-thing.'

'Planning something sounds like I'm twiddling my fingers to-gether in some dank fuckin' lair. I'm liberating people, Rachel.'

Daisy-May noted the flash of anger in the older woman's face, the use of her first name a breaking of protocol that had existed for a millennium. Then it was gone.

'Don't tell me what you're planning. It will only annoy me, which is precisely the reason I chose you. You're the future and I'm the soon-to-be-forgotten past. That's the way it should be. Just try not to change too much too quickly, because then you simply become Hanna.'

'I hear you,' said Daisy-May.

The Duchess sighed appreciatively at the view in front of her. 'There aren't many things I'll miss about this place, or about my old job, but this is one of them. If you ever need to think, or to make a decision you don't want to have to make, there are worse places to find solitude.'

She turned to Daisy-May, holding out a hand. 'Good luck.'

Daisy-May tutted, ignoring the hand and pulling the older woman in for a hug. 'Handshakes are for the dead. We hug it out under my watch.'

The Duchess went stiff, then softened into it a little, patting the girl lightly on the back. 'You seem nervous.'

'That's 'cos I am.'

'It's a place like any other,' said the Duchess. 'Hotter, bleaker and more desolate, perhaps, but still just a place.'

'It wasn't when I was in it,' said Daisy-May. 'That place was all in my mind.'

'This is different. You're a visitor today, rather than an inmate.'

She exhaled, jogging on the spot, psyching herself up.

'He can't hurt you any more,' said the Duchess.

'Easy for you to say; you haven't been swallowed whole by the fucker.'

'You're the warden of the Pen; even he isn't ridiculous enough to harm her.'

They broke apart, the Duchess stepping back, appraising the girl's black leather jacket, Ramones T-shirt, drainpipe jeans and newly scuffed Converse trainers. 'Not the outfit I'd have chosen, but it'll do.'

'You haven't told me where you're going to go,' said Daisy-May. 'Feels like the sort of thing I need to know.'

'It's absolutely the sort of thing you mustn't. Last thing the new leader needs is the old one peering over their shoulder, clucking disapprovingly, because believe me, I would.'

'Give me a hint,' said Daisy-May. 'Hate to think you off in the wilderness for forty days and forty nights.'

The Duchess picked up a backpack and slung it over her shoulder. 'I have family business to attend to on the soil.'

'The white-haired girl?'

She nodded. 'I won't be able to rest until I find her. She's dangerous, and I don't like her running around up there unchecked.'

'How are you going to get through the Gloop, seeing as you poisoned it?'

'Why don't you leave that to me?'

The Duchess snapped off a salute.

'Good luck, Daisy-May, although really, I should offer that platitude to the Xylophone Man. I have a feeling that after you're done with him, he'll need it.'

Really, he should enjoy this more.

Joe Lazarus was sweating pain and endless torment, and for the Xylophone Man, there was absolutely no smell sweeter. Why then did it leave such a sour taste?

It was because he wasn't the girl.

The girl had been the *ruin* of him.

That delicious teenage flower, trapped within her own rotting body, with her genuine, shine-a-light goodness. He didn't get such delicacies in the Pit; the morsels he was thrown were the Joe Lazaruses of this world, their souls wizened and blackened by the wrong turns they'd made during their soil lives. Joe was fast food, a dirty, sometimes necessary meal that left you hungry ten minutes later; Daisy-May had been the choicest prime rib he'd ever tasted, one he should, by rights, have been able to feast on forever.

It had been incredible that Lazarus had willingly changed places with her. In all his time in the Pit, the Xylophone Man had never known it to happen. The souls he got were usually warped by evil and betrayal, not hell-bent on redemption. Still, that wasn't what had unsettled him so much. It was the fact that she had come back.

The Xylophone Man – although he'd never felt more like his soil name, Oliver – clenched his fists, waiting at the entrance of the Pit. He wished it was more intimidating; the cliché of seas of flames and hundred-foot winged monsters couldn't have been further from the truth. Hell was boring, a featureless, joyless scar in the ground, a kingdom that was nothing of the sort. It was all in the mind. There was the Pen, though, and the Next Place, so there had to be a tangible *something*. It surprised him, still, after all this time, what a nuts-and-bolts pragmatist the Almighty was.

There was a booming knock from the slab of granite facing him, and the Xylophone Man grimaced.

His guest had arrived.

'Impossible.'

'Yeah, she said you'd say that.'

Daisy-May watched as the creature with the elephant skull shifted on its feet, as if it were trying to choke down some primeval urge. He can smell me, she thought, and it's driving him fucking crazy.

'His soul is mine, bought and paid for. You left, he stayed. A simple arrangement it is impossible to complicate.'

'Yeah, that's the thing with me, I'm a fucking ninja at complication.' She inspected a nail. 'Sort of made it into an art form.'

She took a step closer to the Xylophone Man, rattling the cage of her fear. Suck me up, she thought, smiling. I fucking dare you.

'Is this what I can expect from your rule of the Pen? Ignorance of the natural order of things? I know it's full of mongoloids and halfwits, but I expected rather better from its newly crowned warden.'

Daisy-May looked around at the featureless landscape surrounding them. It reminded her of the moon, with its grey, dusty texture and bled-dry-of-life atmosphere. 'And I expected more from hell. The best tunes? You haven't even got a Starbucks, mate.'

The Xylophone Man quivered in front of her, barely containing his rage.

'Now here's what's going to happen. You're going to show me where you've got Joe, and then you're going to release him into my custody.'

The Xylophone Man took a step forward, the two of them only inches apart. 'And why would I do that?'

She told him, and when she'd finished speaking the monster screamed in frustration, ravaging the surrounding landscape, ripping up chunks of rock, desecrating further the already unholy ground, brought low by frustration, anger, pain and the knowledge that he had to say yes.

It sounded like a door opening, but it couldn't be, because as far as Joe could remember, people rarely entered your subconscious by lock and key. Until recently, he hadn't believed it was possible for people to enter your subconscious at all. But as he watched, the door opened, throwing a pool of sickly yellow light onto the tile-less floor.

His stomach plunged when he saw Daisy-May enter.

'Close your gob, Joey, you're scaring the flies.'

Joe mouthed silently at her.

'What a reunion. Keep the waterworks to a minimum though, yeah? Nothing more undignified than a crying ghost.'

He looked past her to the half-open door. 'You're not real.'

Daisy-May slapped herself in the face. 'Someone should tell my body. Besides, the devil couldn't conjure up an imaginary me. He doesn't have the fucking wit. Only one of me, Joey.'

'It's Joe,' he said automatically. He continued to stare past her.

'Oh, don't worry about old Xylophone Chops,' she said, crouching down in front of him and looking disdainfully at the featureless, colourless room. 'He's taking a piss.'

'How are you here?'

'Question you should ask is *why* am I here, being as you were the arsehole that helped get me killed.'

Joe dipped his head, his eyes finding the floor. 'You know.'

'I do. Wasn't so long ago that I was in my own padded cell,

getting drip-fed that horror film by the lanky shit-house out-side. Big joke, when you think about it, us working together like we'd never met.'

'One without a punchline.'

'Oh, it had one,' said Daisy-May, inspecting a nail. 'It just weren't funny.'

Joe raised his head, looking at her properly for the first time. 'You seem different. You did it, didn't you? You saved exist-ence.'

'Think people are over-egging that pudding,' she said, the leather of her jacket sighing as she slouched down next to him. 'Not that I'm not a tramp when it comes to compliments. And you changing places with me? Seems to me that makes us even.'

'We're not, not by a long shot. Four months you spent rot-ting away in that safe room. Four months I knew about it, because I helped put you there. The things I did, the person I was – I am – there's no squaring that. No forgetting it, no living with it.'

'That's your punishment for the things you've done, same way me helping to kill my grandma – the things I did after that – is *my* punishment. None of us gets out of life clean. For me, the afterlife is like leaving school and starting uni. New set of clothes, a new look, a chance to be someone different, if not better. And the Joe I know? The one who worked for the Dying Squad? He was one of the good guys.'

Joe looked at her, wanting to believe what she was saying, but struggling to get there.

'He wasn't one of the bad guys, anyway,' conceded Daisy-May. 'He was in the middle, and isn't that what purgatory is, when it comes down to it? A place for people in the middle?'

'Say I believed you, so what? I'm trapped here,' said Joe, his shoulders slumping. 'Think that bastard outside is just going to let me out?'

Daisy-May got to her feet and held out a hand.

'Yeah, well, that's one of the perks that comes with the new job – you get to use the odd get-out-of-jail-free card.'

'Like the Duchess used with Mabel?' said Joe incredulously. 'You only get one of those.'

'That's what they tell me.'

Hope flowered on Joe's face, the first time it had taken root since he'd been imprisoned in hell.

It died just as quickly.

'You can't use it on me,' he said. 'I'm not worth it.'

'I can do what I like. I'm in charge.'

He got to his feet, struggling to believe. 'I can really just go?'

'You can,' said Daisy-May, 'but there's a catch.'

Joe tried on a smile. 'When isn't there? What is it?'

'I've got a job for you, back in the Pen.'

Joe frowned. 'A job? Weird, considering that you've seen my CV.'

Daisy-May grinned at him. 'It's a weird job.'

Considering how large it had loomed over everything, it occurred to Joe how little time he'd spent in the Pen. Absence hadn't made it any prettier.

The same cauldron of clouds billowed overhead, pushed and pulled by unfelt wind, the landscape, almost as flat as his home county, blasted clean by some unseen, ancient force.

Like it's half damned, he thought. Like the devil got bored halfway through building it, or God got bored halfway through tearing it down.

Still, it wasn't exactly the same. There were signs of civilisation. Shabby settlements. Something that was considerably better than the nothing of before.

'It ain't much,' said Daisy-May, 'but it's home.'

They'd decamped to the control room, Daisy-May eschewing

the grand throne favoured by the Duchess, instead perching herself on one of the grunts' empty desks. Joe frowned, pointing at the far-right monitor and the view of the Pen it was displaying. 'Are those *houses*?'

Daisy-May nodded. 'Seemed to make sense to make the Dispossessed feel, you know, *not* dispossessed? 'Cos me, I reckon four walls and a roof is all that people really want, alive or dead. That and a job.' She punched Joe's shoulder. 'And that's where you come in, Joey.'

He rubbed his arm, frowning. 'It's Joe. What do you mean?'

The newly anointed purgatory head jumped to her feet, grinning. 'People need a purpose, they need to feel pride, and the Dying Squad's going to be the way we do it. Up till now, it's been cliquey as fuck. An old boys' – and old girls' – club. We're opening up the membership.'

She marched to the corner of the room, leaning on the handle of a thick slab of door and levering it open.

'Come on in,' she said, to someone out of Joe's eyeline. 'Time for you to meet your guv'nor.'

Five members of the Dispossessed walked uncertainly into the room, looking at the whirling technology all around them. Three men and two women, with the same translucent quality as their brethren outside, but dressed in matching outfits of shirt, pencil-thin black tie and weathered leather jacket.

Daisy-May nodded to them. 'What do you think?'

'What do I think of what?'

'Your new team,' she said.

Joe laughed. 'My new team of *what*?'

'Dying Squad recruits. You're going to train these beautiful people, teach them everything you know about police work. Shouldn't take long.'

'How can they learn anything without their memories?'

'That's the thing,' said Daisy-May. 'Dispossessed are changing.

They're smarter than they were yesterday, and twice as smart as the day before that. It's a brave new world, mate.'

'Everything I know about police work is a fucking lie, Daisy-May,' said Joe, looking down. 'I'm no more a detective than you are.'

'Then you'll fit right in. New broom, Joey, that's what this world needs. You're playing a part, a new casting where you're the good copper rather than the bent one. You get to do things right this time.'

He shook his head and peered closer at the recruits. 'They're all dressed like you.'

'Course they are, I've got kick-ass taste. You'll be wearing the same.'

'I fucking won't.'

'You fucking will.' Daisy-May placed her hands on her hips. 'Souls that need saving – that need someone to help them move on, by righting the wrong that was done to them – there's a backlog of cases, and I need all the help I can get to clear it.'

'But what about balance?' said Joe. 'If the Dispossessed get more autonomy, won't that throw things in the Pen out of whack?'

'That's what the Duchess always reckoned,' said Daisy-May, 'but I think she reckoned wrong. We give these people their freedom, they won't let us down. Never been as sure of anything in my life.'

Joe tutted, taking in the merry band. 'They've got a lot to learn, in not much time. Think they're up to it? Think they're even capable of it?'

'Are you?' asked Daisy-May, a small smile on her lips.

He did, and so they talked about what came next, about how they would reclaim the Gloop from the environmental disaster it had suffered, and about her hopes for the new world she had been tasked with building. And as she spoke, something flared in Daisy-May's chest, something new, something she had never felt before in her young life, but something she could absolutely get used to.

Hope.

Acknowledgements

I spent a lot of days in cafes (when I should have been writing) idly dreaming about this bit. That I'm finally able to write acknowledgements is massively down to Harry Illingworth. Always there to chat about plot problems (or be the recipient of football abuse), he's the kind of hungry-fighter agent I always wanted but was beginning to fear I'd never actually get. Thanks for the leap of faith, mate. I won't let you down.

Before you get to the agent stage, though, you have to inflict your work in progress on other people. Thanks to my brother, Robin, and James Briggs for their kind words, and great notes. Christa Larwood for the critiquing, and for also teaching me English. Dan Woodall, for saying nice things about the book, and also listening to me moan a lot too. John Humphries for taking the time to read it, giving great feedback, and copy editing; you're a hell of an uncle. And my dad, for never countenancing something wasn't possible, or being anything less than hugely supportive. I reckon my mum would have thought this book was alright, too. Though she probably wouldn't have been mad keen on the swearing.

A huge thanks to everyone at Gollancz, and in particular, Rachel Winterbottom. It's hard to imagine a better editor or anyone more fun to work with. Editing this together in a rough-as-old-boots 2020 was easily the highlight of my year.

To you, the reader. You picked this up off the shelf when there are a thousand other books to read, and ten thousand other things to watch. I've waited a long time for someone to make that choice: thanks for making it. It means a lot.

And finally, to my partner in crime, critique in residence and wife, Kirsty Eyre. Always my first reader and the person I want to impress the most, Kirsty gives it to me straight, and has zero tolerance for my tantrums. Her notes are stellar and she's always there when I need picking up or setting straight. We make a great team, but I'm in no doubt who the Most Valuable Player is. Those boys we whipped up together aren't too shabby, either.

Credits

Adam Simcox and Gollancz would like to thank everyone at Orion who worked on the publication of *The Dying Squad* in the UK.

Editorial
Rachel Winterbottom
Brendan Durkin

Copy editor
Jane Selley

Audio
Paul Stark
Amber Bates

Contracts
Anne Goddard
Paul Bulos
Jake Alderson

Publicity
Will O'Mullane

Design
Lucie Stericker
Tomas Almeida
Joanna Ridley
Nick May

Editorial Management
Charlie Panayiotou
Jane Hughes

Marketing
Brittany Sankey

Operations
Jo Jacobs
Sharon Willis
Lisa Pryde
Lucy Brem